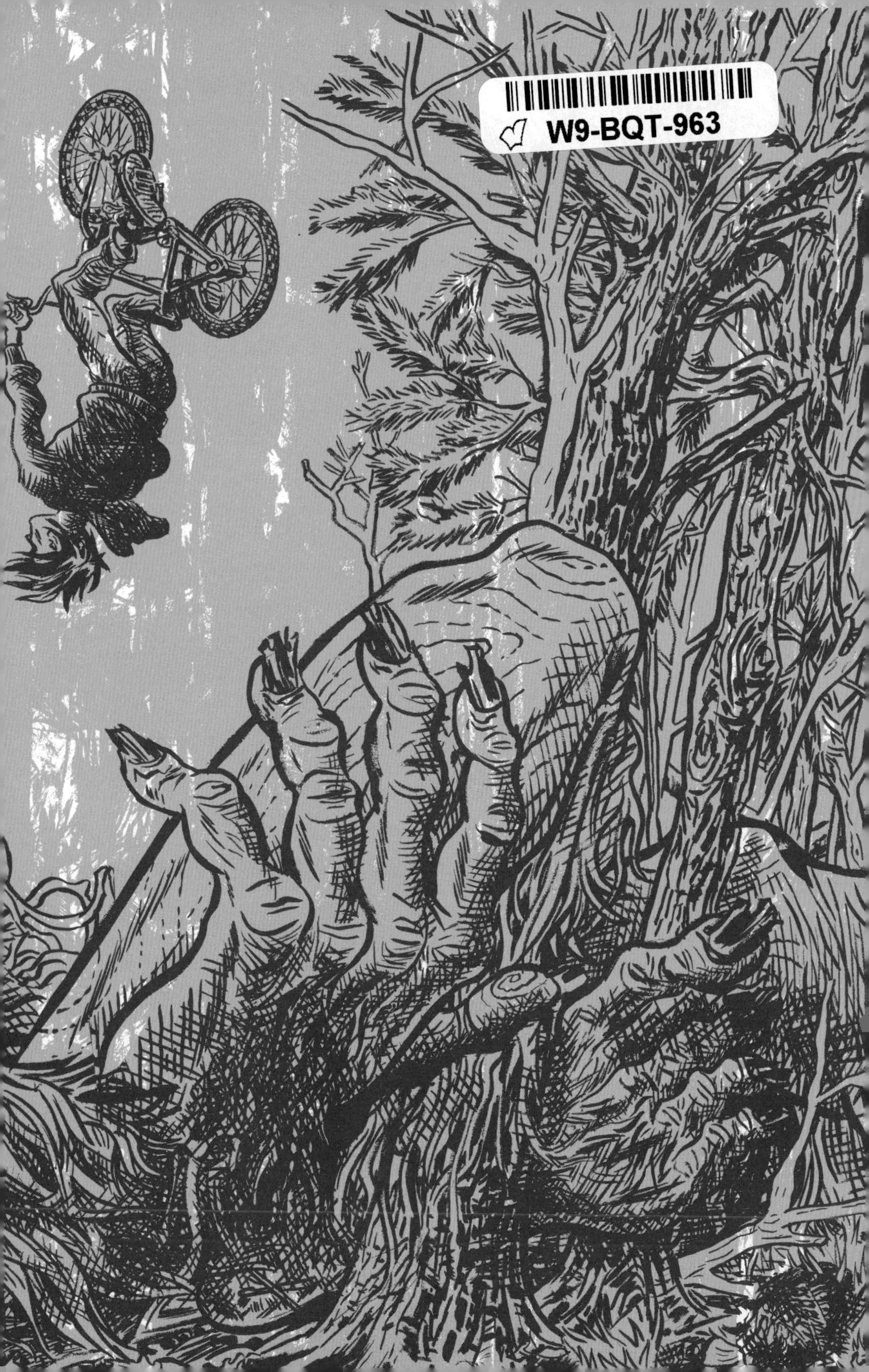

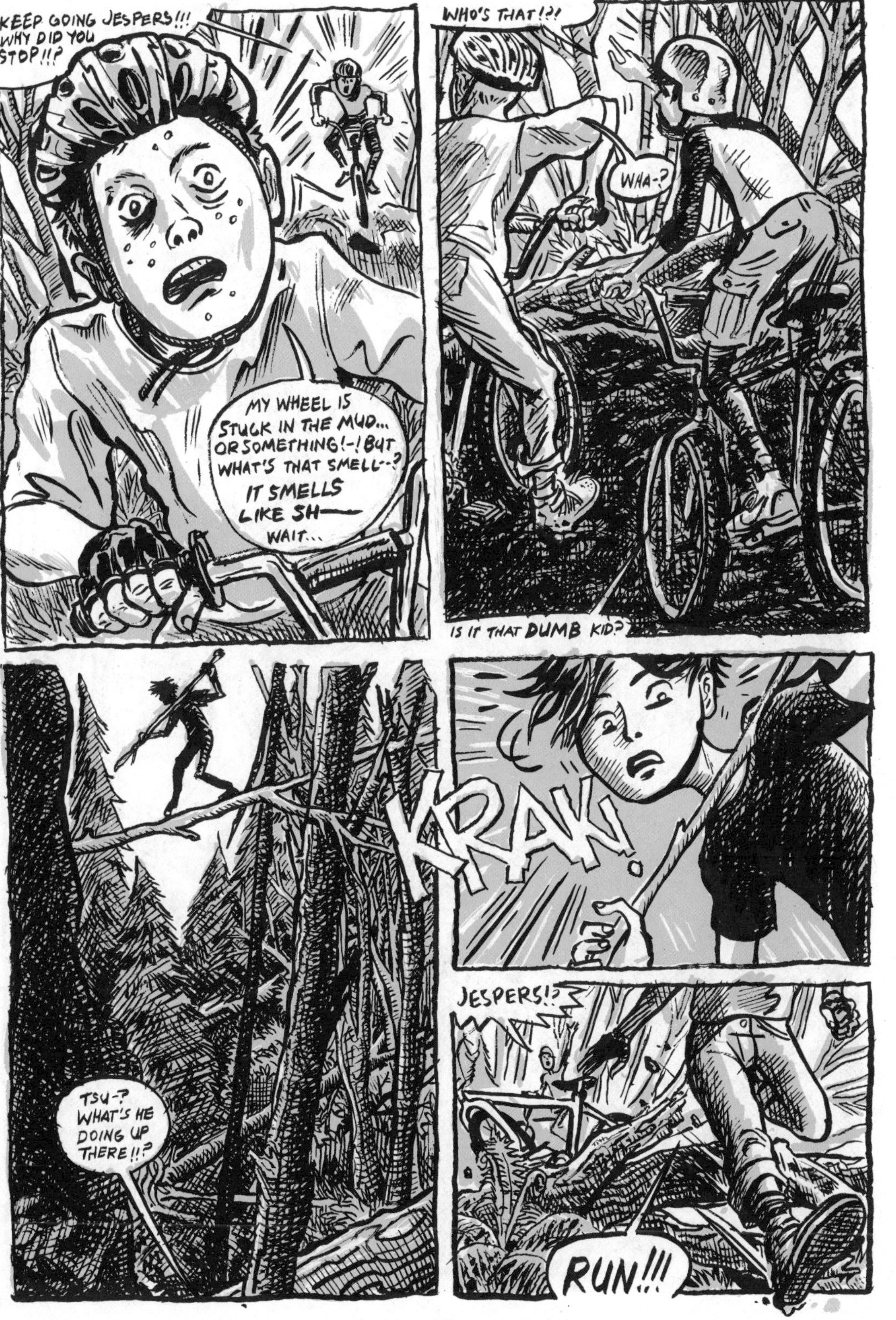

KEEP GOING JESPERS!!! WHY DID YOU STOP!!?
MY WHEEL IS STUCK IN THE MUD... OR SOMETHING!-! BUT WHAT'S THAT SMELL--? IT SMELLS LIKE SH— WAIT...
WHO'S THAT!?!
WHA-?
IS IT THAT DUMB KID?
KRAK!
TSU-? WHAT'S HE DOING UP THERE!!?
JESPERS!?
RUN!!!

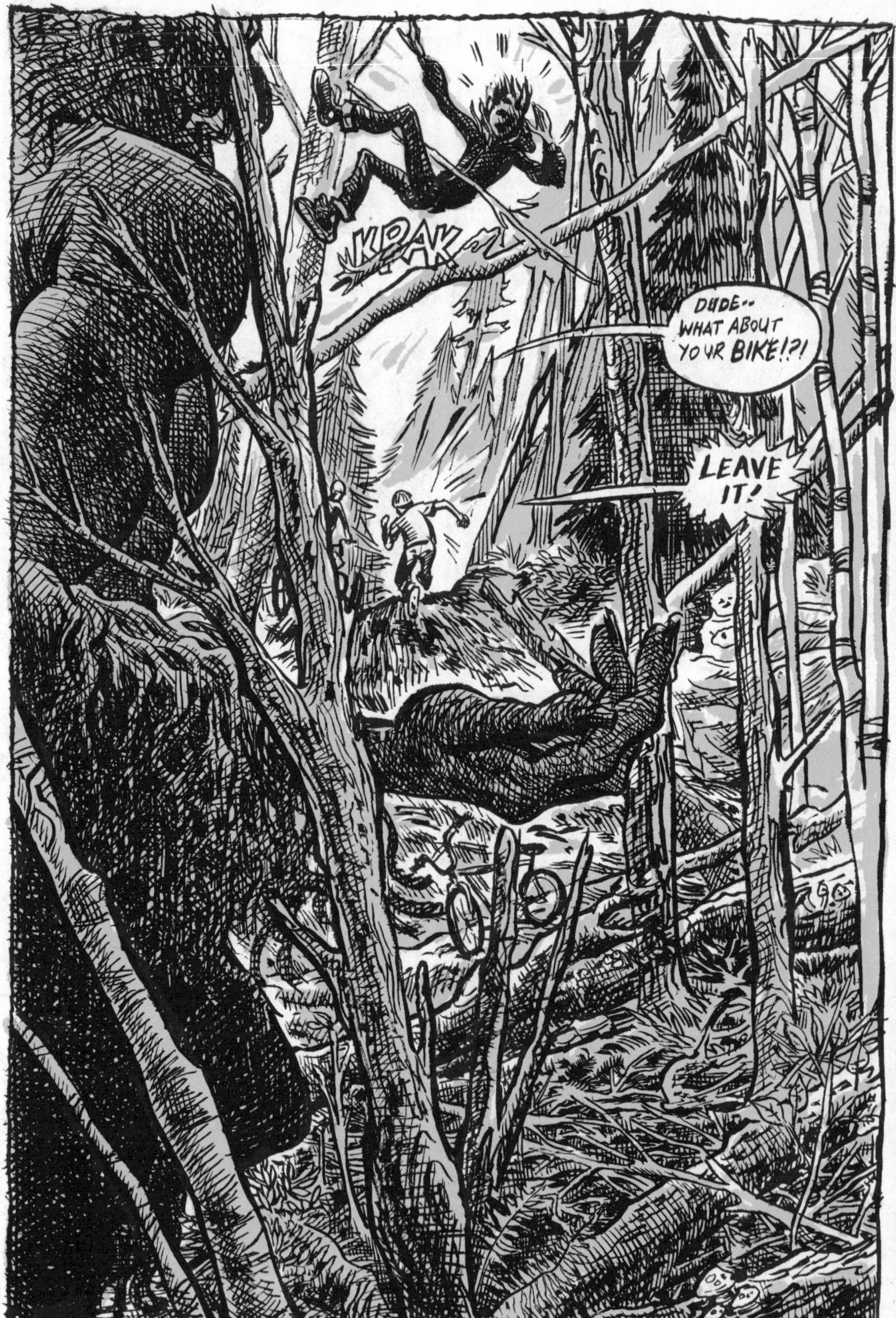
KRAK
DUDE-- WHAT ABOUT YOUR BIKE!?!
LEAVE IT!

TSU AND THE OUTLIERS

Tsu and the Outliers
by E. Eero Johnson

Editor: Tom Kaczynski   Color Assist: Puck Saint

ODOD Books / Uncivilized Books
P.O. Box 6534
Minneapolis, MN 55406 USA
uncivilizedbooks.com ododbooks.com
First Edition, May 2018

10 9 8 7 6 5 4 3 2 1

ISBN 978-1-941250-24-2

DISTRIBUTED TO THE TRADE BY:
Consortium Book Sales Distribution, LLC.
34 Thirteenth Ave. NE, Suite 101
Minneapolis, MN 55413-1007
cbsd.com
Orders: (800) 283-3572

Printed in Canada

Chapter 1.

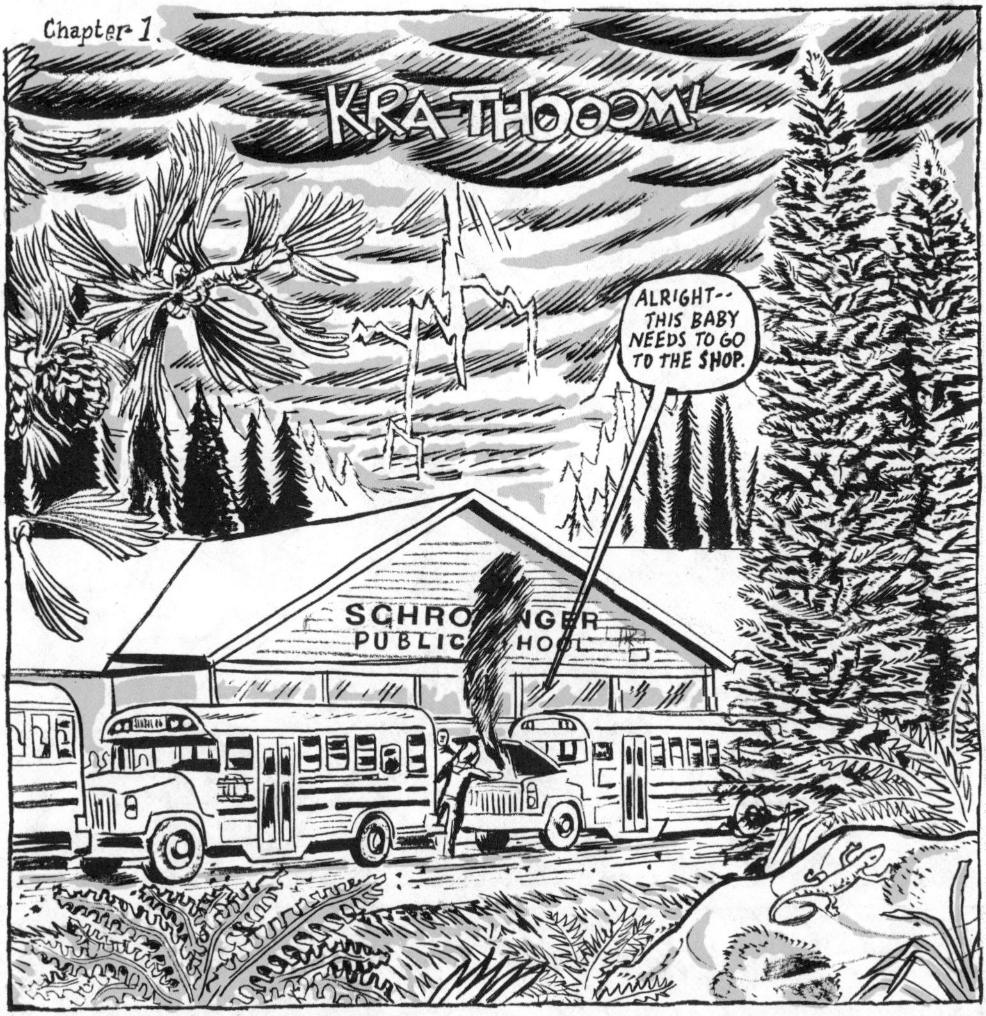
KRA-THOOOM!
ALRIGHT-- THIS BABY NEEDS TO GO TO THE SHOP.

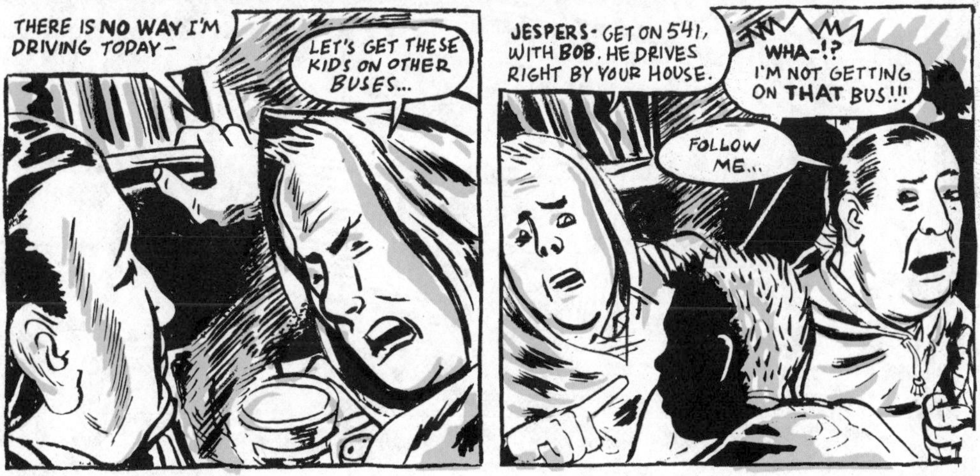
THERE IS NO WAY I'M DRIVING TODAY-
LET'S GET THESE KIDS ON OTHER BUSES...
JESPERS- GET ON 541, WITH BOB. HE DRIVES RIGHT BY YOUR HOUSE.
WHA-!? I'M NOT GETTING ON THAT BUS!!!
FOLLOW ME...

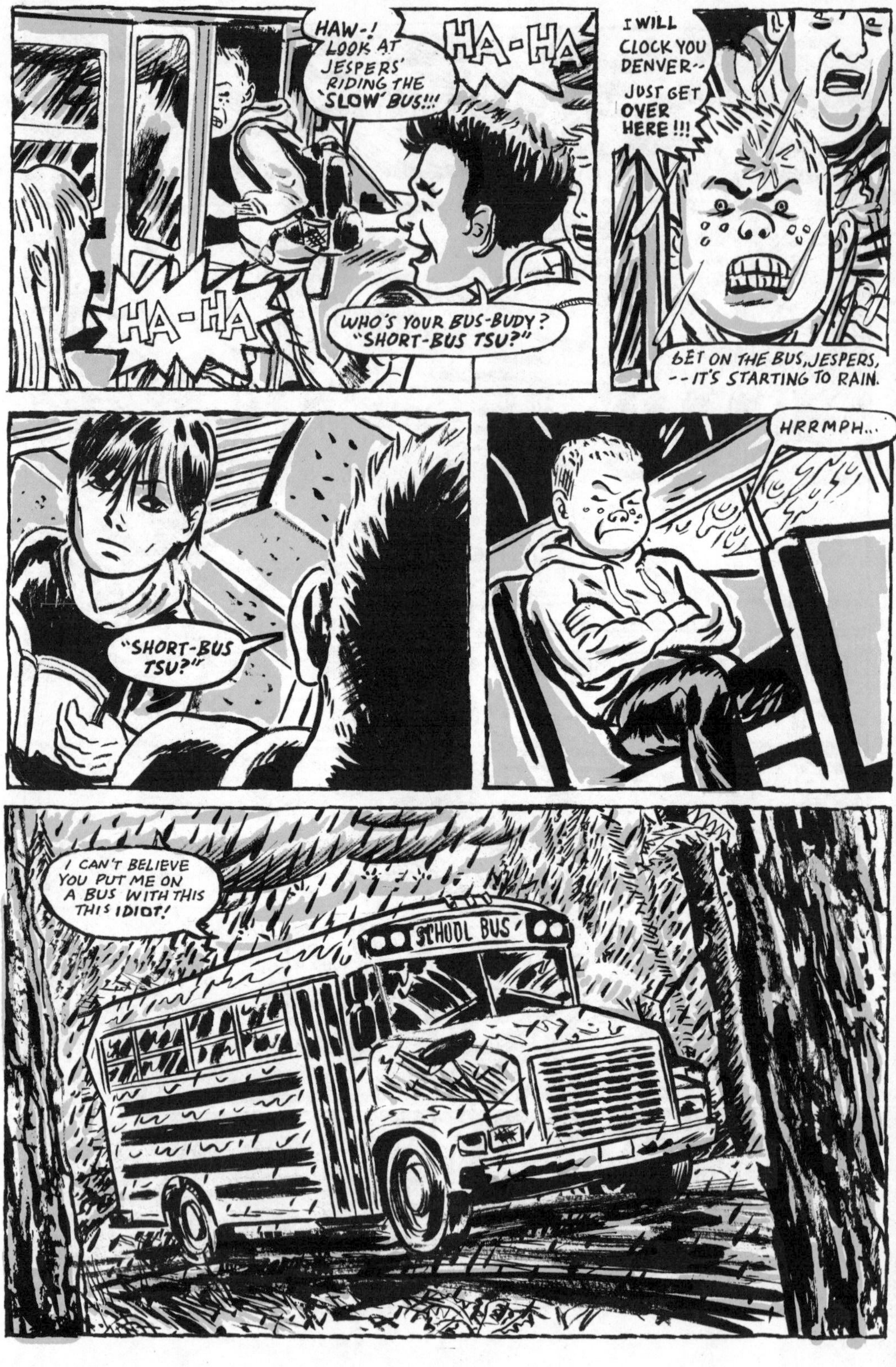
HAW-! LOOK AT JESPERS' RIDING THE 'SLOW' BUS!!!
HA-HA
HA-HA
WHO'S YOUR BUS-BUDY? "SHORT-BUS TSU?"
I WILL CLOCK YOU DENVER-- JUST GET OVER HERE!!!
GET ON THE BUS, JESPERS, --IT'S STARTING TO RAIN.
"SHORT-BUS TSU?"
HRRMPH...
I CAN'T BELIEVE YOU PUT ME ON A BUS WITH THIS THIS IDIOT!
SCHOOL BUS

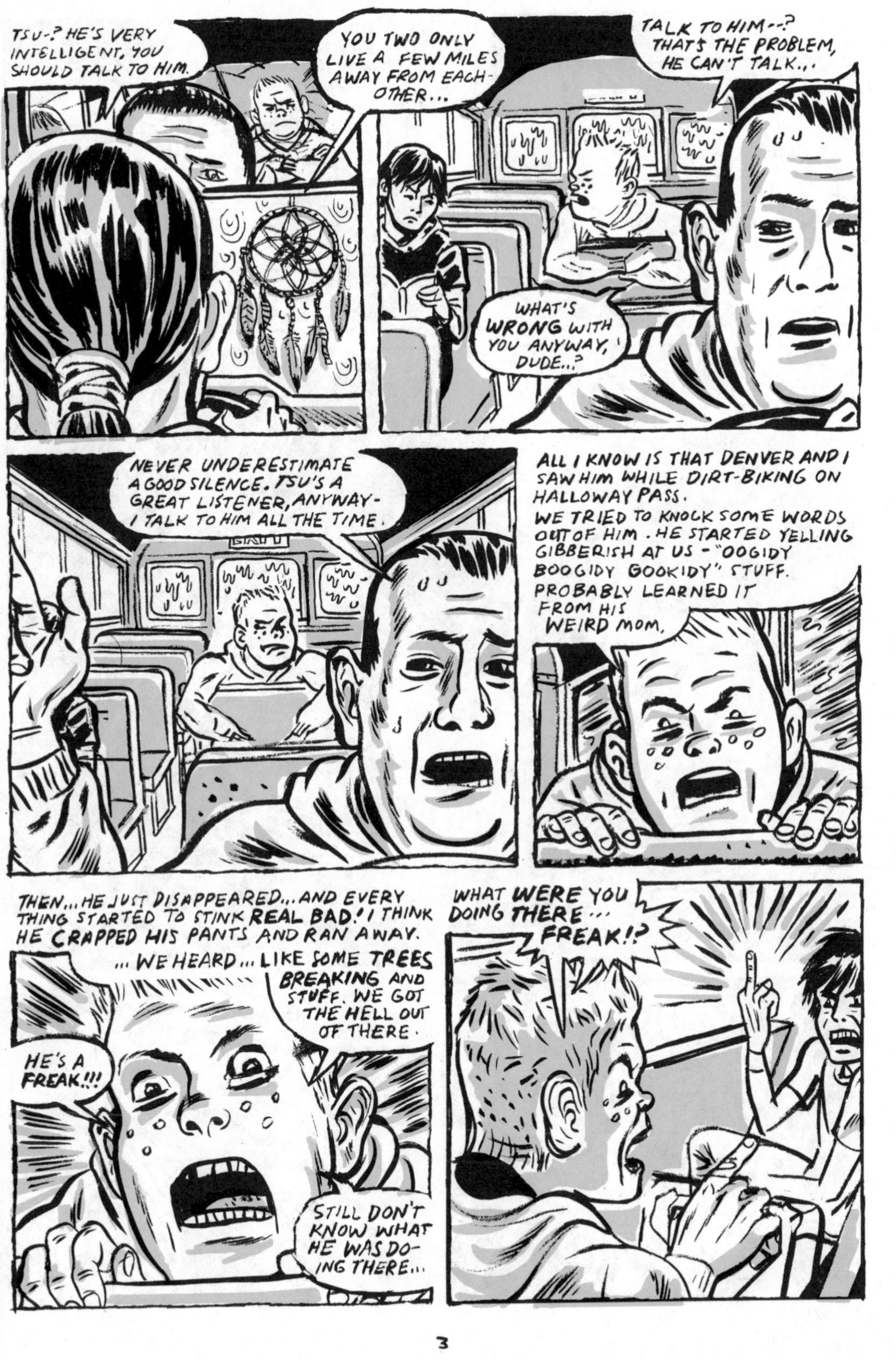
TSU-? HE'S VERY INTELLIGENT. YOU SHOULD TALK TO HIM.
YOU TWO ONLY LIVE A FEW MILES AWAY FROM EACH-OTHER...
TALK TO HIM--? THAT'S THE PROBLEM, HE CAN'T TALK...
WHAT'S WRONG WITH YOU ANYWAY, DUDE...?
NEVER UNDERESTIMATE A GOOD SILENCE. TSU'S A GREAT LISTENER, ANYWAY- I TALK TO HIM ALL THE TIME.
ALL I KNOW IS THAT DENVER AND I SAW HIM WHILE DIRT-BIKING ON HALLOWAY PASS.
WE TRIED TO KNOCK SOME WORDS OUT OF HIM. HE STARTED YELLING GIBBERISH AT US - "OOGIDY BOOGIDY GOOKIDY" STUFF.
PROBABLY LEARNED IT FROM HIS WEIRD MOM.
THEN... HE JUST DISAPPEARED... AND EVERY THING STARTED TO STINK REAL BAD! I THINK HE CRAPPED HIS PANTS AND RAN AWAY.
... WE HEARD... LIKE SOME TREES BREAKING AND STUFF. WE GOT THE HELL OUT OF THERE.
HE'S A FREAK!!!
STILL DON'T KNOW WHAT HE WAS DOING THERE...
WHAT WERE YOU DOING THERE... FREAK!?

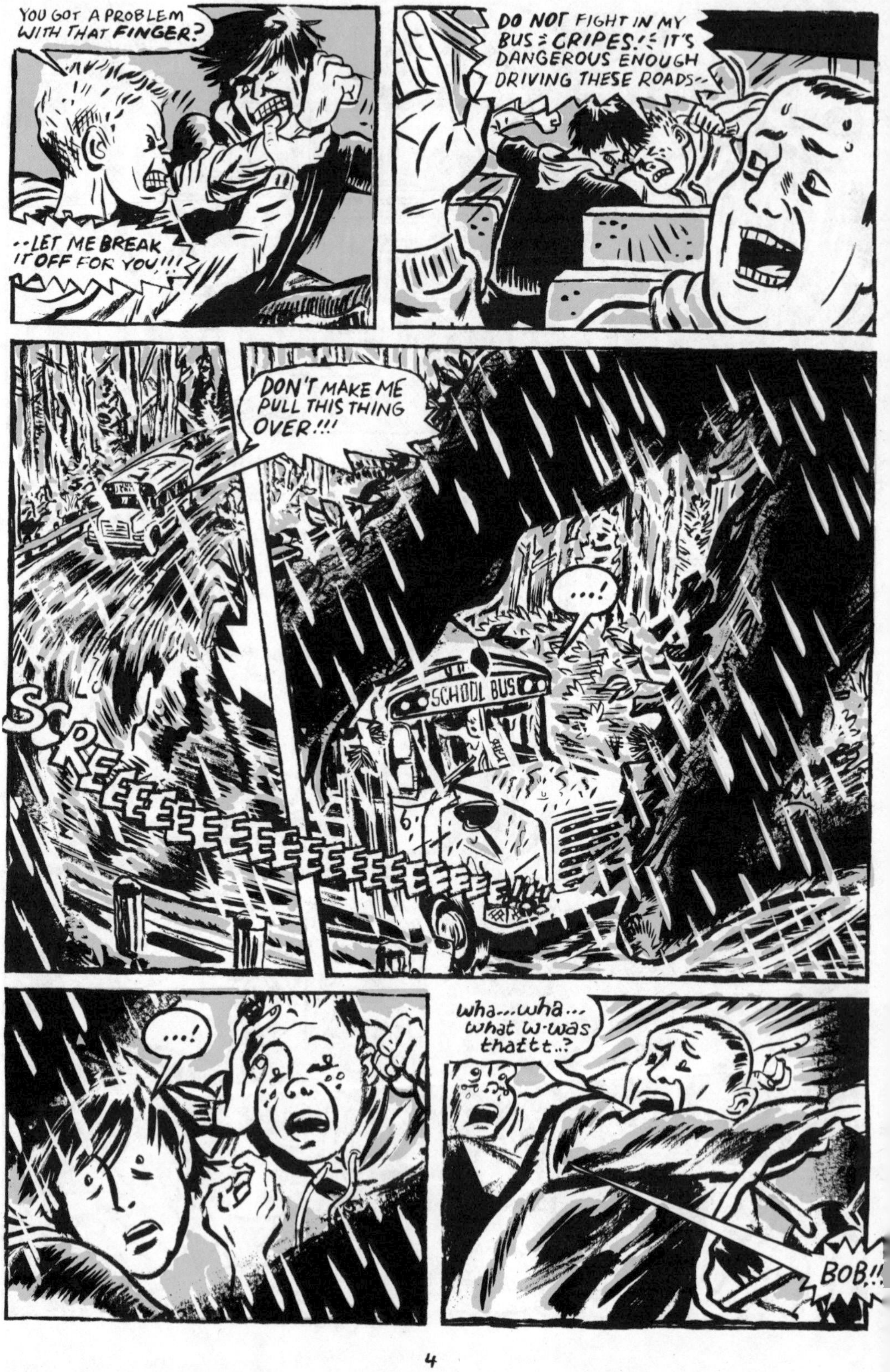
YOU GOT A PROBLEM WITH THAT FINGER?
--LET ME BREAK IT OFF FOR YOU!!!
DO NOT FIGHT IN MY BUS = GRIPES! = IT'S DANGEROUS ENOUGH DRIVING THESE ROADS--
DON'T MAKE ME PULL THIS THING OVER!!!
...!
SCHOOL BUS
SCREEEEEEEEEEEEEEEEEEEE
...!
wha...wha... what w-was thattt..?
BOB!!

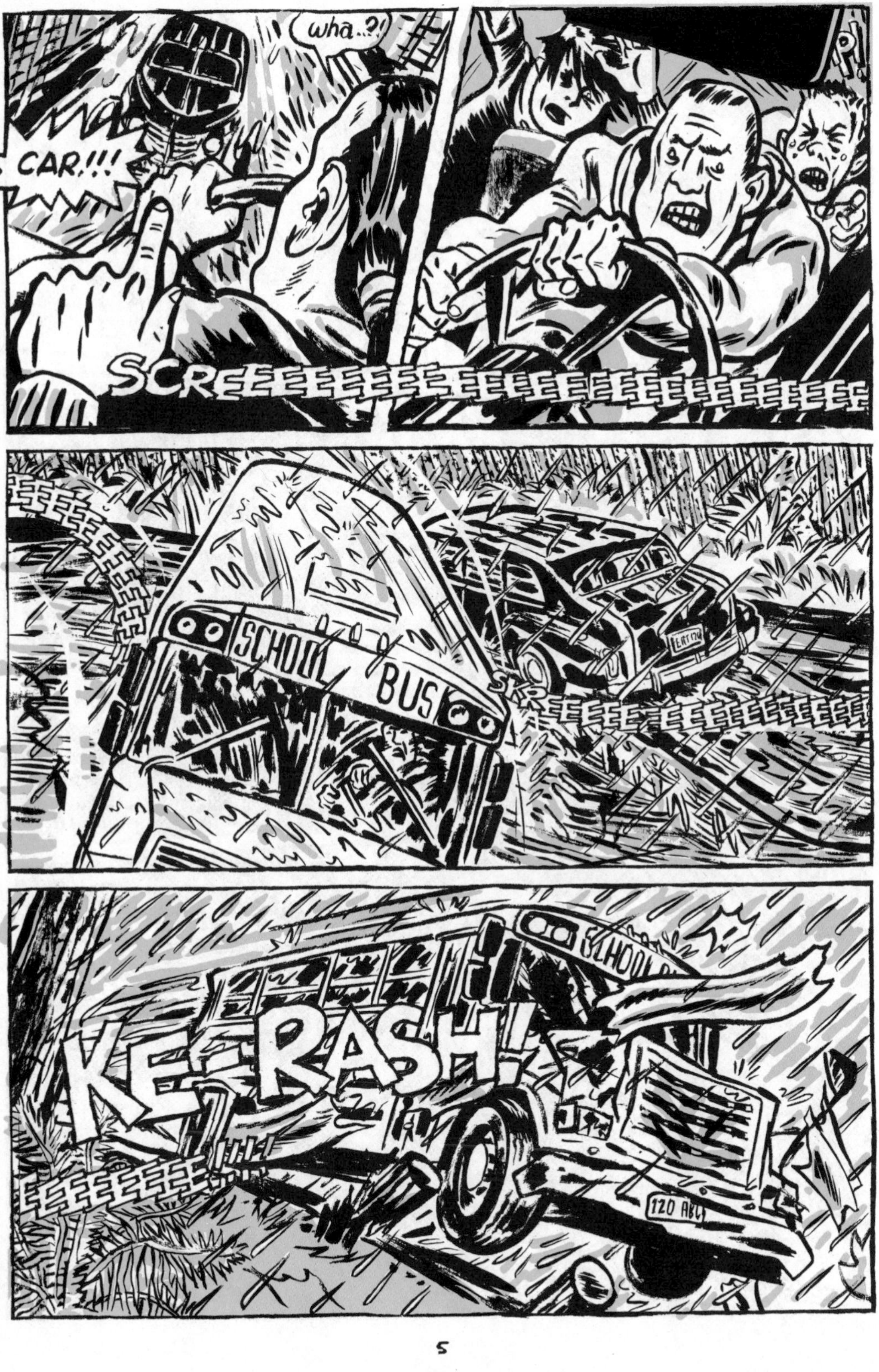
CAR!!!
whã..?!
SCREEEEEEEEEEEEEEEEEEEEEEEEEEEE
SCHOOL BUS
KE-RASH!
120 ABL

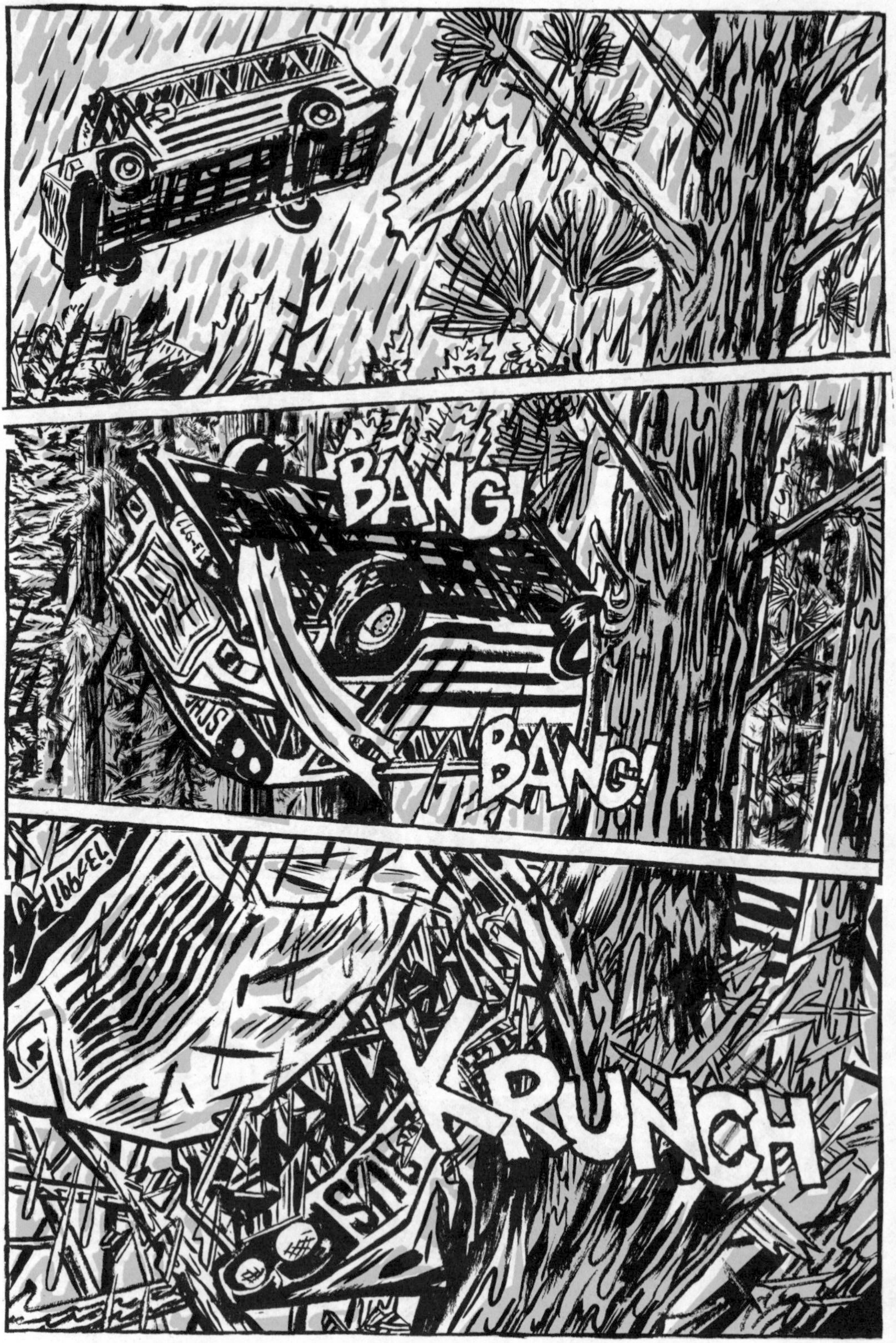
BANG!
BANG!
KRUNCH

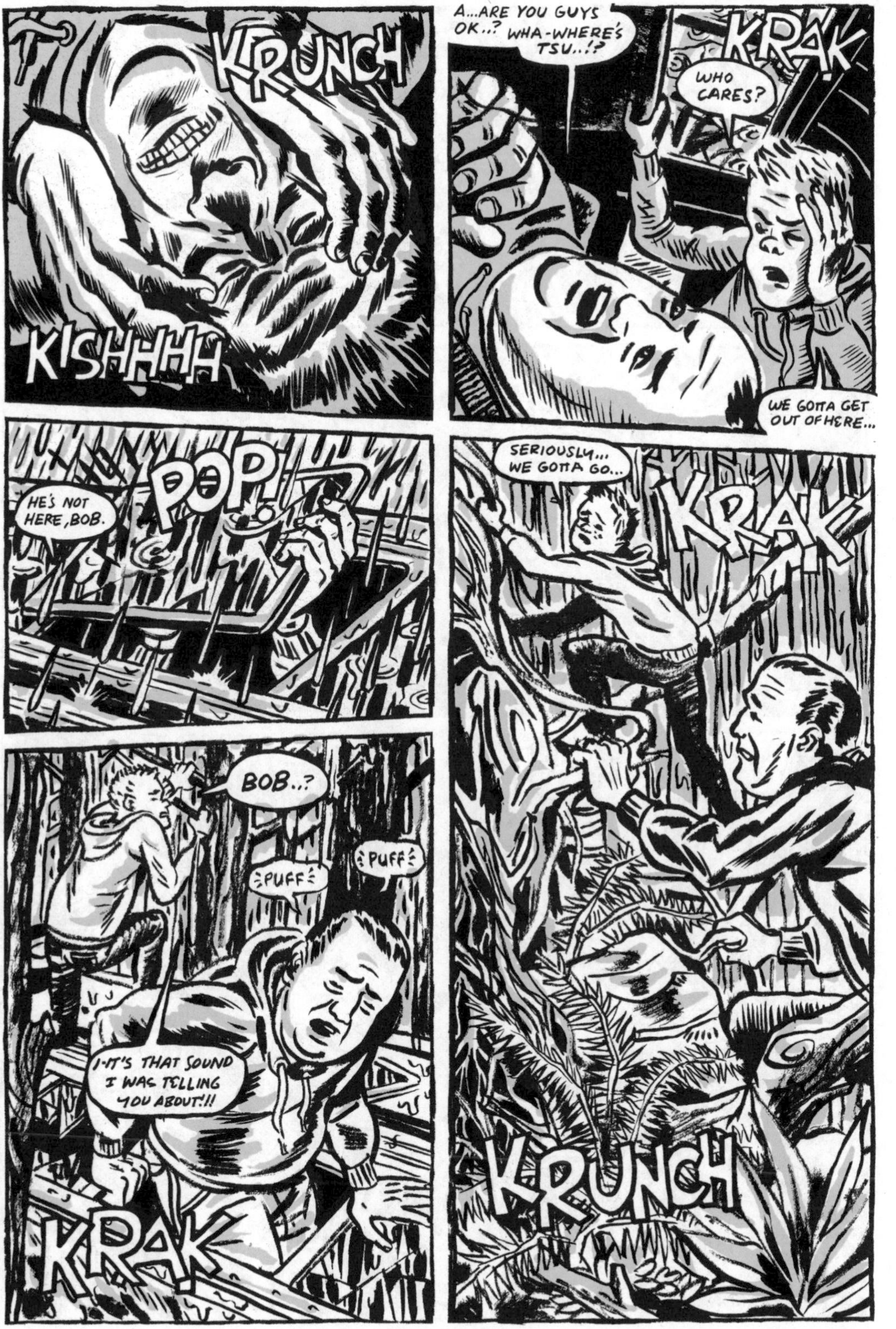
KRUNCH
KISHHHH
A...ARE YOU GUYS OK..? WHA-WHERE'S TSU..!?
KRAK
WHO CARES?
WE GOTTA GET OUT OF HERE...
POP
HE'S NOT HERE, BOB.
SERIOUSLY... WE GOTTA GO...
KRAK
BOB..?
PUFF
PUFF
I-IT'S THAT SOUND I WAS TELLING YOU ABOUT!!!
KRAK
KRUNCH

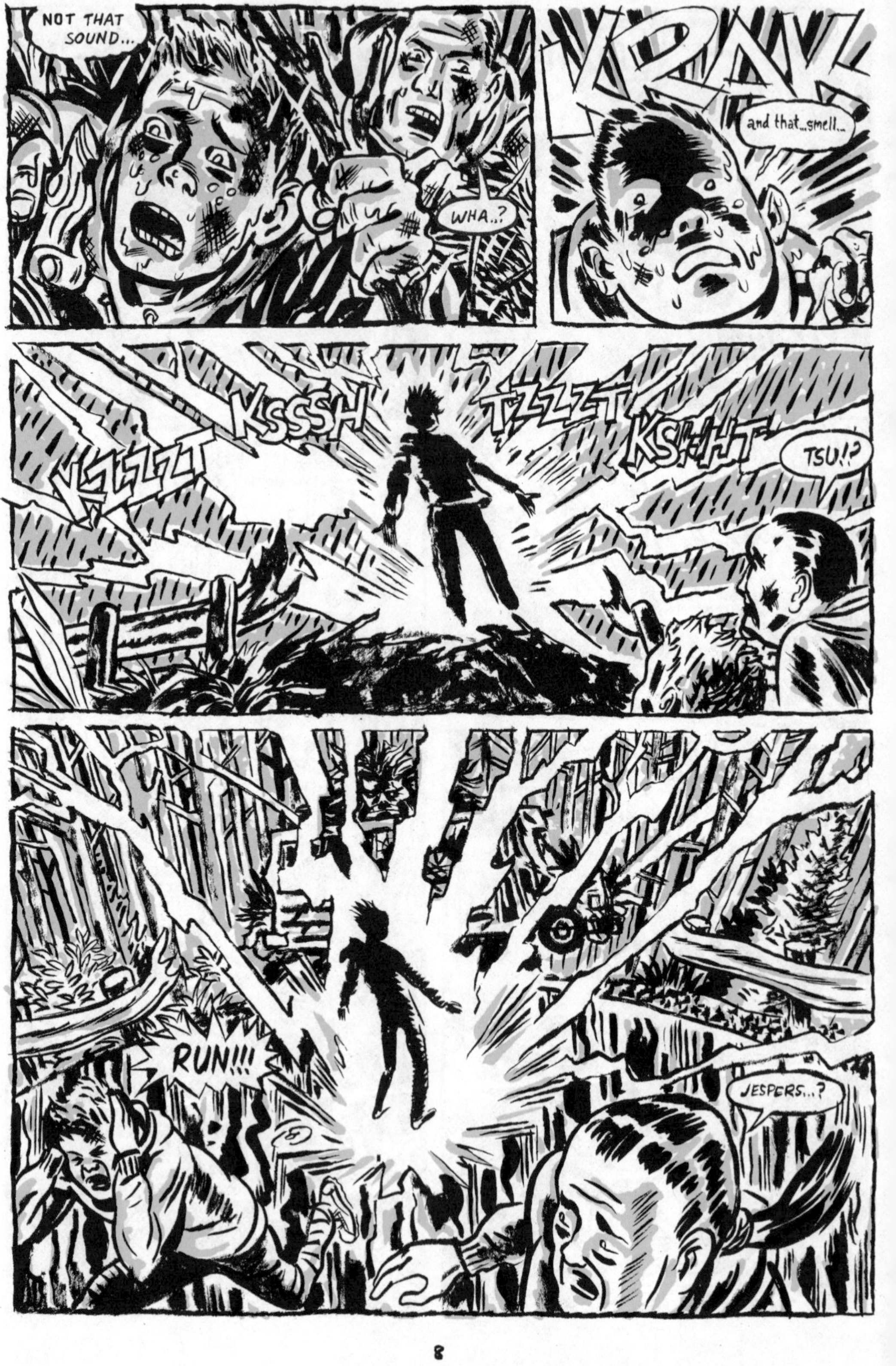
NOT THAT SOUND...
WHA..?
KRAK!
and that...smell...
KSSSH
TZZZZT
TSU!?
RUN!!!
JESPERS...?

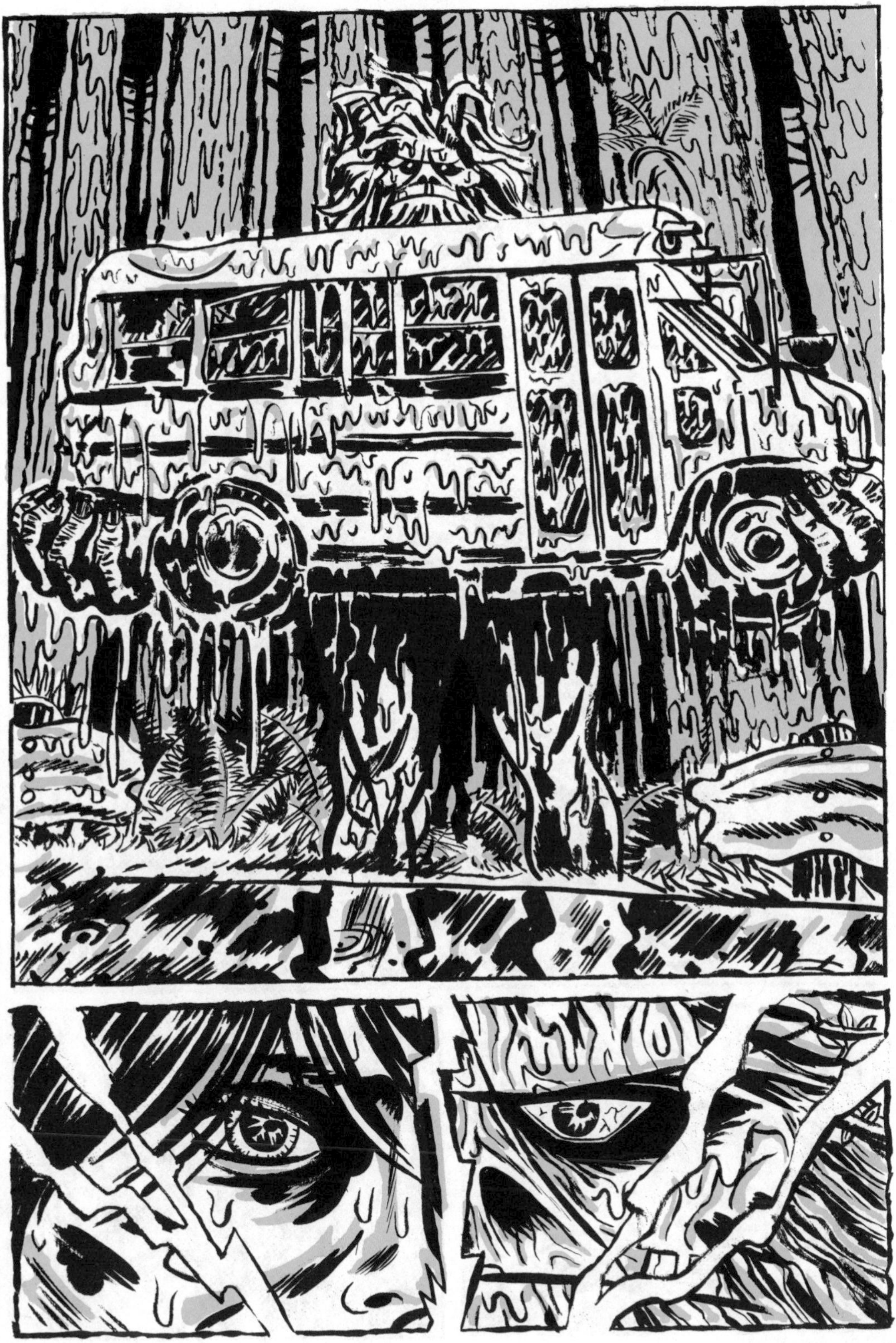

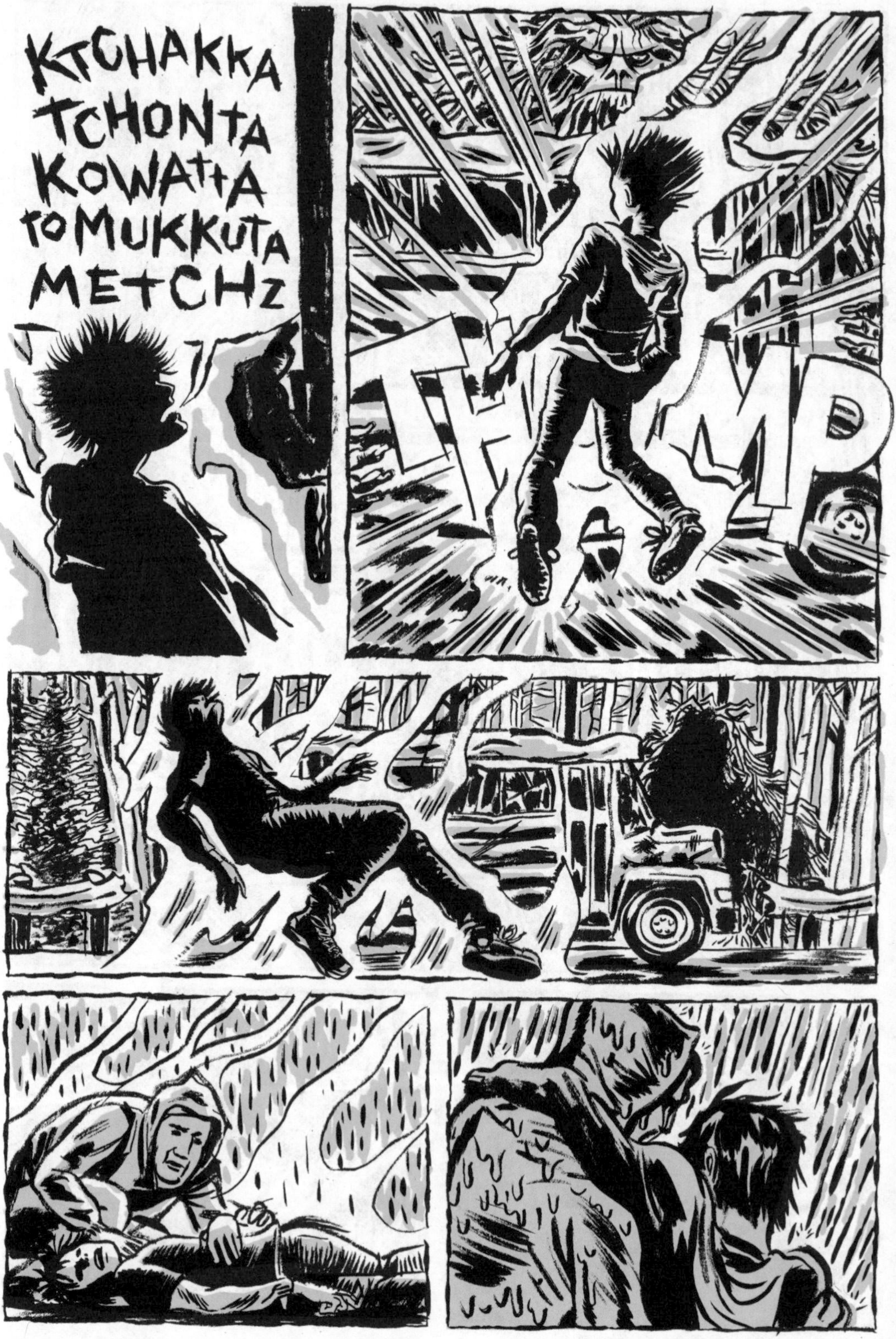
KTCHAKKA
TCHONTA
KOWATTA
TOMUKKUTA
METCHZ
THMP

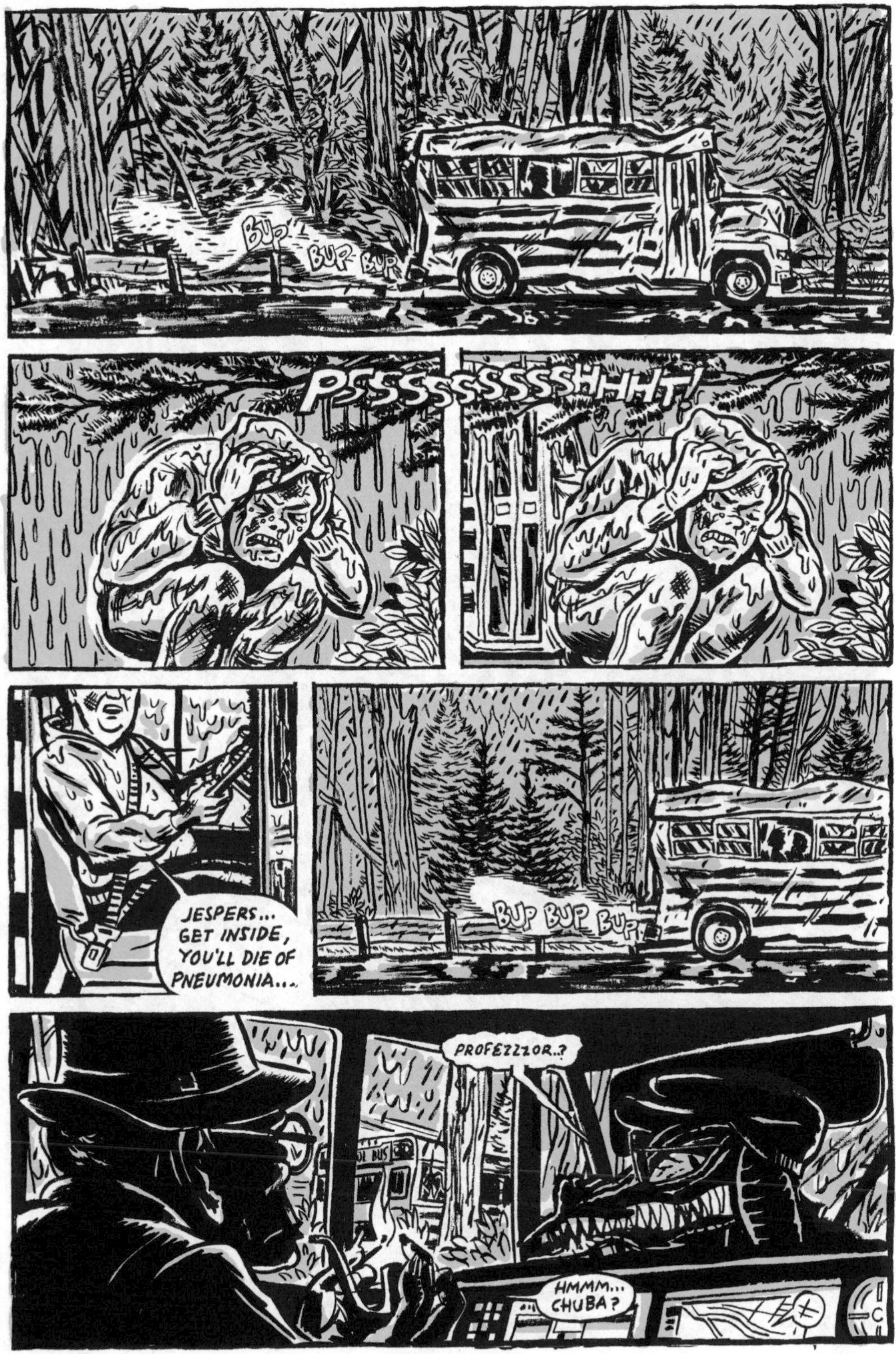
BUP BUP BUP
PSSSSSSSSHHHT!
JESPERS... GET INSIDE, YOU'LL DIE OF PNEUMONIA...
BUP BUP BUP
PROFEZZZOR..?
HMMM... CHUBA?

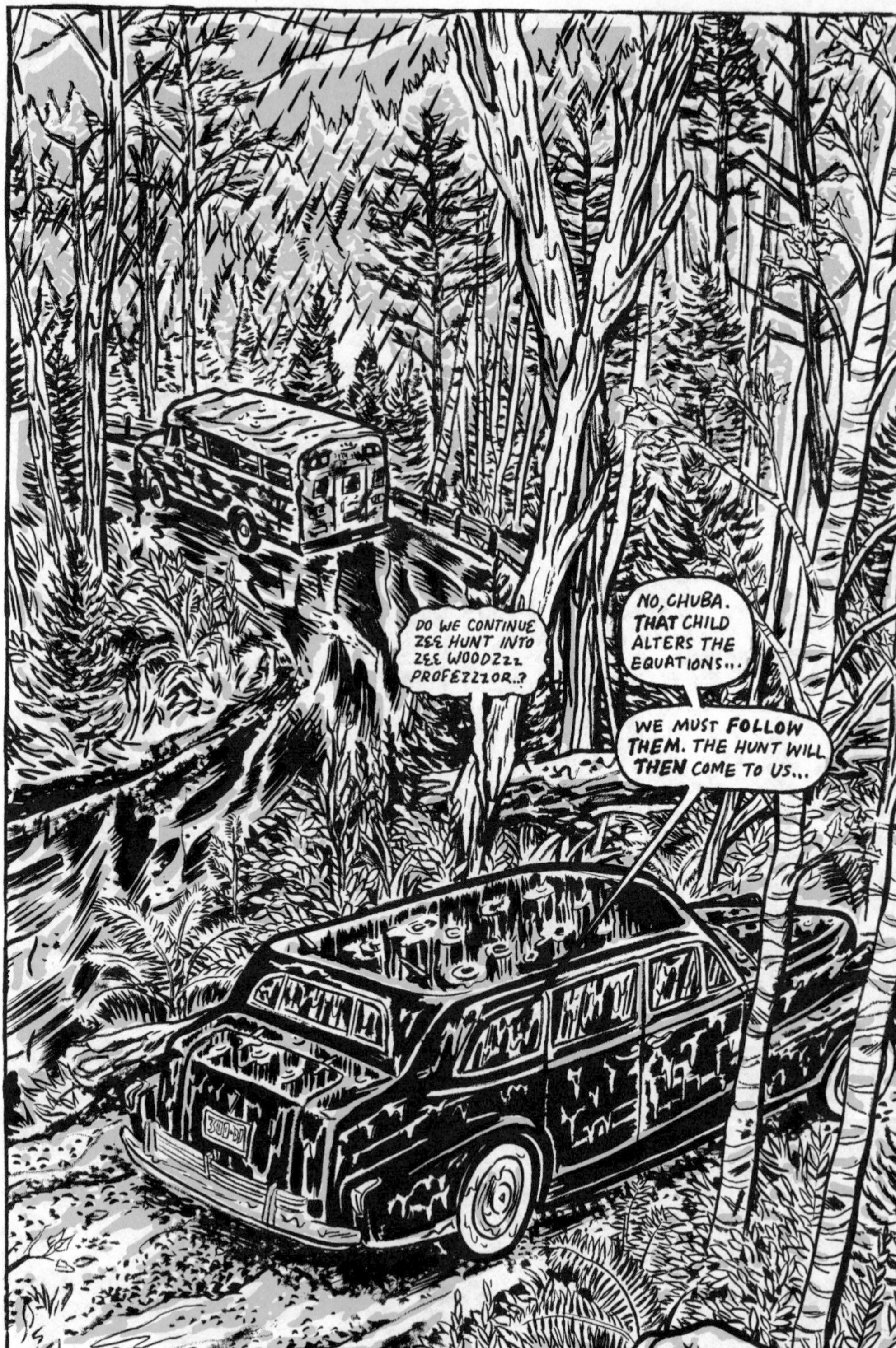
DO WE CONTINUE ZEE HUNT INTO ZEE WOODZzz PROFEZZZOR..?
NO, CHUBA. THAT CHILD ALTERS THE EQUATIONS...
WE MUST FOLLOW THEM. THE HUNT WILL THEN COME TO US...

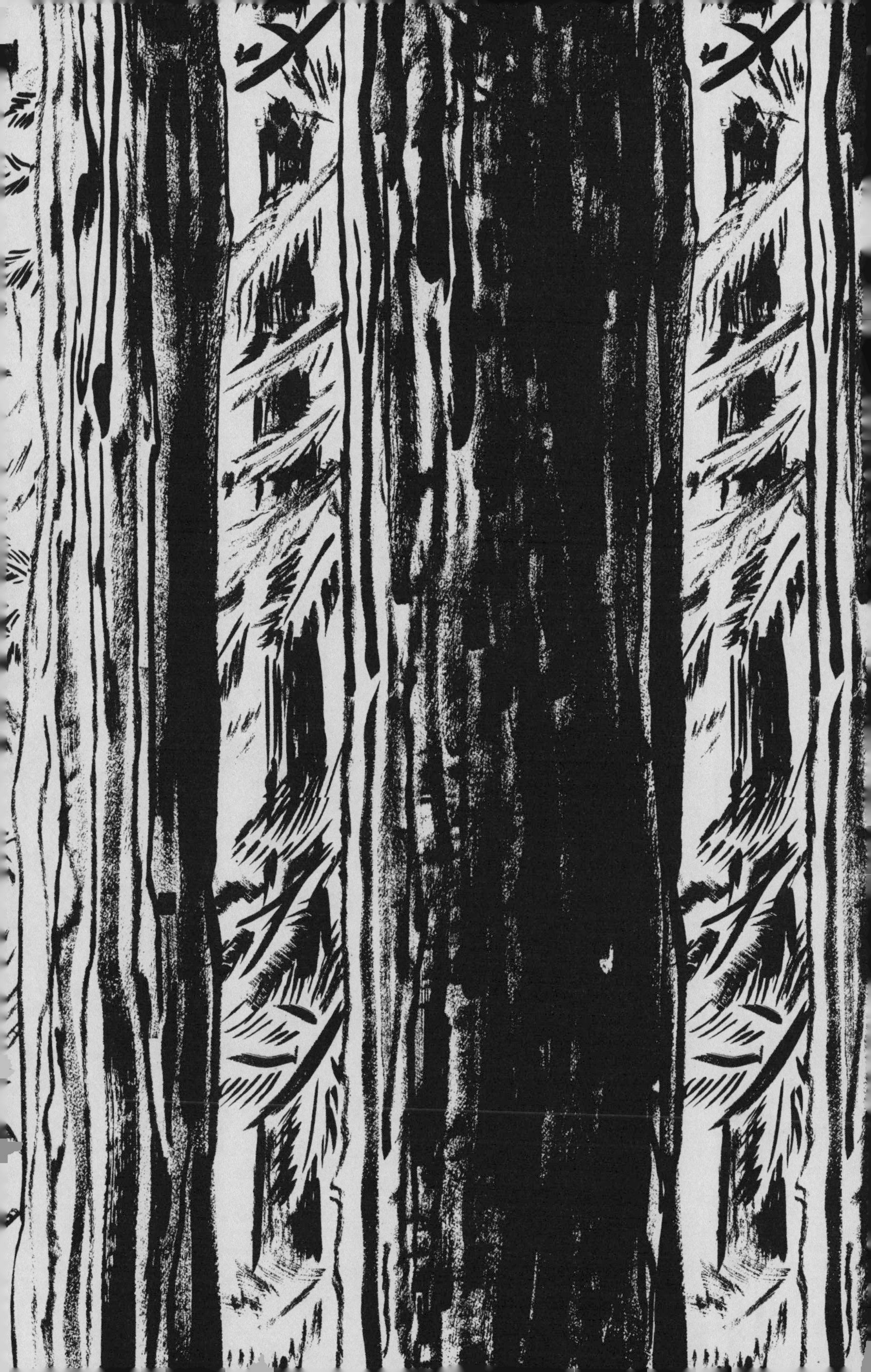

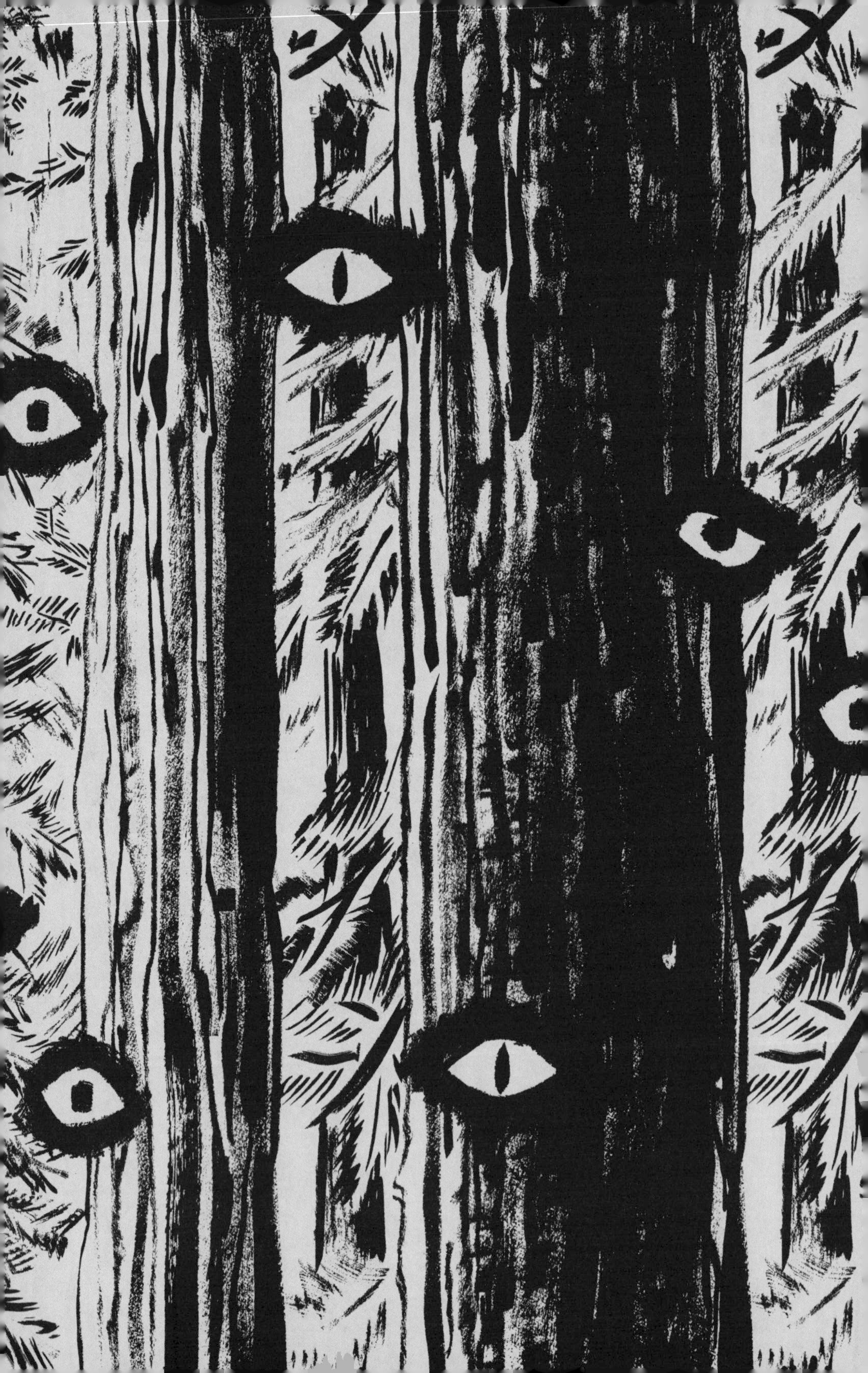

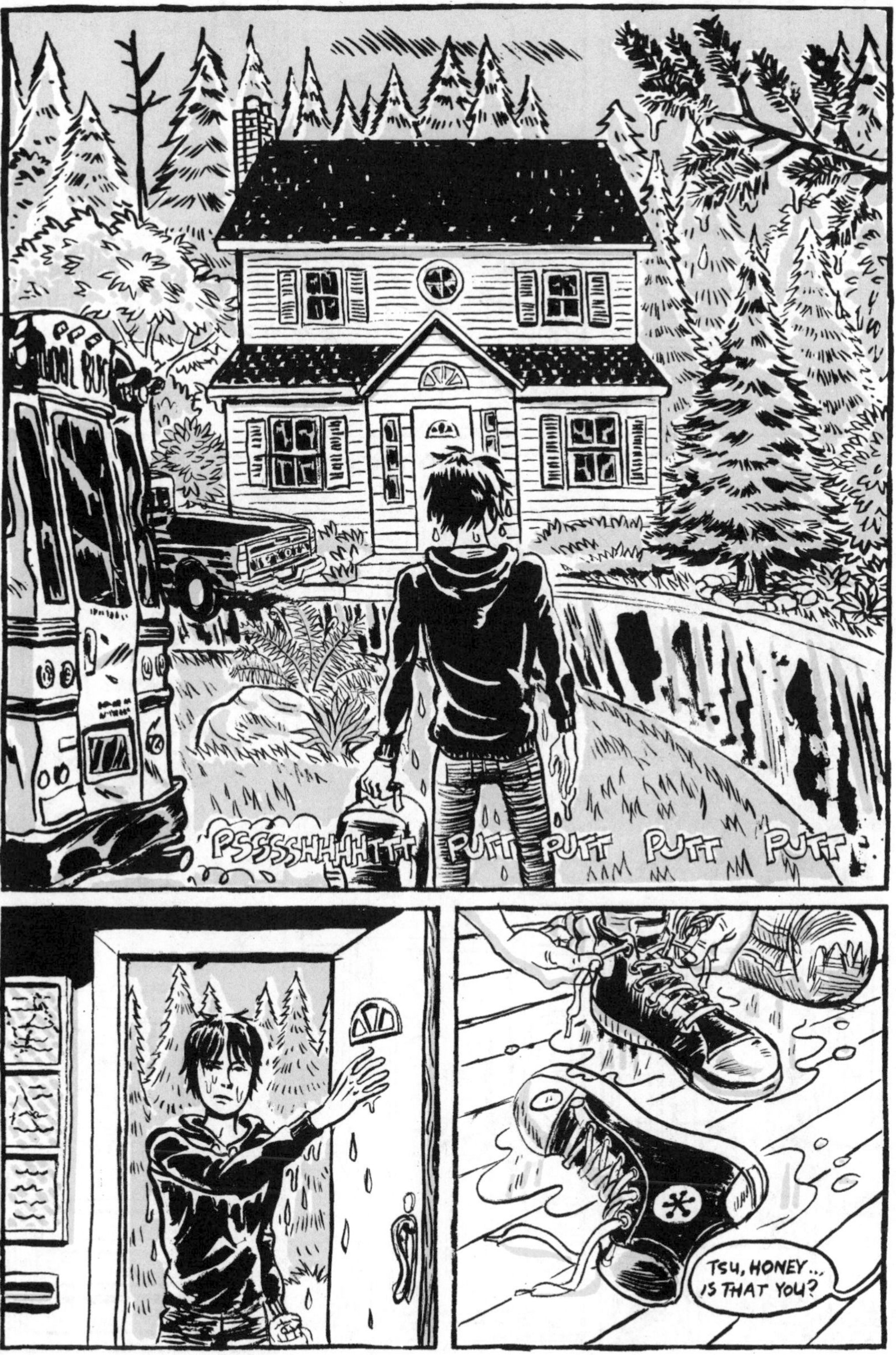
PSSSSHHHHTTT
PUTT
PUTT
PUTT
PUTT
TSU, HONEY... IS THAT YOU?

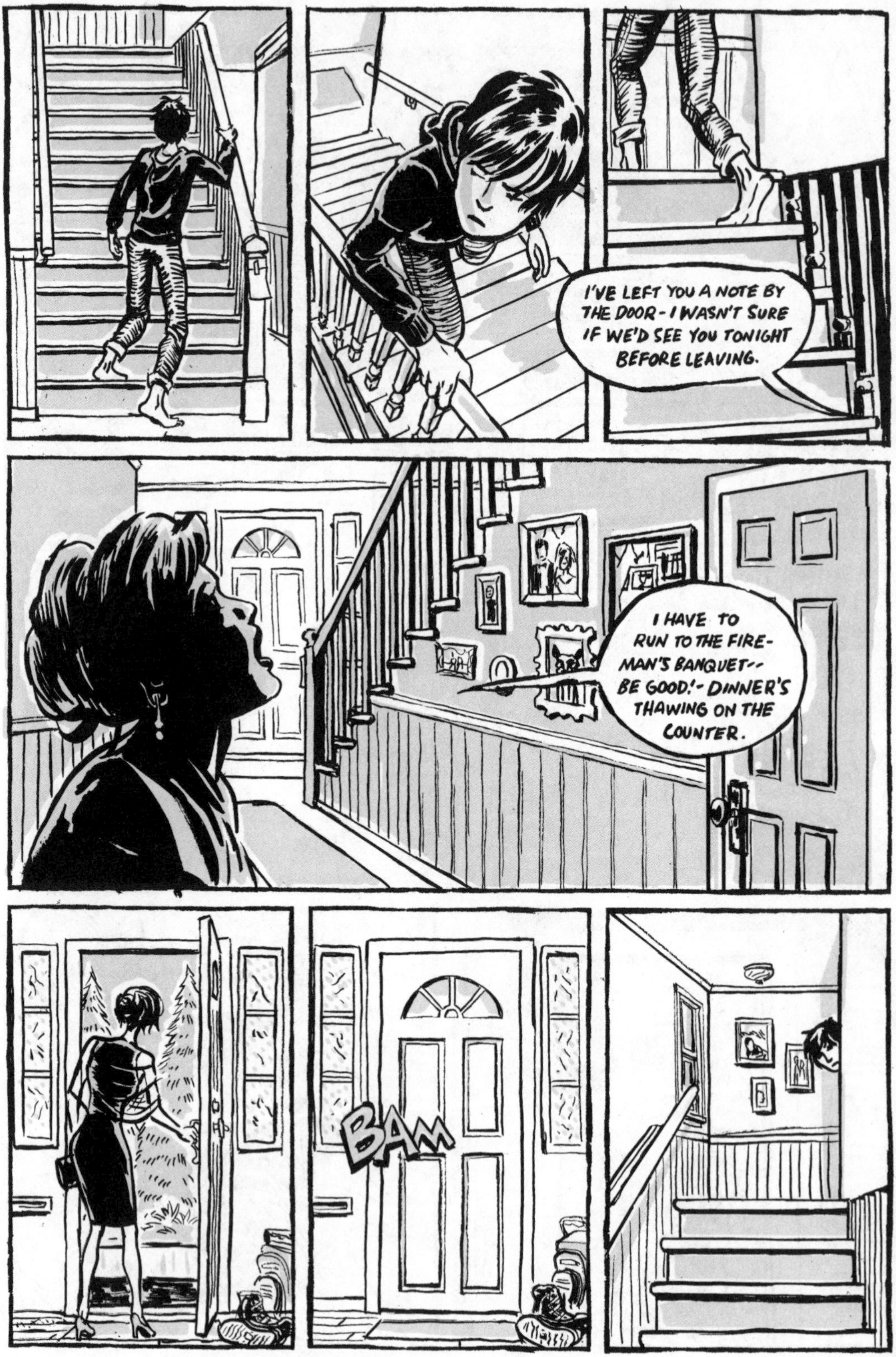
I'VE LEFT YOU A NOTE BY THE DOOR - I WASN'T SURE IF WE'D SEE YOU TONIGHT BEFORE LEAVING.
I HAVE TO RUN TO THE FIRE-MAN'S BANQUET-- BE GOOD!- DINNER'S THAWING ON THE COUNTER.
BAM

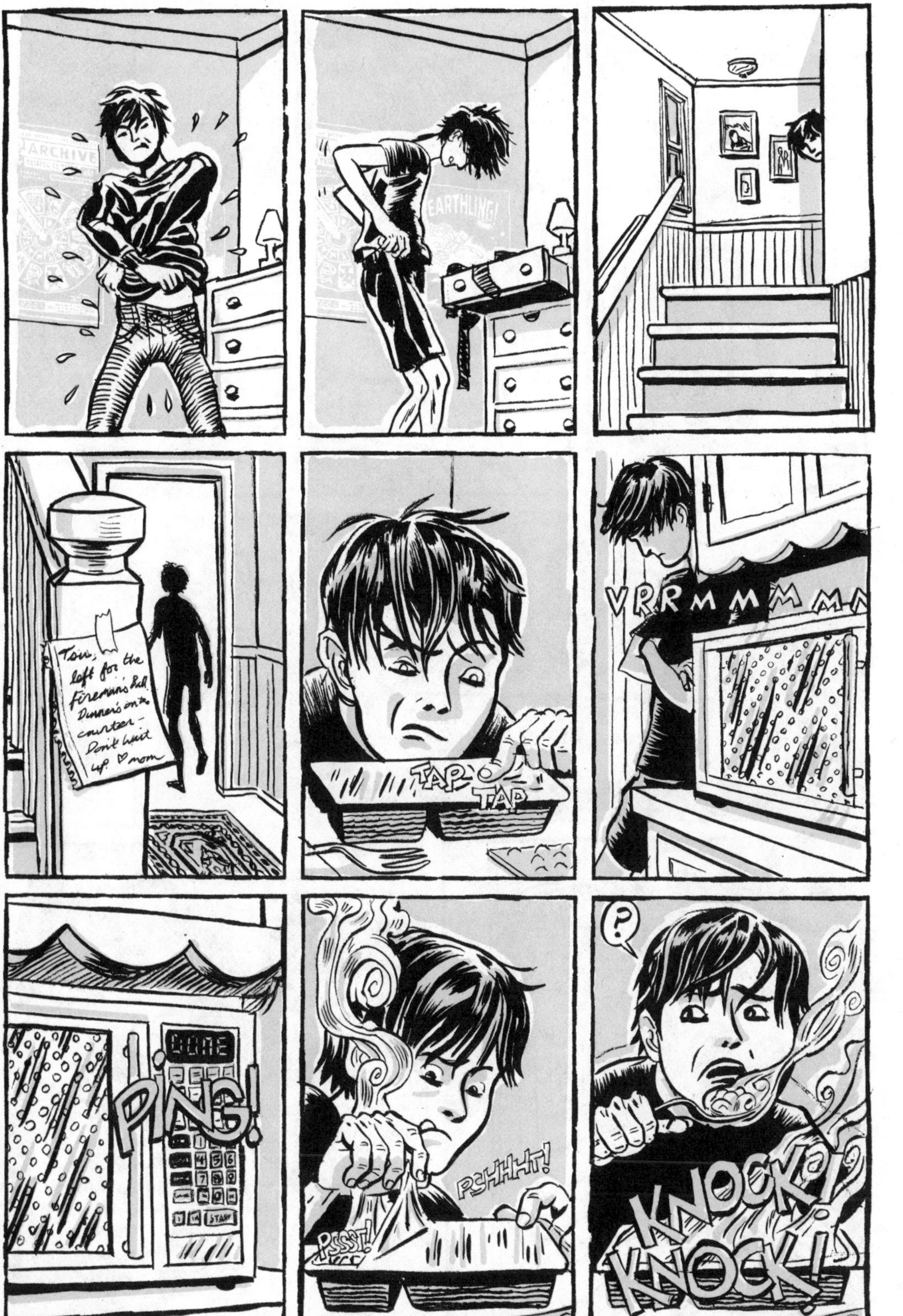
ARCHIVE
EARTHLING!
Tsu, left for the Fireman's Ball. Dinner's on the counter - Don't wait up. ♡ mom
TAP TAP
VRRMMMMM
PING!
PSSST!
PSHHHT!
?
KNOCK! KNOCK!

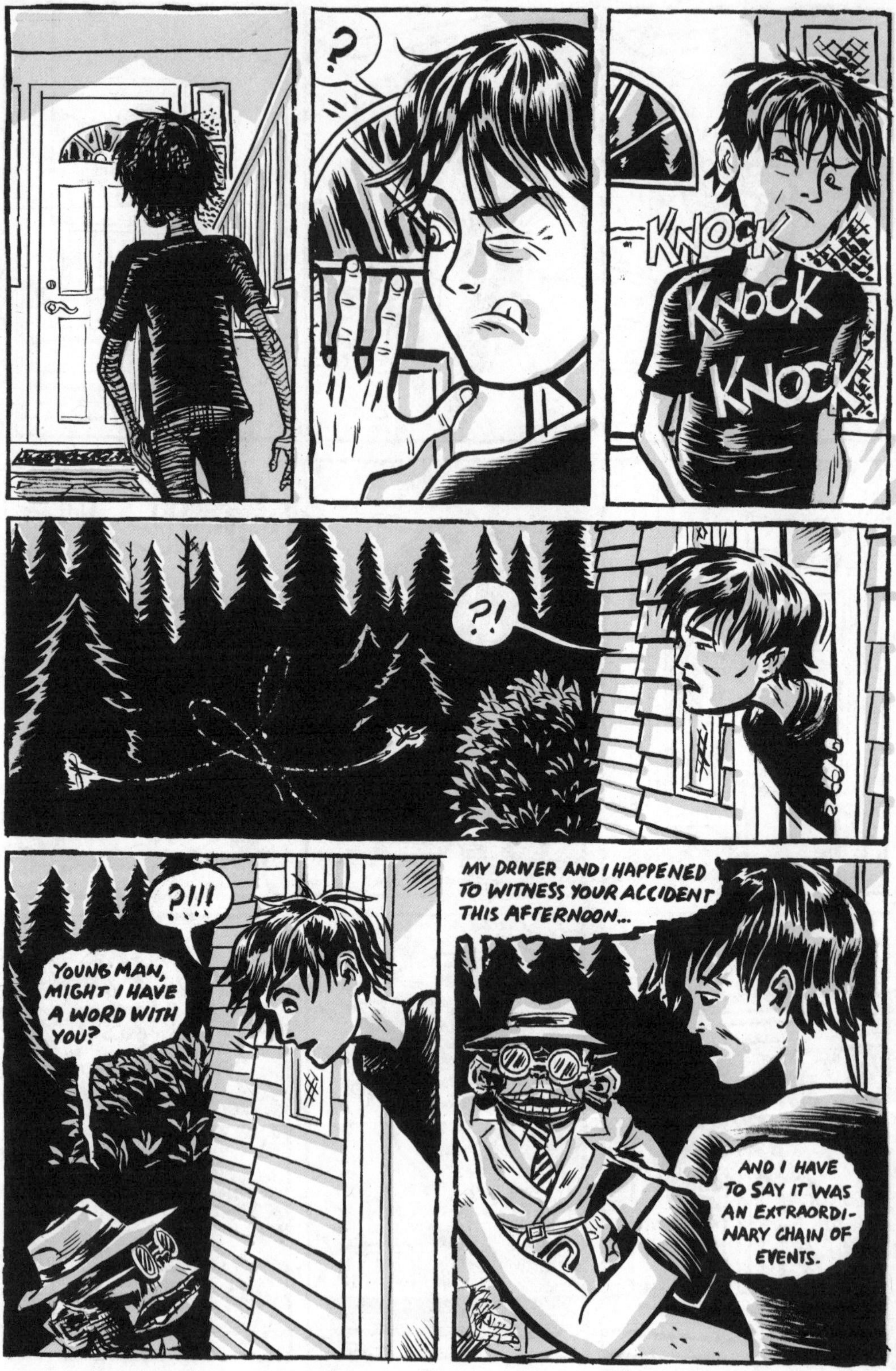
?
KNOCK
KNOCK
KNOCK
?!
?!!!
YOUNG MAN, MIGHT I HAVE A WORD WITH YOU?
MY DRIVER AND I HAPPENED TO WITNESS YOUR ACCIDENT THIS AFTERNOON...
AND I HAVE TO SAY IT WAS AN EXTRAORDINARY CHAIN OF EVENTS.

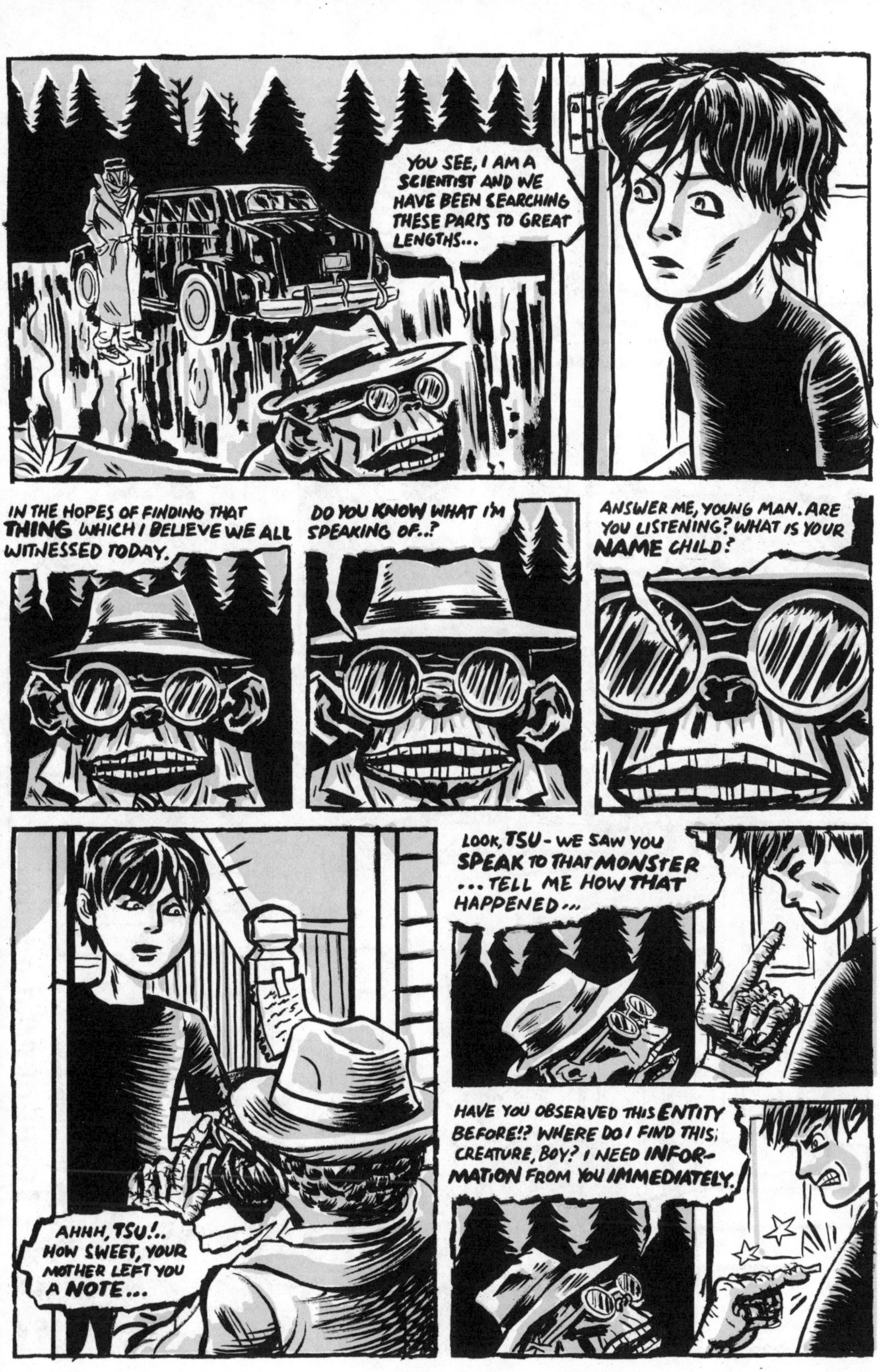
YOU SEE, I AM A SCIENTIST AND WE HAVE BEEN SEARCHING THESE PARTS TO GREAT LENGTHS...
IN THE HOPES OF FINDING THAT THING WHICH I BELIEVE WE ALL WITNESSED TODAY.
DO YOU KNOW WHAT I'M SPEAKING OF..?
ANSWER ME, YOUNG MAN. ARE YOU LISTENING? WHAT IS YOUR NAME CHILD?
AHHH, TSU!.. HOW SWEET, YOUR MOTHER LEFT YOU A NOTE...
LOOK, TSU - WE SAW YOU SPEAK TO THAT MONSTER ...TELL ME HOW THAT HAPPENED...
HAVE YOU OBSERVED THIS ENTITY BEFORE!? WHERE DO I FIND THIS; CREATURE, BOY? I NEED INFORMATION FROM YOU IMMEDIATELY.

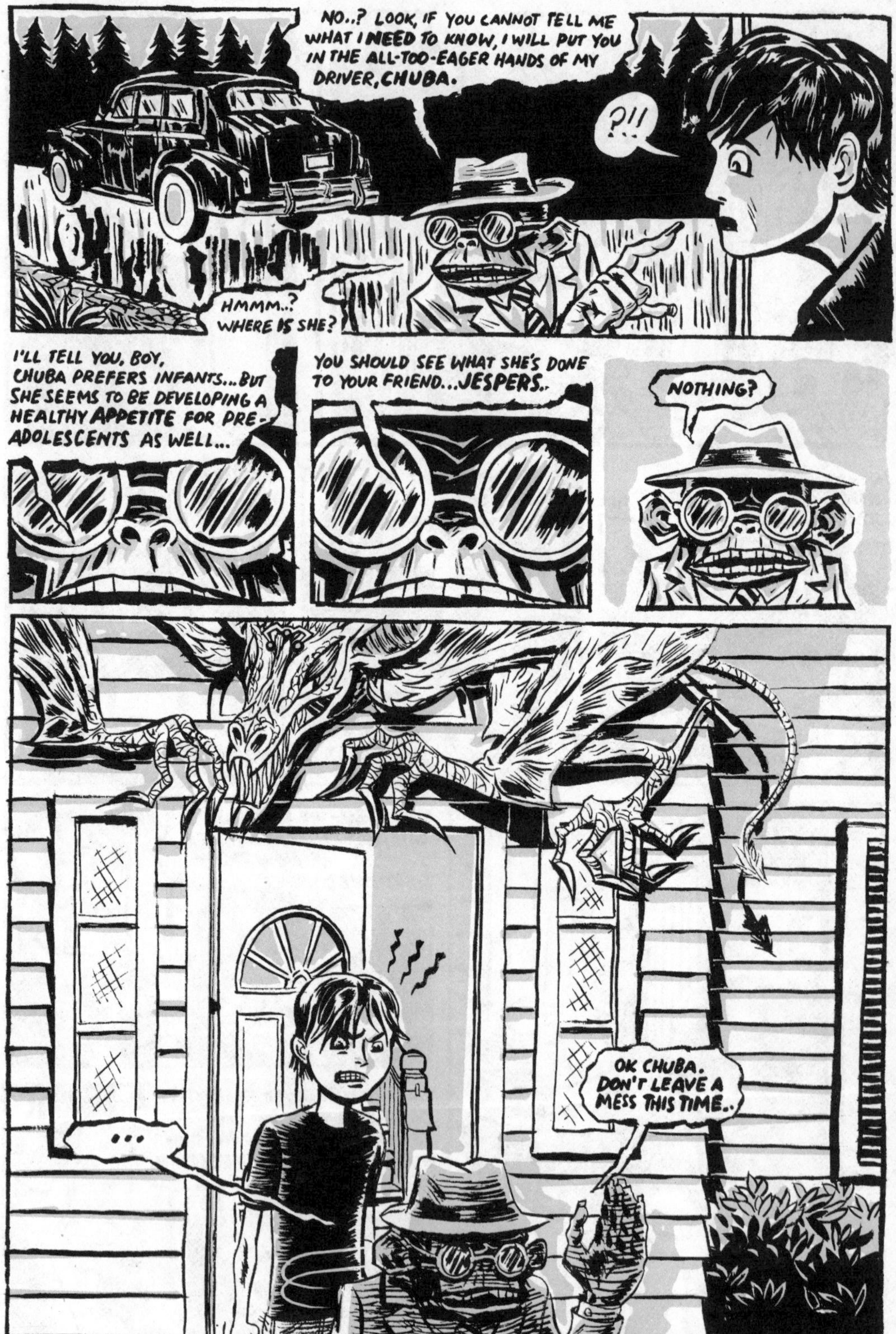
NO..? LOOK, IF YOU CANNOT TELL ME WHAT I NEED TO KNOW, I WILL PUT YOU IN THE ALL-TOO-EAGER HANDS OF MY DRIVER, CHUBA.
?!!
HMMM..? WHERE IS SHE?
I'LL TELL YOU, BOY, CHUBA PREFERS INFANTS... BUT SHE SEEMS TO BE DEVELOPING A HEALTHY APPETITE FOR PRE-ADOLESCENTS AS WELL...
YOU SHOULD SEE WHAT SHE'S DONE TO YOUR FRIEND... JESPERS..
NOTHING?
...
OK CHUBA. DON'T LEAVE A MESS THIS TIME..

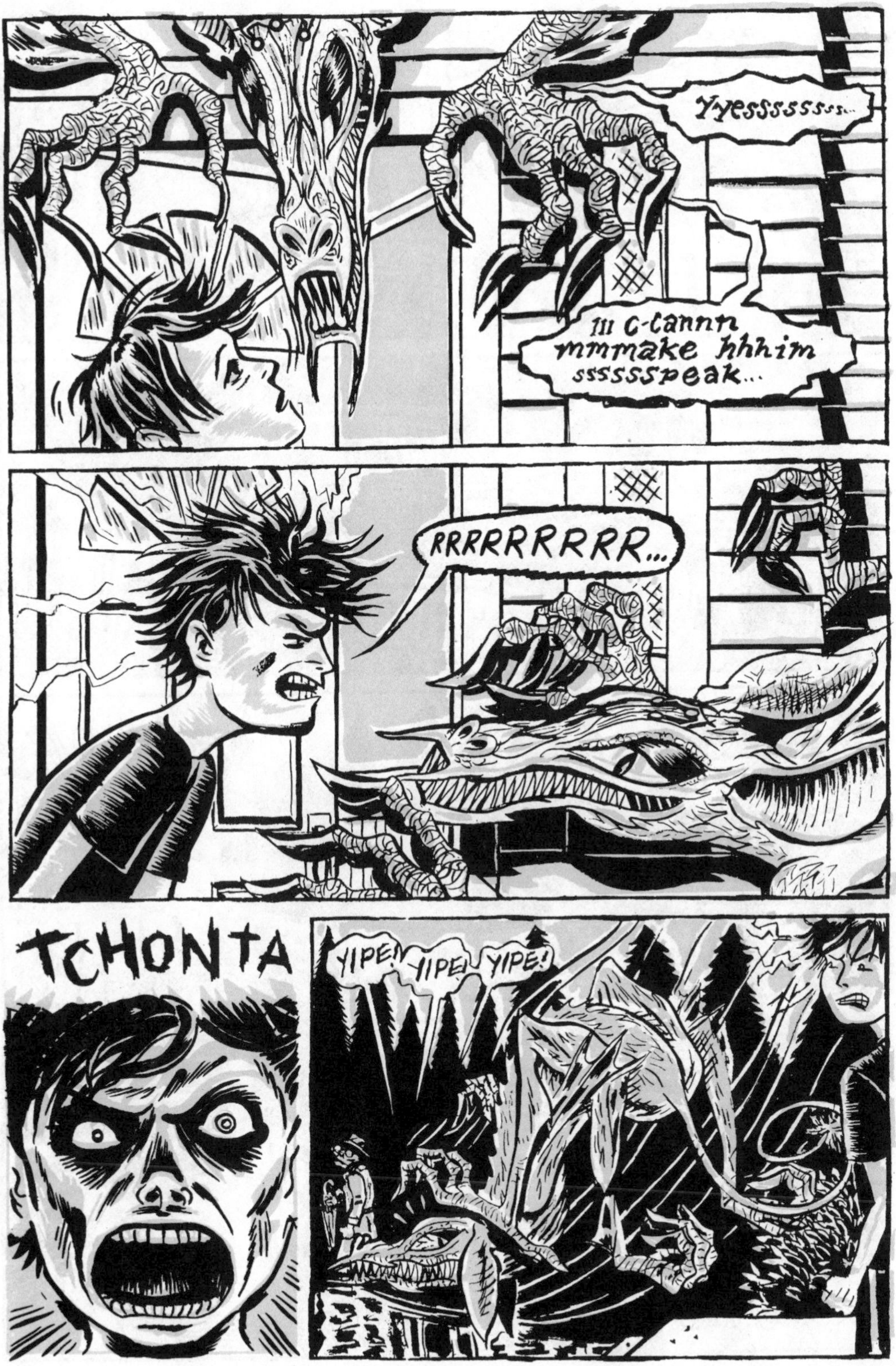
Yyessssssss...
III C-cannn mmmake hhhim sssssspeak...
RRRRRRRRR...
TCHONTA
YIPE! YIPE! YIPE!

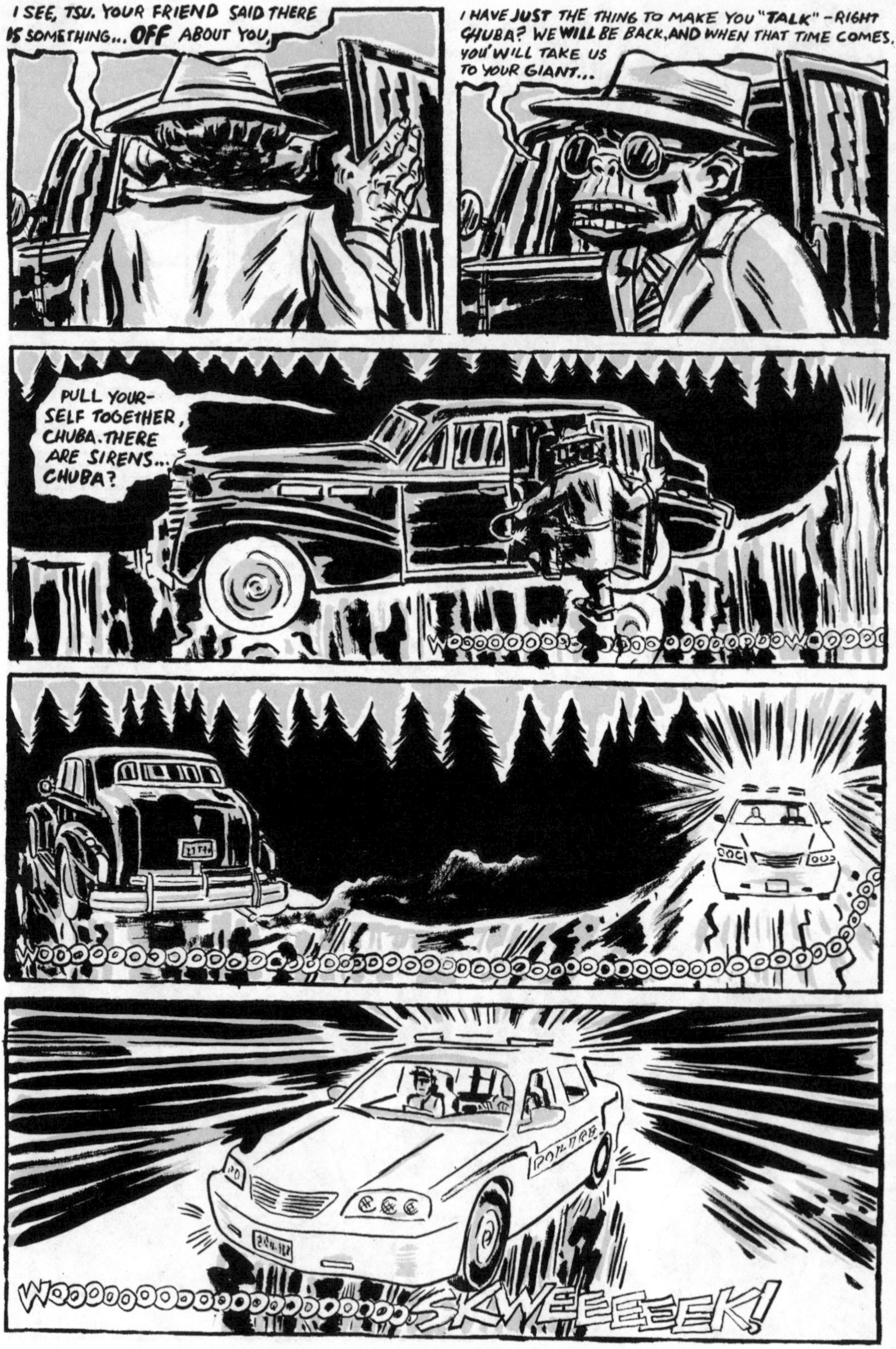
I SEE, TSU. YOUR FRIEND SAID THERE IS SOMETHING... OFF ABOUT YOU.
I HAVE JUST THE THING TO MAKE YOU "TALK" - RIGHT CHUBA? WE WILL BE BACK, AND WHEN THAT TIME COMES, YOU WILL TAKE US TO YOUR GIANT...
PULL YOURSELF TOGETHER, CHUBA. THERE ARE SIRENS... CHUBA?
WOOOOOOOOOOOOOOOOOOOOOOOOOOOOO
WOOOOOOOOOOOOOOOOOOOOOOOOOOOOOOOOOOOOOOOOOOOO
WOOOOOOOOOOOOOOOOOOOOOOOOOO SKWEEEEEK!

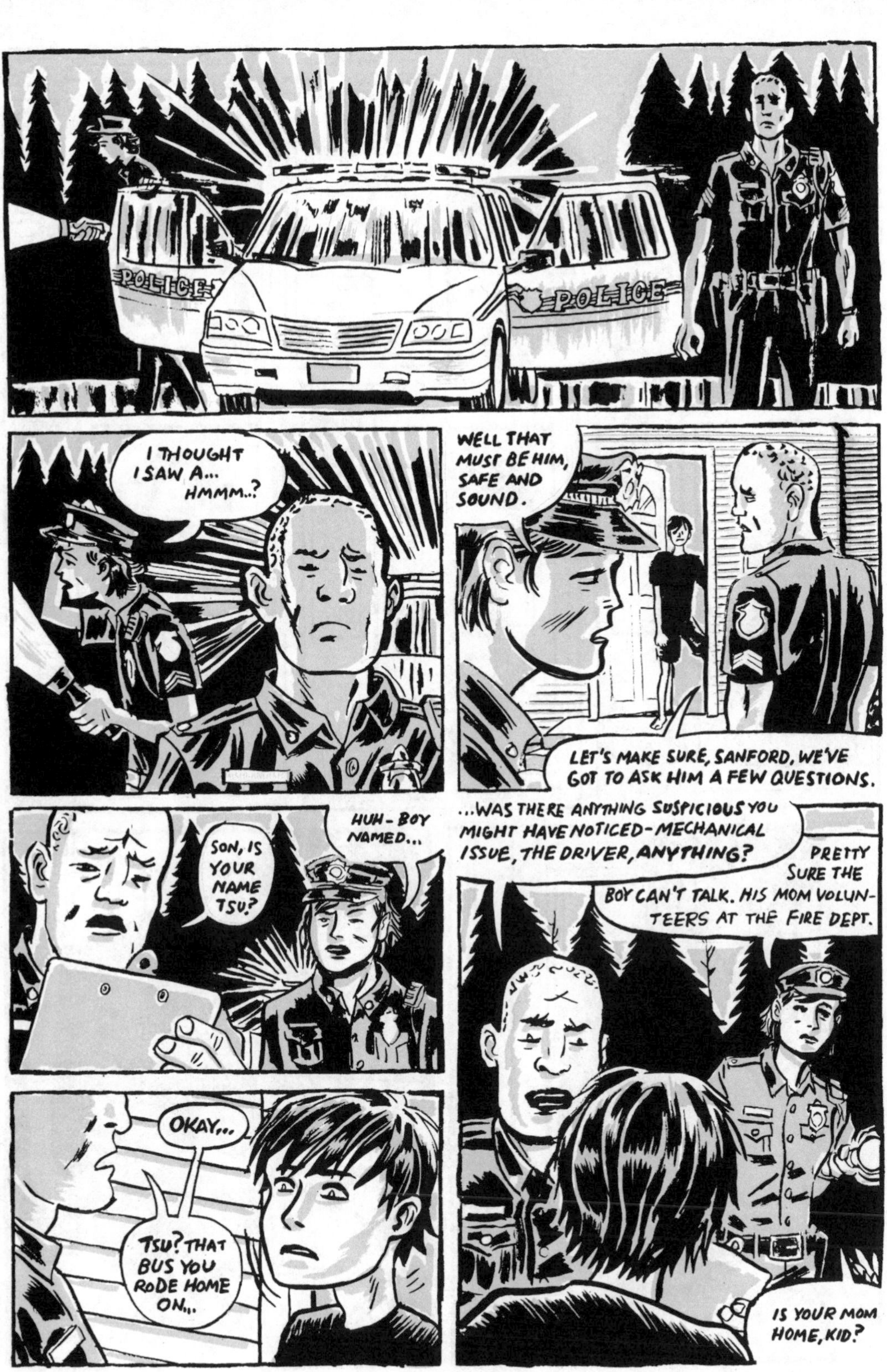
I THOUGHT I SAW A... HMMM..?
WELL THAT MUST BE HIM, SAFE AND SOUND.
LET'S MAKE SURE, SANFORD, WE'VE GOT TO ASK HIM A FEW QUESTIONS.
SON, IS YOUR NAME TSU?
HUH - BOY NAMED...
...WAS THERE ANYTHING SUSPICIOUS YOU MIGHT HAVE NOTICED - MECHANICAL ISSUE, THE DRIVER, ANYTHING?
PRETTY SURE THE BOY CAN'T TALK. HIS MOM VOLUNTEERS AT THE FIRE DEPT.
OKAY...
TSU? THAT BUS YOU RODE HOME ON...
IS YOUR MOM HOME, KID?

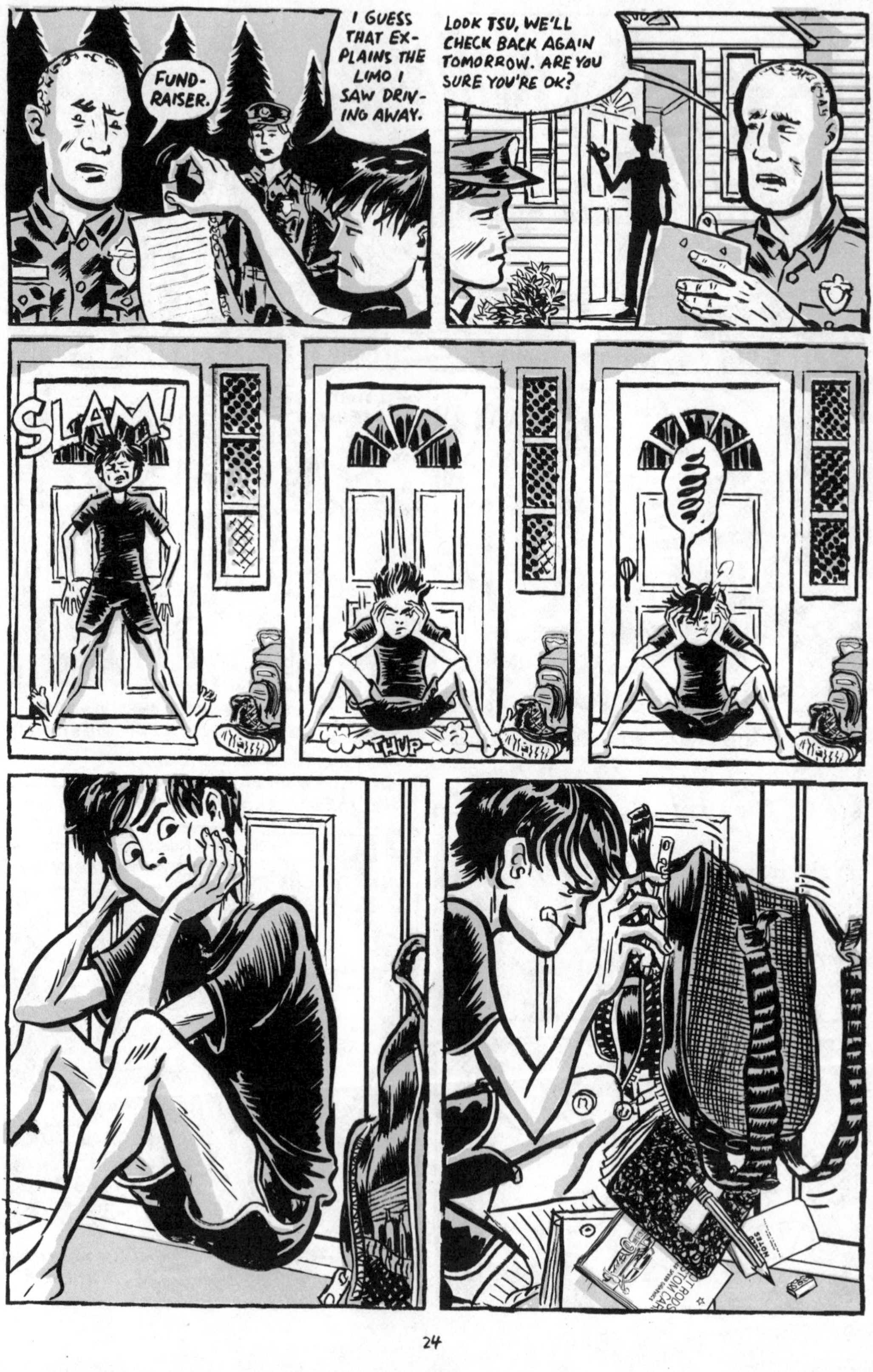
FUND-RAISER.
I GUESS THAT EX-PLAINS THE LIMO I SAW DRIV-ING AWAY.
LOOK TSU, WE'LL CHECK BACK AGAIN TOMORROW. ARE YOU SURE YOU'RE OK?
SLAM!
THUP

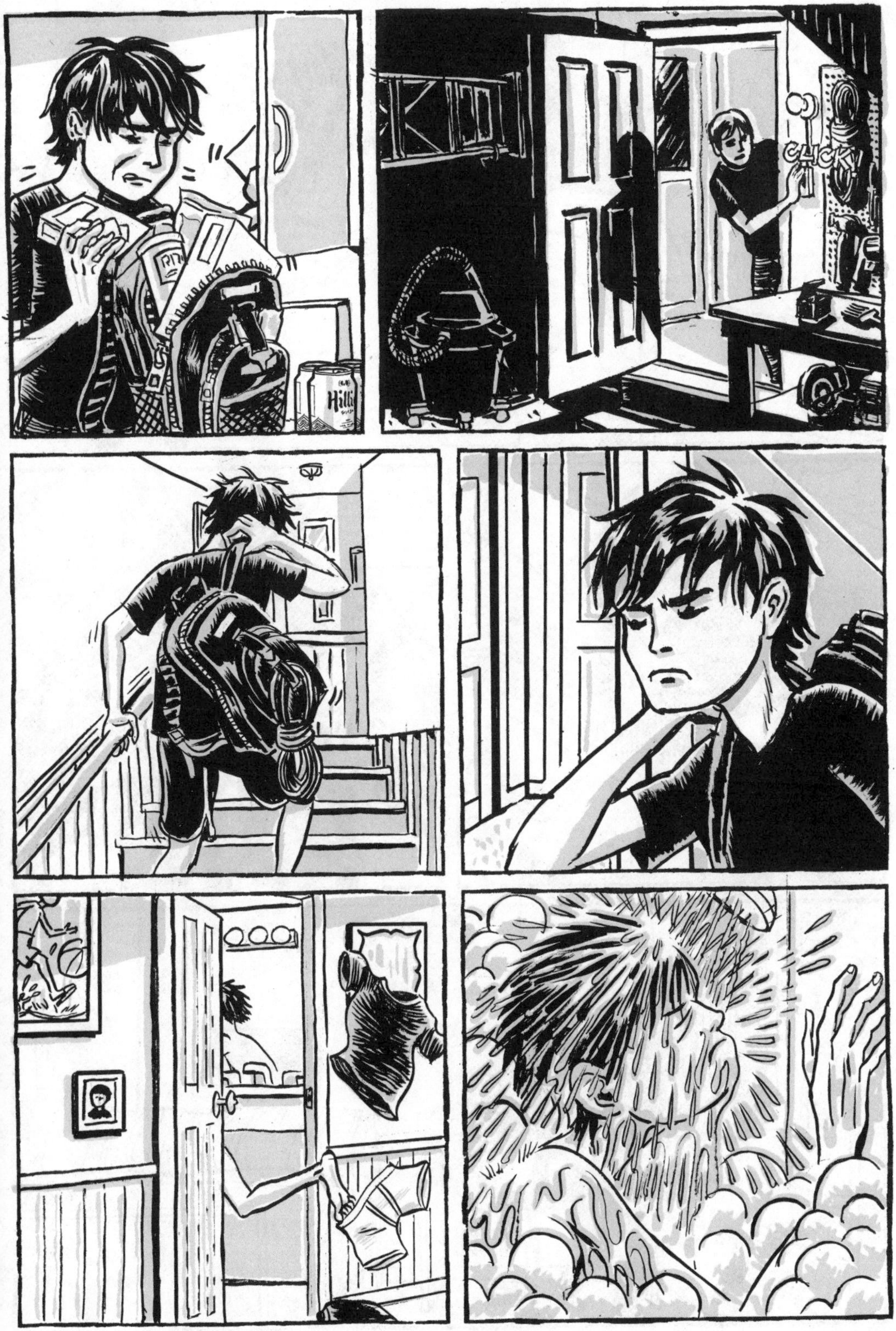
CLICK!

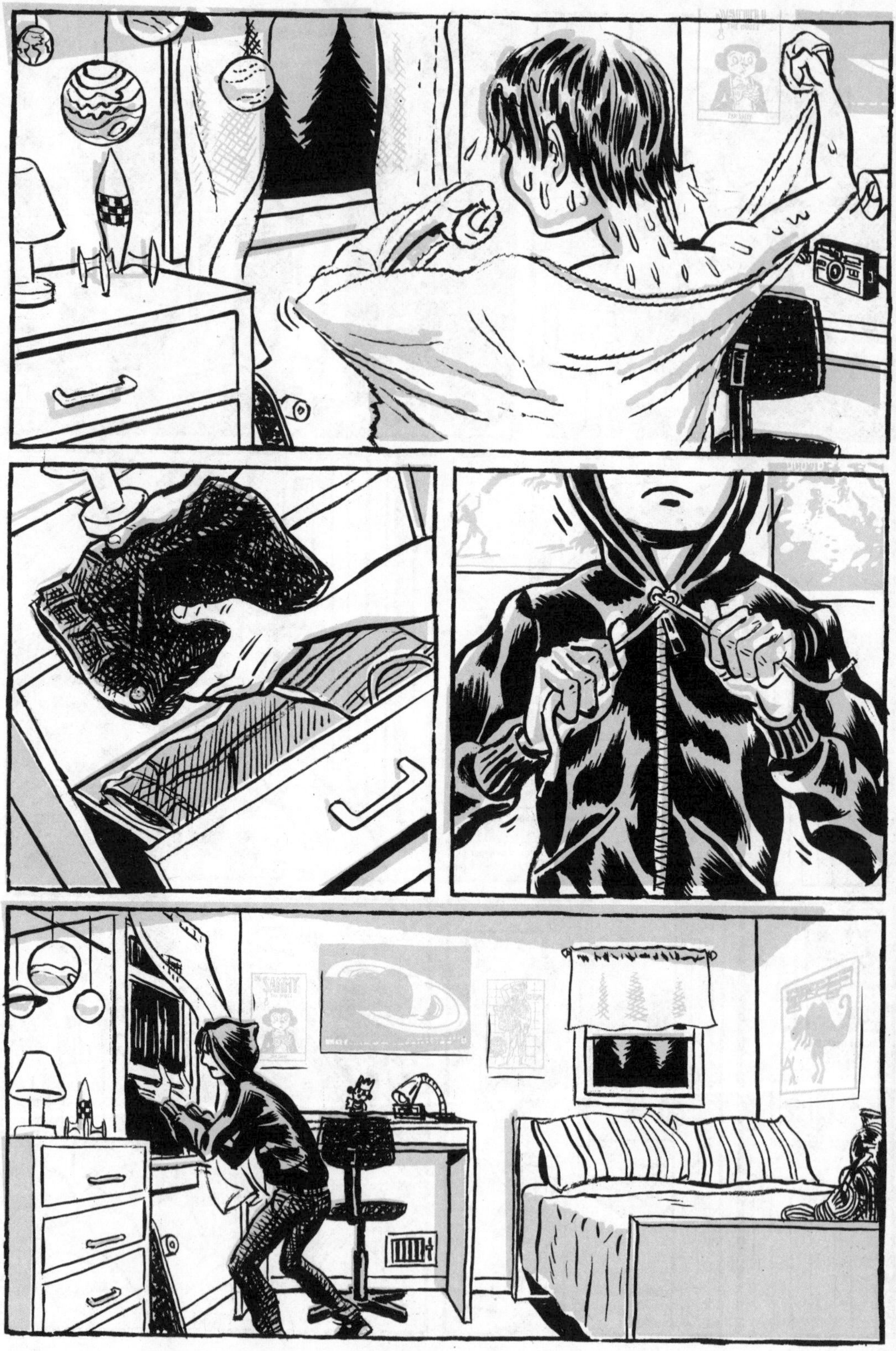
SAMMY

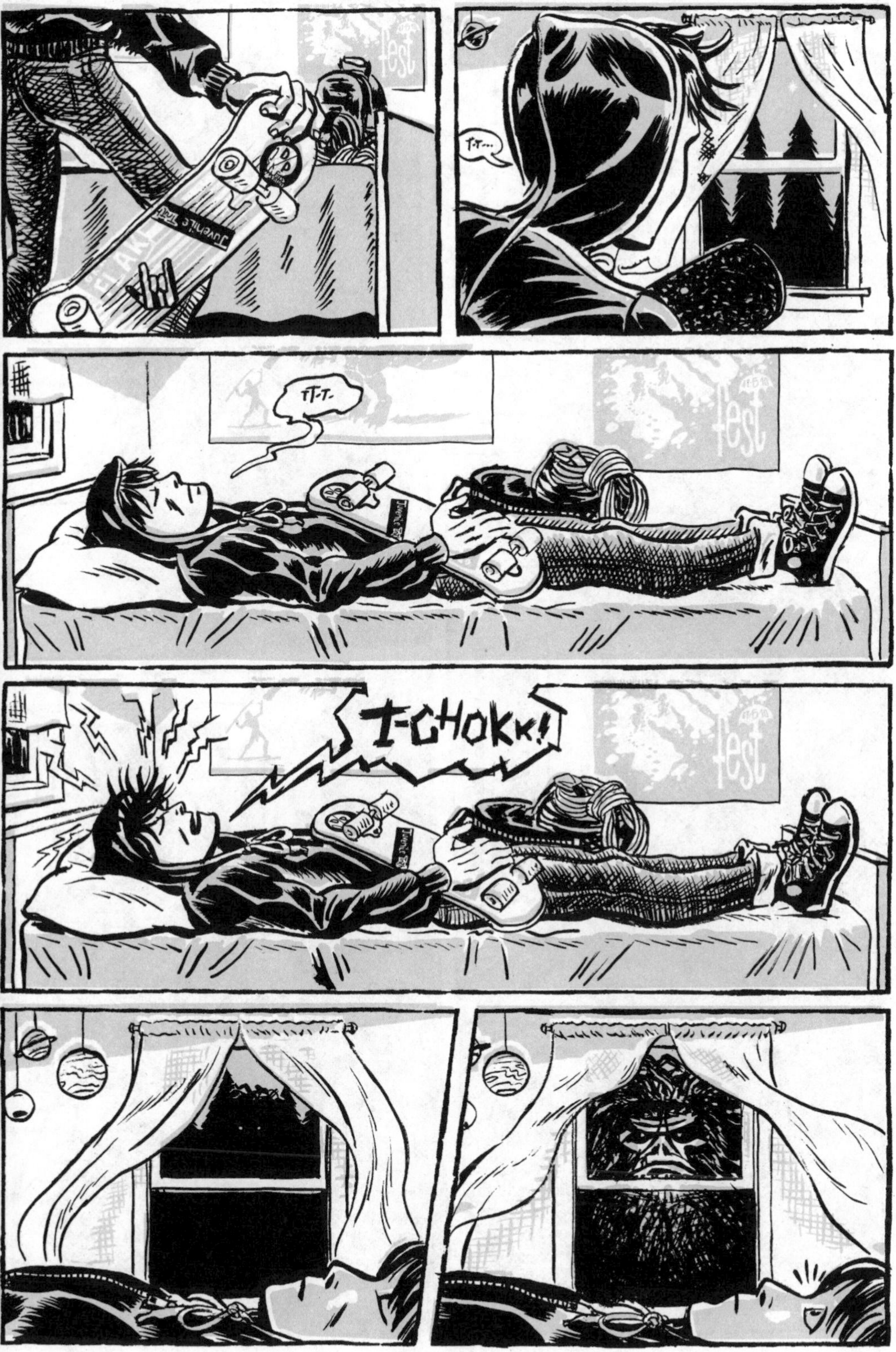

Juvenile
fest
T-T...
TT-T-
fest
T-CHOKK!
fest

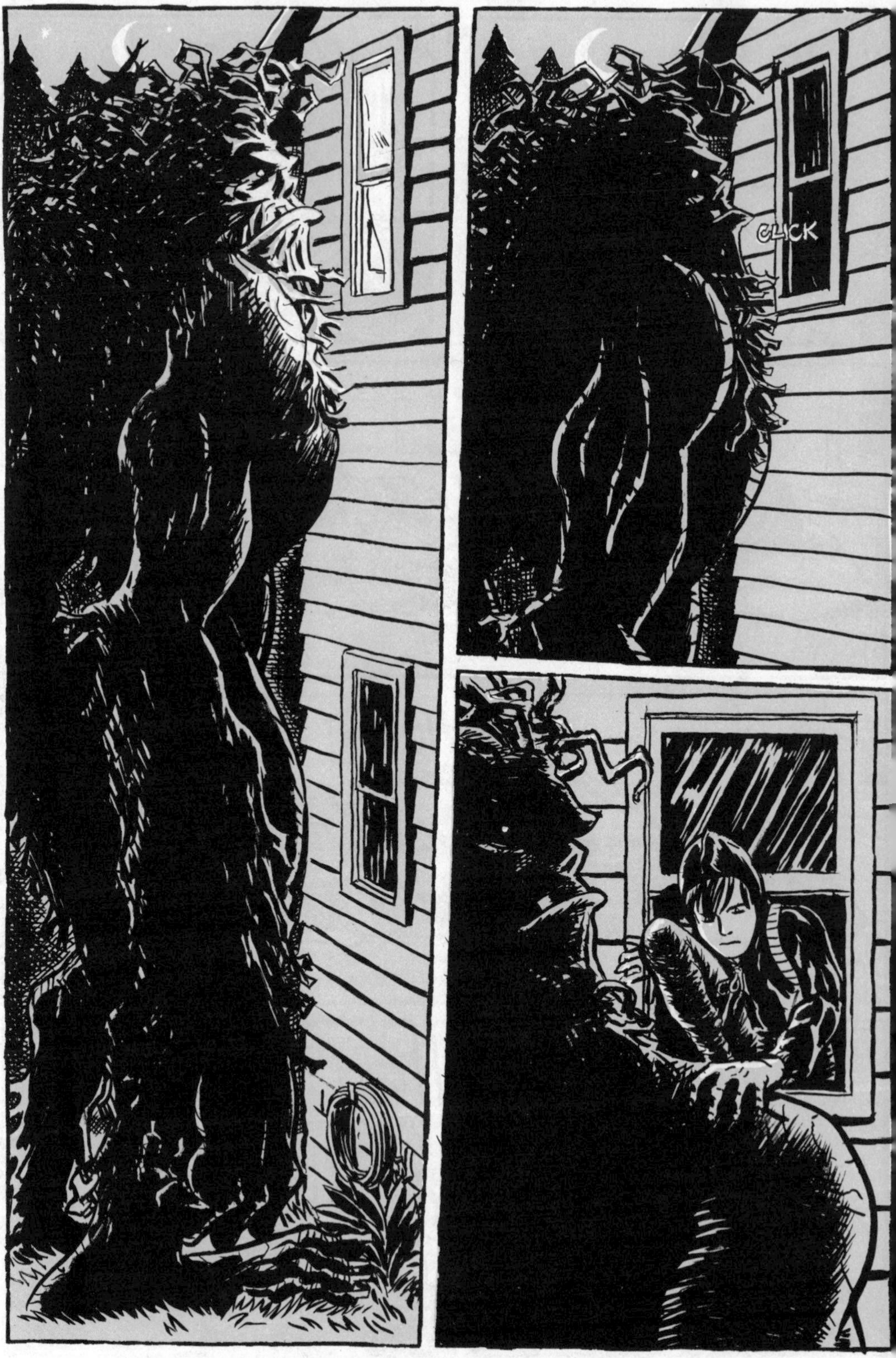
CLICK

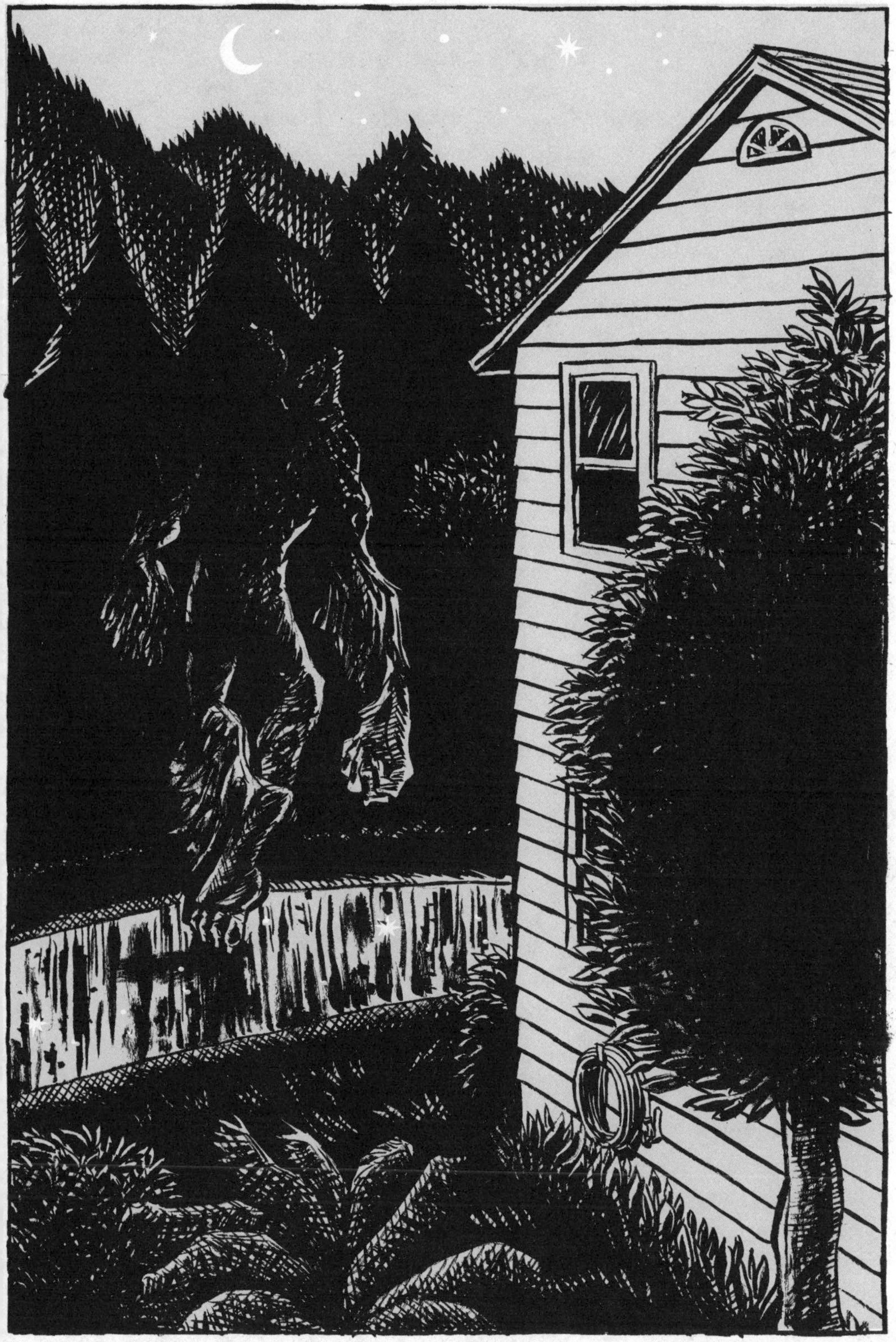

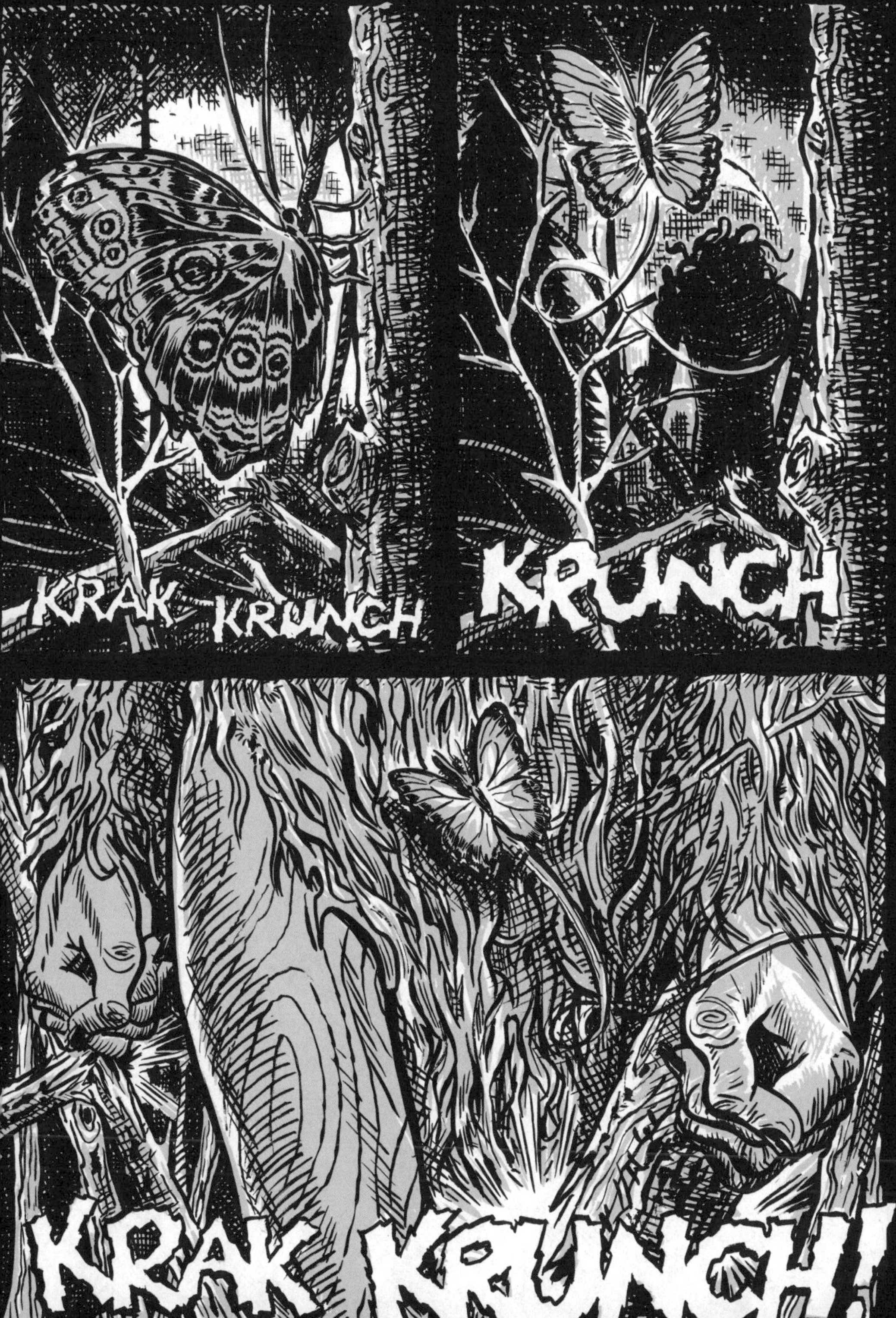
KRAK KRUNCH
KRUNCH
KRAK KRUNCH!

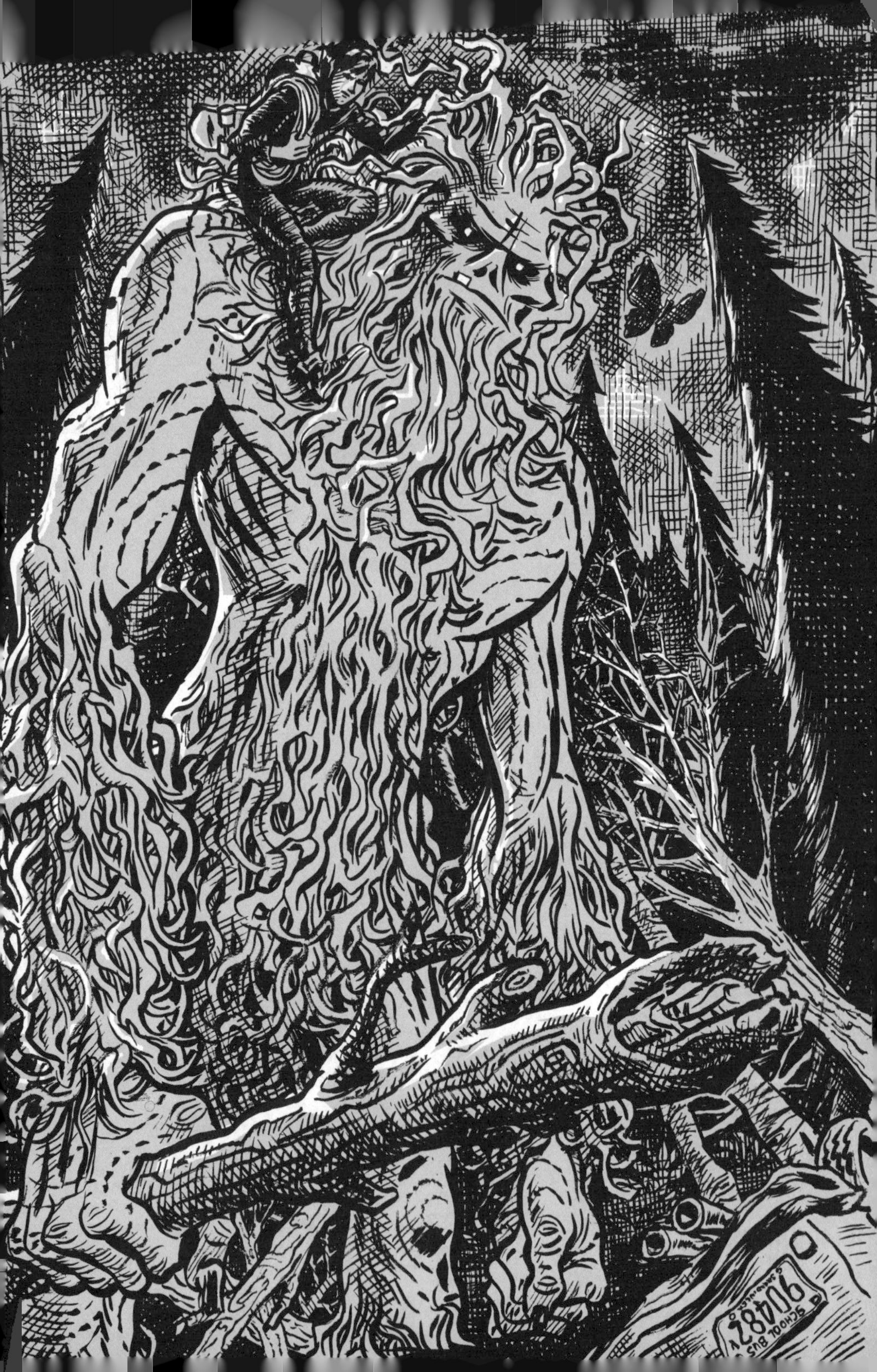
9U482
SCHOOL BUS

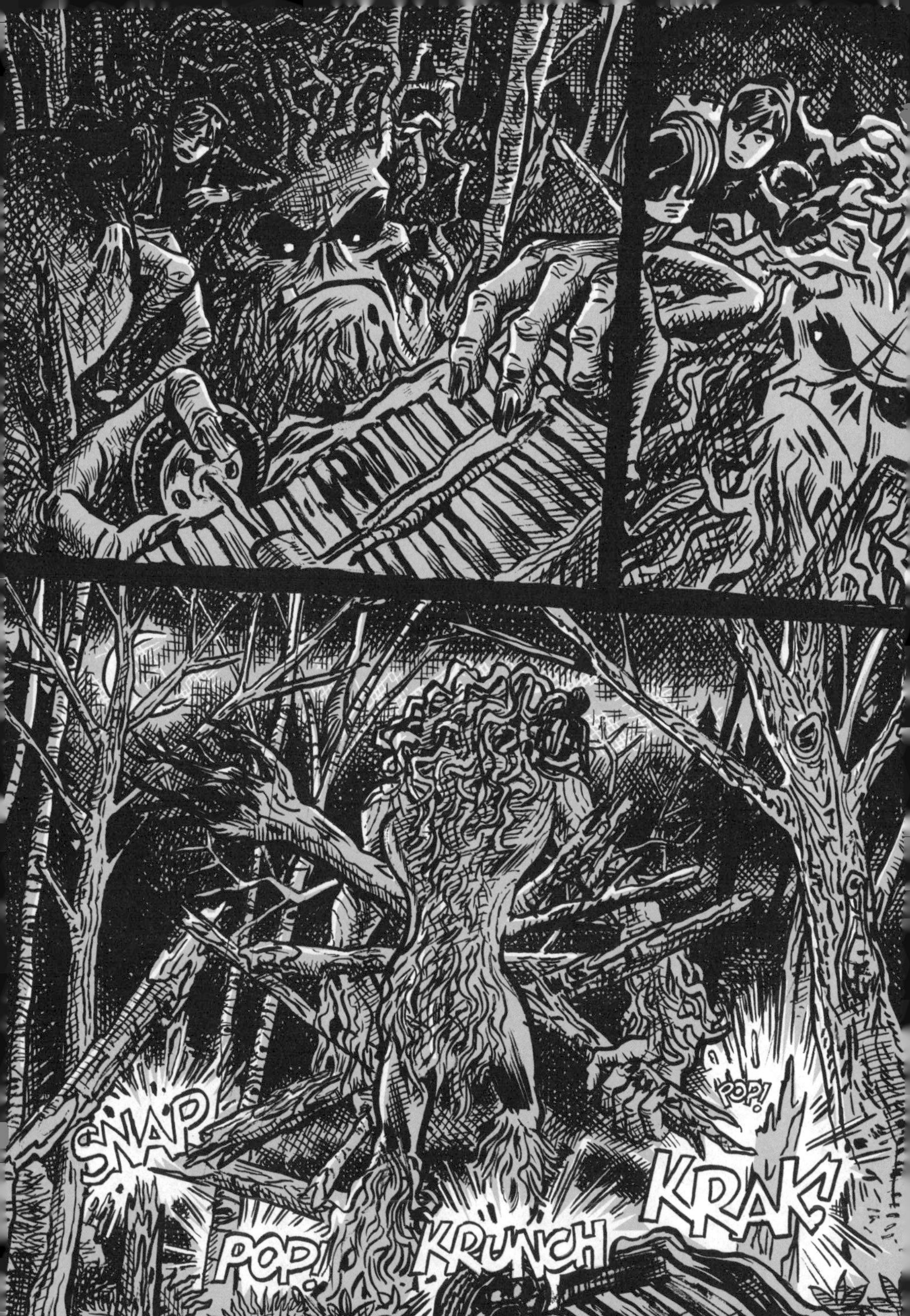
SNAP
POP!
KRUNCH
POP!
KRAK!

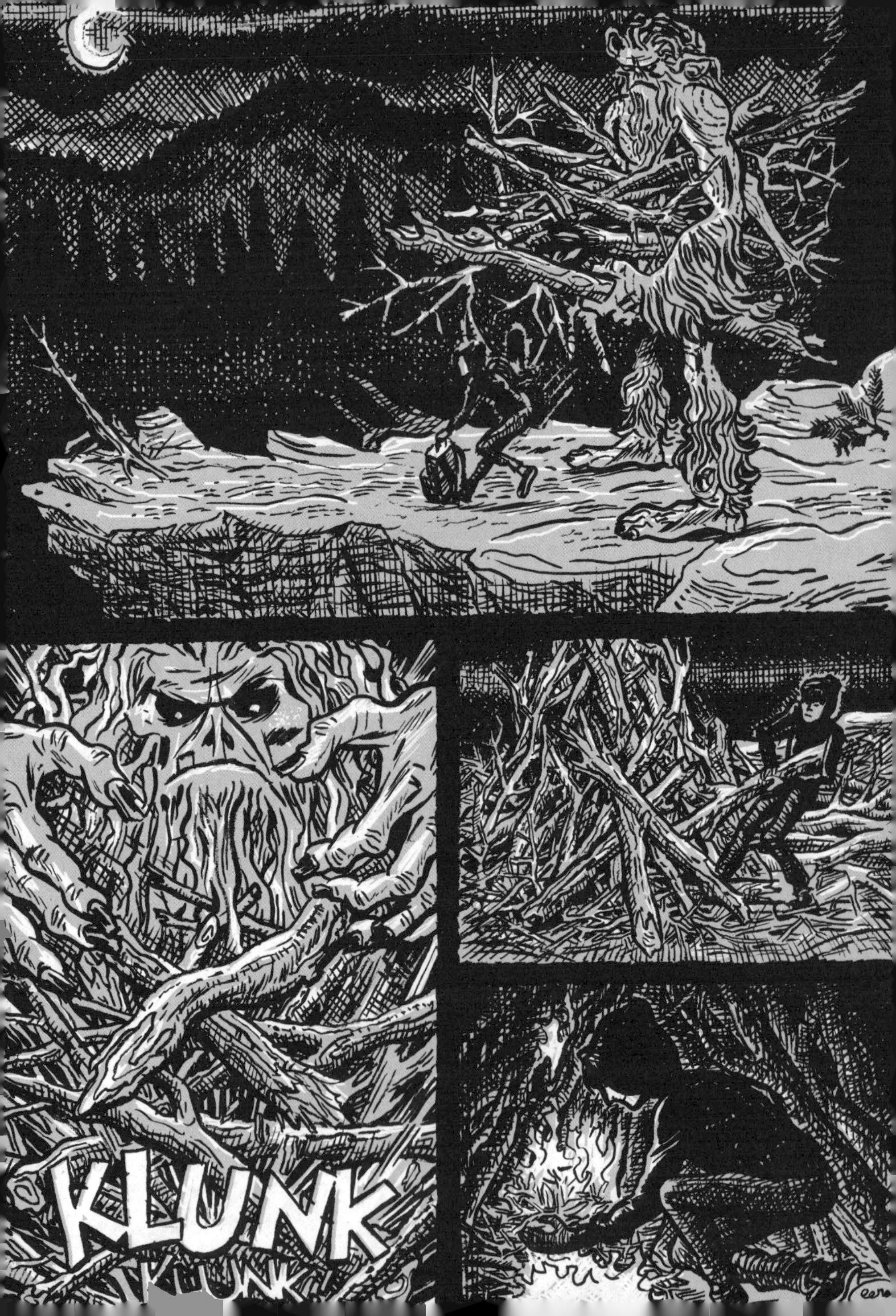
KLUNK

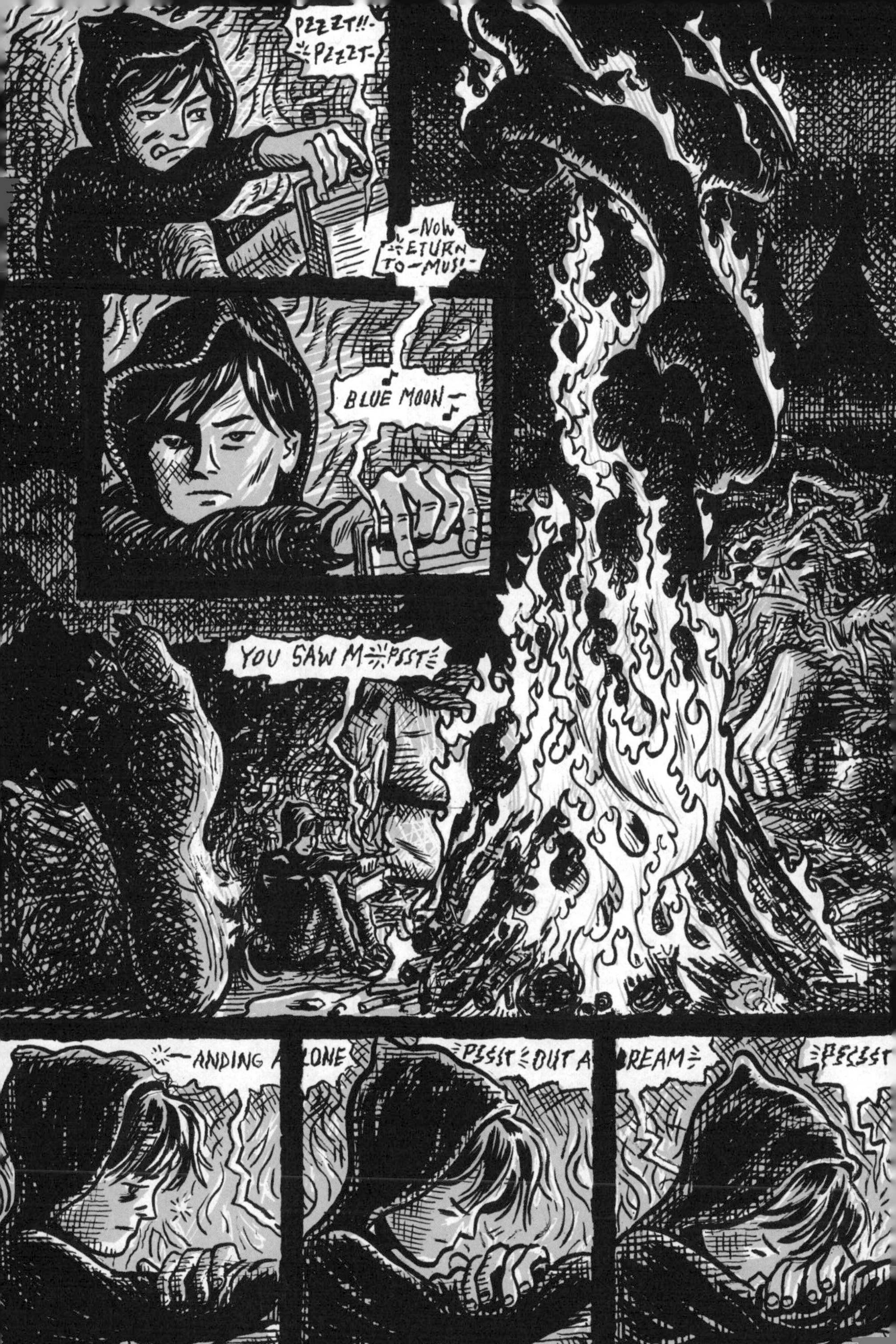

PZZZT!!-
PZZZT-
-NOW
ETURN
TO-MUS
BLUE MOON
YOU SAW M PSSST
ANDING A LONE
PSSST OUT A REAM
PSSSST

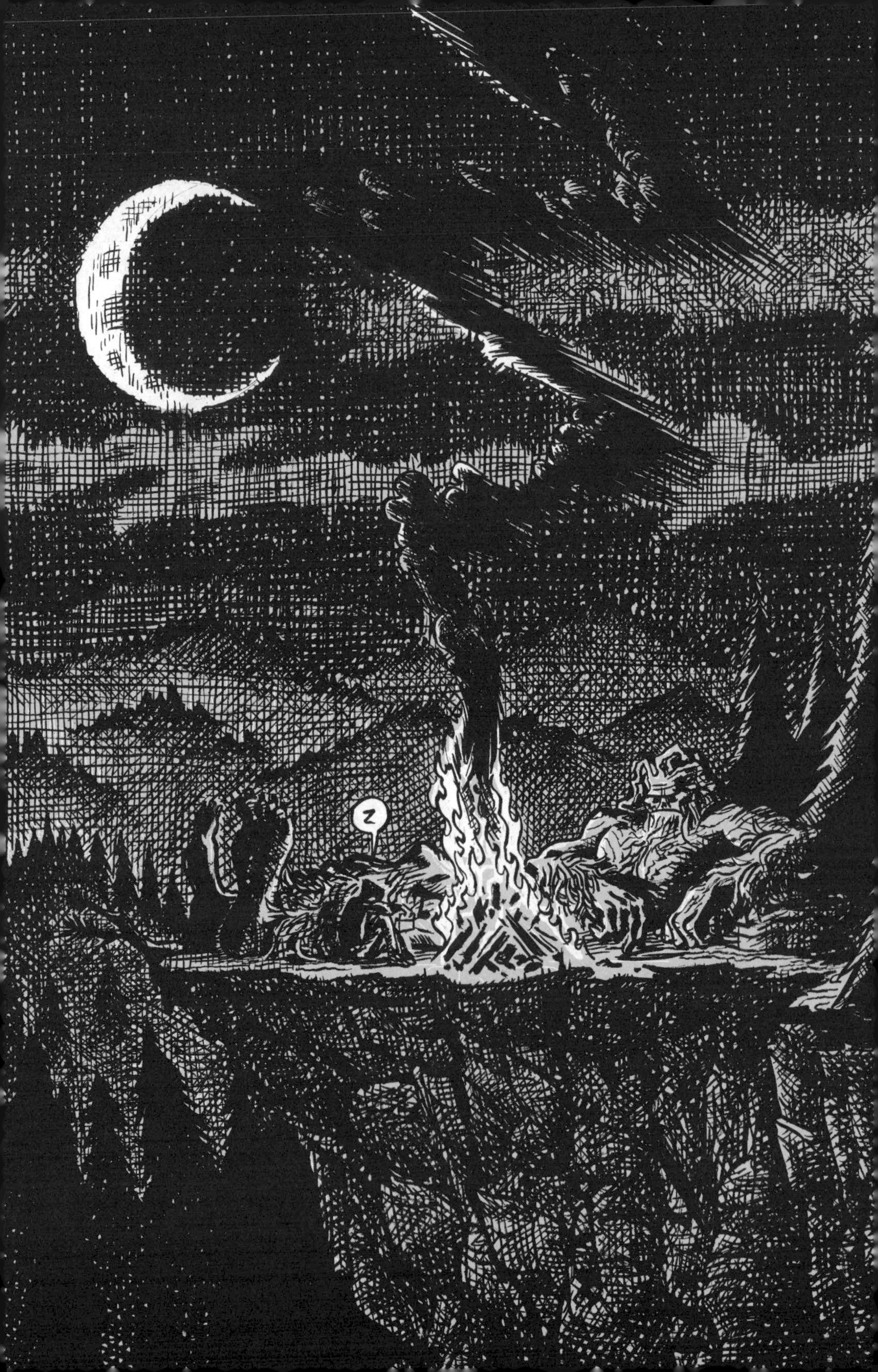
Z

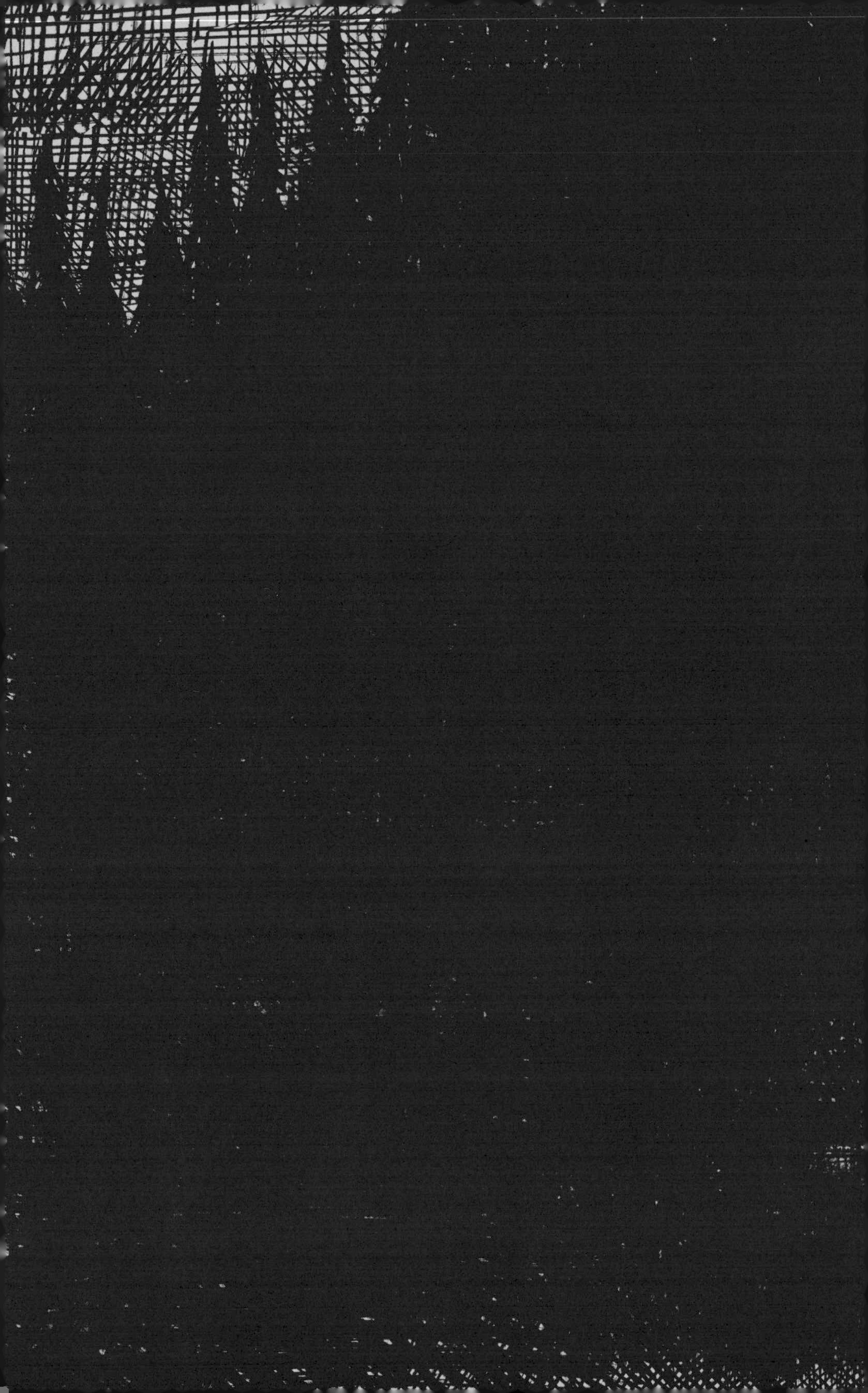

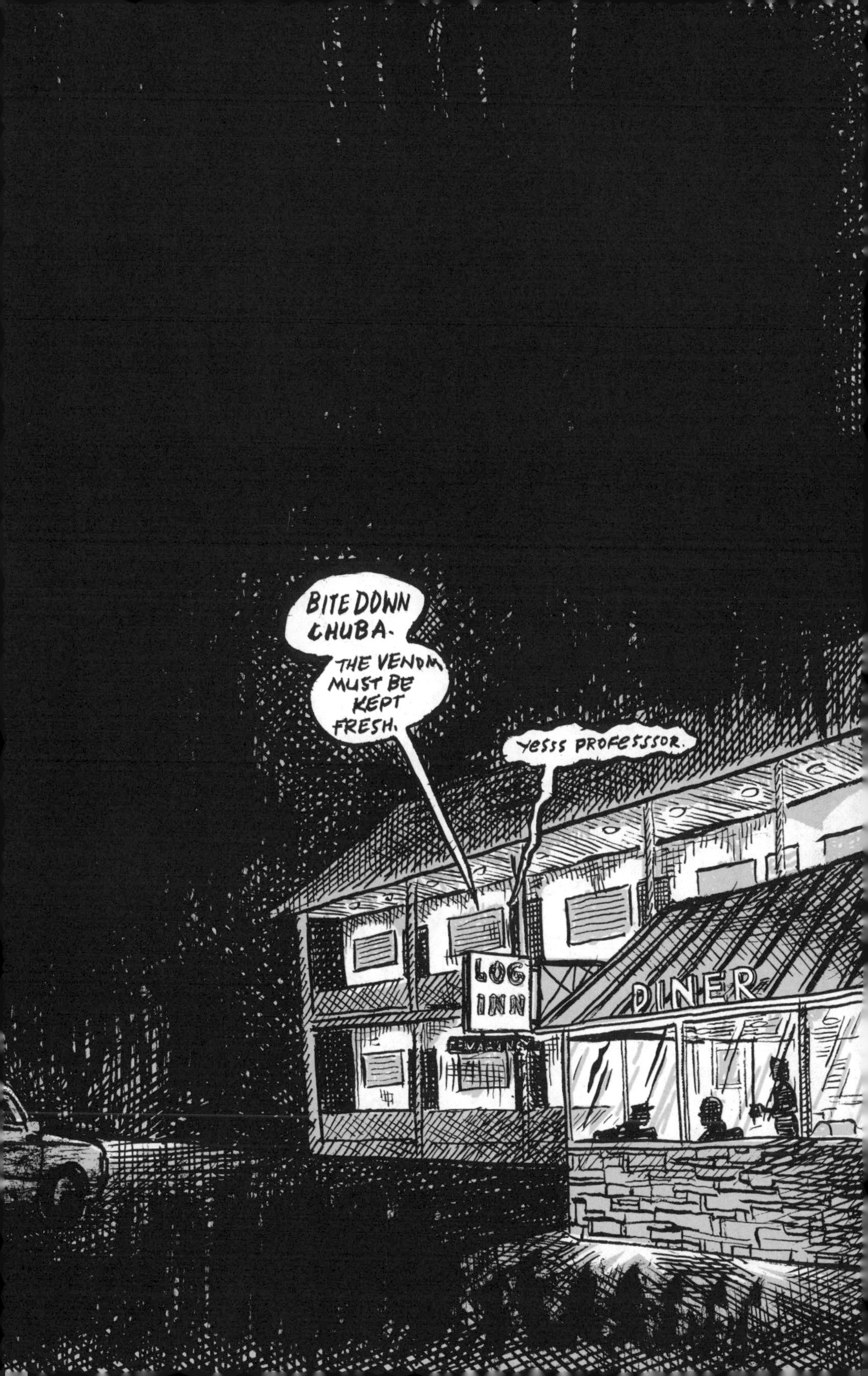
BITE DOWN CHUBA.
THE VENOM MUST BE KEPT FRESH.
YESSS PROFESSSOR.
LOG INN
DINER

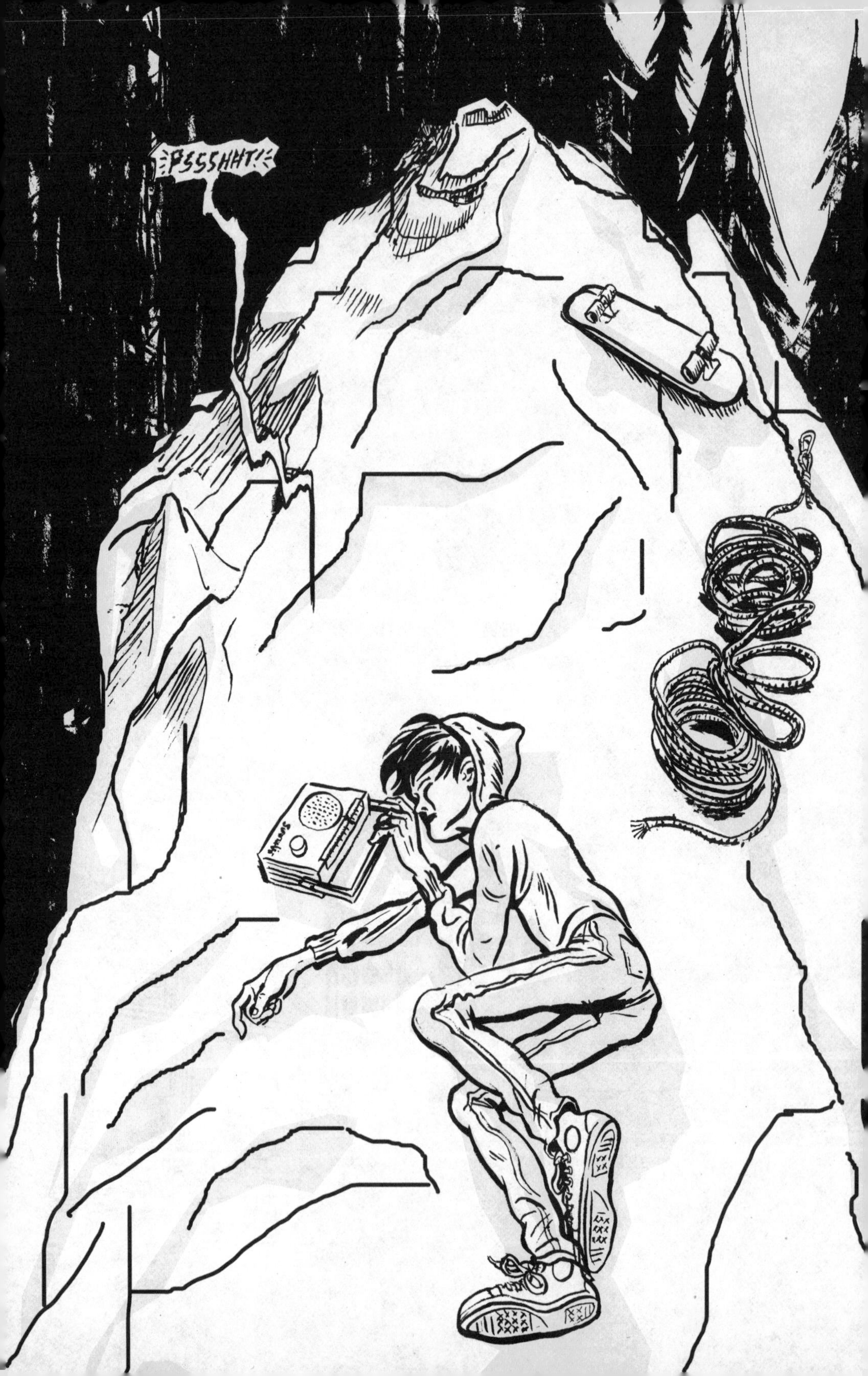
PSSSHHT!

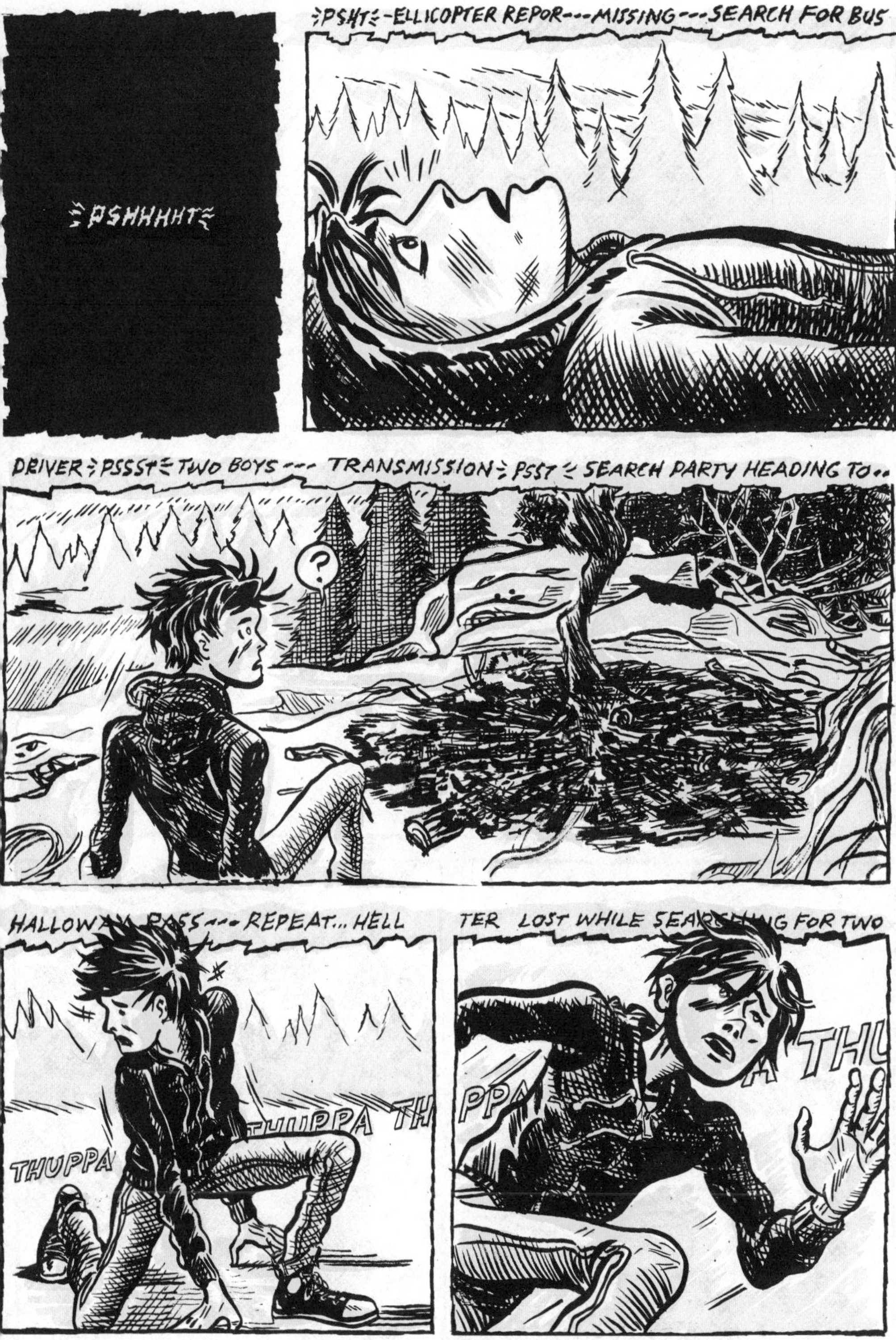
PSHHHHT
PSHT -ELLICOPTER REPOR--- MISSING --- SEARCH FOR BUS
DRIVER PSSST TWO BOYS --- TRANSMISSION PSST SEARCH PARTY HEADING TO..
?
HALLOWAY PASS --- REPEAT... HELL
THUPPA
THUPPA TH
TER LOST WHILE SEARCHING FOR TWO
THU
PPA

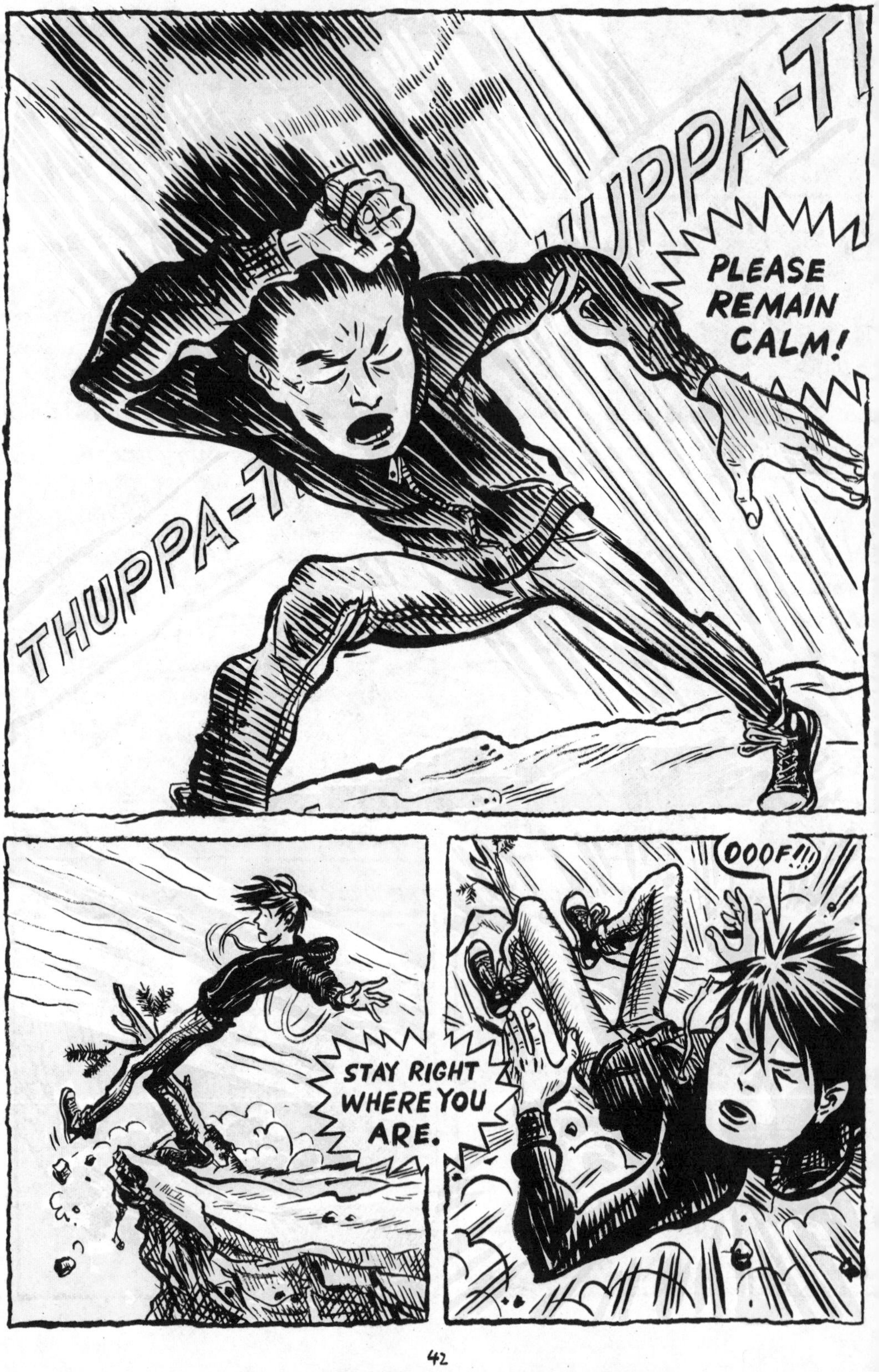
HUPPA-T
PLEASE REMAIN CALM!
THUPPA-T
STAY RIGHT WHERE YOU ARE.
OOOF!!!

THUPPA THUPPA THUP! PPA

THUPPA TH... THUP!

THUPPA THUPP THUPPA THUPPA THUPPA

A SEARCH PARTY IS ON IT'S WAY.

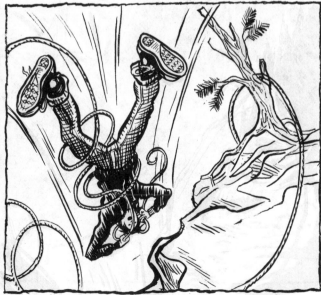

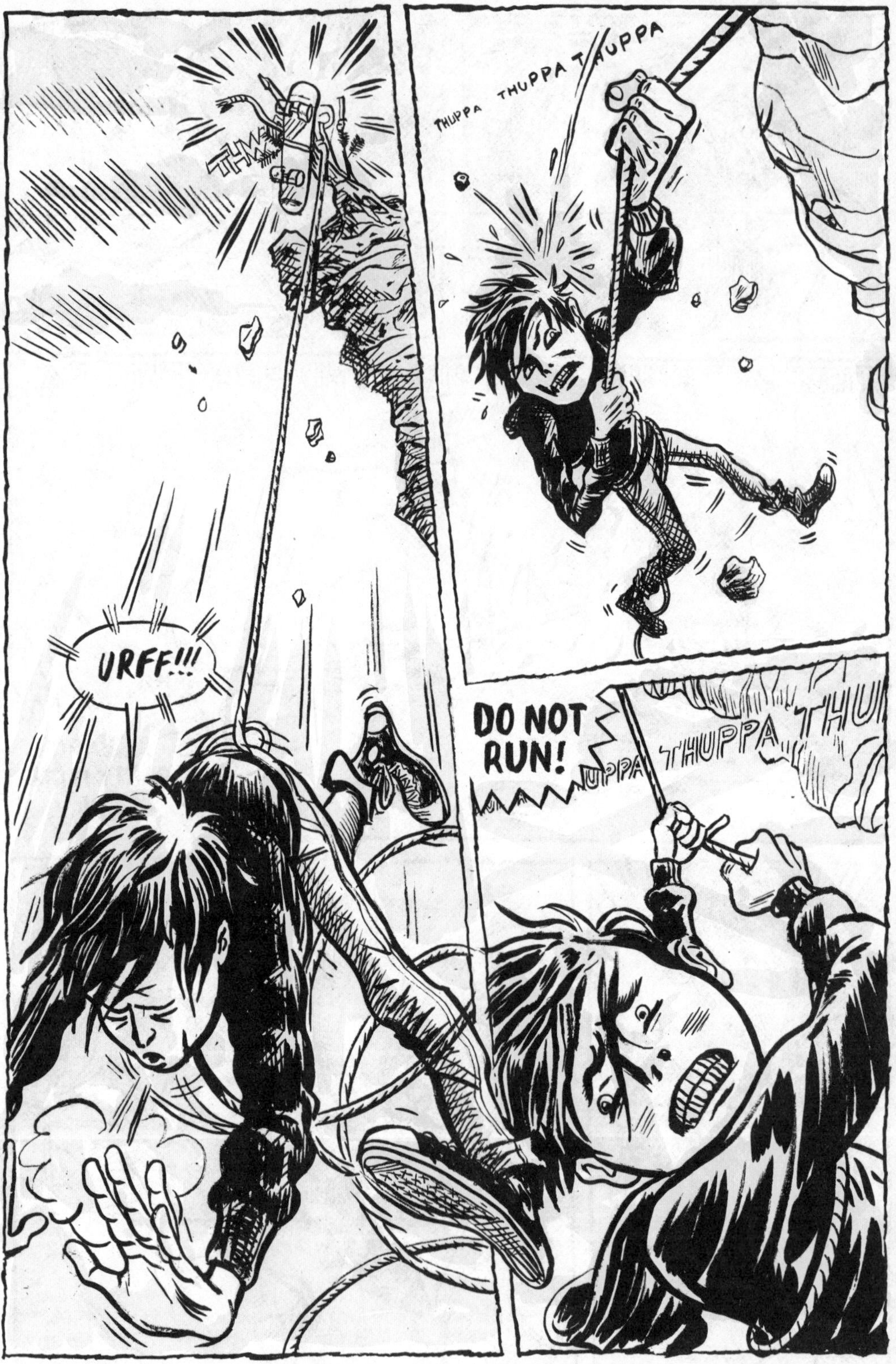
URFF!!!
THUPPA THUPPA THUPPA THUPPA
DO NOT RUN!
THUPPA

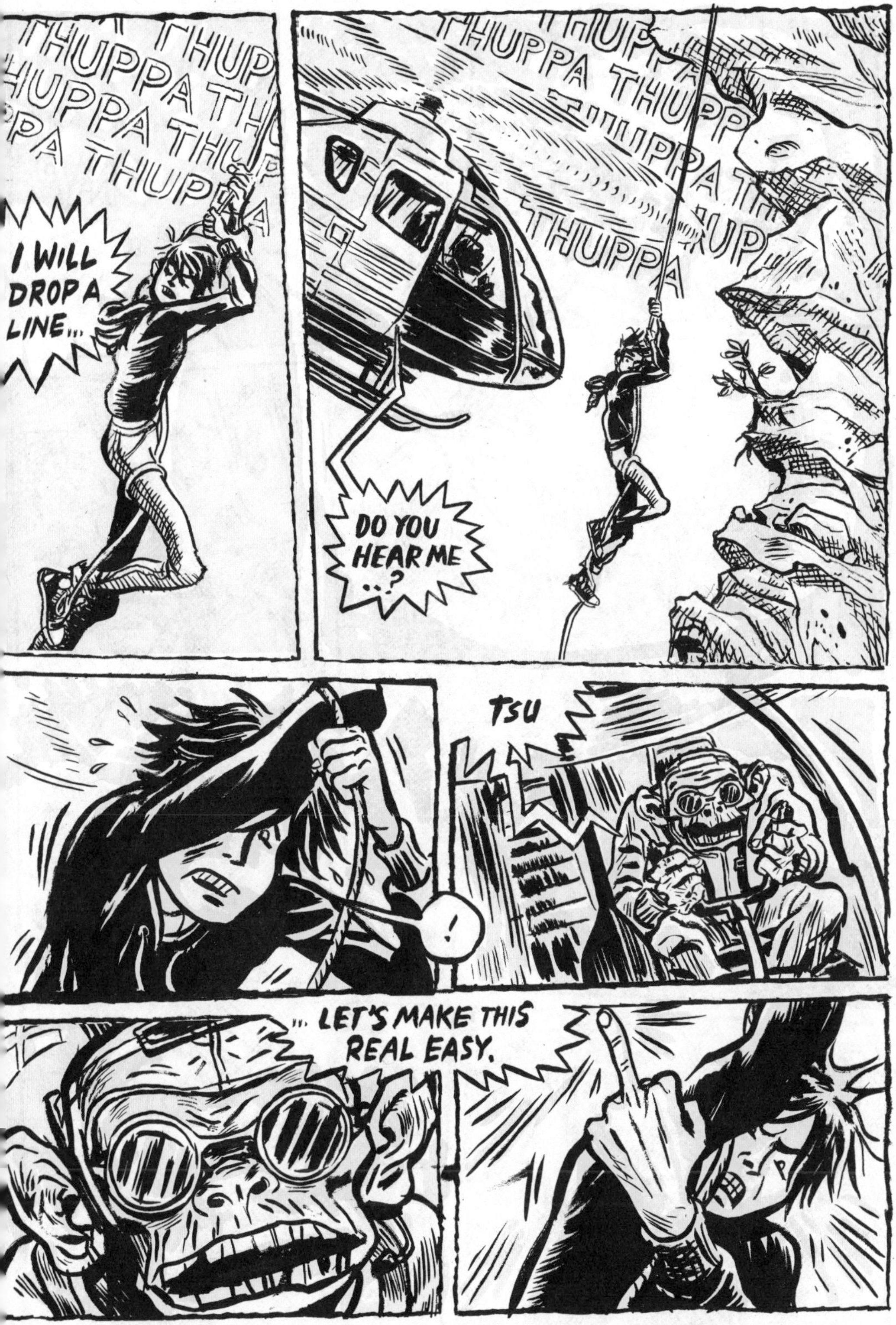
THUPPA THUPPA THUPPA THUPPA THUP
I WILL DROP A LINE...
THUPPA THUPPA THUPPA THUPPA THUP
DO YOU HEAR ME ...?
!
TSU
...LET'S MAKE THIS REAL EASY.

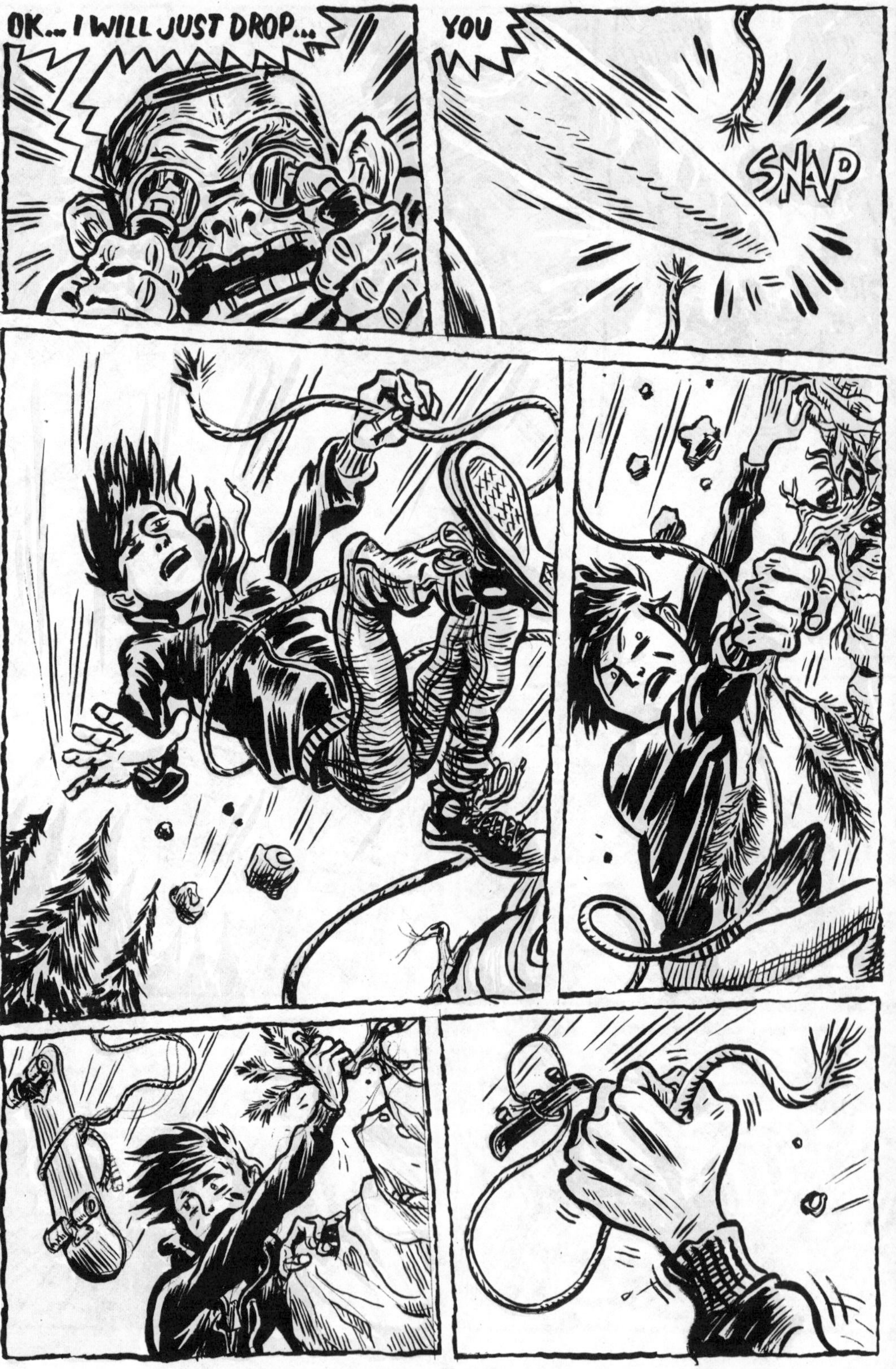
OK... I WILL JUST DROP...
YOU
SNAP

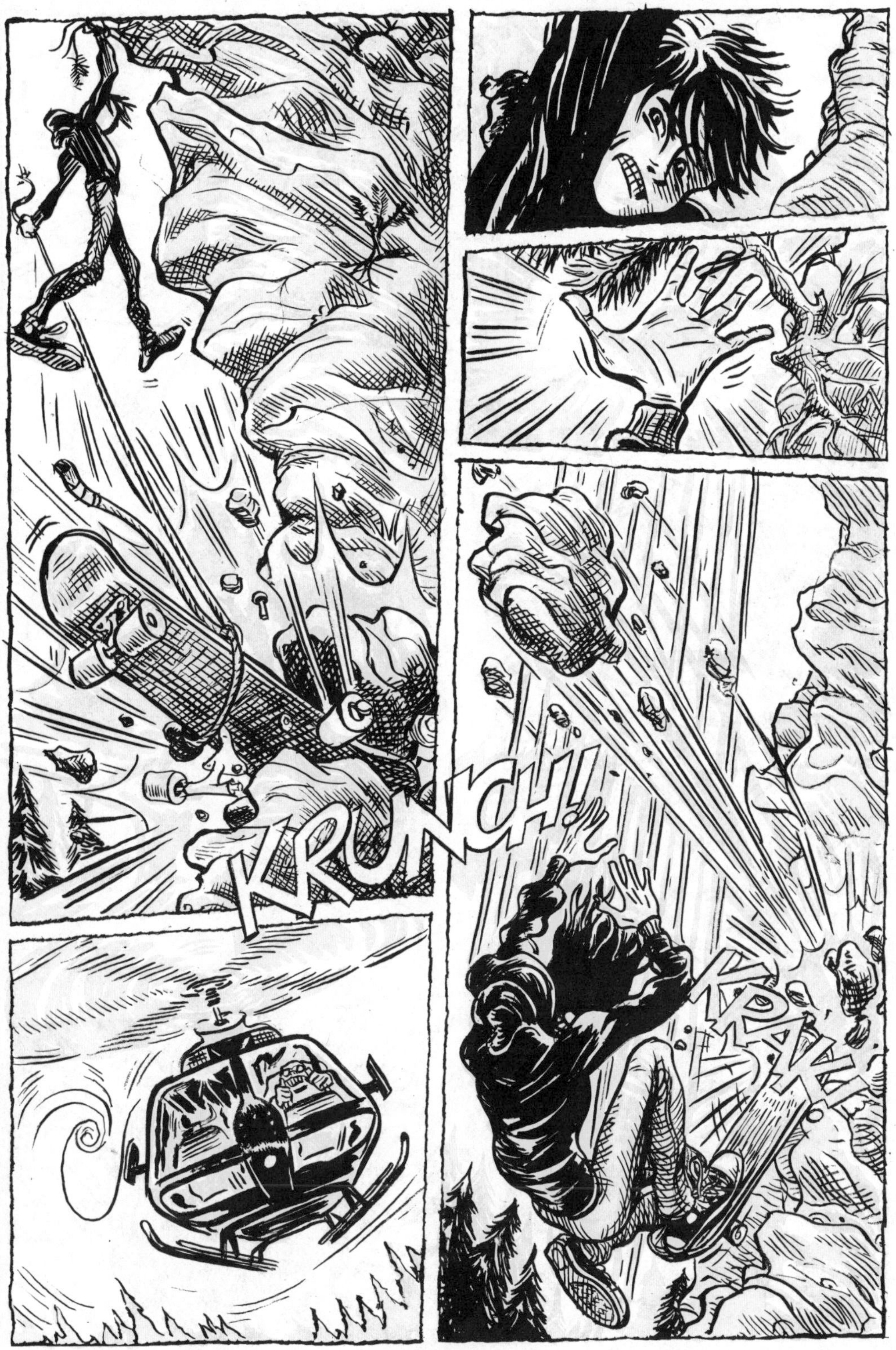
KRUNCH!
KRAKK!

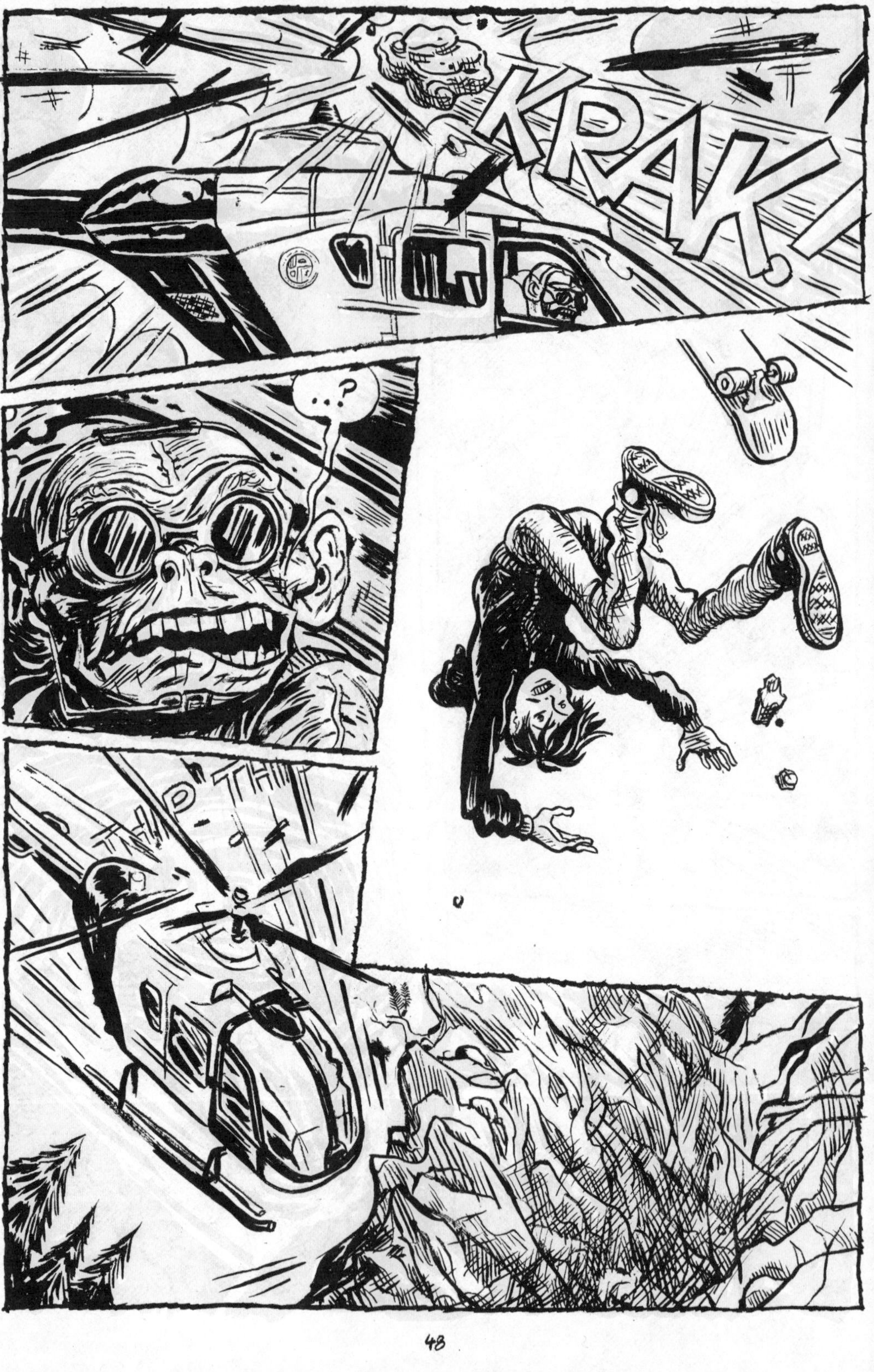
KRAK!
..?
THIP THIP

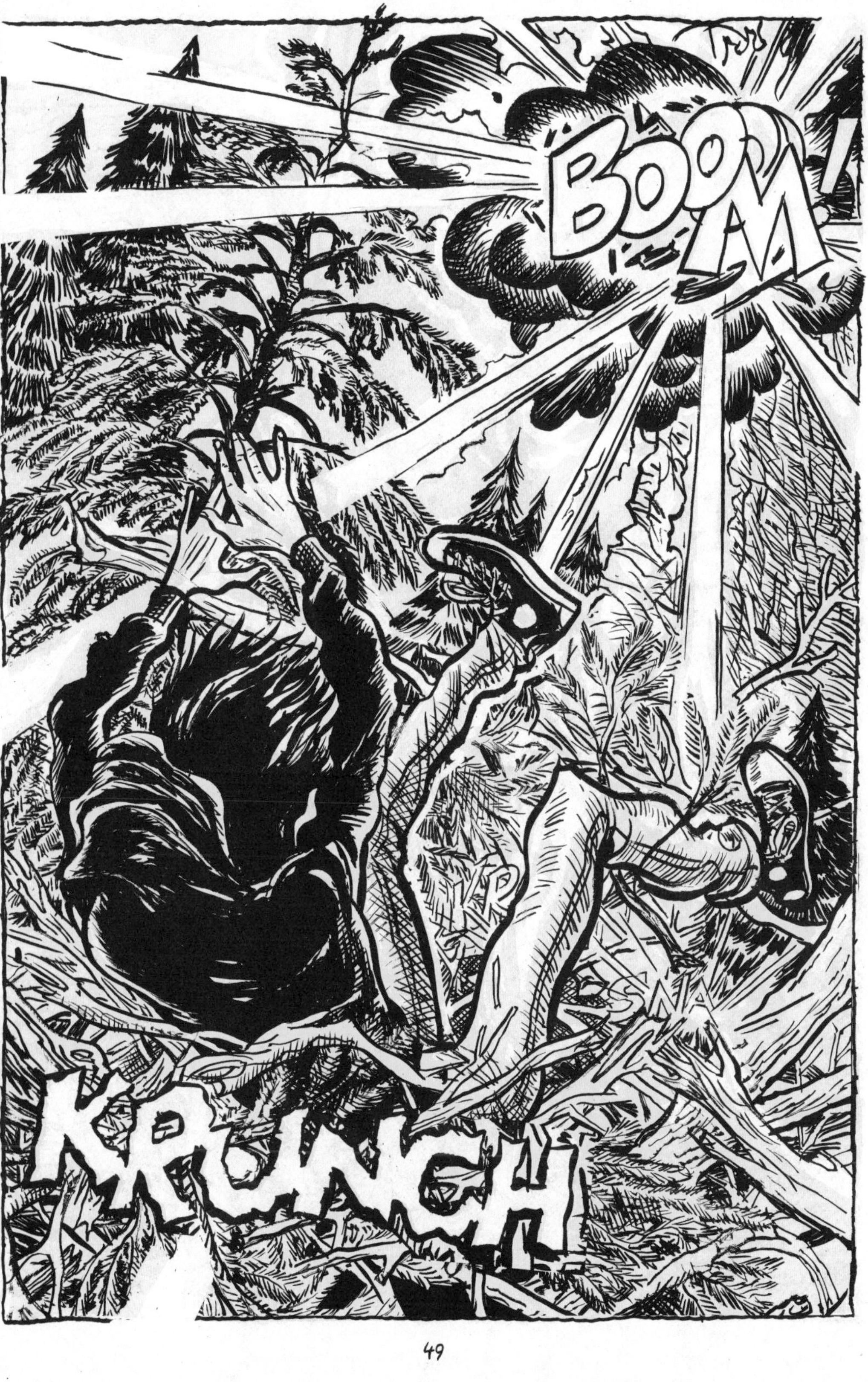
BOOM!
KRUNCH

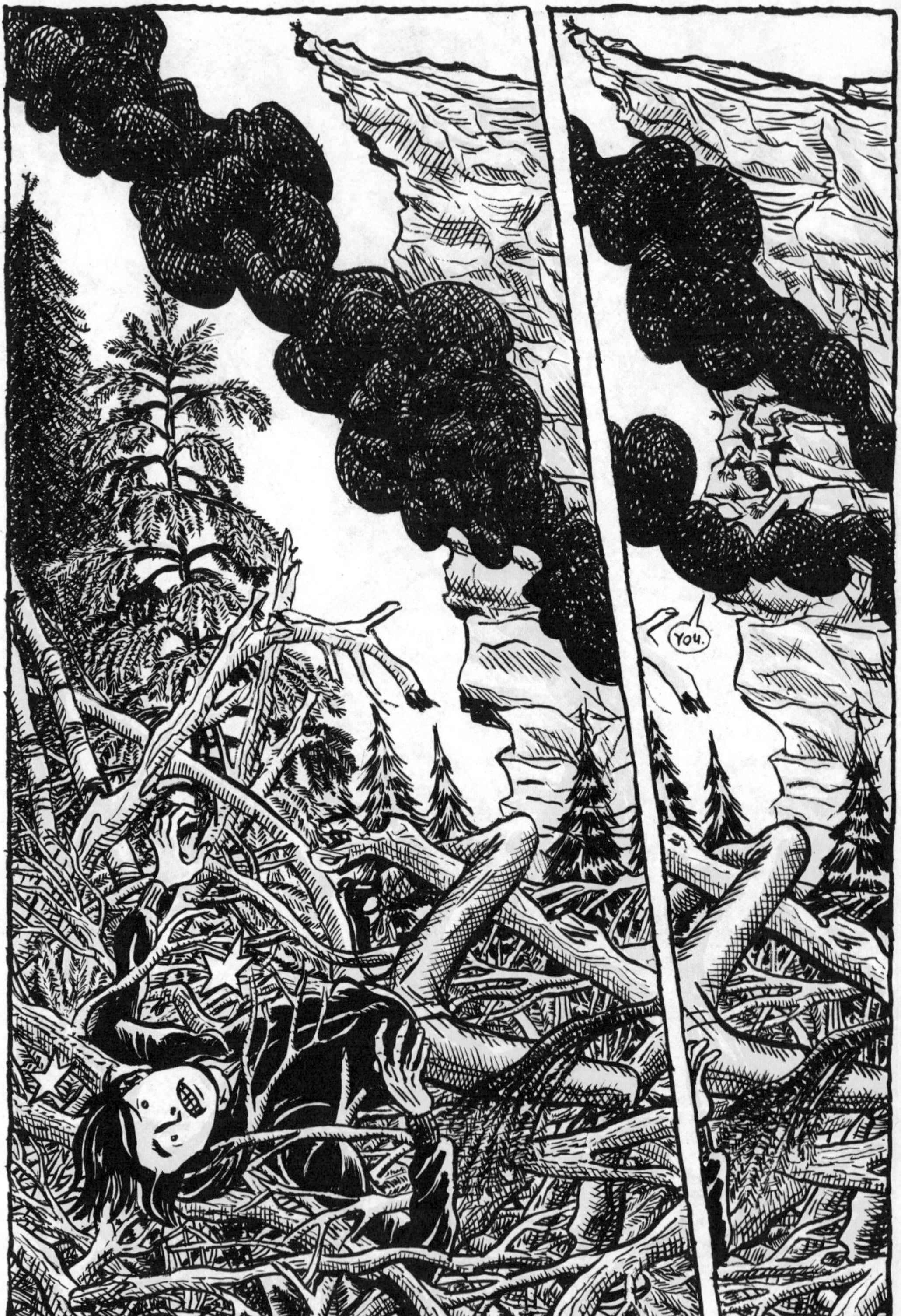
YOU.

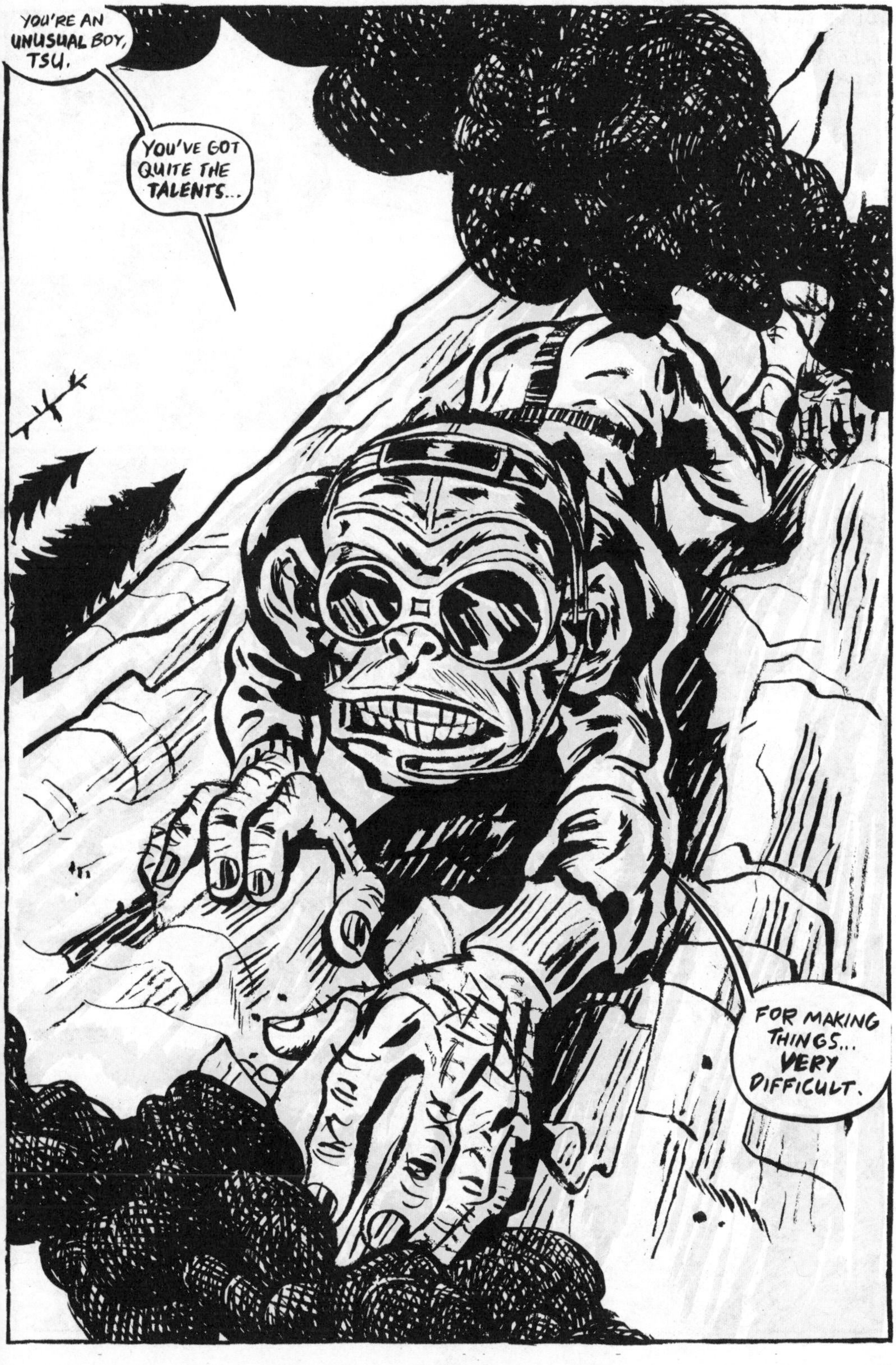
YOU'RE AN UNUSUAL BOY, TSU.
YOU'VE GOT QUITE THE TALENTS...
FOR MAKING THINGS... VERY DIFFICULT.

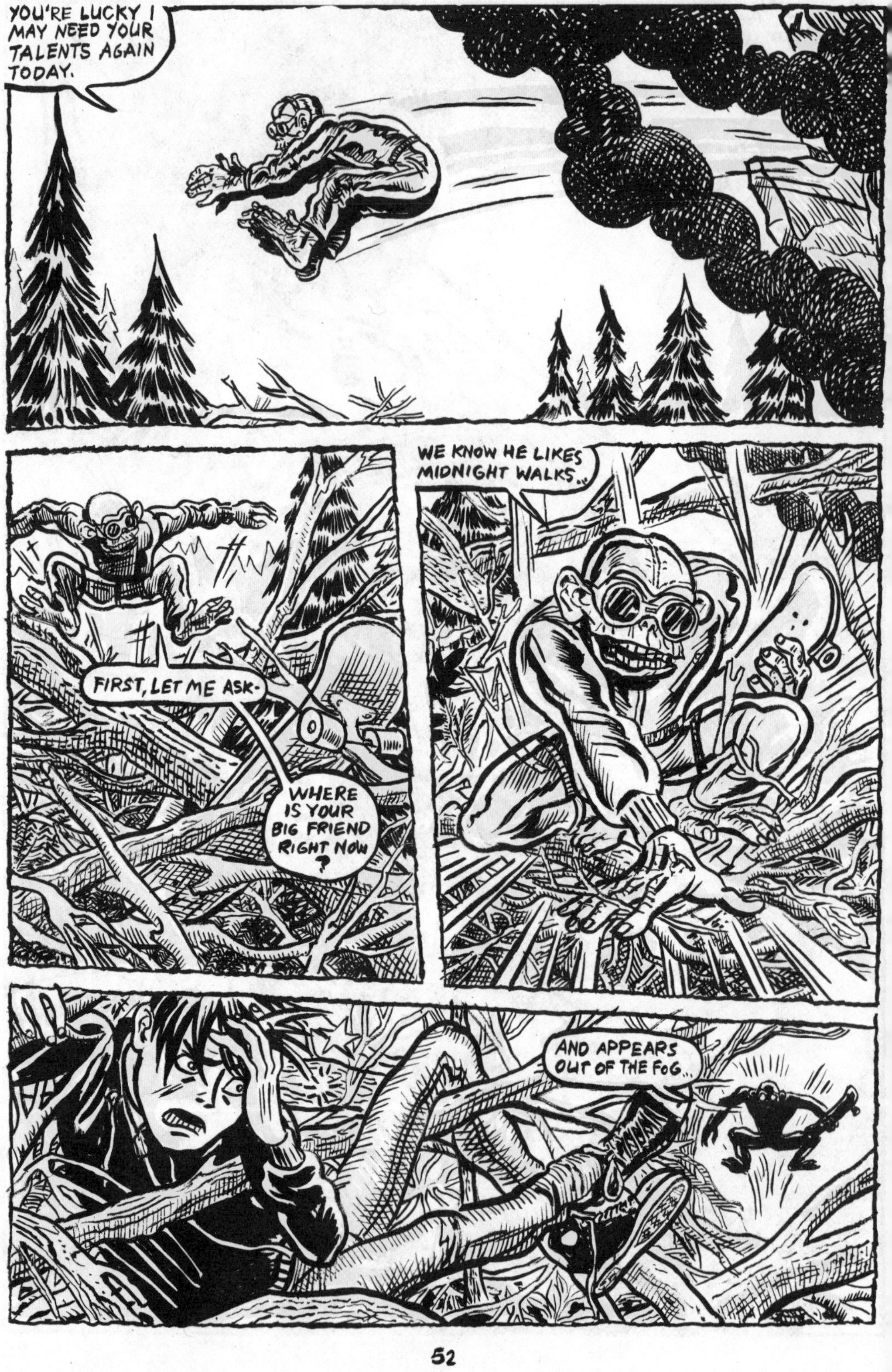
YOU'RE LUCKY I MAY NEED YOUR TALENTS AGAIN TODAY.
FIRST, LET ME ASK-
WHERE IS YOUR BIG FRIEND RIGHT NOW ?
WE KNOW HE LIKES MIDNIGHT WALKS..
AND APPEARS OUT OF THE FOG..

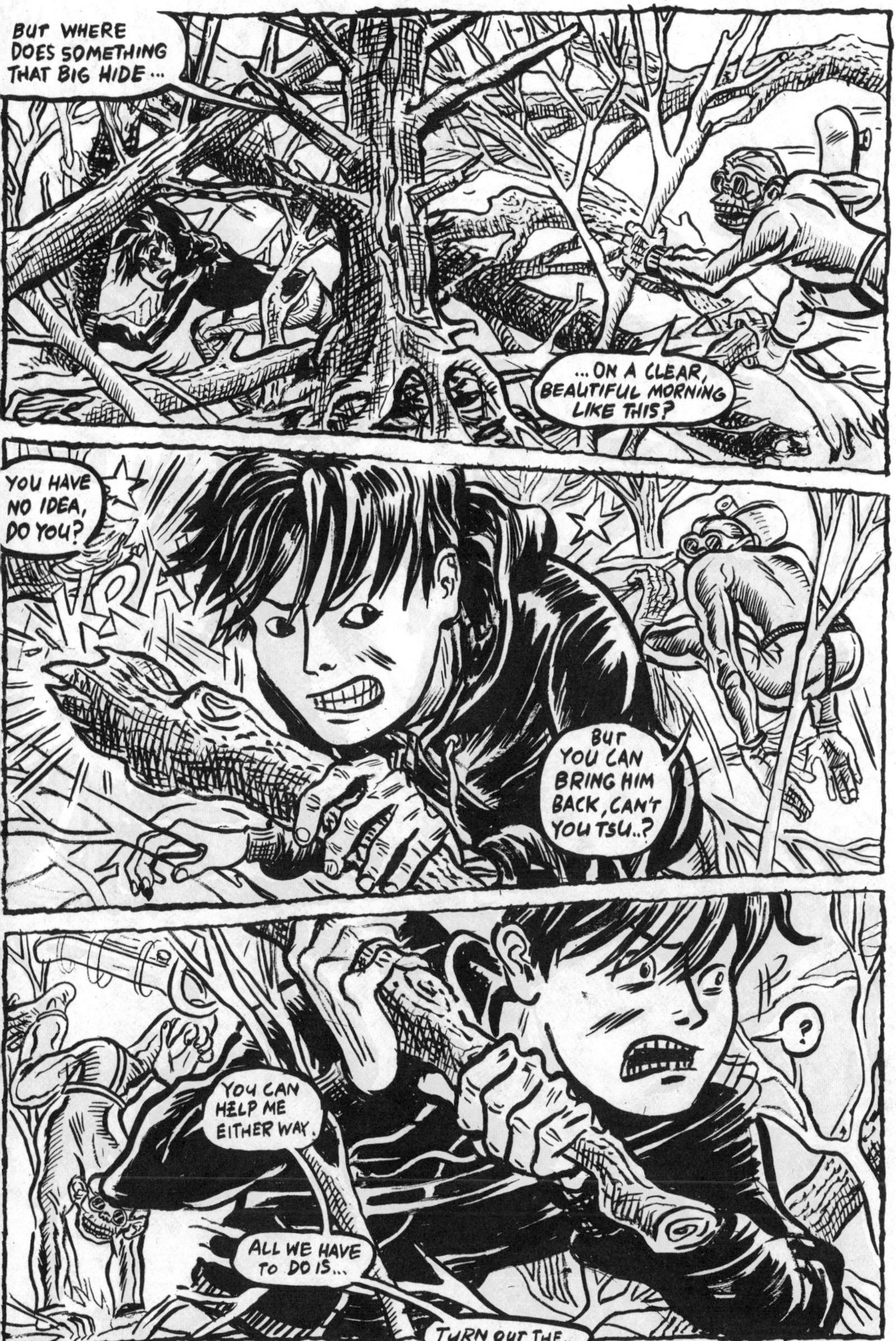
BUT WHERE DOES SOMETHING THAT BIG HIDE...
...ON A CLEAR, BEAUTIFUL MORNING LIKE THIS?
YOU HAVE NO IDEA, DO YOU?
BUT YOU CAN BRING HIM BACK, CAN'T YOU TSU..?
?
YOU CAN HELP ME EITHER WAY.
ALL WE HAVE TO DO IS...
TURN OUT THE...

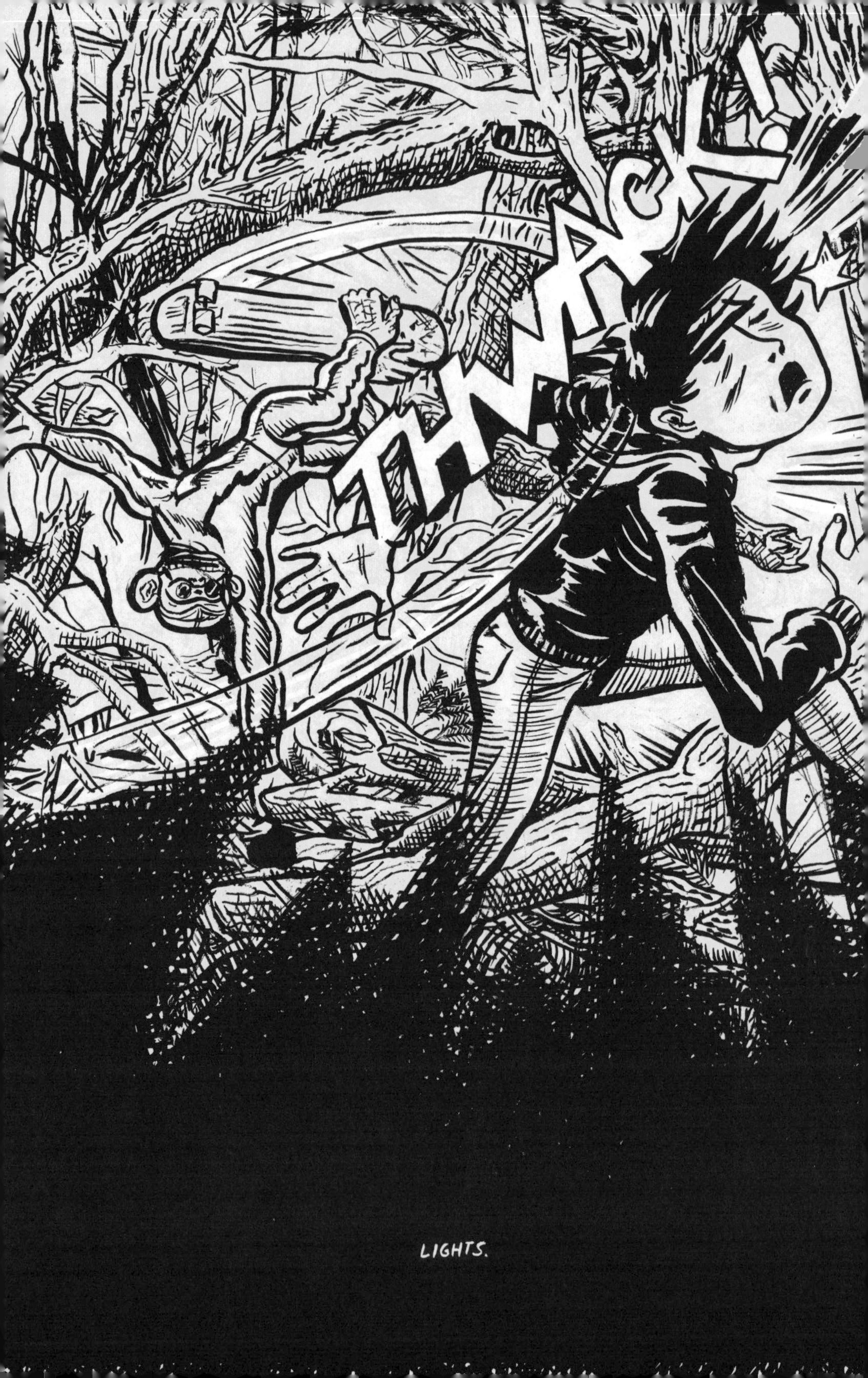
THWACK!
LIGHTS.

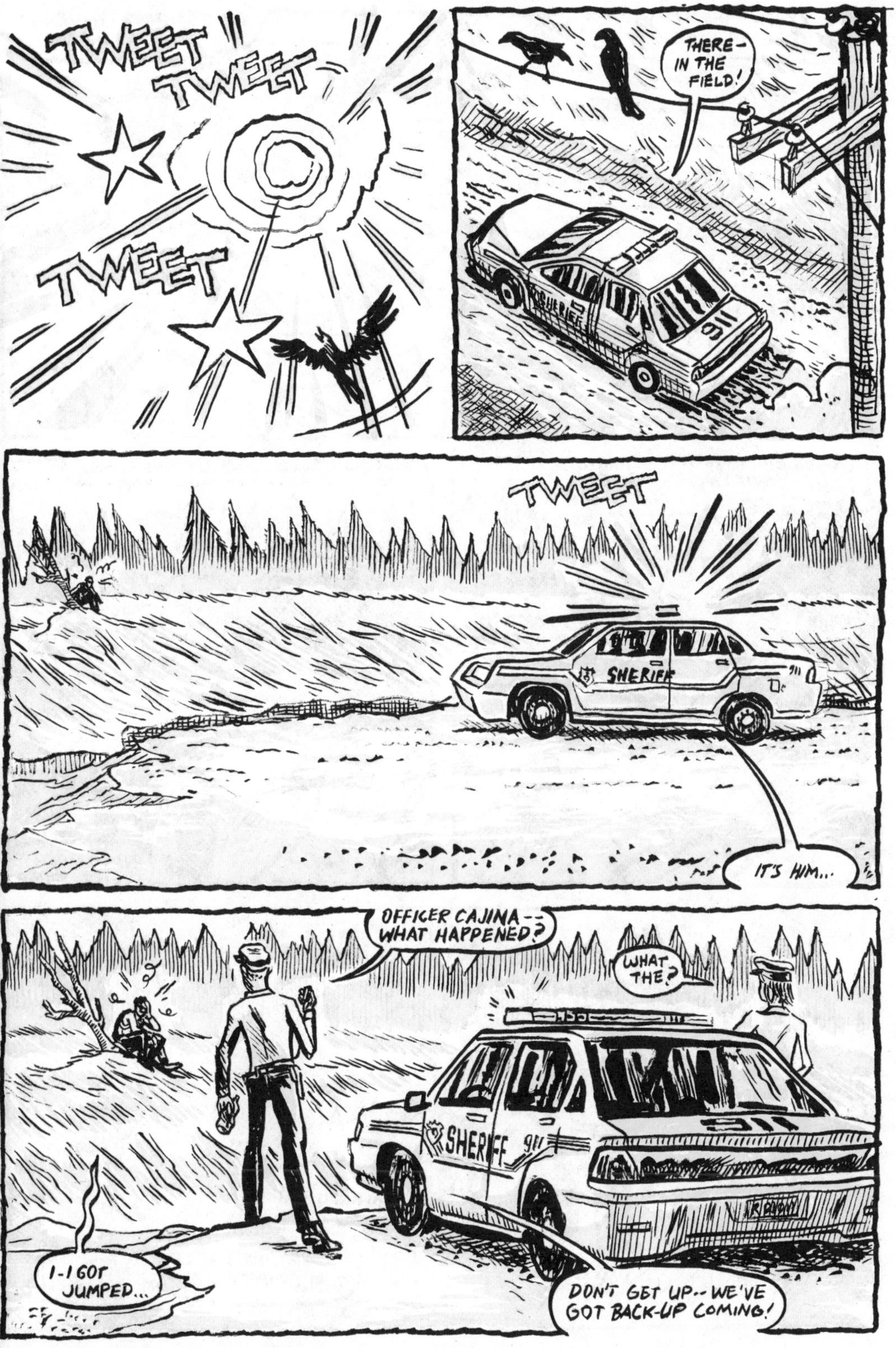
TWEET TWEET
TWEET
THERE- IN THE FIELD!
TWEET
IT'S HIM...
OFFICER CAJINA-- WHAT HAPPENED?
WHAT THE?
I-I GOT JUMPED...
DON'T GET UP-- WE'VE GOT BACK-UP COMING!

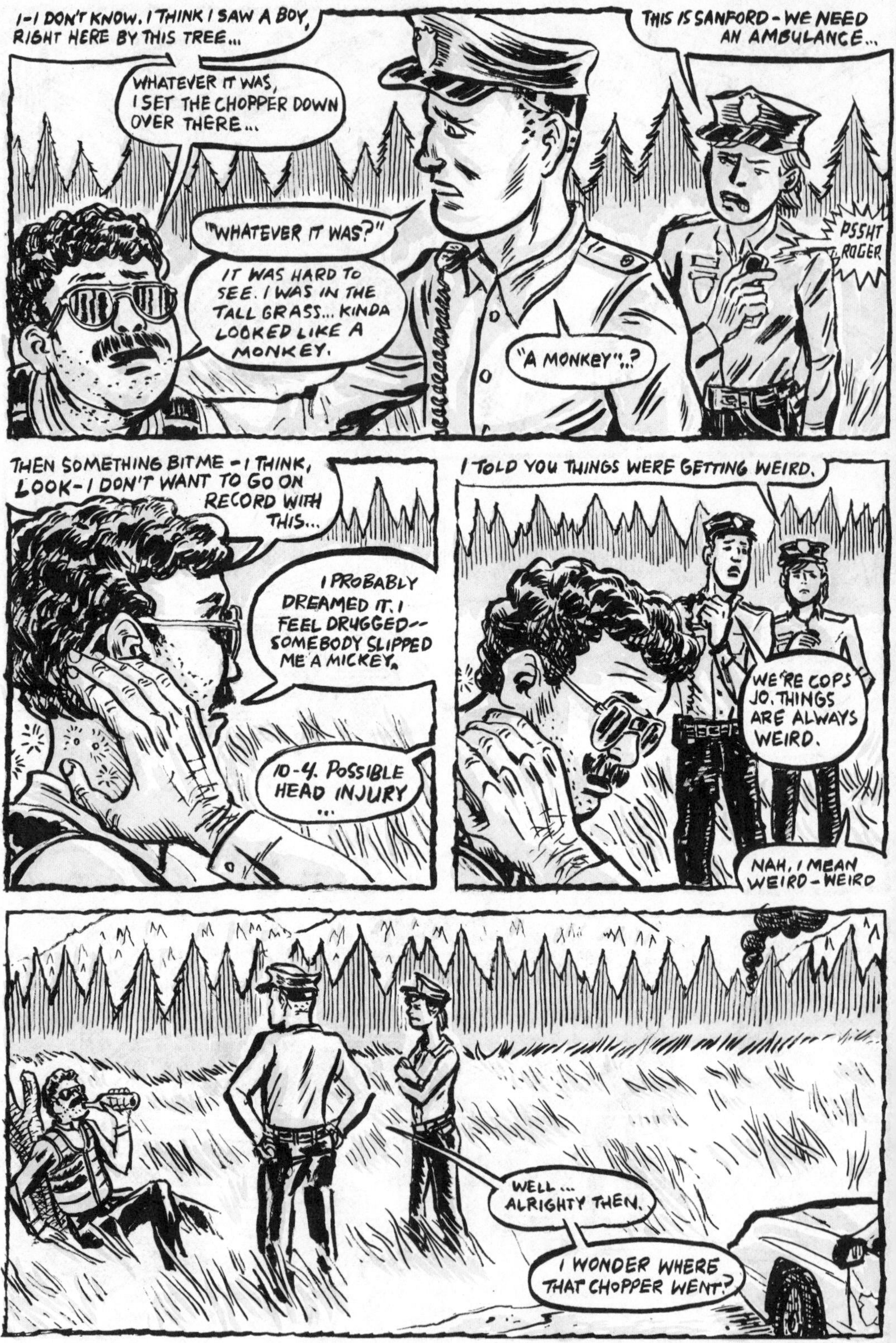

I-I DON'T KNOW. I THINK I SAW A BOY, RIGHT HERE BY THIS TREE...
WHATEVER IT WAS, I SET THE CHOPPER DOWN OVER THERE...
"WHATEVER IT WAS?"
IT WAS HARD TO SEE. I WAS IN THE TALL GRASS... KINDA LOOKED LIKE A MONKEY.
"A MONKEY"..?
THIS IS SANFORD - WE NEED AN AMBULANCE...
PSSHT ROGER
THEN SOMETHING BIT ME - I THINK, LOOK - I DON'T WANT TO GO ON RECORD WITH THIS...
I PROBABLY DREAMED IT. I FEEL DRUGGED-- SOMEBODY SLIPPED ME A MICKEY.
10-4. POSSIBLE HEAD INJURY ...
I TOLD YOU THINGS WERE GETTING WEIRD.
WE'RE COPS JO. THINGS ARE ALWAYS WEIRD.
NAH, I MEAN WEIRD - WEIRD
WELL ... ALRIGHTY THEN.
I WONDER WHERE THAT CHOPPER WENT?

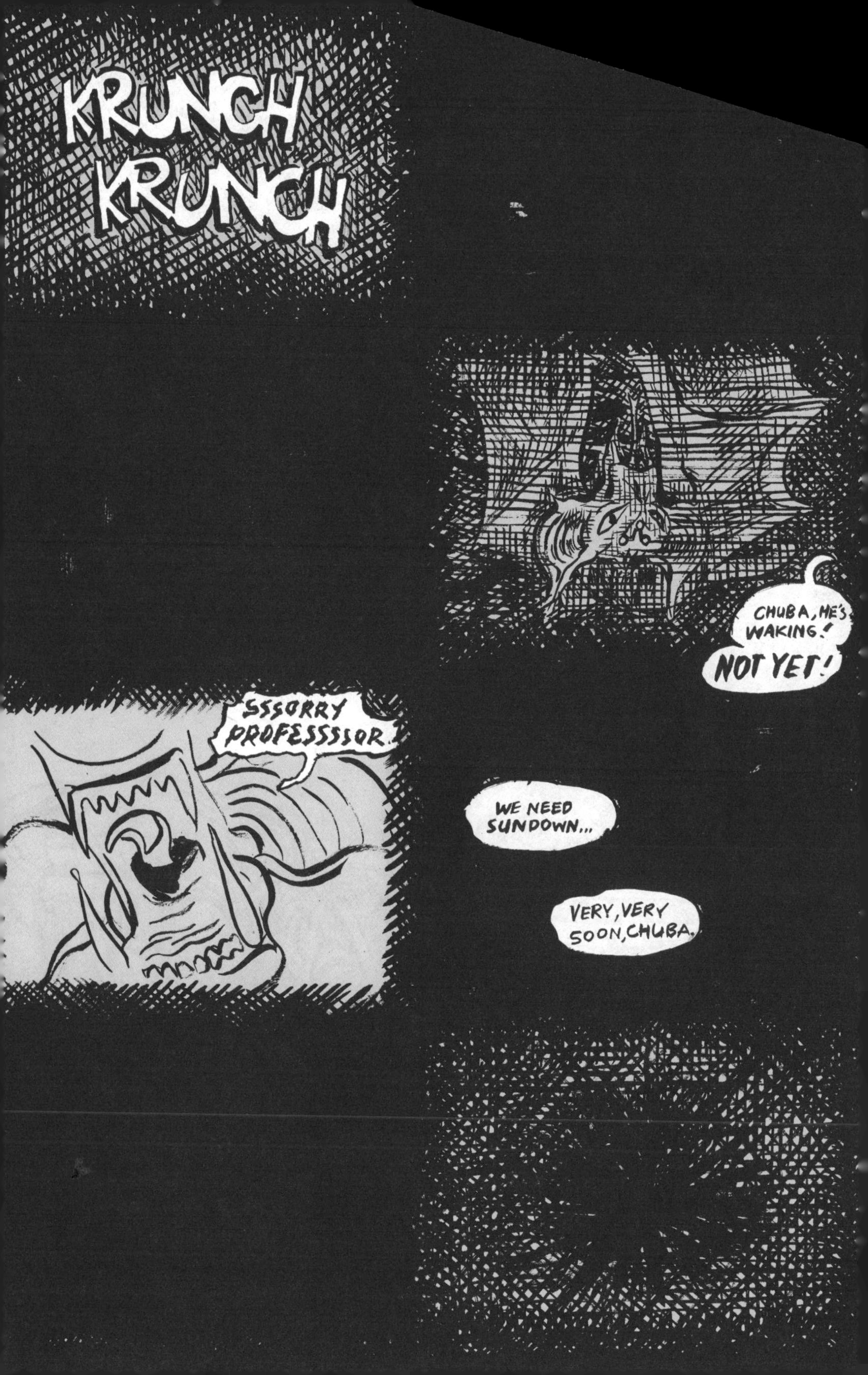
KRUNCH KRUNCH
CHUBA, HE'S WAKING!
NOT YET!
SSSORRY PROFESSSSSOR.
WE NEED SUNDOWN...
VERY, VERY SOON, CHUBA.

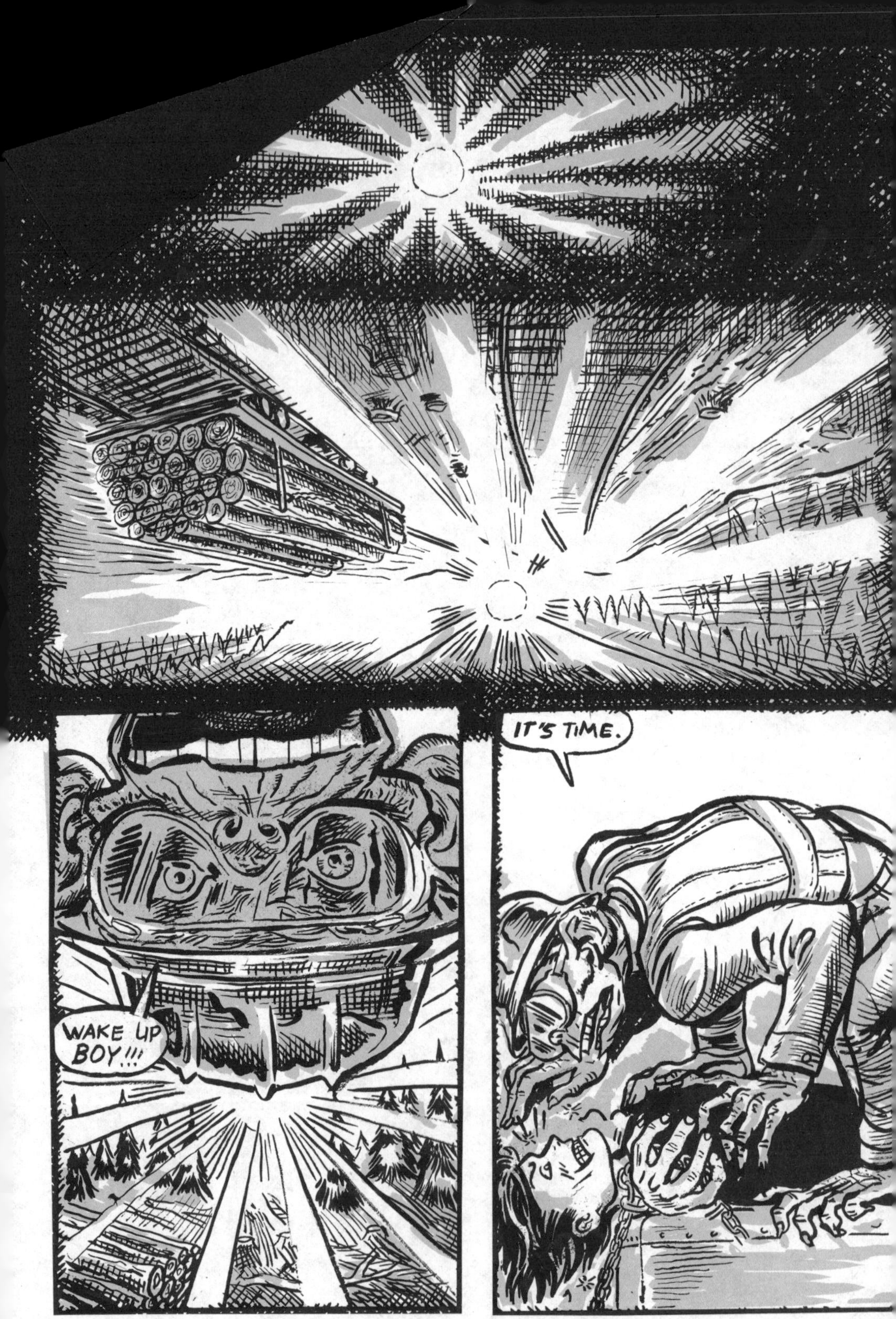
WAKE UP BOY!!!
IT'S TIME.

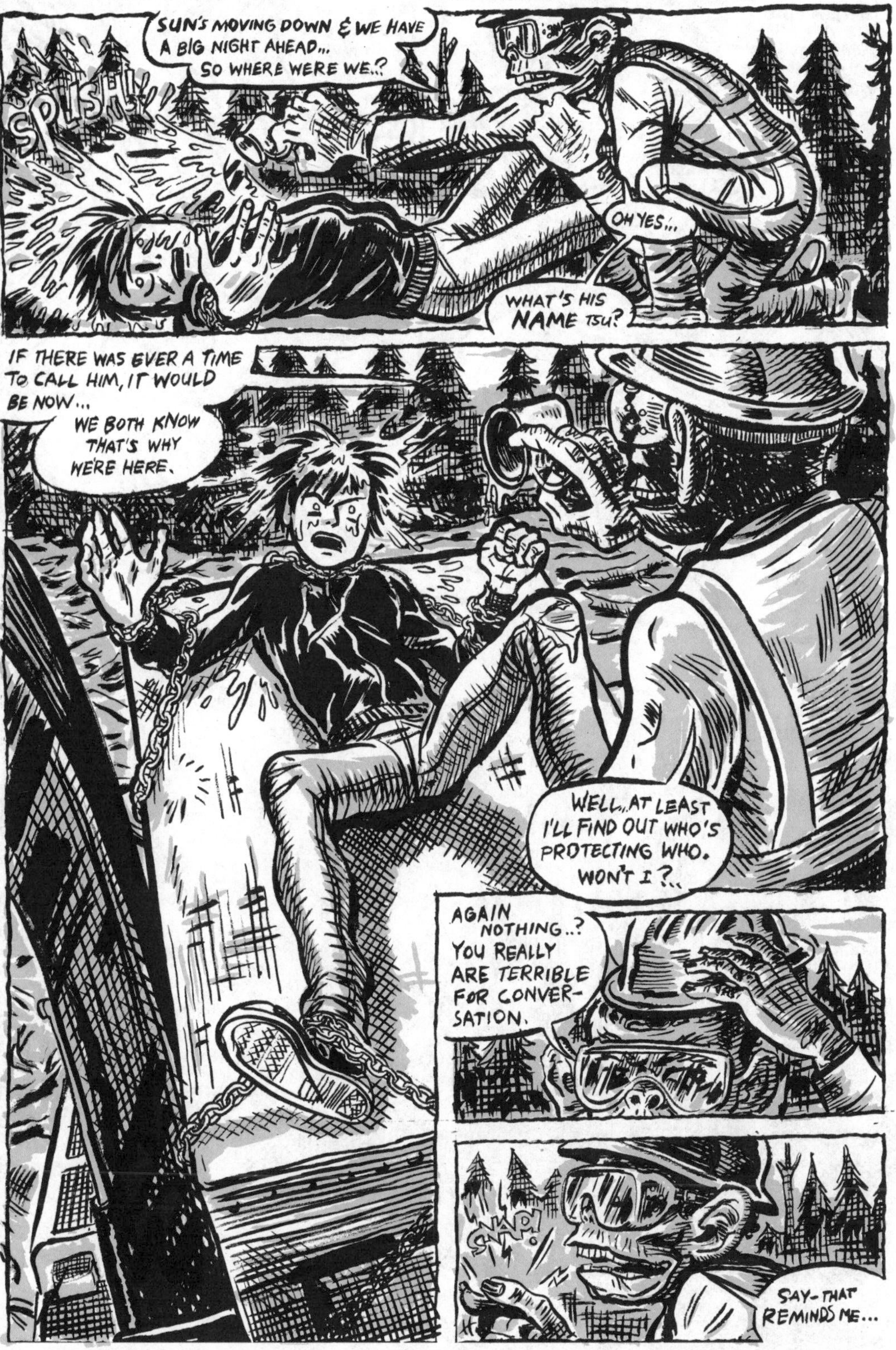
SPLISH!
SUN'S MOVING DOWN & WE HAVE A BIG NIGHT AHEAD... SO WHERE WERE WE..?
OH YES...
WHAT'S HIS NAME TSU?
IF THERE WAS EVER A TIME TO CALL HIM, IT WOULD BE NOW...
WE BOTH KNOW THAT'S WHY WE'RE HERE.
WELL.. AT LEAST I'LL FIND OUT WHO'S PROTECTING WHO. WON'T I?..
AGAIN NOTHING..? YOU REALLY ARE TERRIBLE FOR CONVER-SATION.
SNAP!
SAY-THAT REMINDS ME...

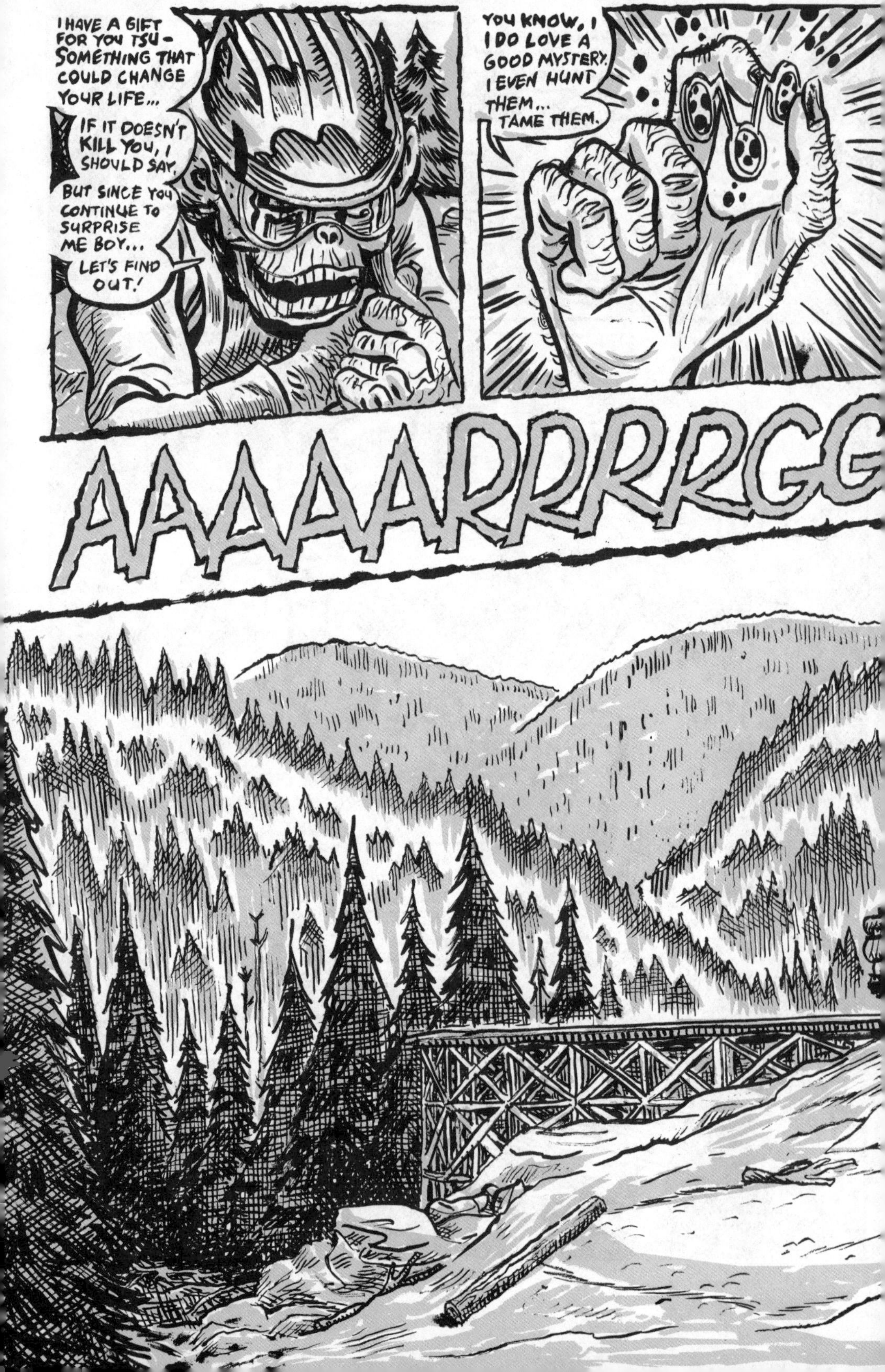
I HAVE A GIFT FOR YOU TSU - SOMETHING THAT COULD CHANGE YOUR LIFE...
IF IT DOESN'T KILL YOU, I SHOULD SAY.
BUT SINCE YOU CONTINUE TO SURPRISE ME BOY...
LET'S FIND OUT!
YOU KNOW, I DO LOVE A GOOD MYSTERY. I EVEN HUNT THEM... TAME THEM.
AAAAARRRRGG

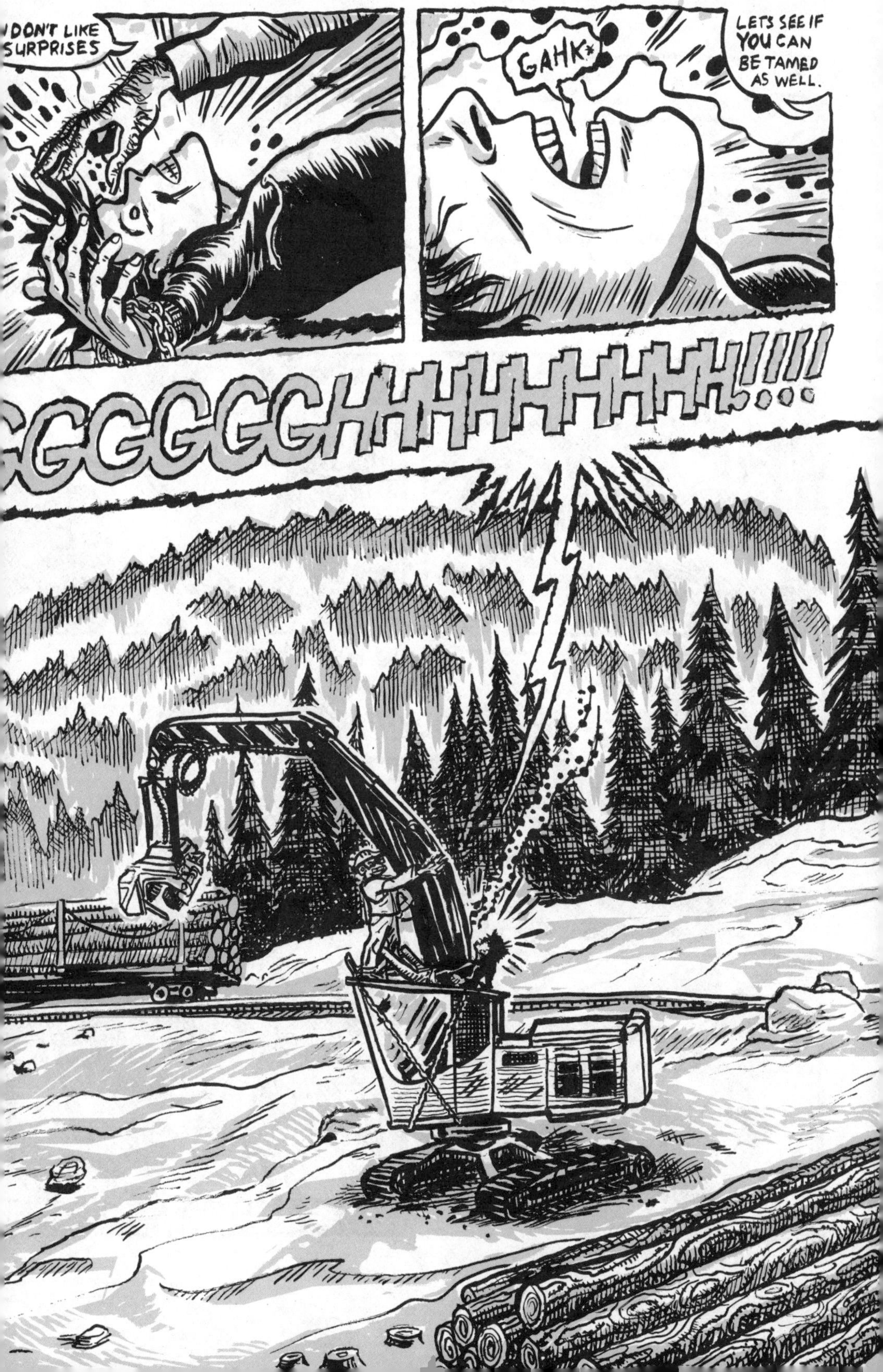
I DON'T LIKE SURPRISES
GAHK*
LETS SEE IF YOU CAN BE TAMED AS WELL.
GGGGGGHHHHHHHHHHH!!!!!

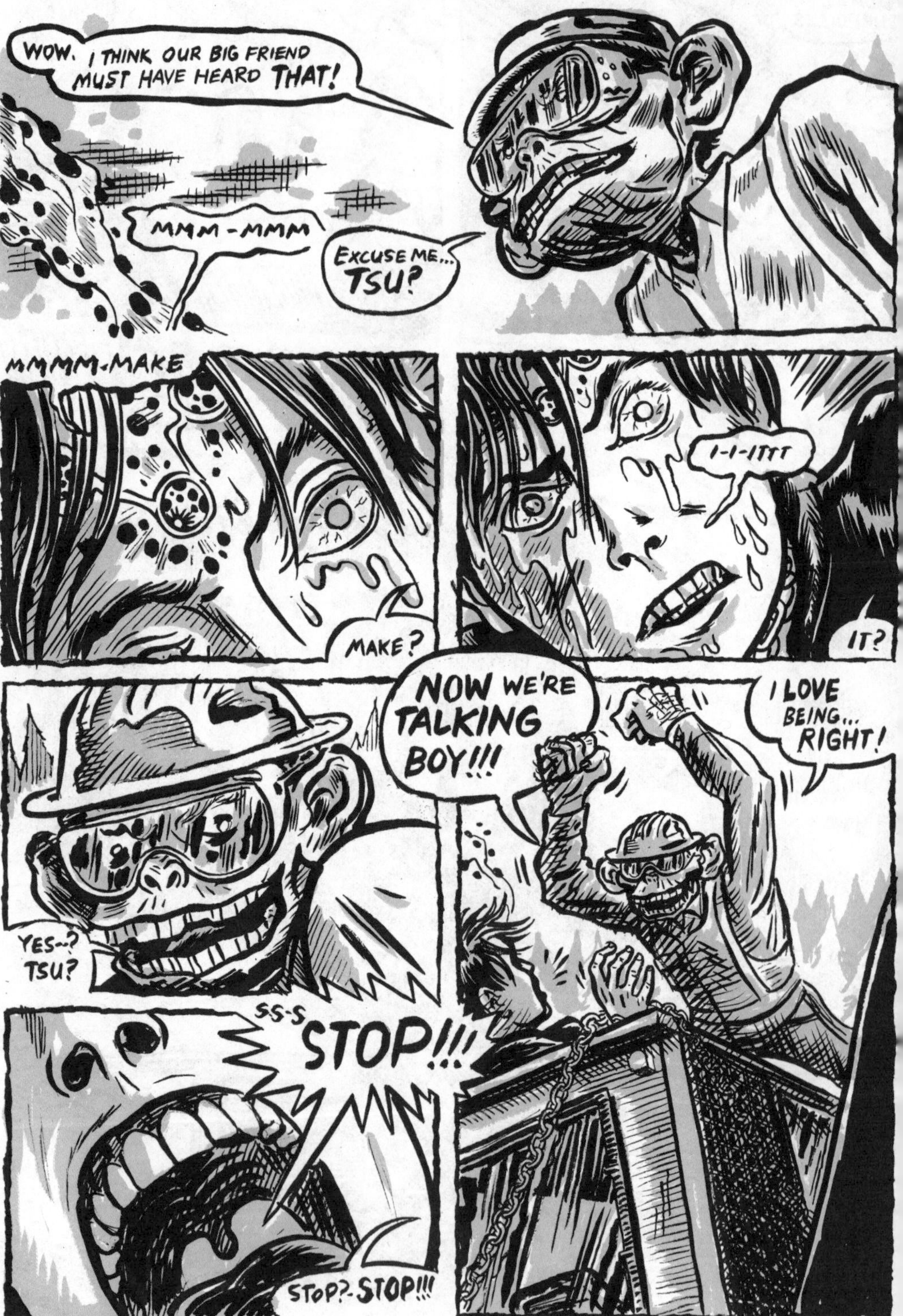
WOW. I THINK OUR BIG FRIEND MUST HAVE HEARD THAT!
MMM-MMM
EXCUSE ME... TSU?
MMMM-MAKE
MAKE?
I-I-ITTT
IT?
NOW WE'RE TALKING BOY!!!
I LOVE BEING... RIGHT!
YES--? TSU?
S-S-S STOP!!!
STOP?-STOP!!!

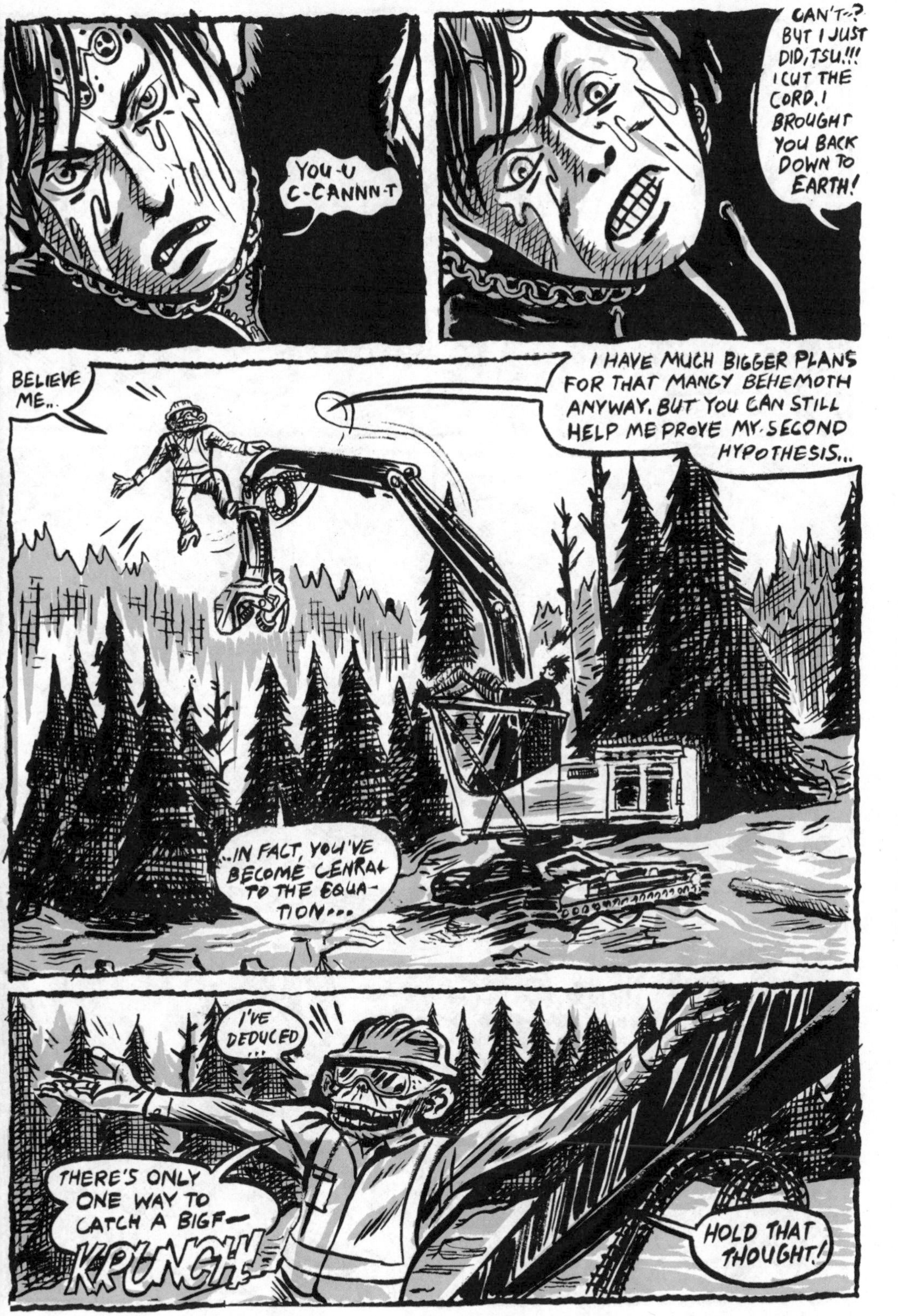
YOU-U C-CANNN-T
CAN'T--? BUT I JUST DID, TSU!!! I CUT THE CORD. I BROUGHT YOU BACK DOWN TO EARTH!
BELIEVE ME..
I HAVE MUCH BIGGER PLANS FOR THAT MANGY BEHEMOTH ANYWAY. BUT YOU CAN STILL HELP ME PROVE MY SECOND HYPOTHESIS...
...IN FACT, YOU'VE BECOME CENRAL TO THE EQUATION...
I'VE DEDUCED...
THERE'S ONLY ONE WAY TO CATCH A BIGF—
KRUNCH!
HOLD THAT THOUGHT!

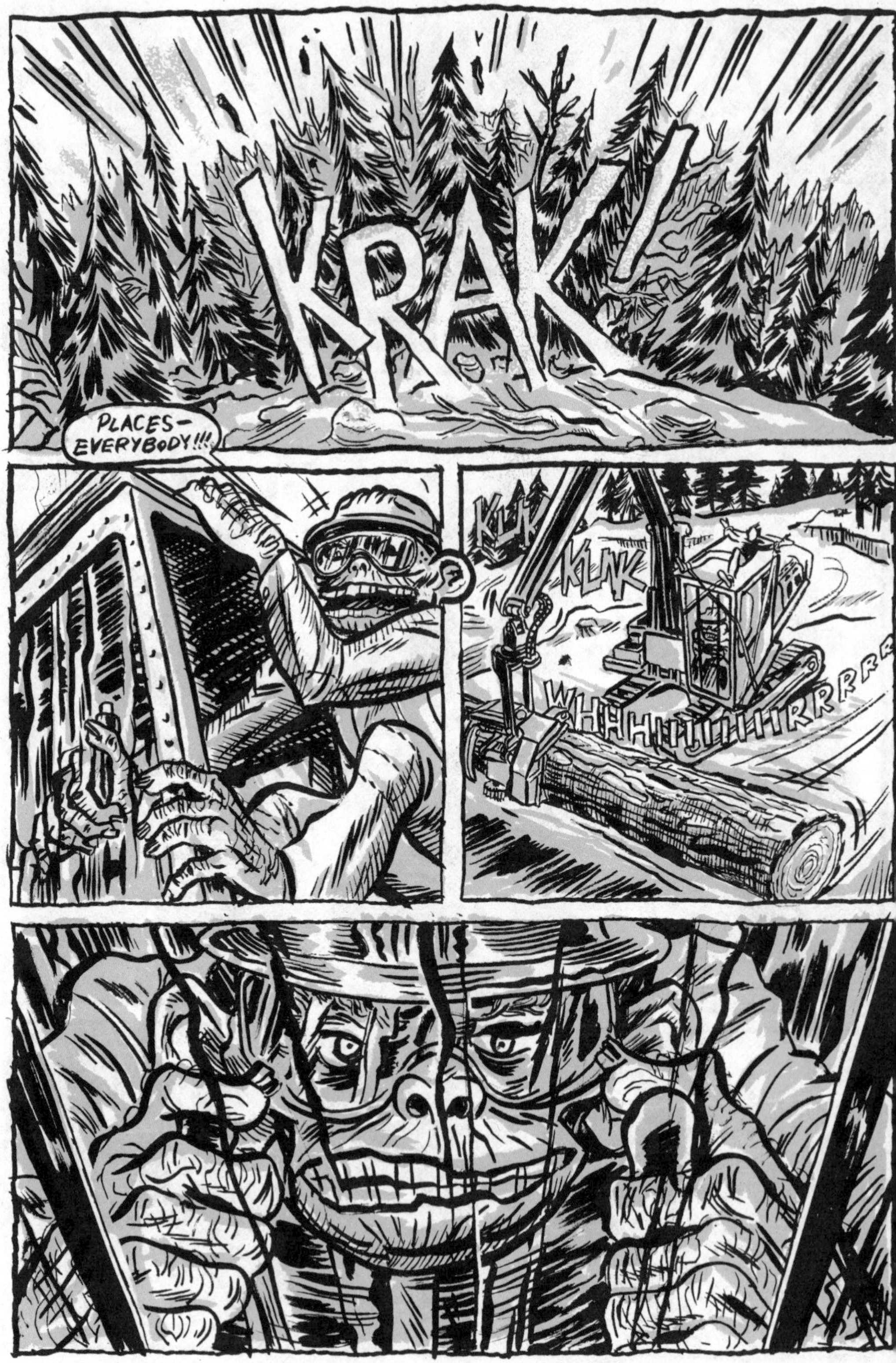
KRAK!
PLACES-
EVERYBODY!!!
KLUNK
KLUNK
WHHHHIIIIIIIIRRRRRR

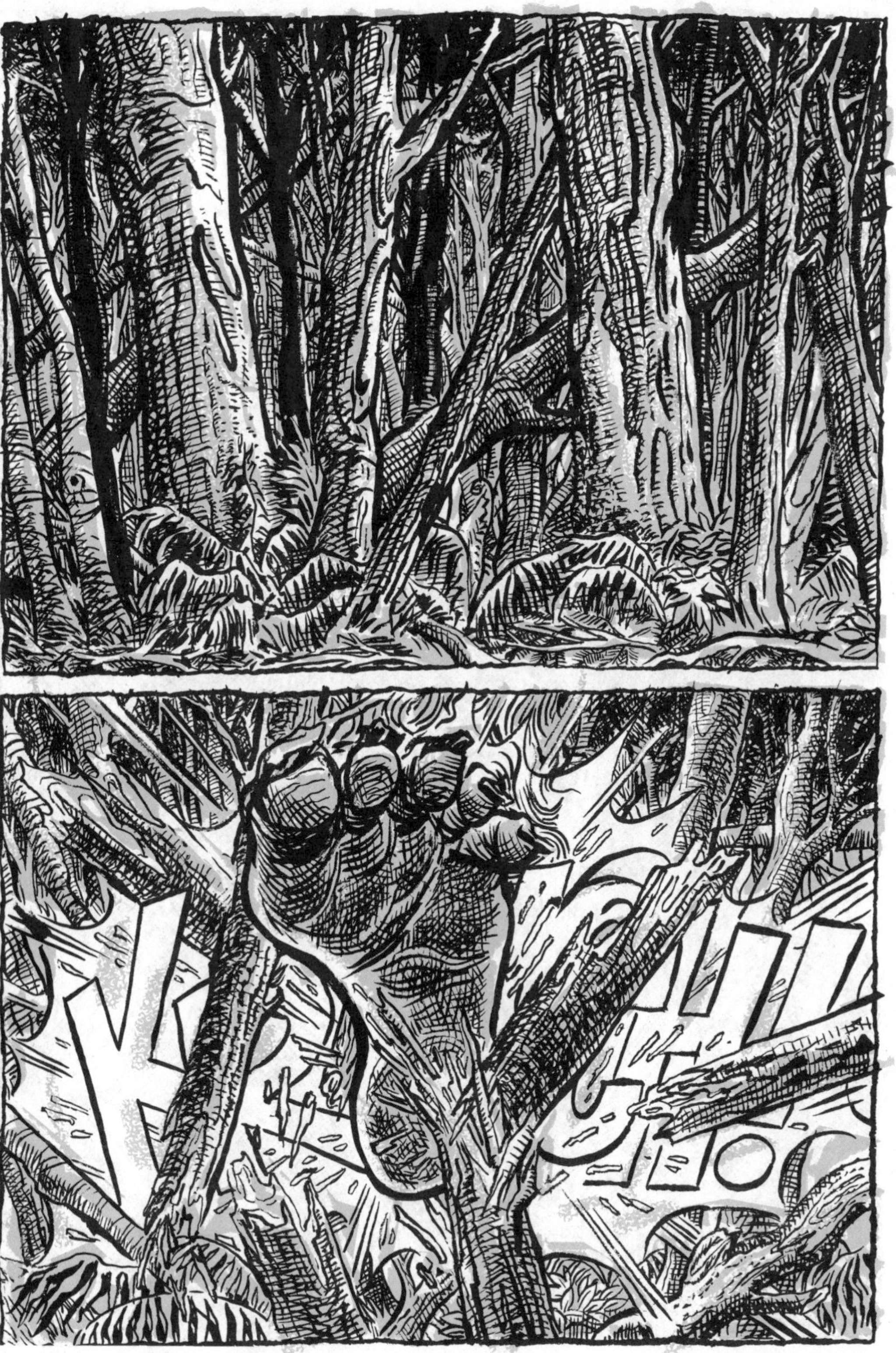

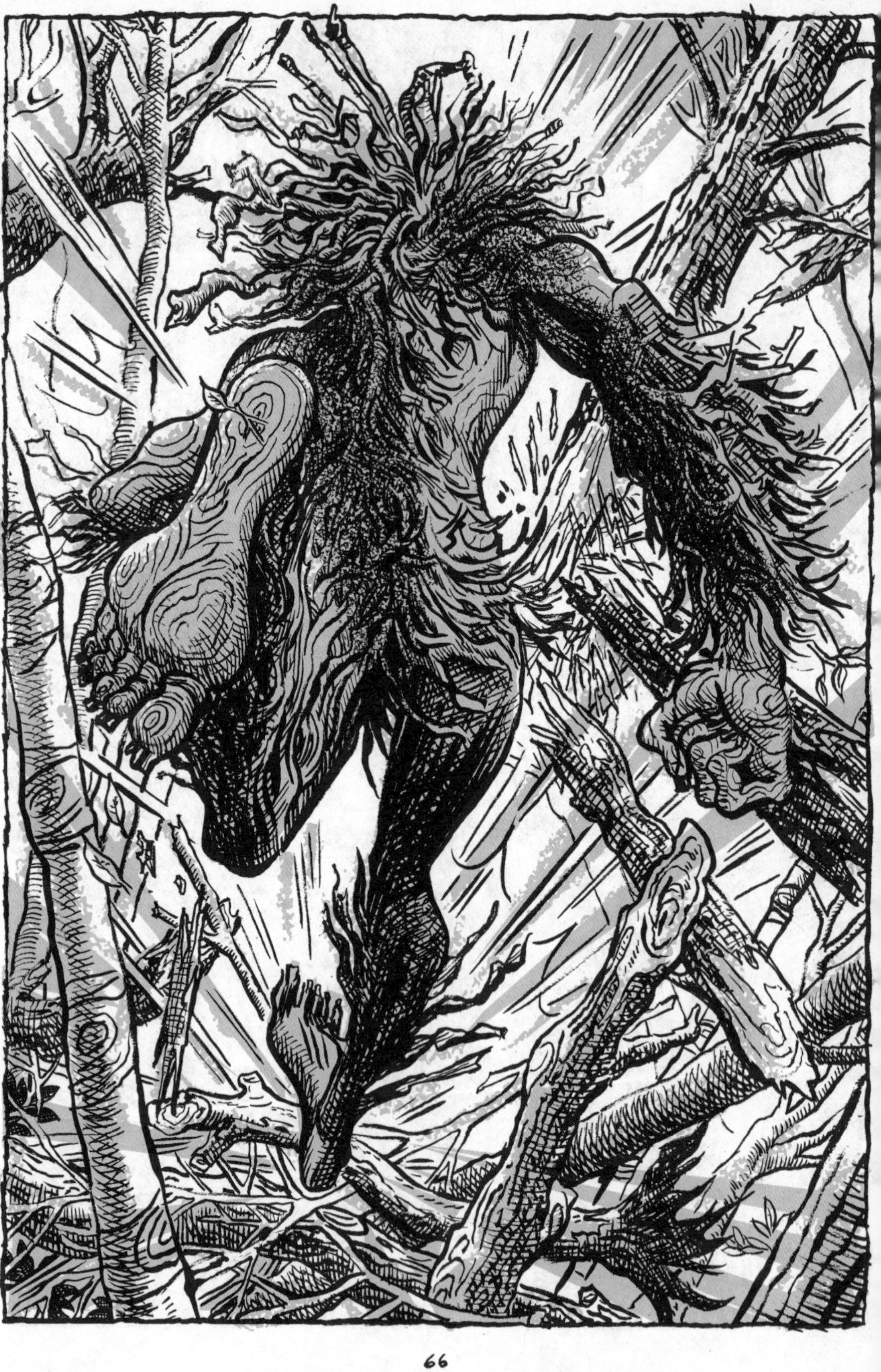

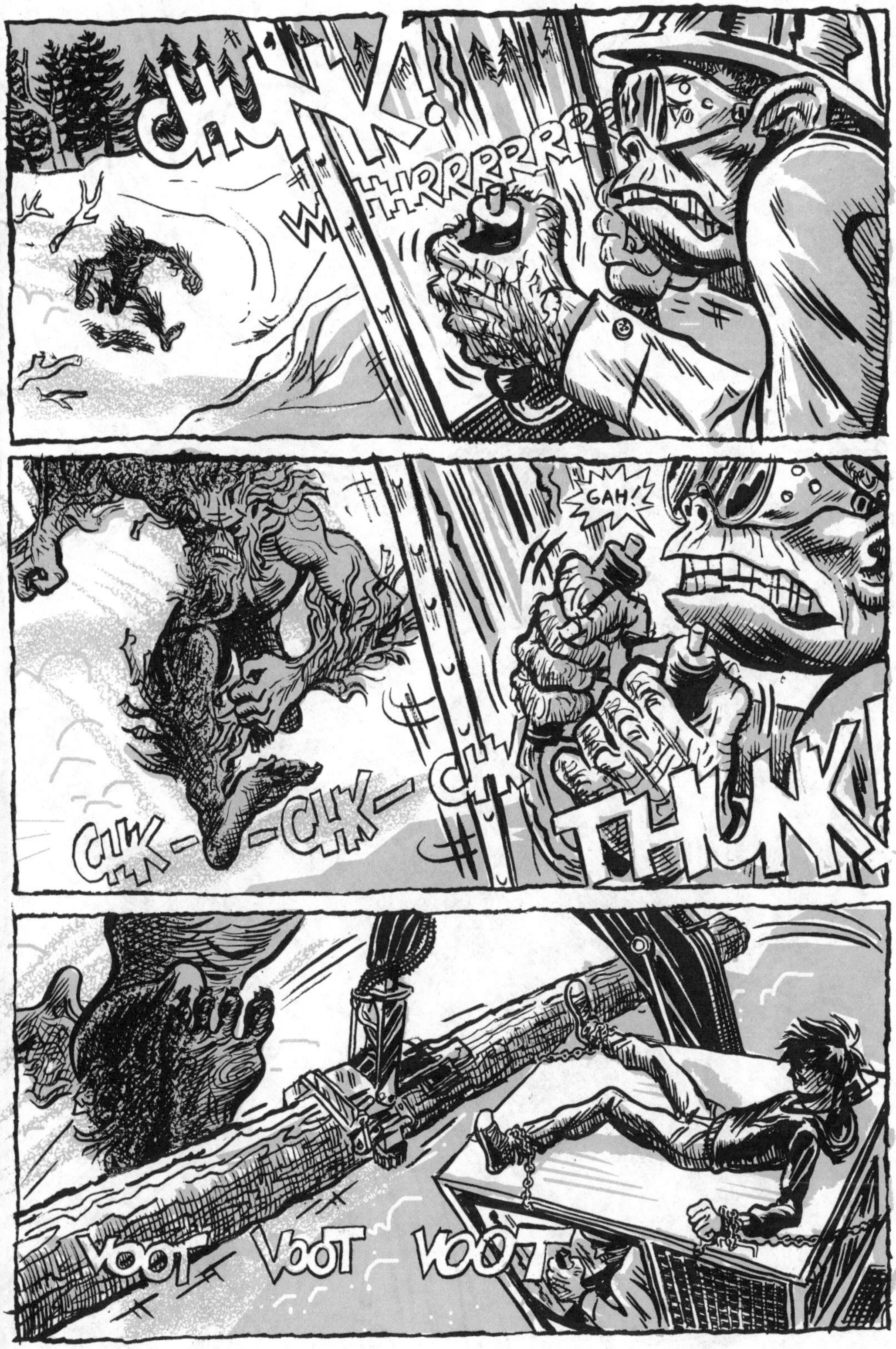
CHUNK!
WHHRRRRRR
GAH!
CHK-CHK-CHK-CHK
THUNK!
VOOT VOOT VOOT

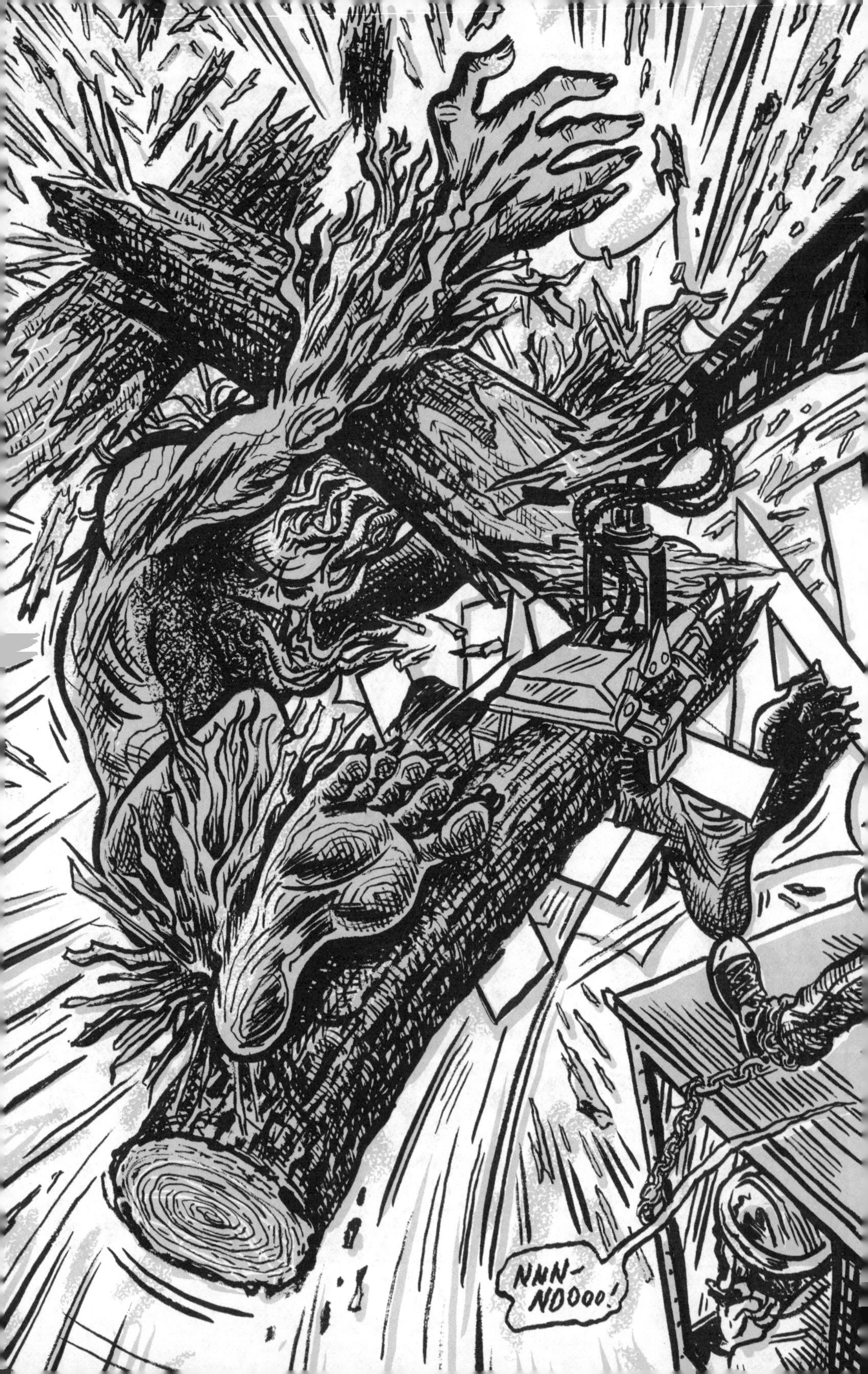
NNN-
NOOoo!

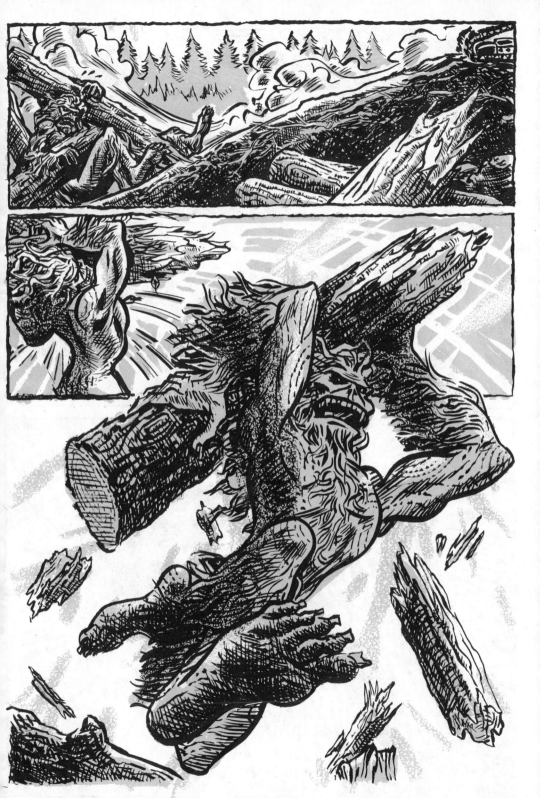

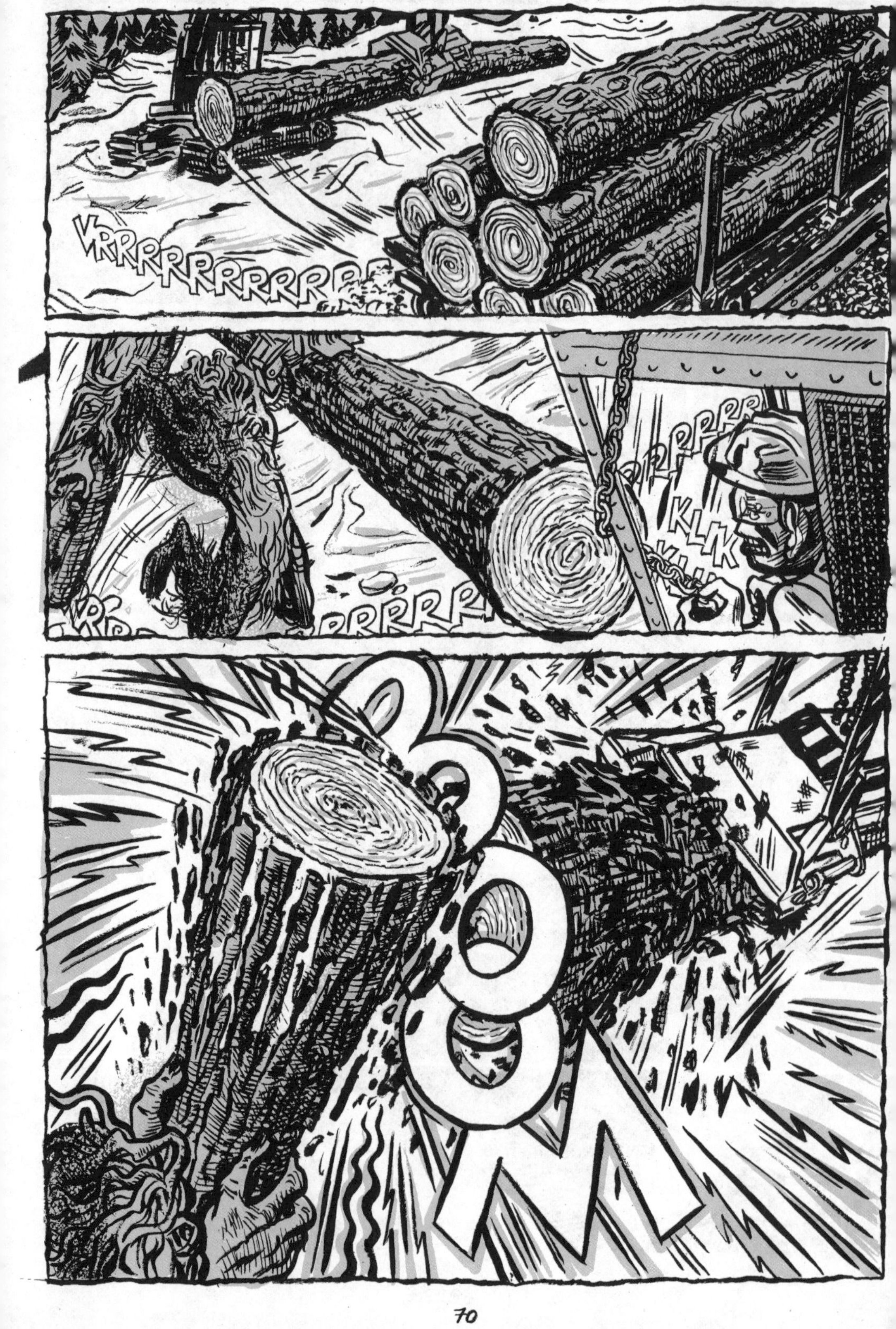
VRRRRRRRRRRRR
RRRRR
KLIK
BOOM

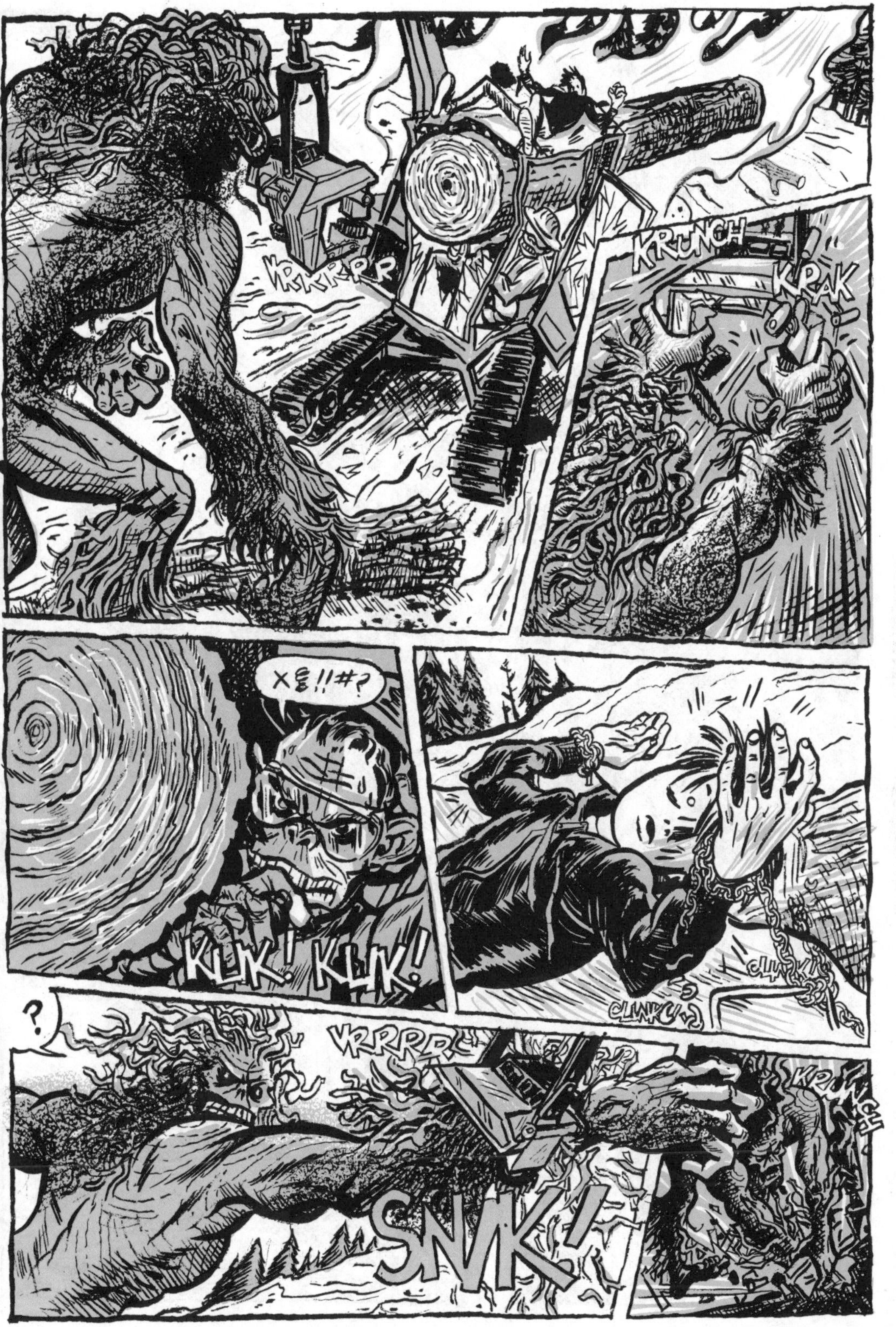
KRUNCH
KRAK
KLIK! KLIK!
?
SNIK!

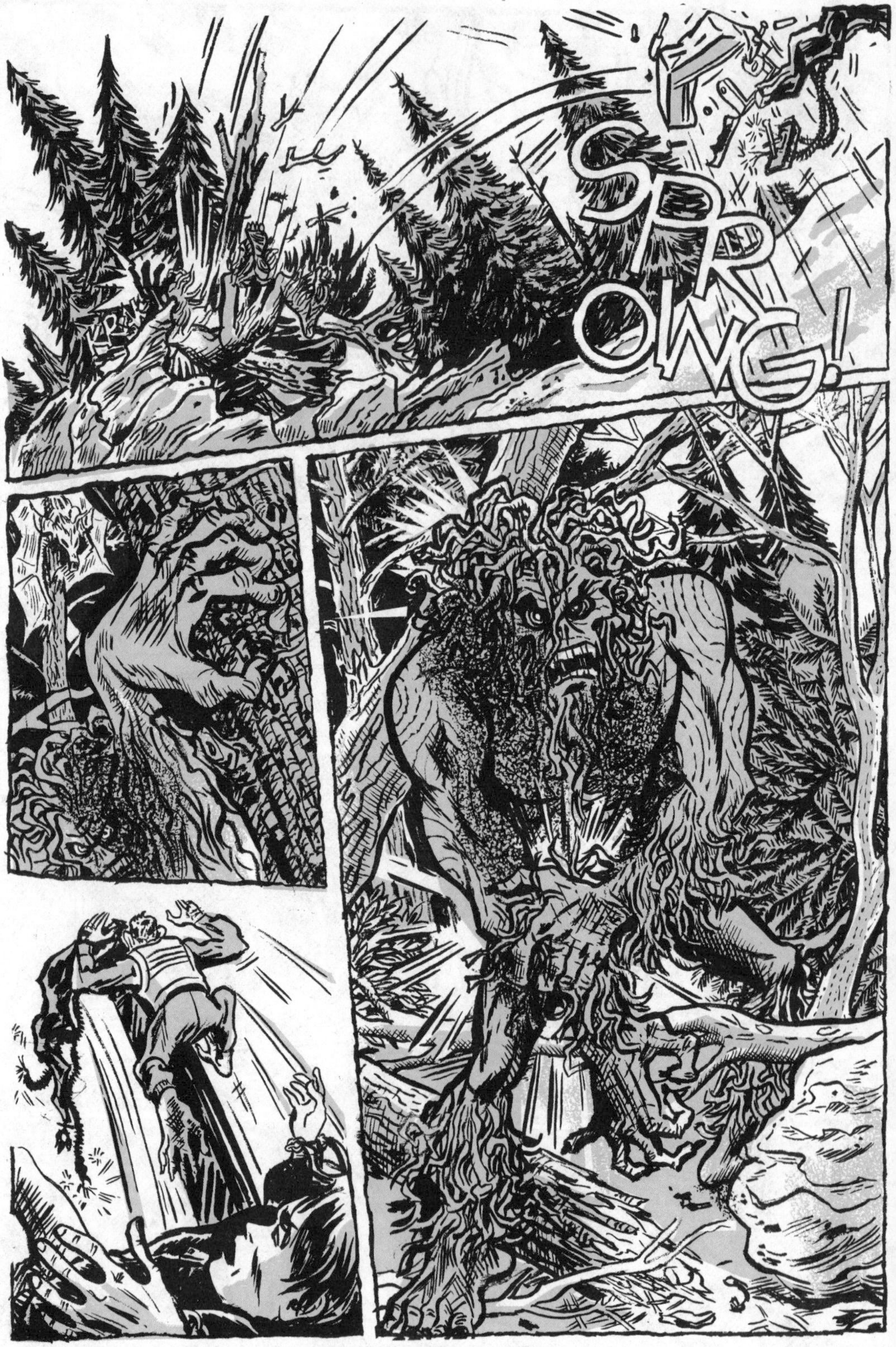
SPROWG!

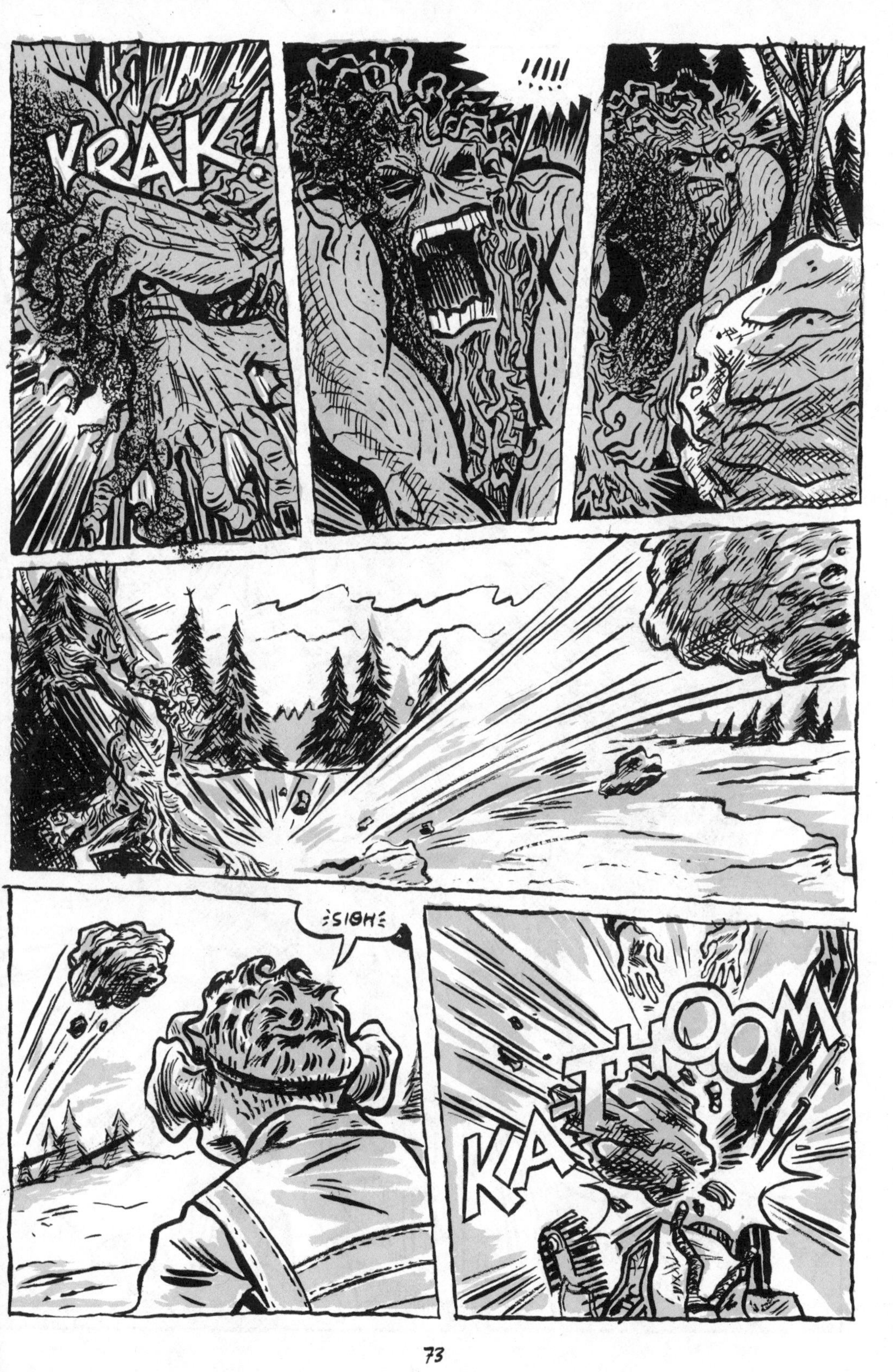
KRAK!
!!!!!!
SIGH
KA-THOOM

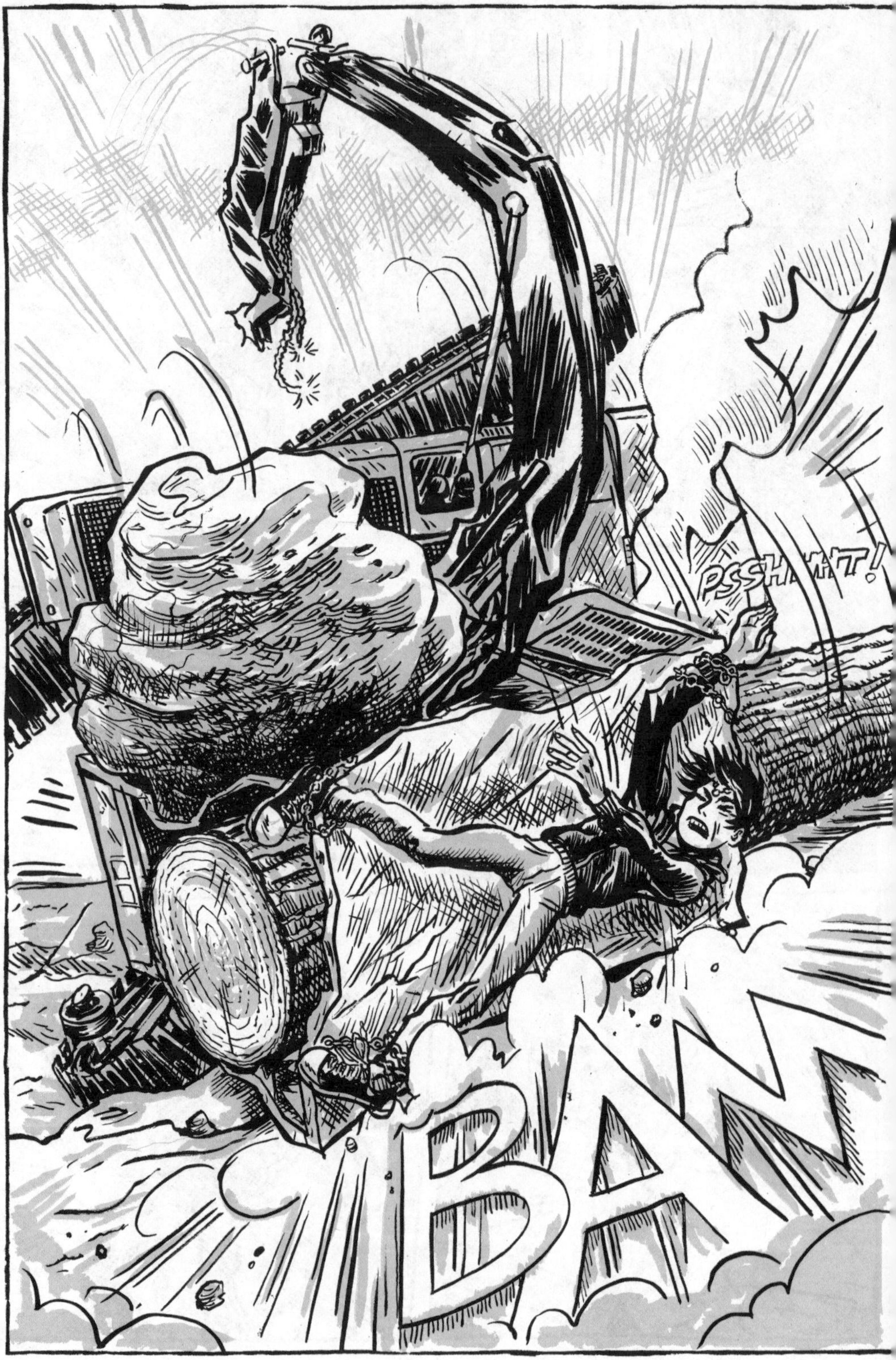
PSSHHHT!
BAM

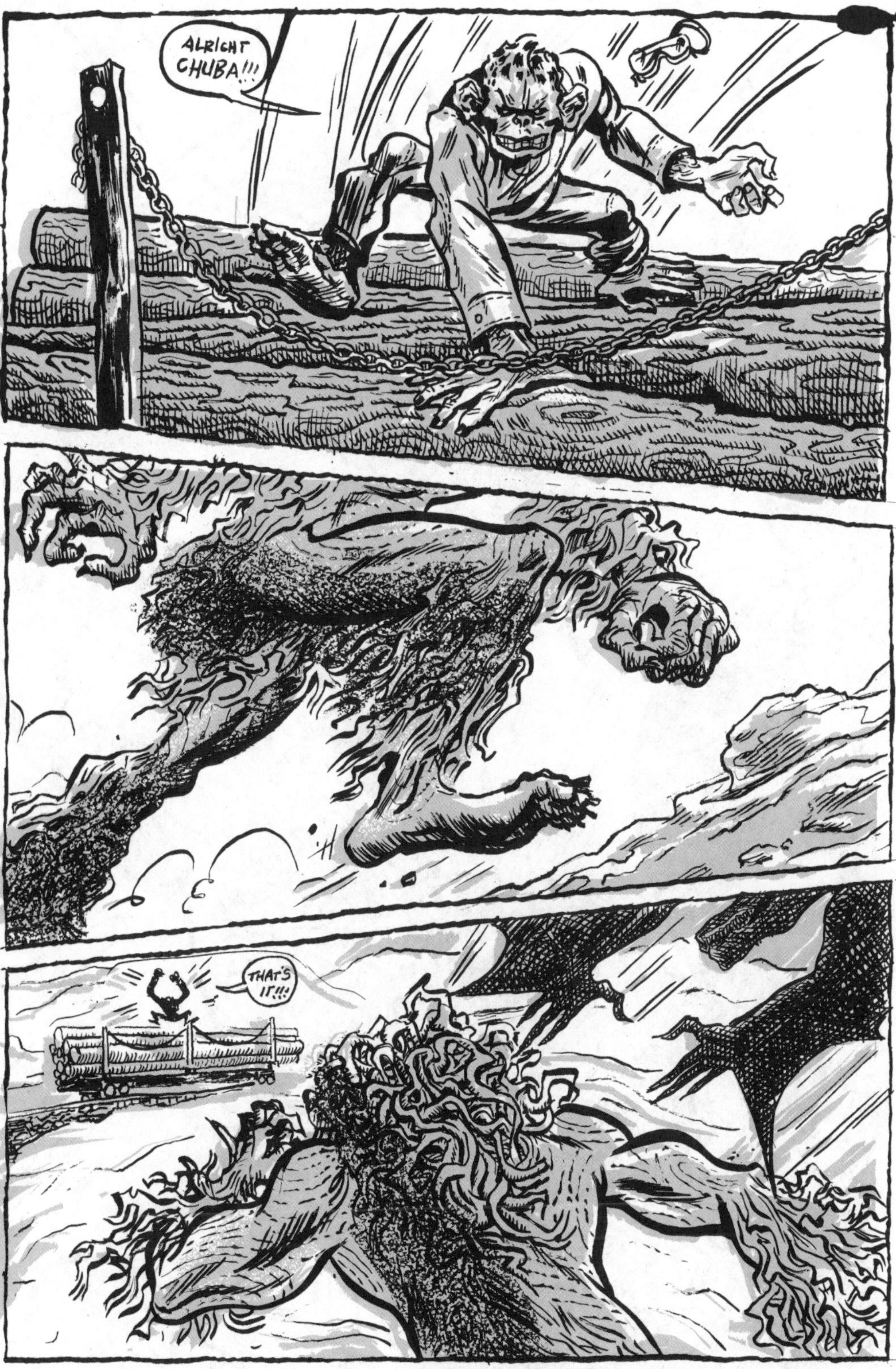
ALRIGHT CHUBA!!!
THAT'S IT!!!

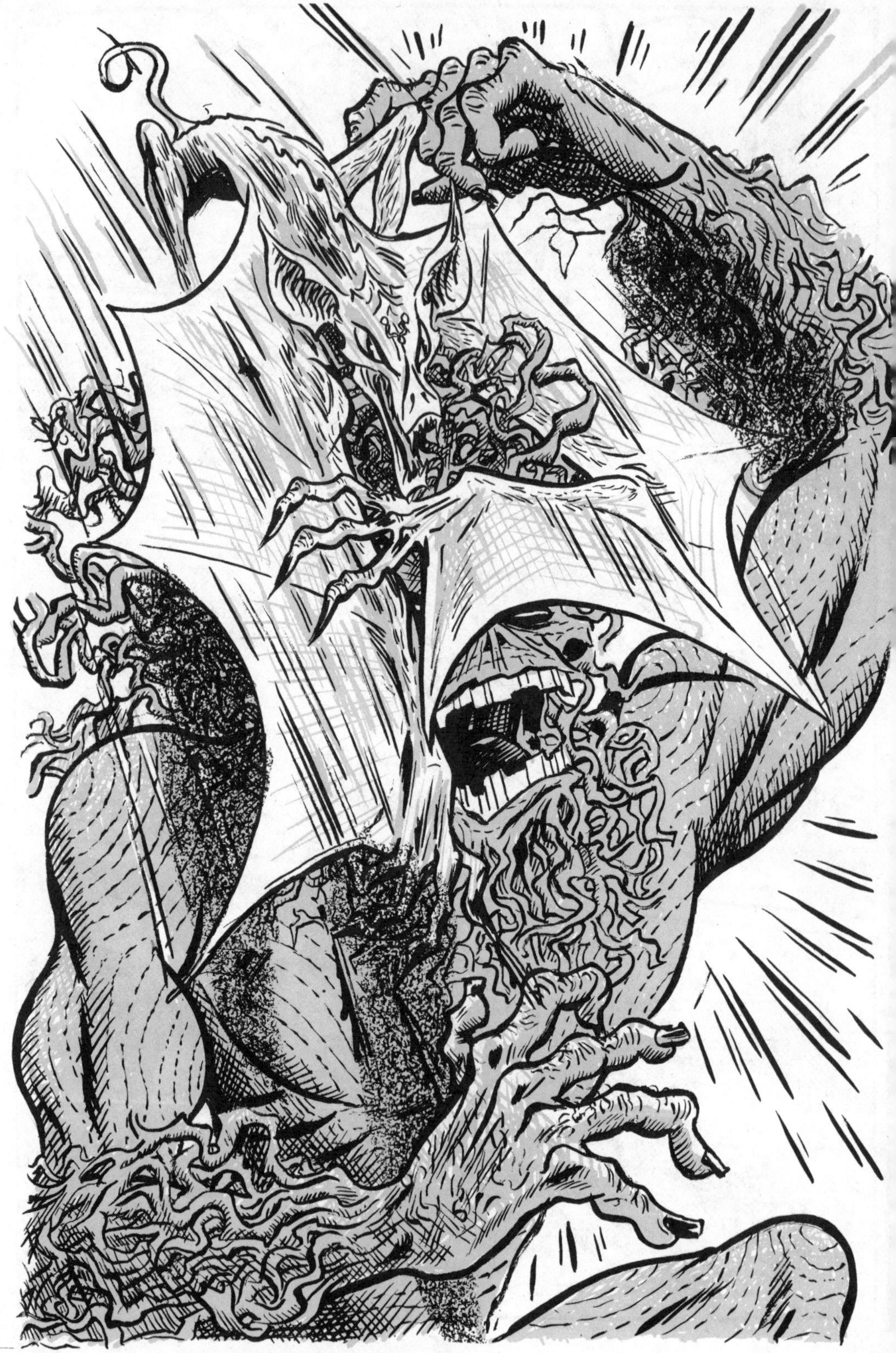

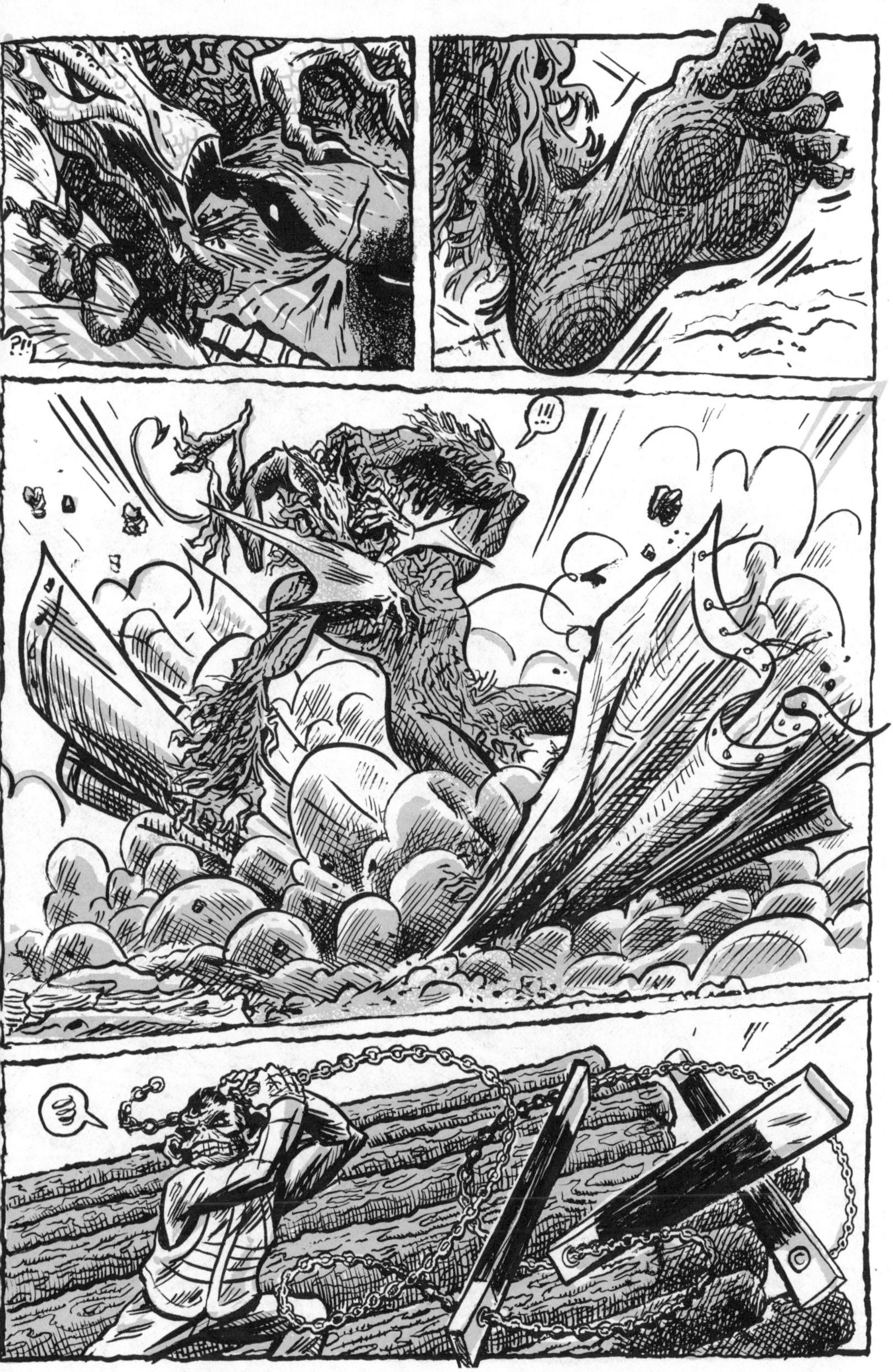
?!!
!!!

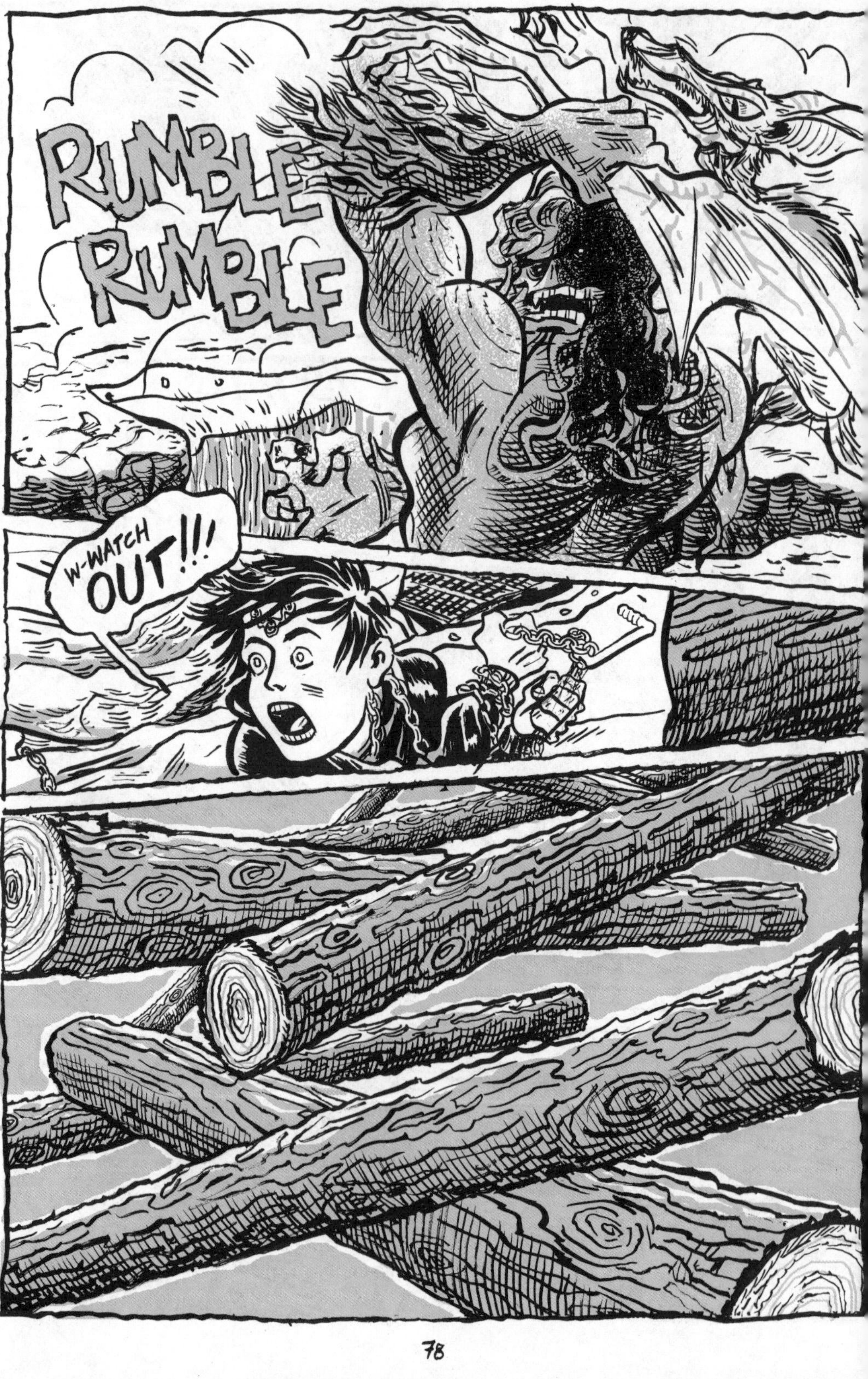
RUMBLE RUMBLE
W-WATCH OUT!!!

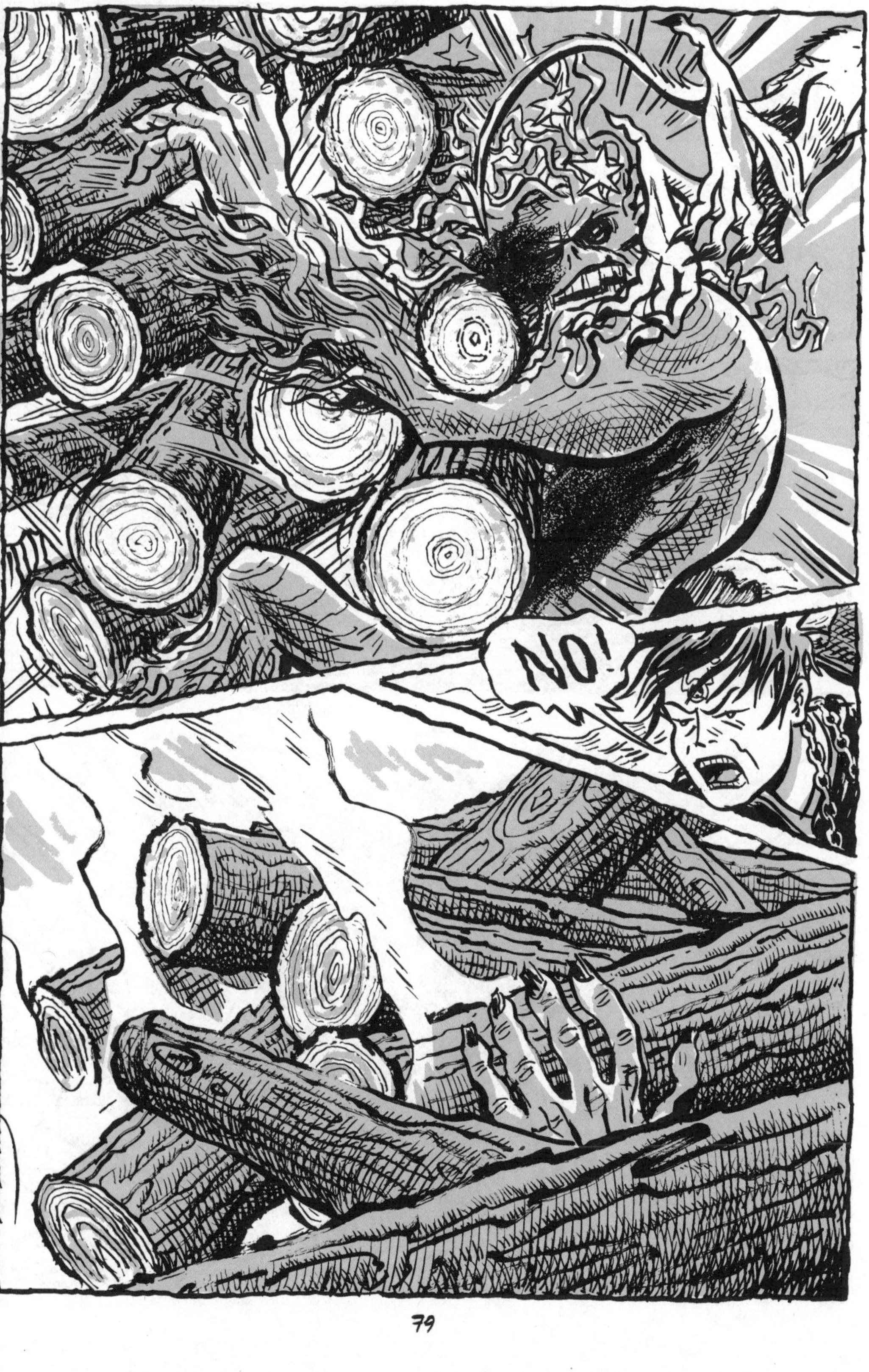
NO!

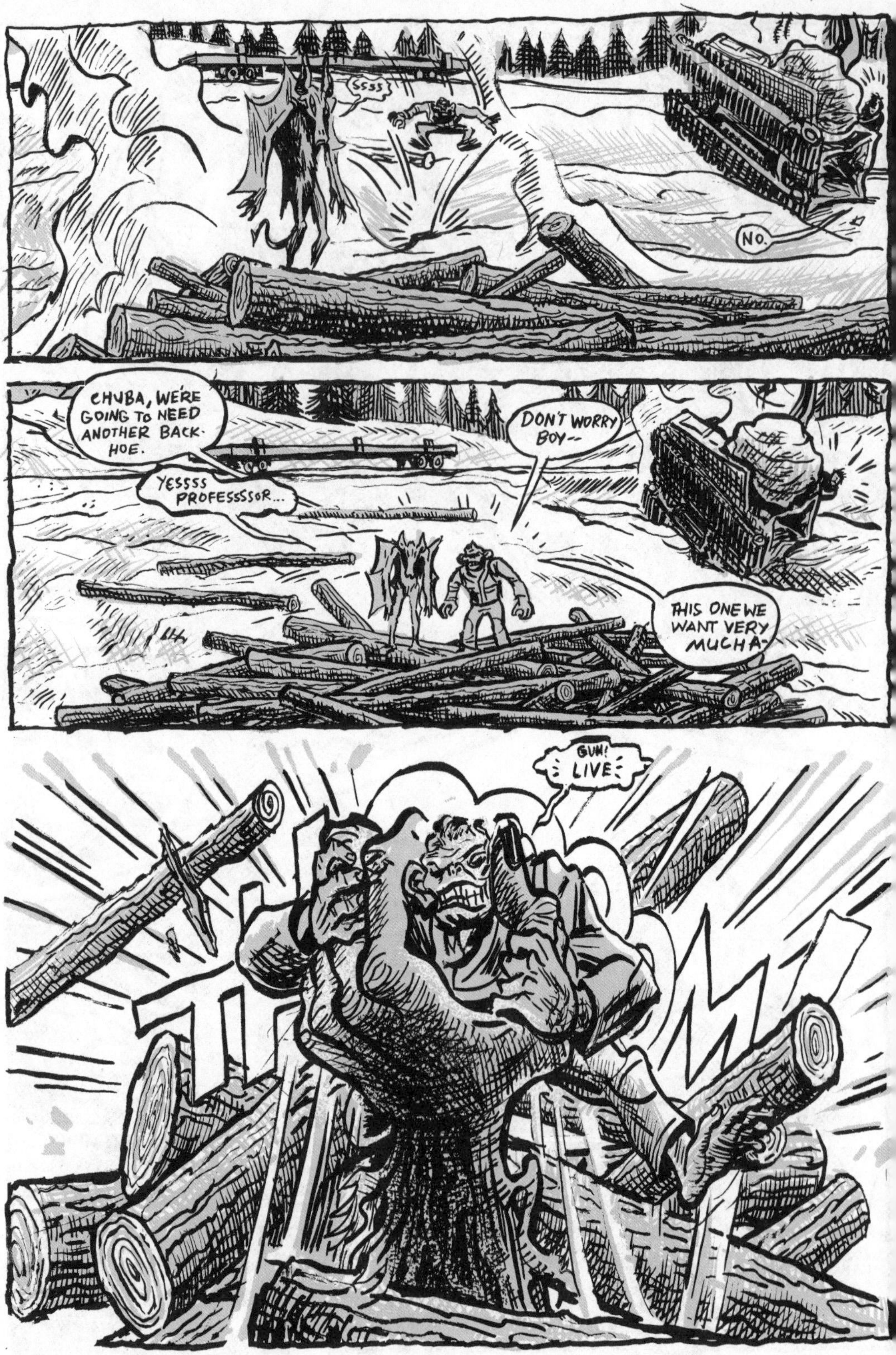
SSSS
NO.
CHUBA, WE'RE GOING TO NEED ANOTHER BACK-HOE.
YESSSS PROFESSSSOR...
DON'T WORRY BOY--
THIS ONE WE WANT VERY MUCHA-
GUH! LIVE

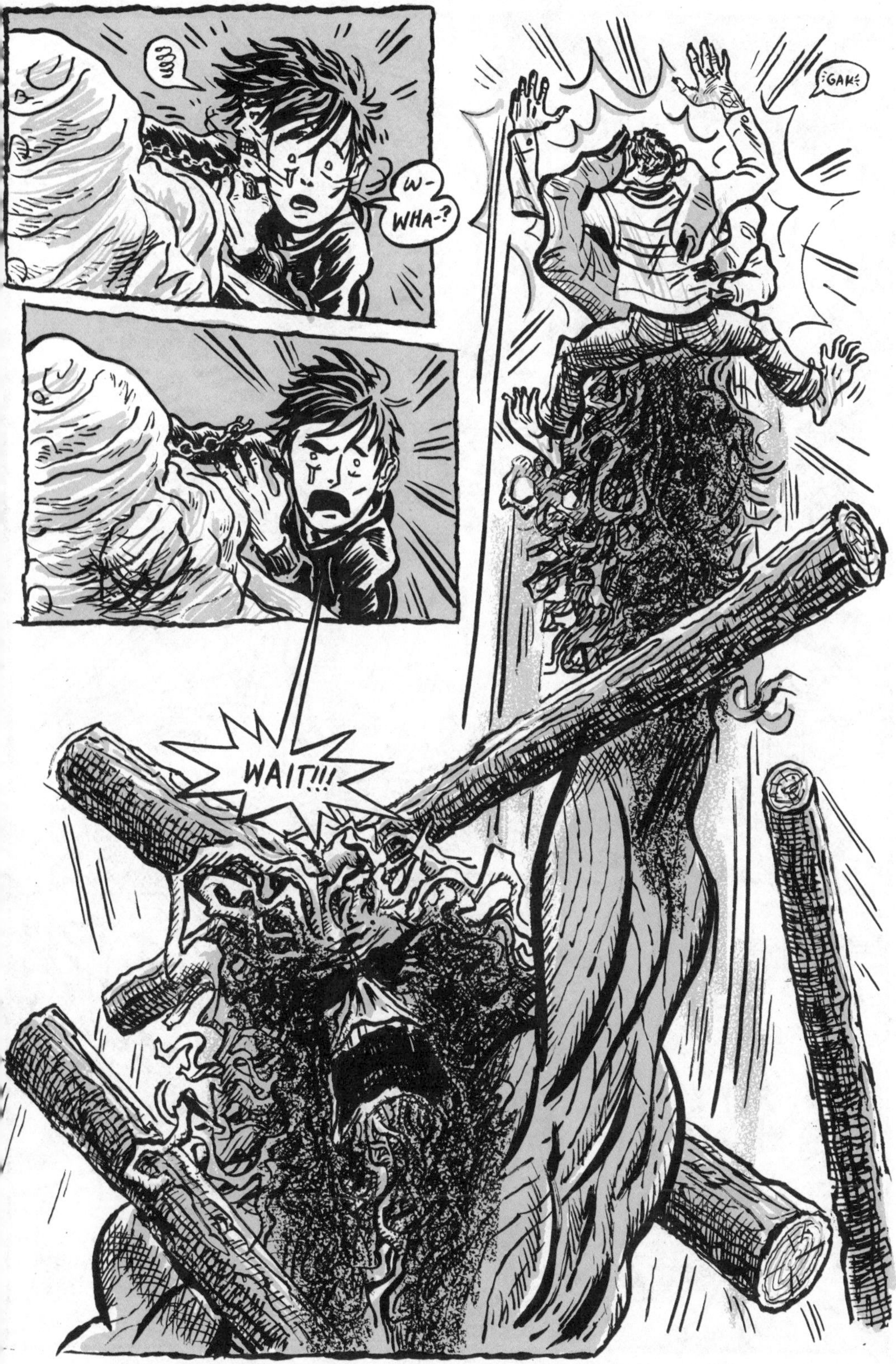
W-
WHA-?
GAK
WAIT!!!

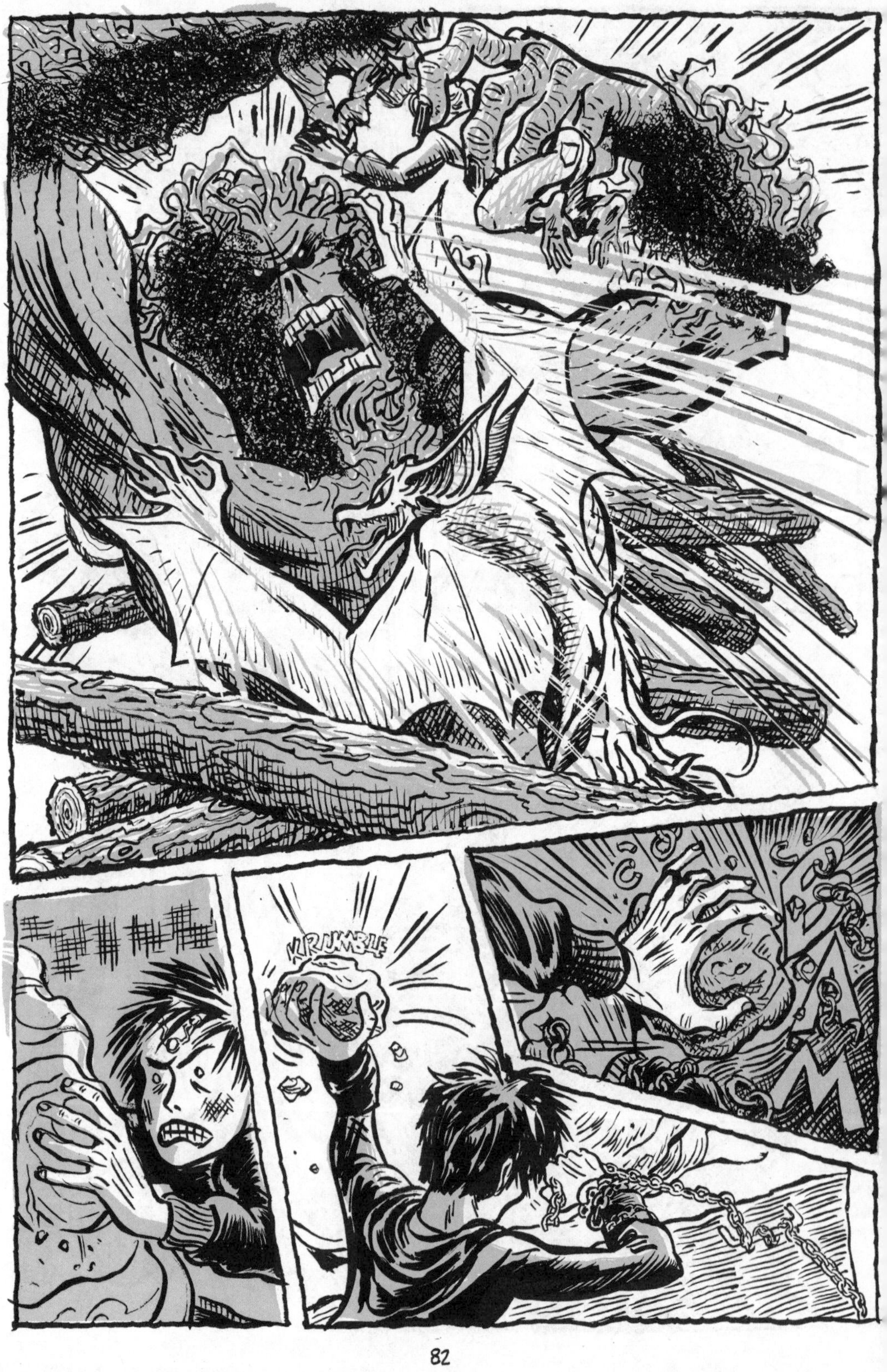
KRUMBLE

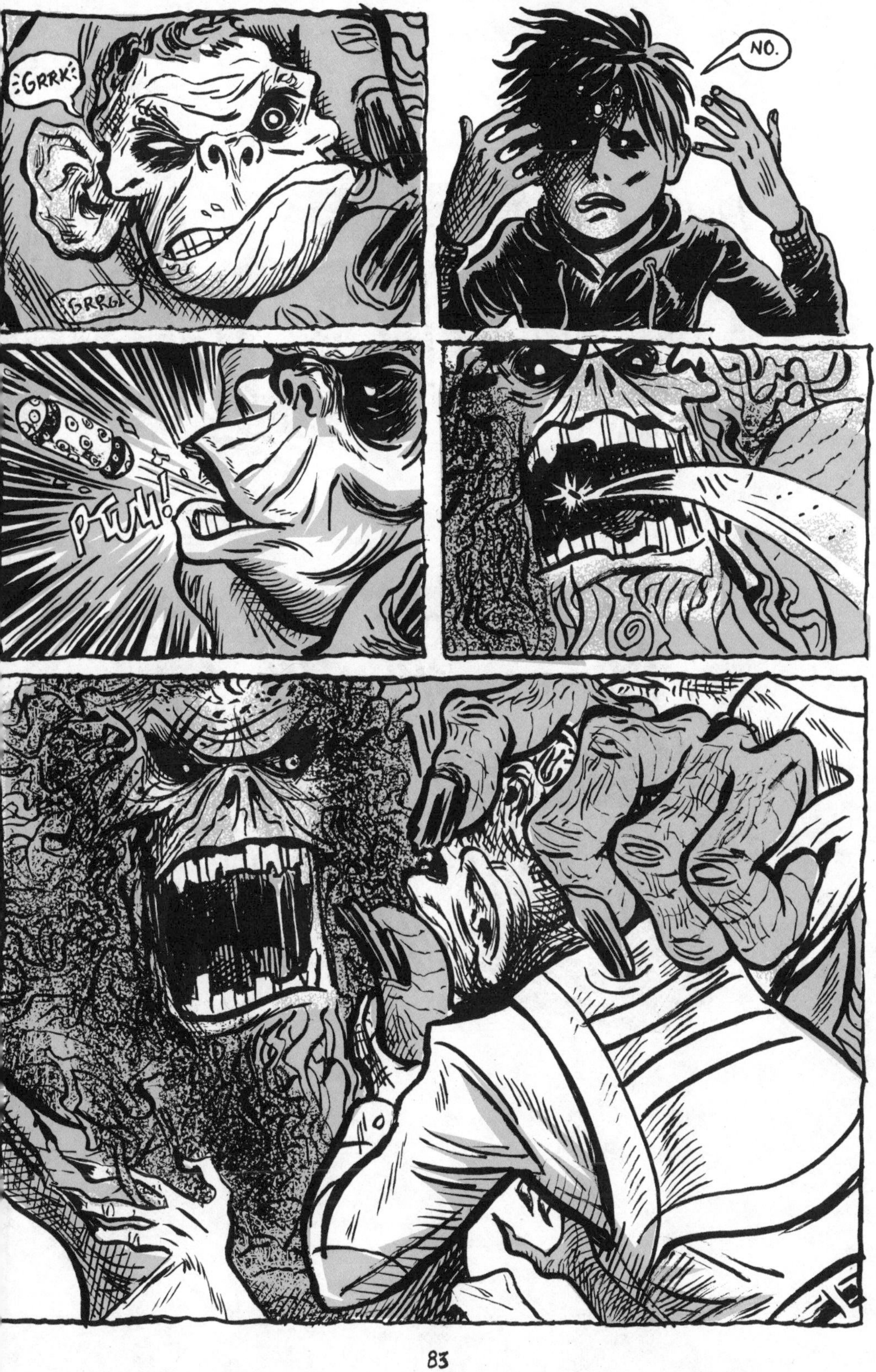
GRRK
GRRGL
NO.
PTUI!

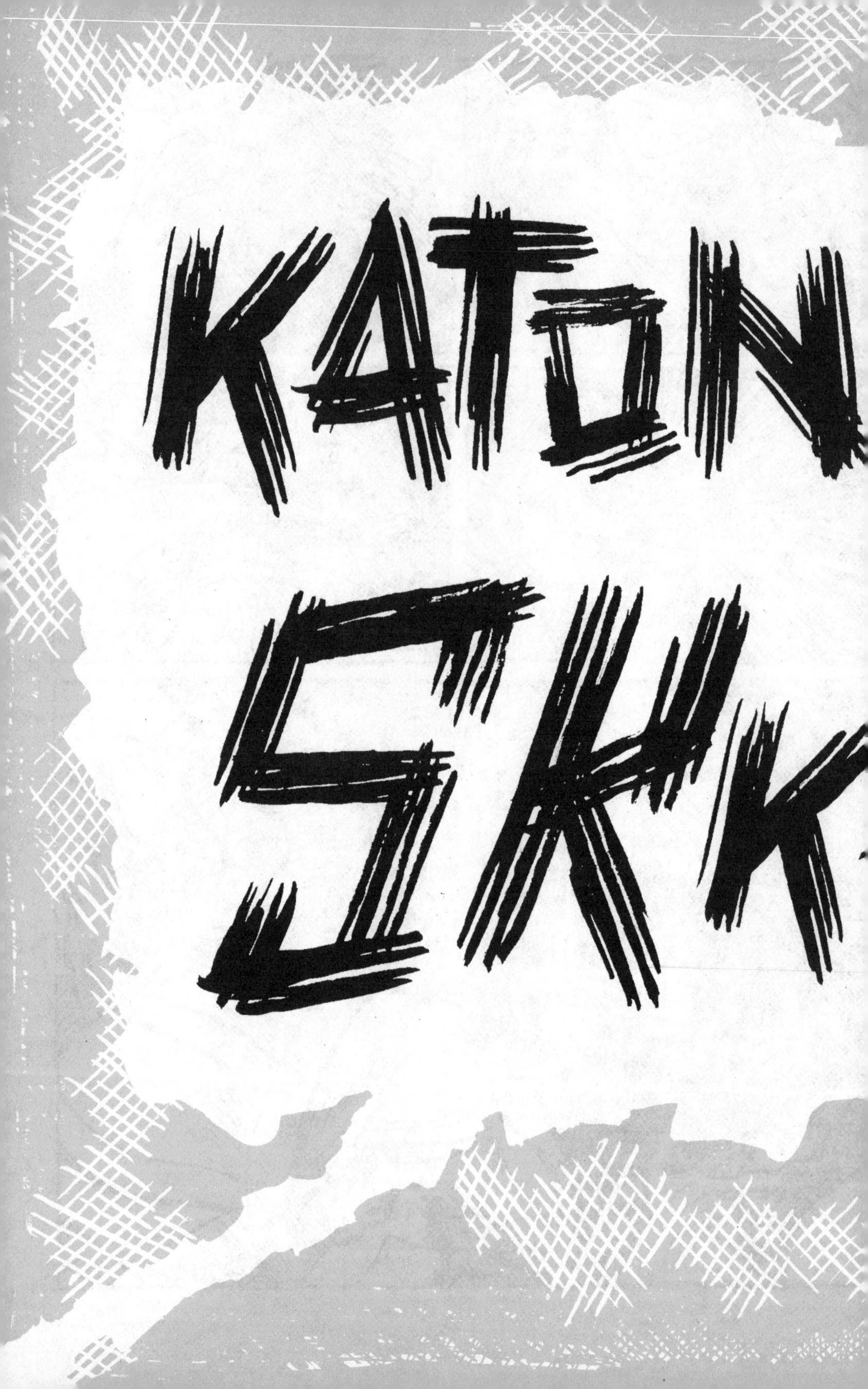
KATON
SHK

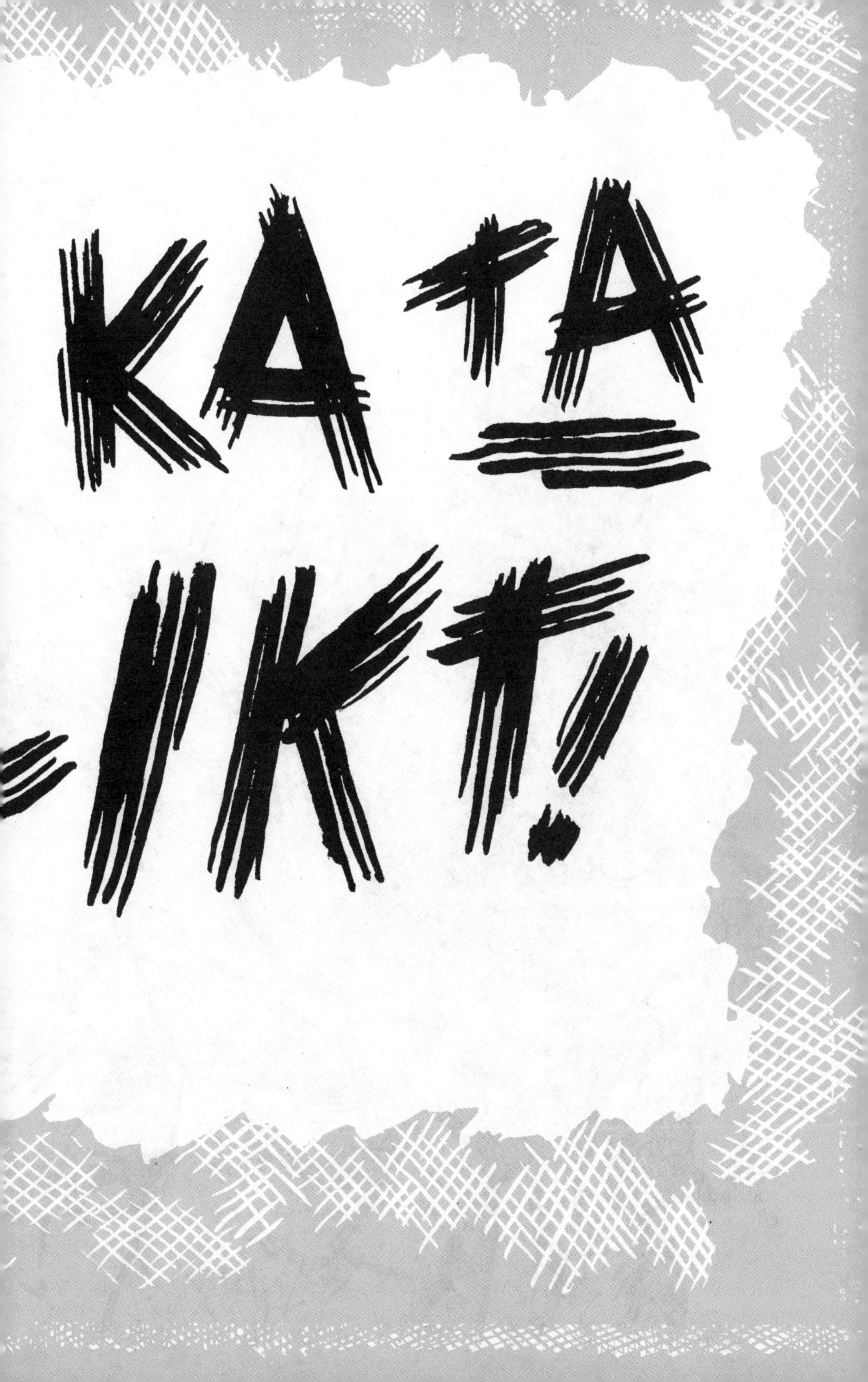
KATA
IKT!

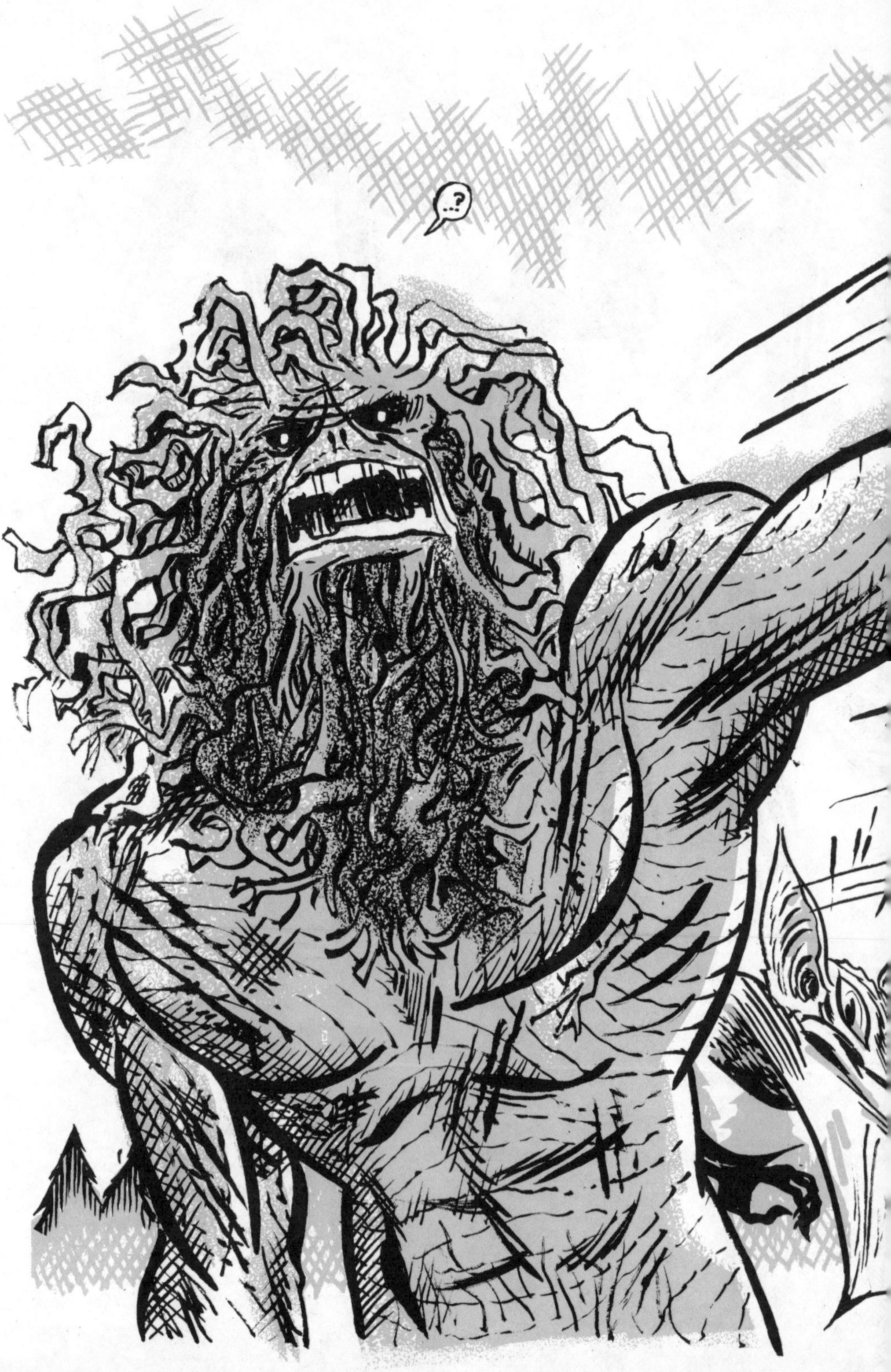

...?

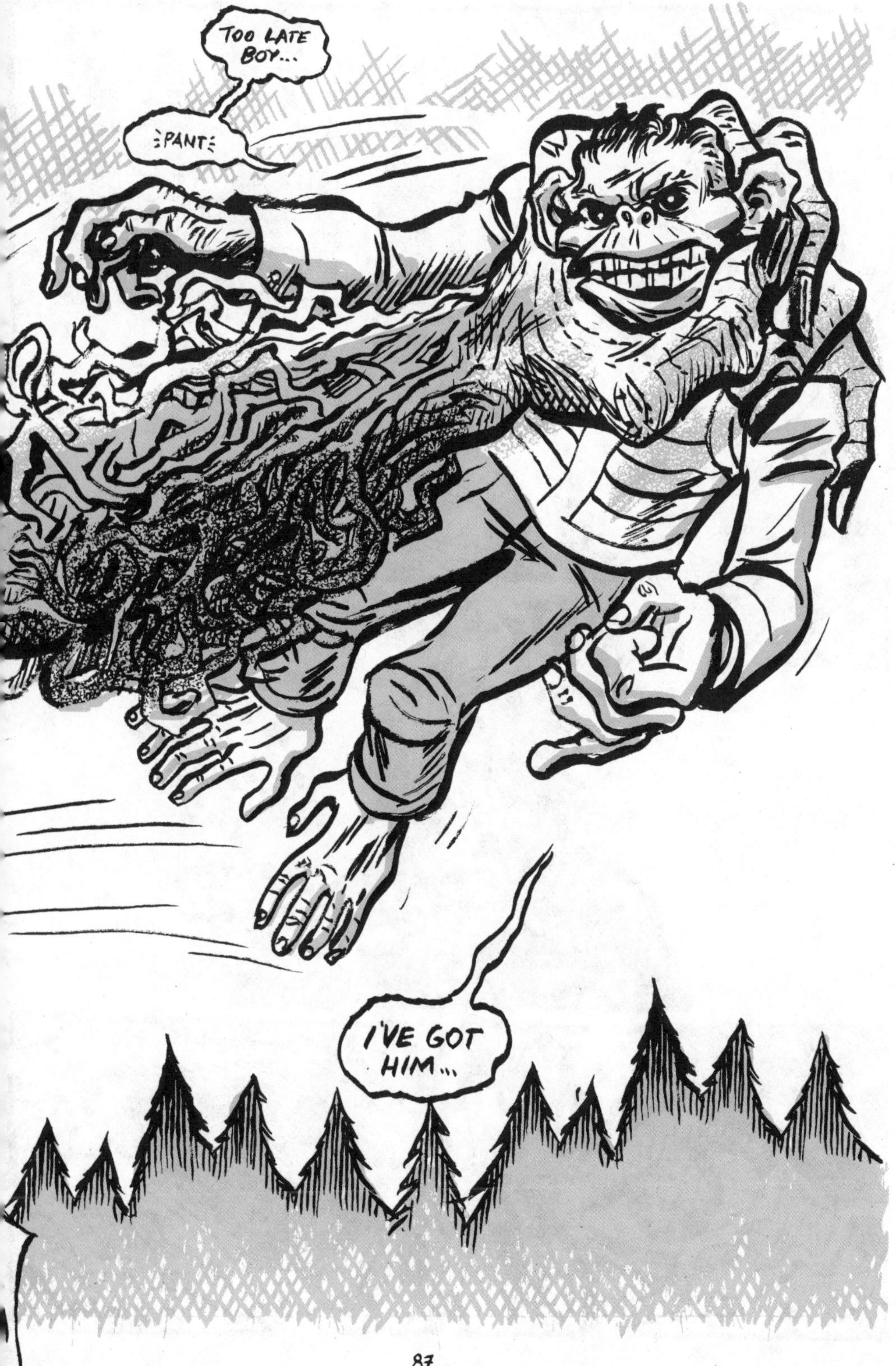
TOO LATE BOY...
PANT
I'VE GOT HIM...

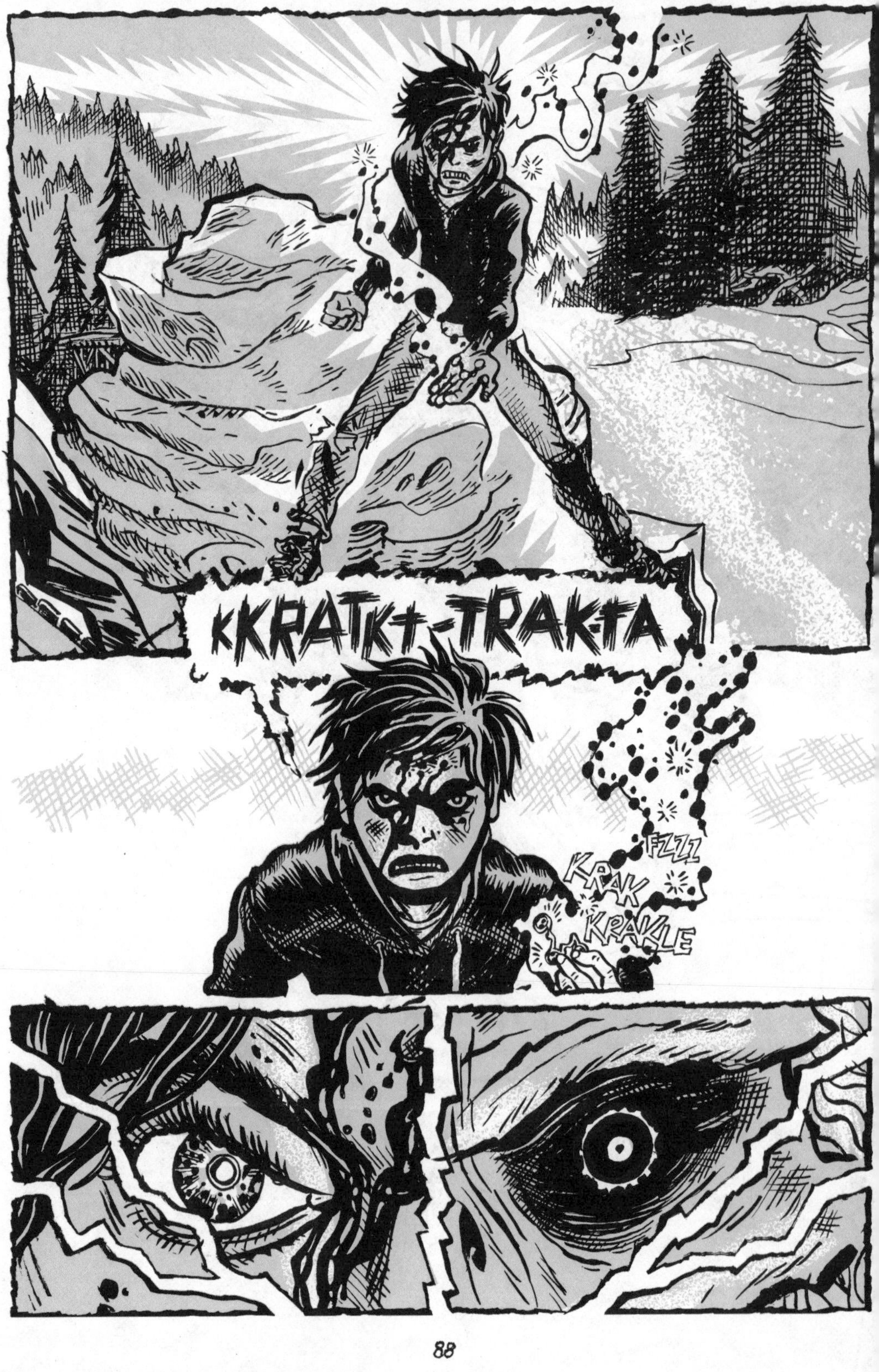
KKRATKT-TRAKTA
FZZZ
KRAK
KRAKLE

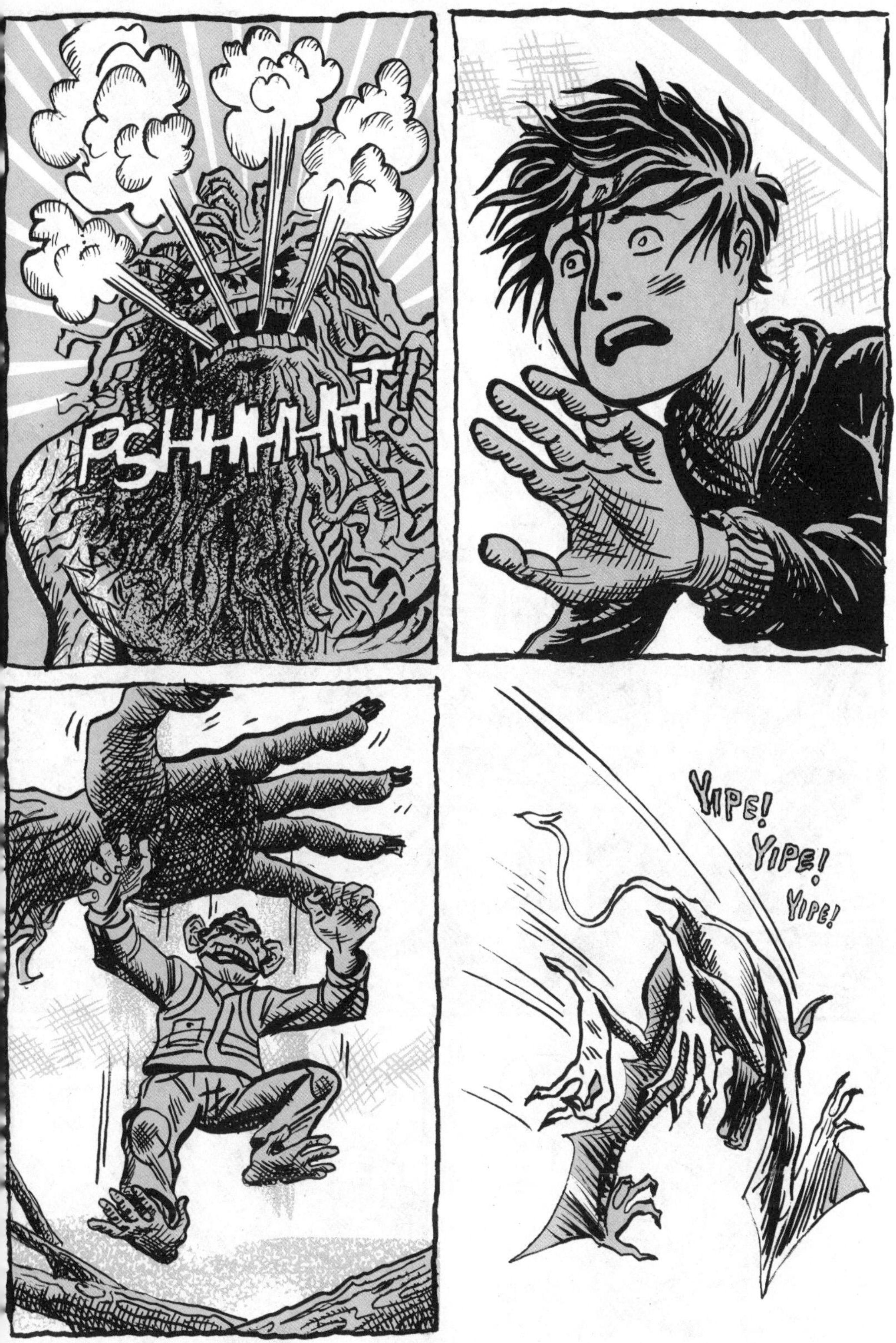
PSHHHHT!
YIPE!
YIPE!
YIPE!

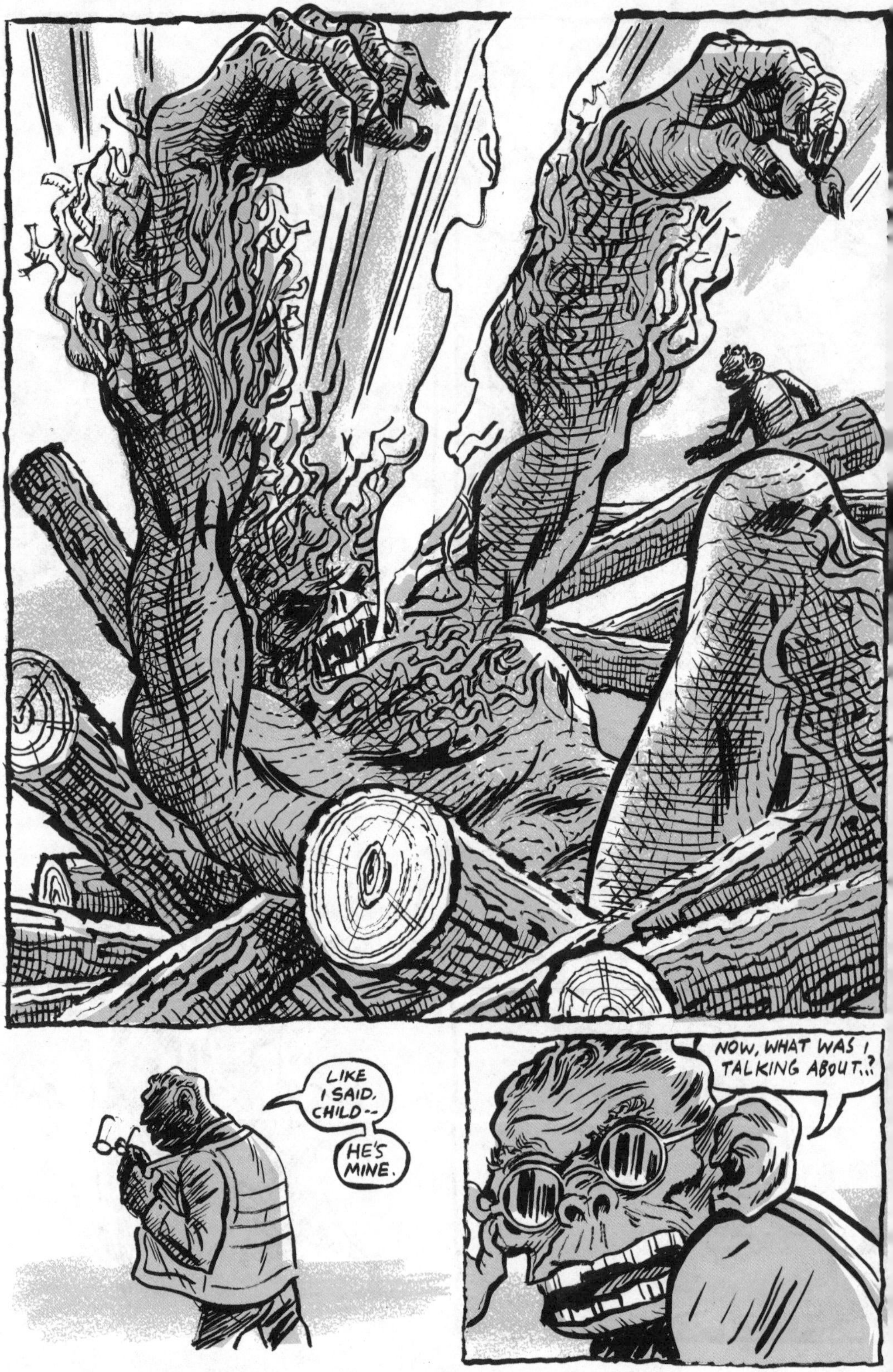
LIKE I SAID, CHILD--
HE'S MINE.
NOW, WHAT WAS I TALKING ABOUT..?

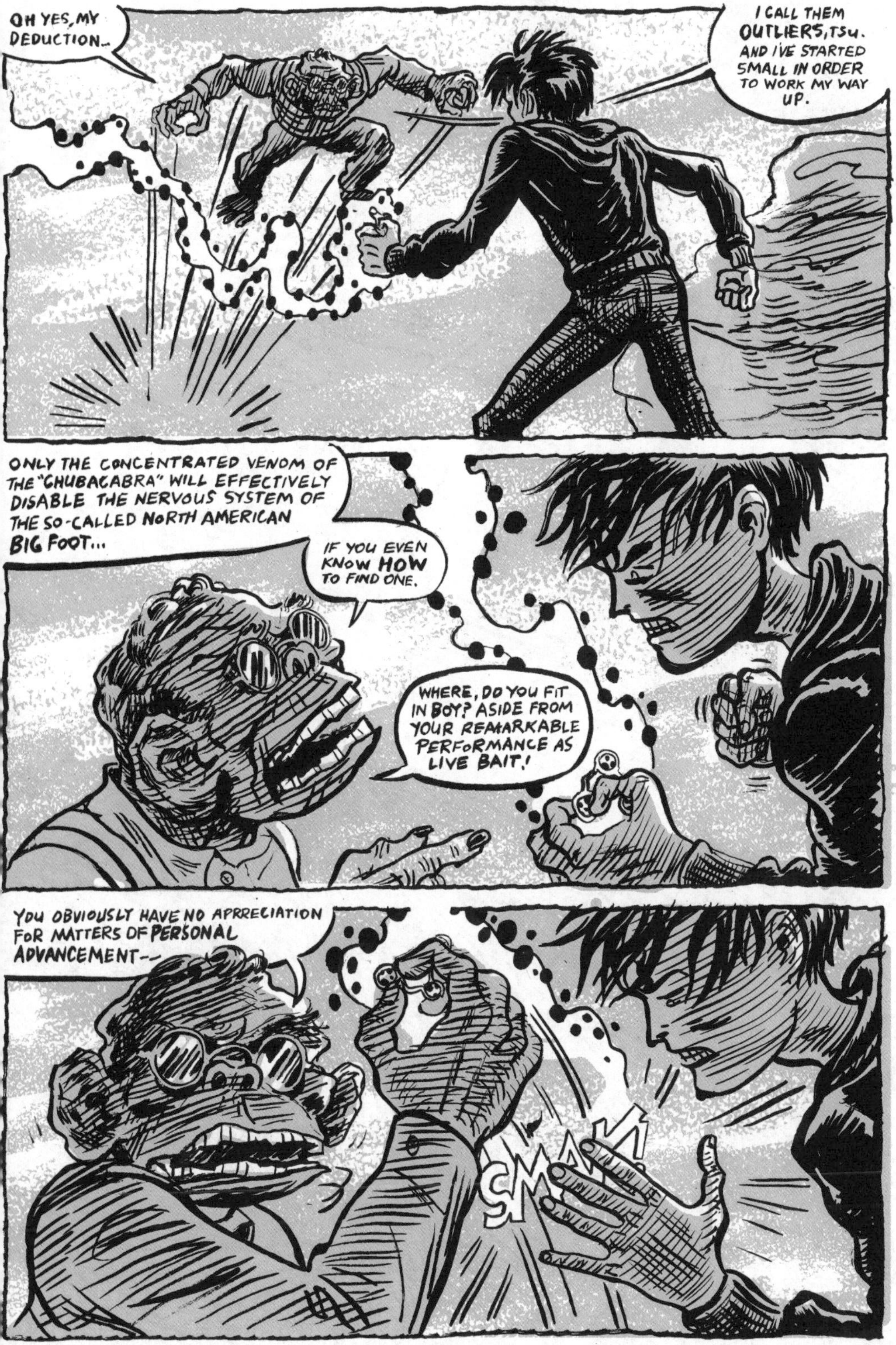
OH YES, MY DEDUCTION...
I CALL THEM OUTLIERS, TSU. AND I'VE STARTED SMALL IN ORDER TO WORK MY WAY UP.
ONLY THE CONCENTRATED VENOM OF THE "CHUBACABRA" WILL EFFECTIVELY DISABLE THE NERVOUS SYSTEM OF THE SO-CALLED NORTH AMERICAN BIG FOOT...
IF YOU EVEN KNOW HOW TO FIND ONE.
WHERE, DO YOU FIT IN BOY? ASIDE FROM YOUR REMARKABLE PERFORMANCE AS LIVE BAIT!
YOU OBVIOUSLY HAVE NO APPRECIATION FOR MATTERS OF PERSONAL ADVANCEMENT--
SMAK

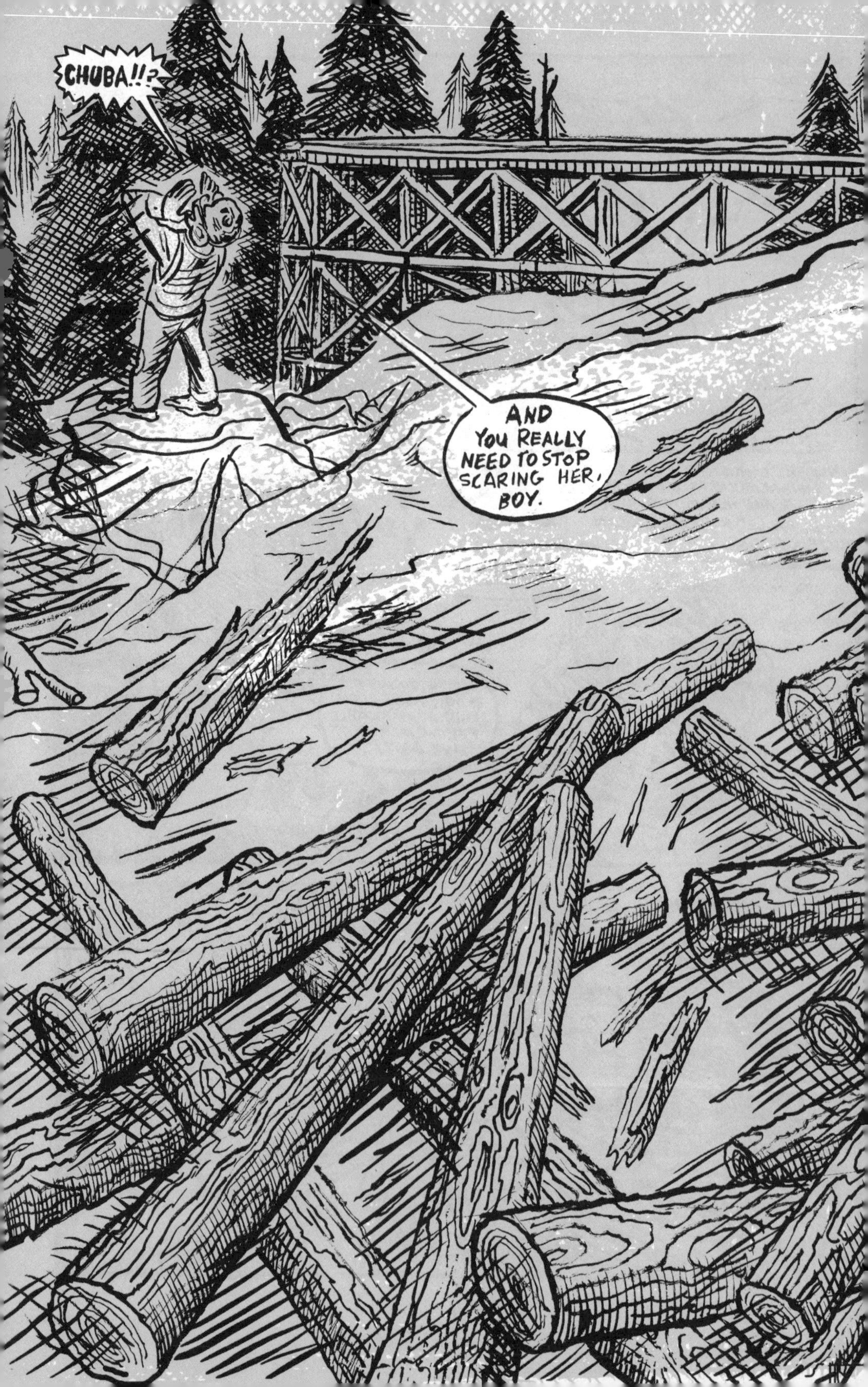
CHUBA!!?
AND YOU REALLY NEED TO STOP SCARING HER, BOY.

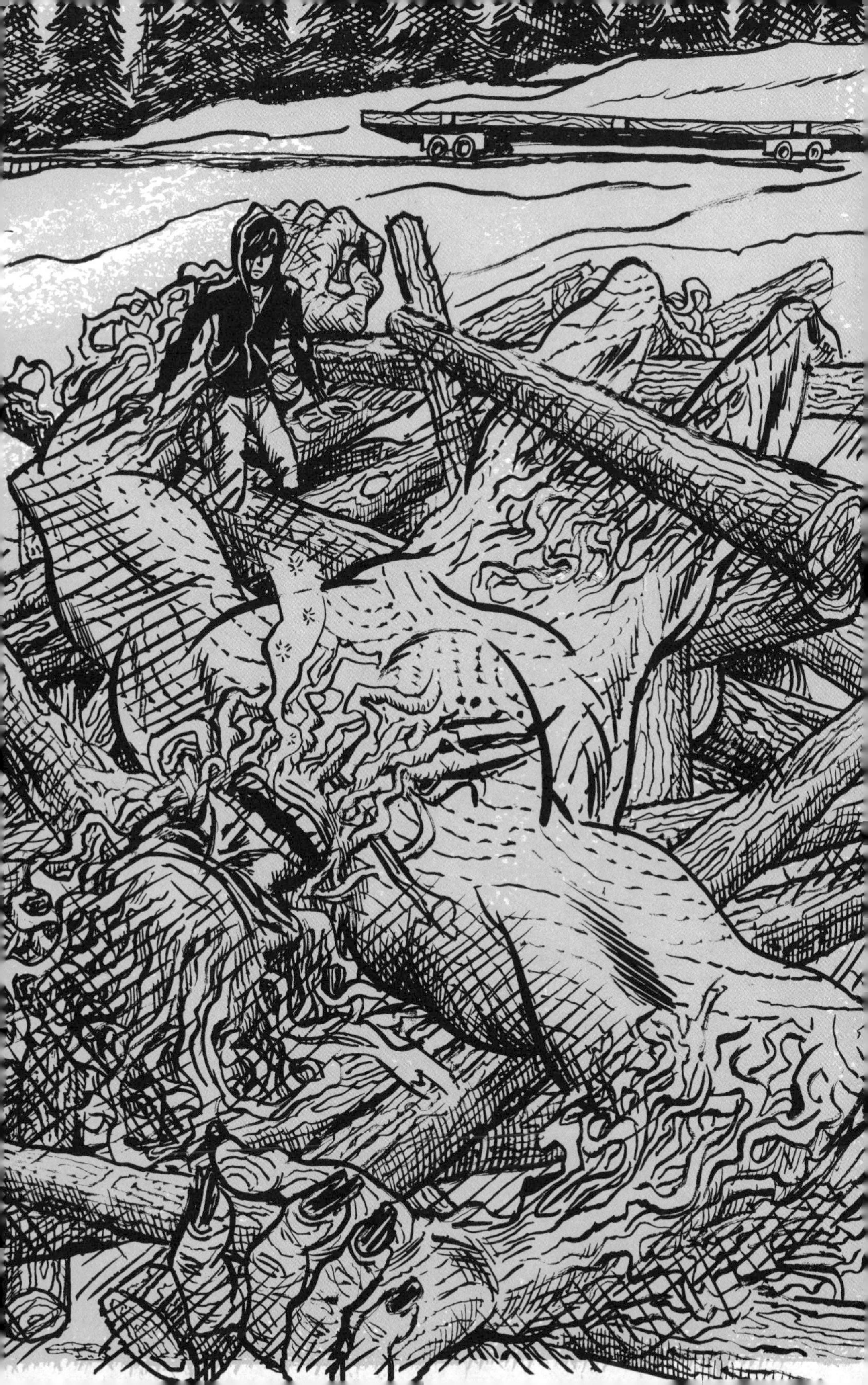

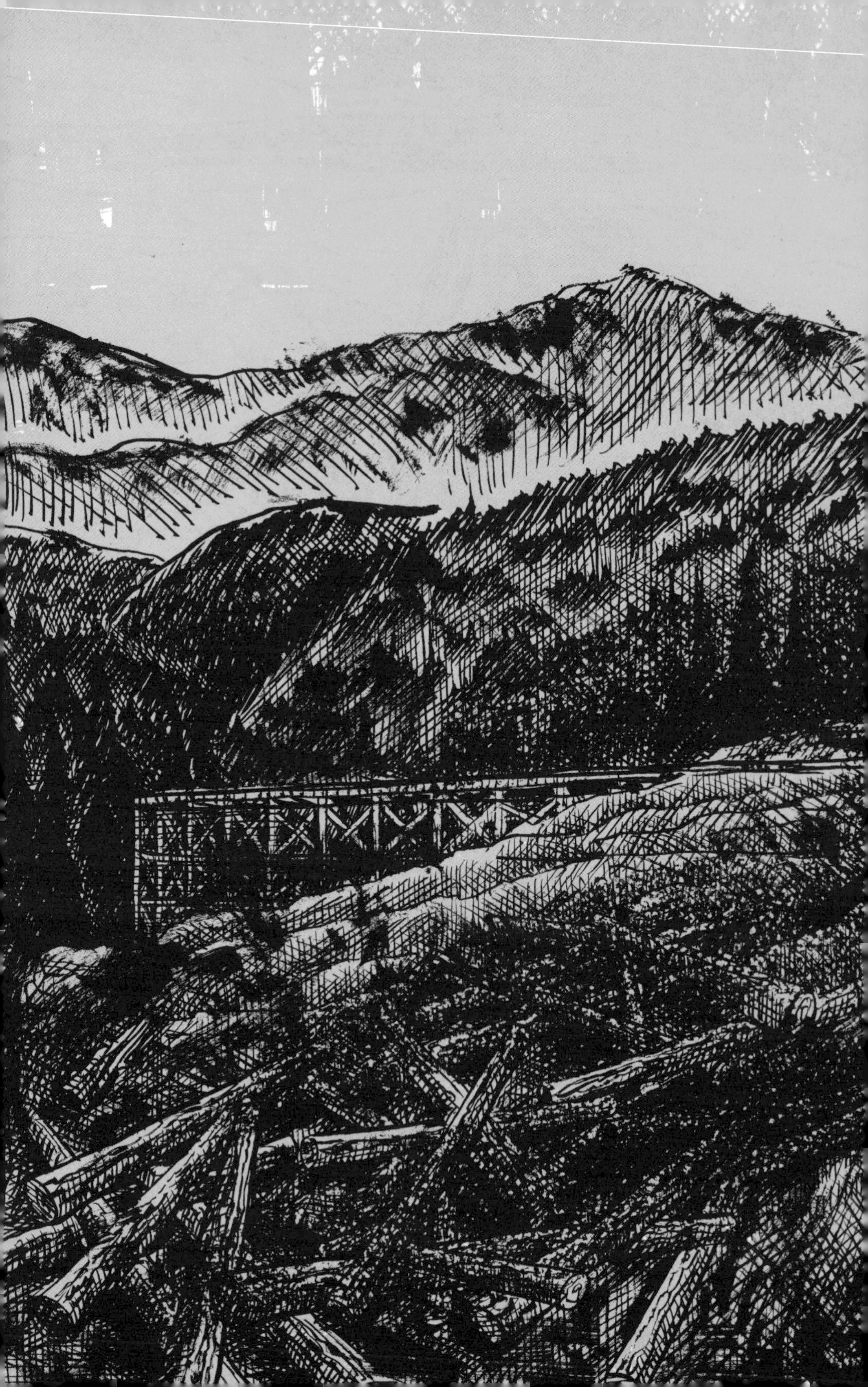

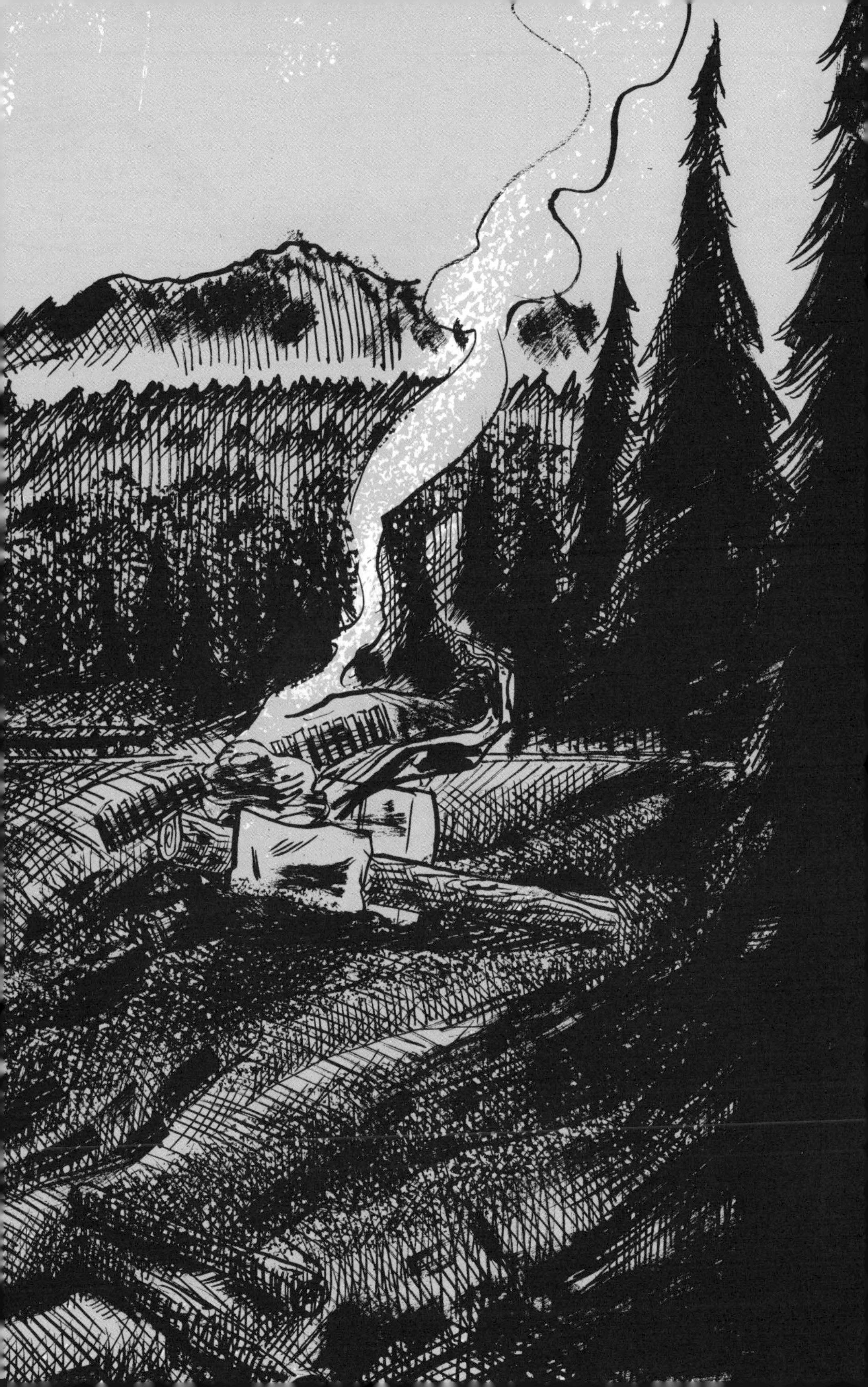

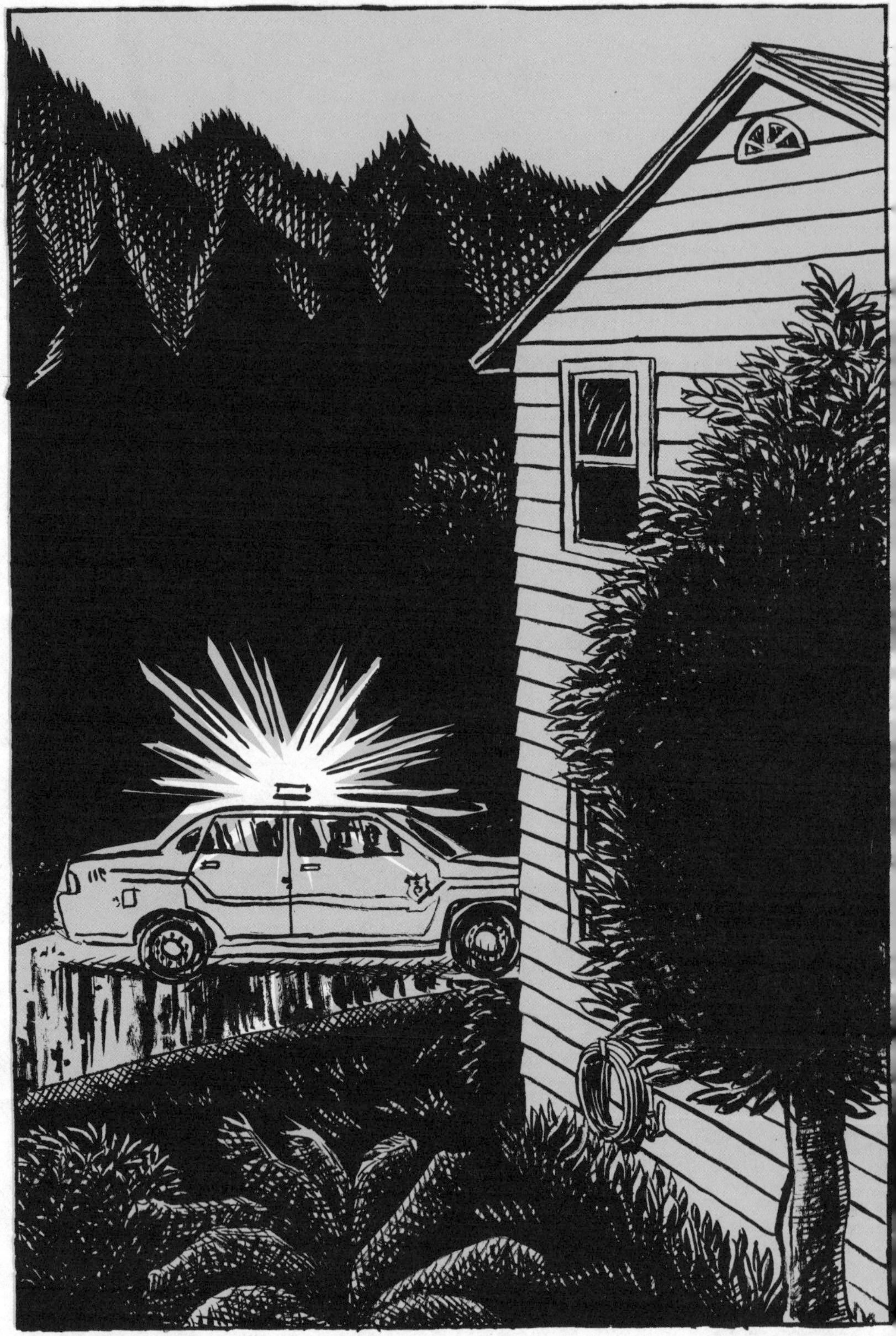

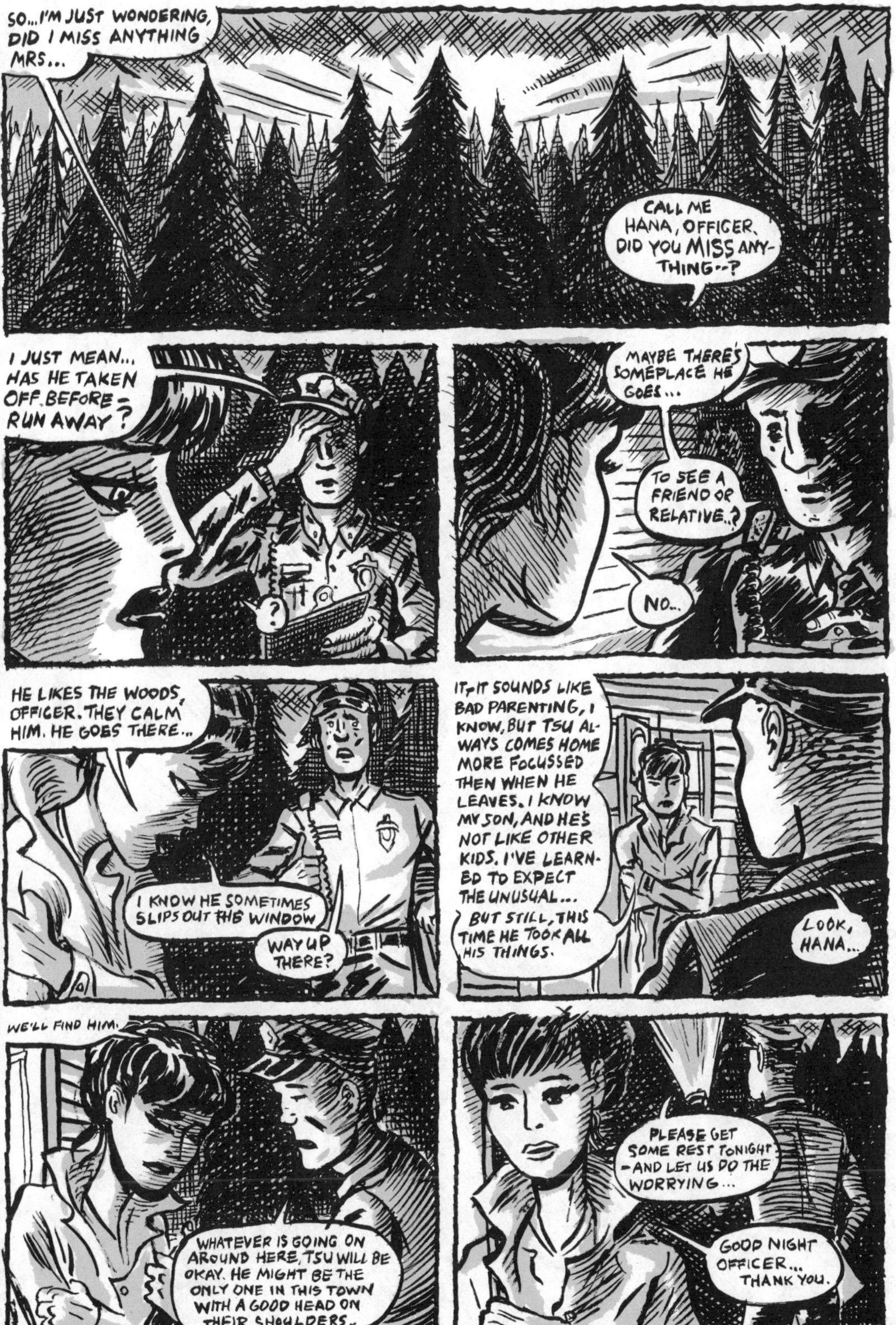
SO... I'M JUST WONDERING, DID I MISS ANYTHING MRS...
CALL ME HANA, OFFICER. DID YOU MISS ANYTHING--?
I JUST MEAN... HAS HE TAKEN OFF BEFORE-RUN AWAY?
?
MAYBE THERE'S SOMEPLACE HE GOES...
TO SEE A FRIEND OR RELATIVE..?
NO...
HE LIKES THE WOODS, OFFICER. THEY CALM HIM. HE GOES THERE...
I KNOW HE SOMETIMES SLIPS OUT THE WINDOW
WAY UP THERE?
IT, IT SOUNDS LIKE BAD PARENTING, I KNOW, BUT TSU ALWAYS COMES HOME MORE FOCUSSED THEN WHEN HE LEAVES. I KNOW MY SON, AND HE'S NOT LIKE OTHER KIDS. I'VE LEARNED TO EXPECT THE UNUSUAL...
BUT STILL, THIS TIME HE TOOK ALL HIS THINGS.
LOOK, HANA...
WE'LL FIND HIM.
WHATEVER IS GOING ON AROUND HERE, TSU WILL BE OKAY. HE MIGHT BE THE ONLY ONE IN THIS TOWN WITH A GOOD HEAD ON THEIR SHOULDERS, RIGHT NOW.
PLEASE GET SOME REST TONIGHT - AND LET US DO THE WORRYING...
GOOD NIGHT OFFICER... THANK YOU.

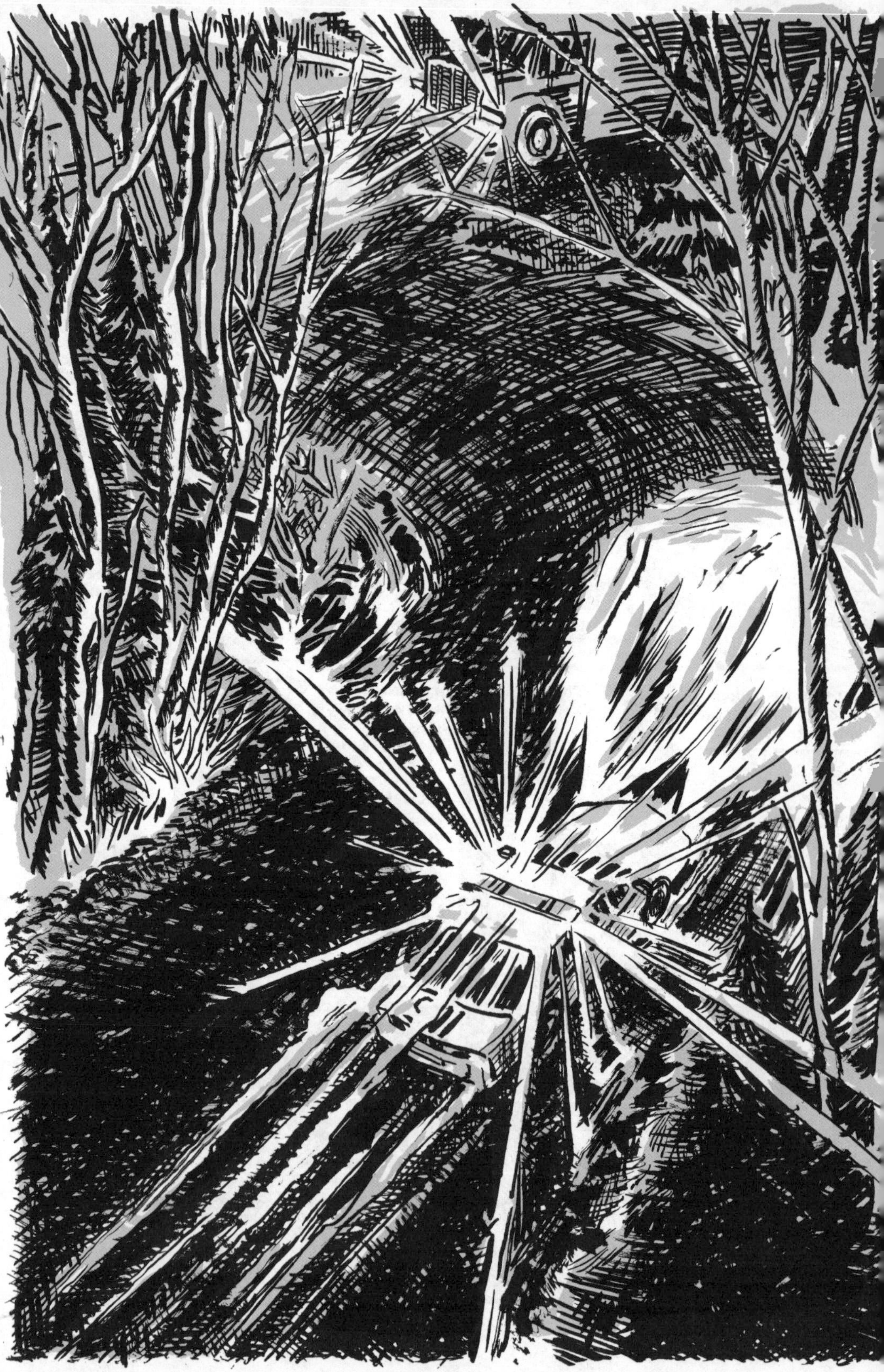

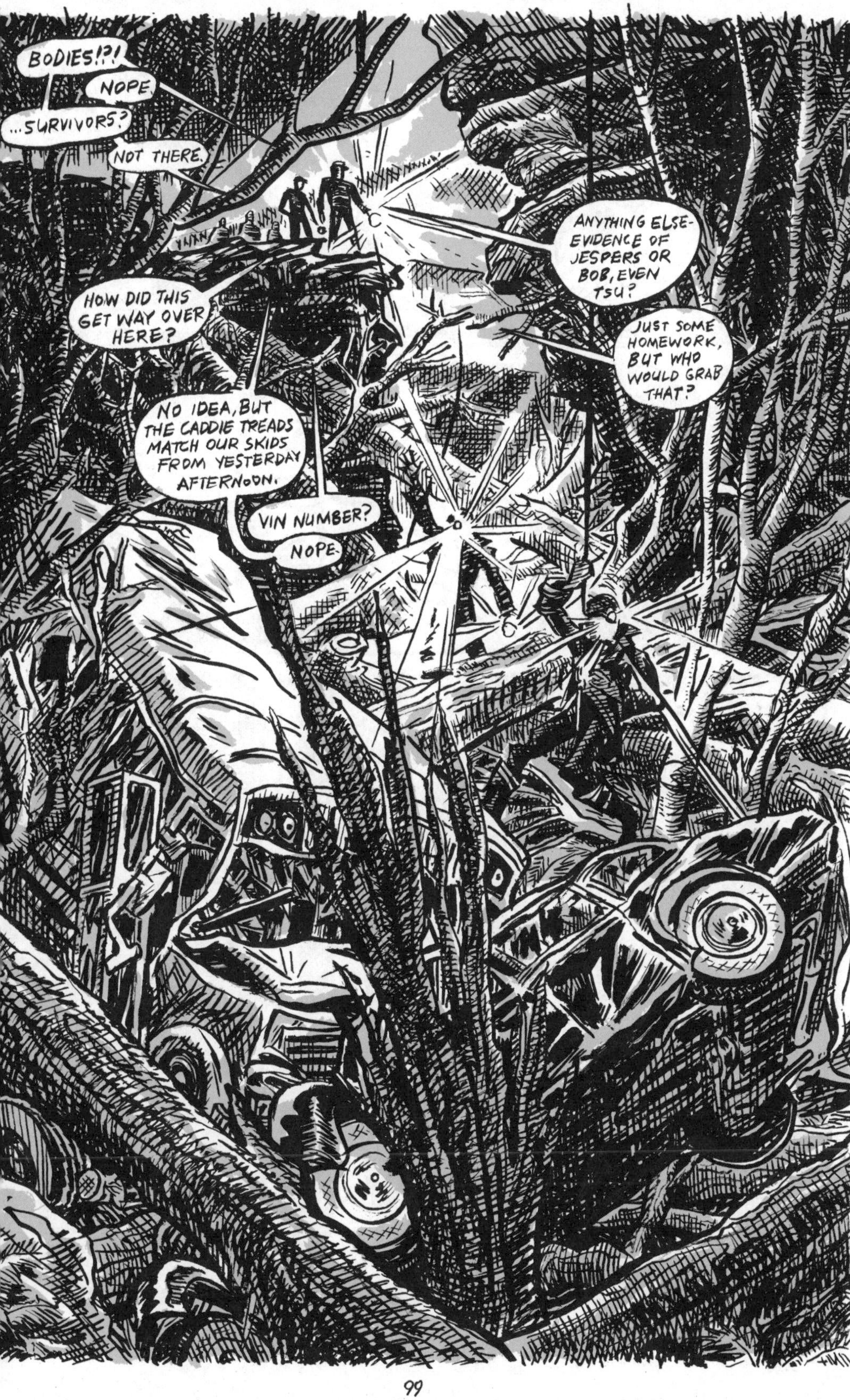
BODIES!?!
NOPE.
...SURVIVORS?
NOT THERE.
HOW DID THIS GET WAY OVER HERE?
NO IDEA, BUT THE CADDIE TREADS MATCH OUR SKIDS FROM YESTERDAY AFTERNOON.
VIN NUMBER?
NOPE.
ANYTHING ELSE- EVIDENCE OF JESPERS OR BOB, EVEN TSU?
JUST SOME HOMEWORK, BUT WHO WOULD GRAB THAT?

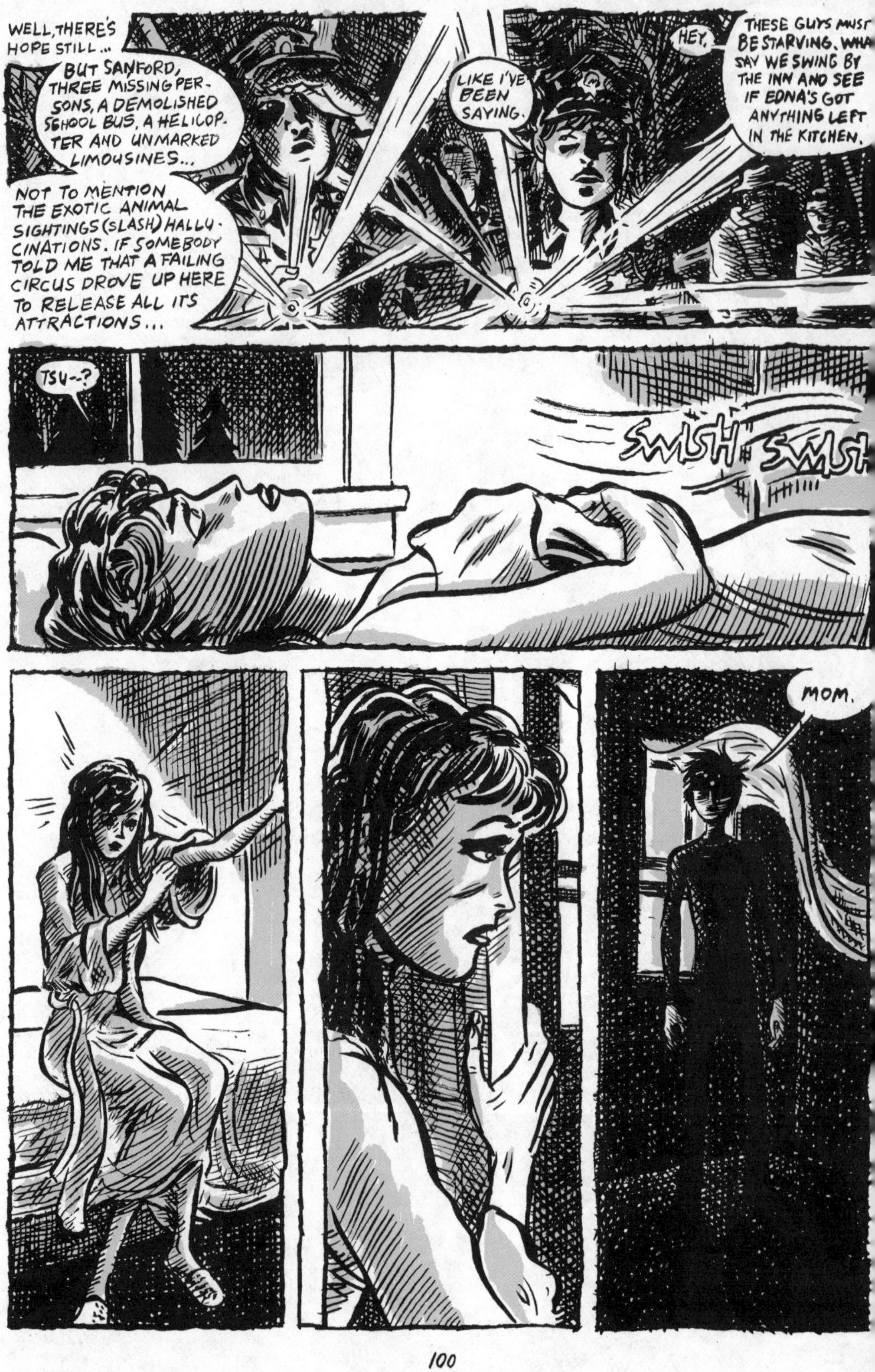
WELL, THERE'S HOPE STILL...
BUT SANFORD, THREE MISSING PERSONS, A DEMOLISHED SCHOOL BUS, A HELICOPTER AND UNMARKED LIMOUSINES...
NOT TO MENTION THE EXOTIC ANIMAL SIGHTINGS (SLASH) HALLUCINATIONS. IF SOMEBODY TOLD ME THAT A FAILING CIRCUS DROVE UP HERE TO RELEASE ALL ITS ATTRACTIONS...
LIKE I'VE BEEN SAYING.
HEY.
THESE GUYS MUST BE STARVING. WHA SAY WE SWING BY THE INN AND SEE IF EDNA'S GOT ANYTHING LEFT IN THE KITCHEN.
TSU--?
SWISH SWISH
MOM.

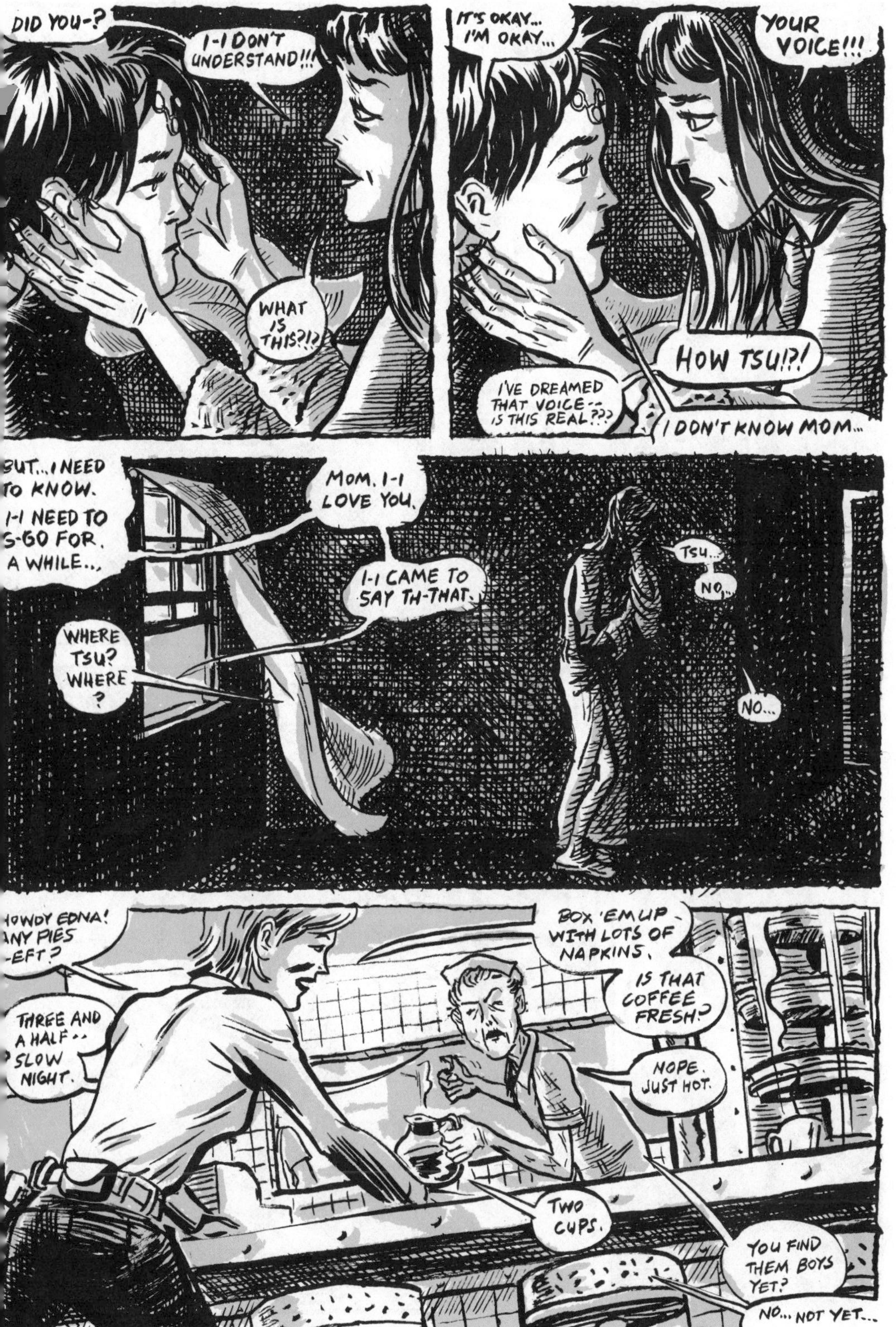
DID YOU-?
I-I DON'T UNDERSTAND!!!
WHAT IS THIS?!?
IT'S OKAY... I'M OKAY...
YOUR VOICE!!!
HOW TSU!?!
I'VE DREAMED THAT VOICE-- IS THIS REAL???
I DON'T KNOW MOM...
BUT... I NEED TO KNOW.
I-I NEED TO G-GO FOR A WHILE...
MOM. I-I LOVE YOU.
I-I CAME TO SAY TH-THAT.
WHERE TSU? WHERE?
TSU...
NO...
NO...
HOWDY EDNA! ANY PIES LEFT?
BOX 'EM UP WITH LOTS OF NAPKINS.
THREE AND A HALF-- SLOW NIGHT.
IS THAT COFFEE FRESH?
NOPE. JUST HOT.
TWO CUPS.
YOU FIND THEM BOYS YET?
NO... NOT YET...

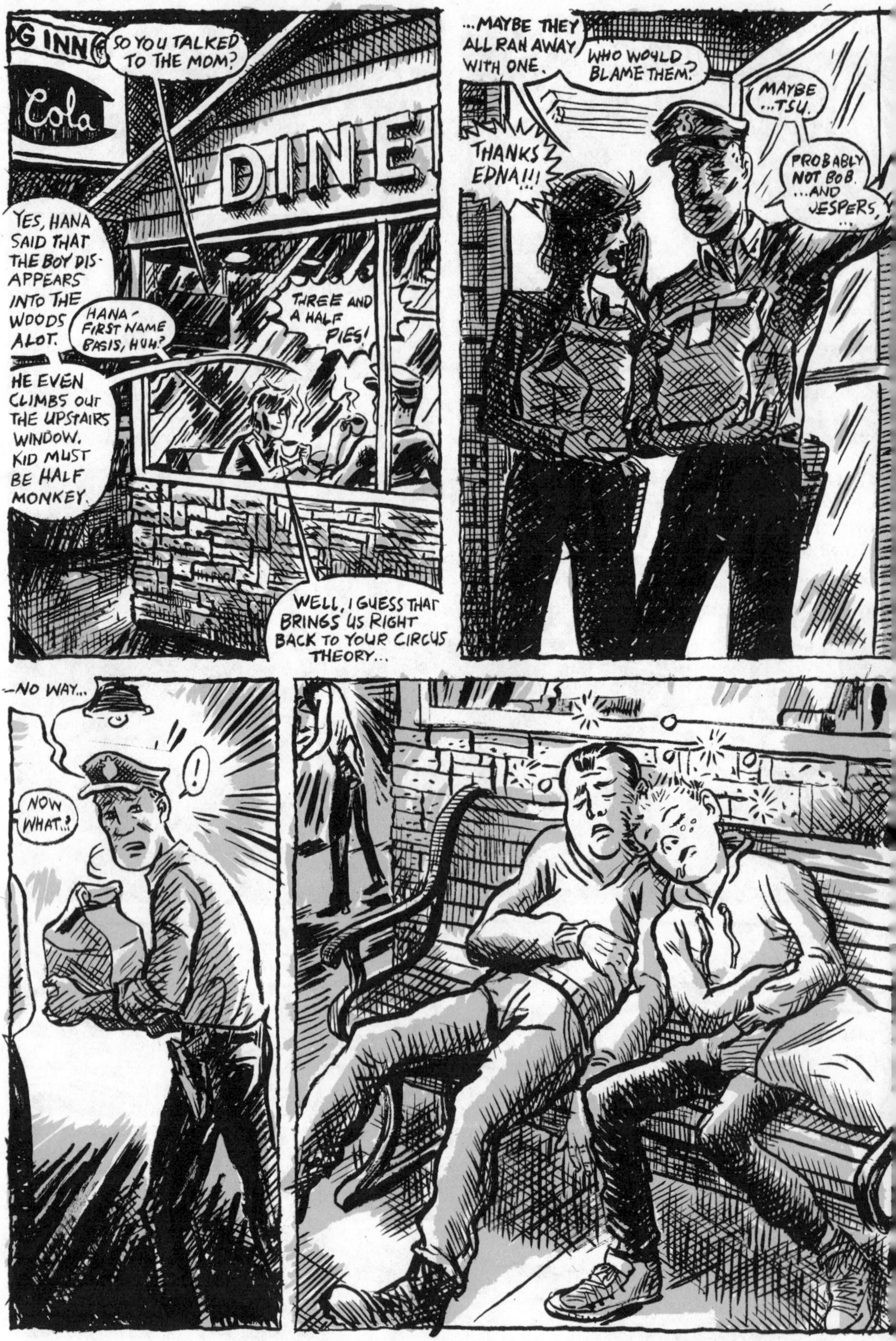
G INN
Cola
DINE
SO YOU TALKED TO THE MOM?
YES, HANA SAID THAT THE BOY DIS-APPEARS INTO THE WOODS ALOT.
HANA-FIRST NAME BASIS, HUH?
THREE AND A HALF PIES!
HE EVEN CLIMBS OUT THE UPSTAIRS WINDOW. KID MUST BE HALF MONKEY.
WELL, I GUESS THAT BRINGS US RIGHT BACK TO YOUR CIRCUS THEORY...
...MAYBE THEY ALL RAN AWAY WITH ONE.
WHO WOULD BLAME THEM?
THANKS EDNA!!!
MAYBE ...TSU.
PROBABLY NOT BOB. ...AND JESPERS. ...
—NO WAY...
NOW WHAT..?
!

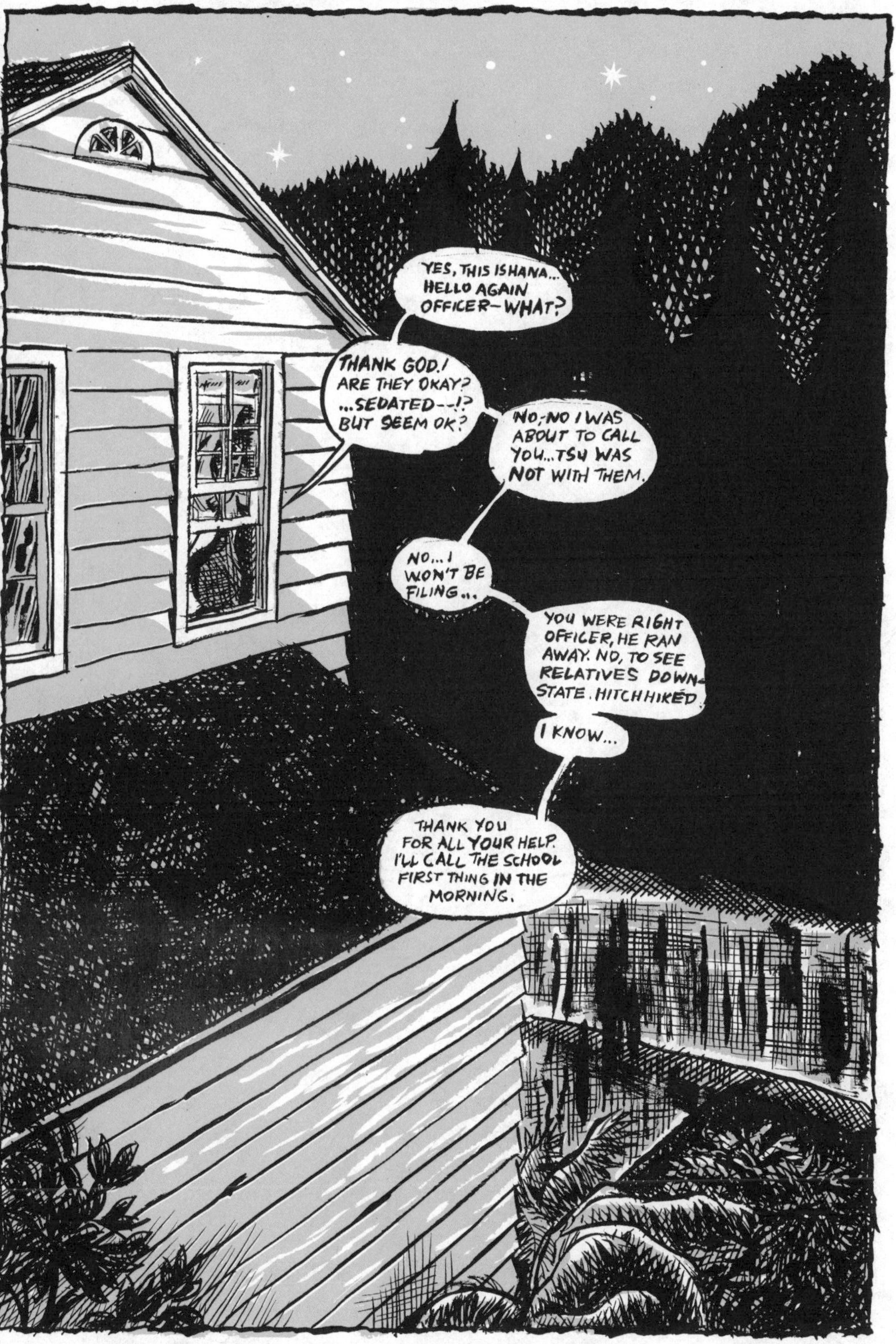
YES, THIS ISHANA... HELLO AGAIN OFFICER—WHAT?
THANK GOD.! ARE THEY OKAY? ...SEDATED--!? BUT SEEM OK?
NO,-NO I WAS ABOUT TO CALL YOU...TSU WAS NOT WITH THEM.
NO... I WON'T BE FILING...
YOU WERE RIGHT OFFICER, HE RAN AWAY. NO, TO SEE RELATIVES DOWN-STATE. HITCHHIKED.
I KNOW...
THANK YOU FOR ALL YOUR HELP. I'LL CALL THE SCHOOL FIRST THING IN THE MORNING.

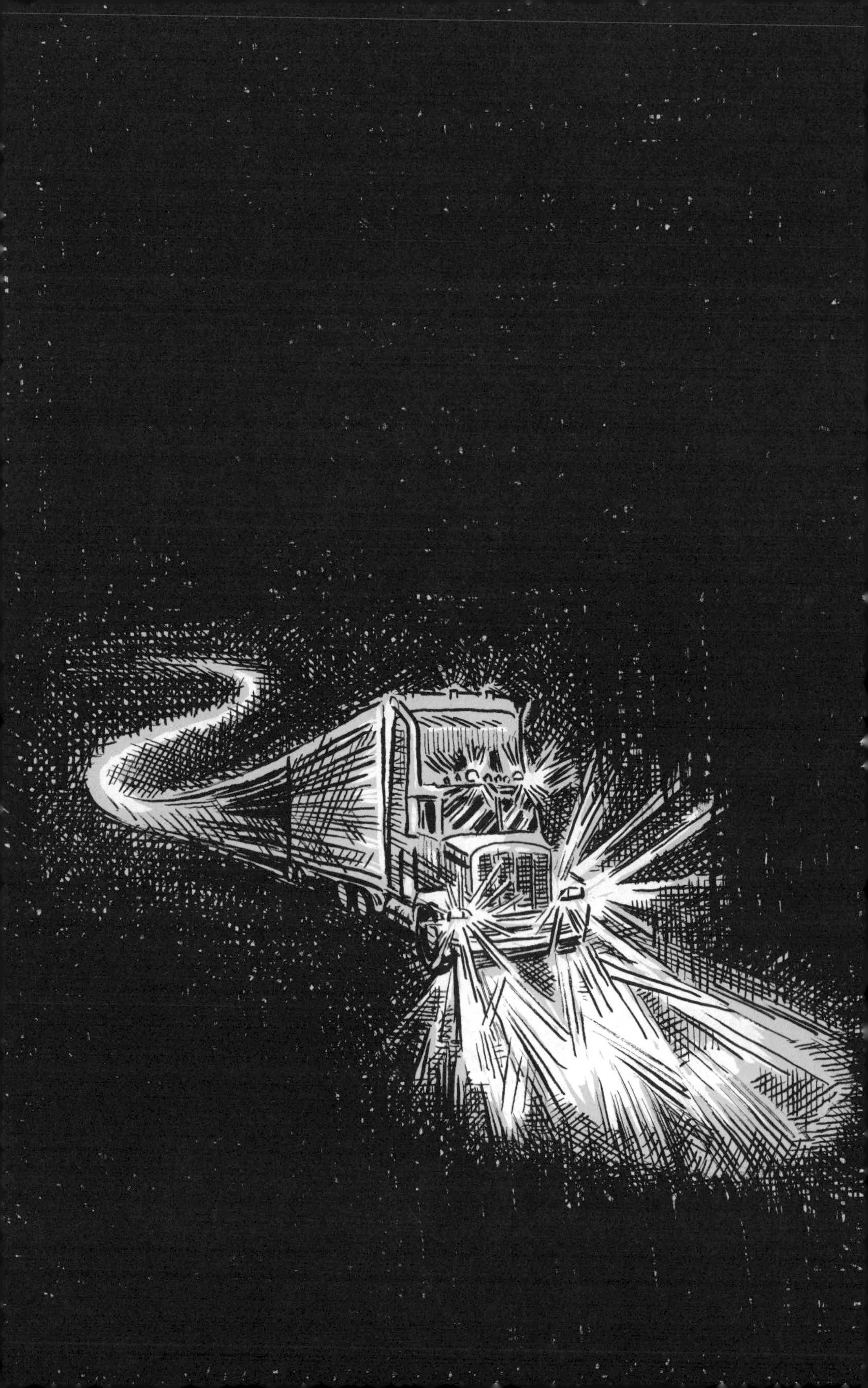

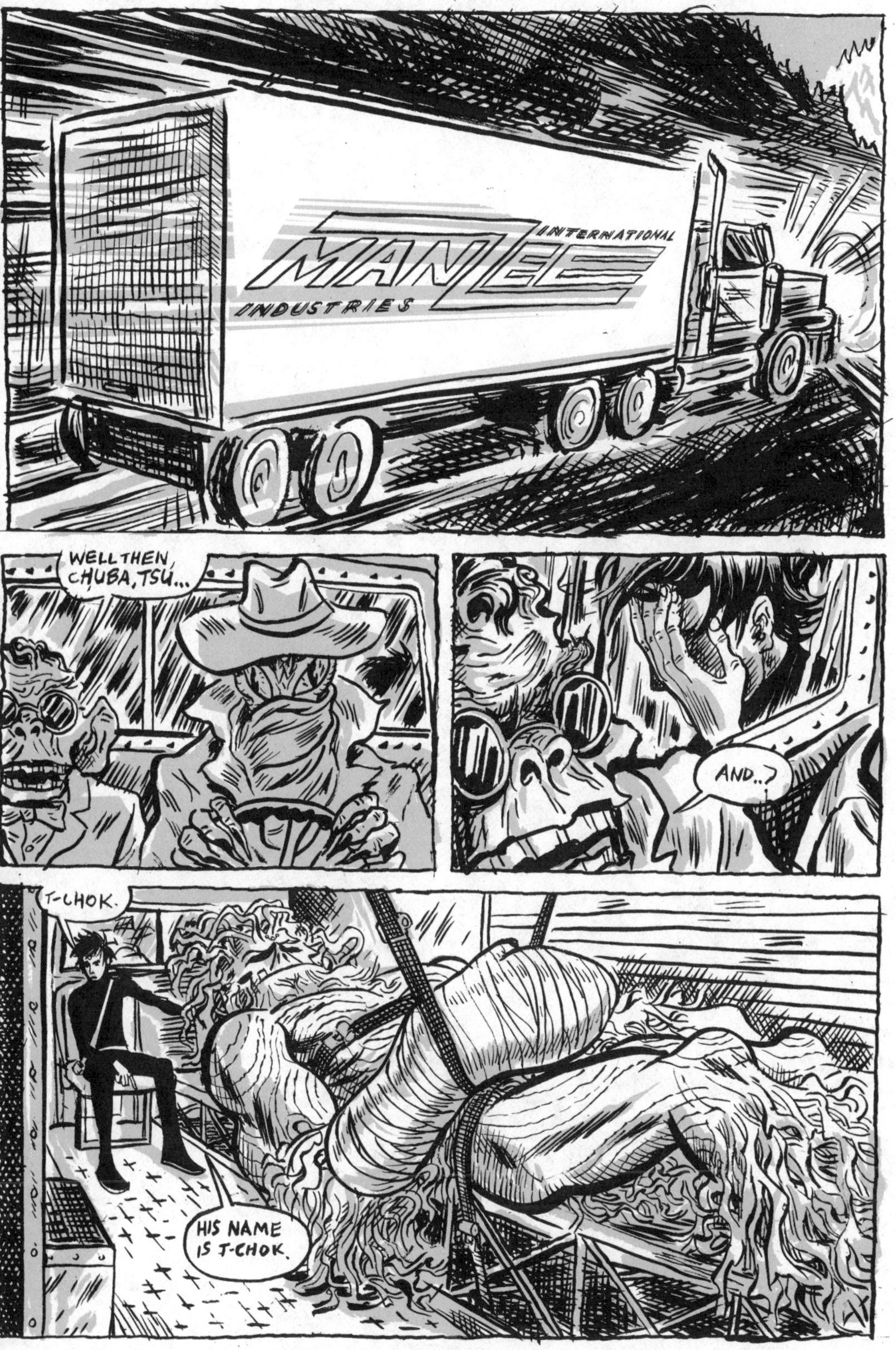
INTERNATIONAL
MANLEE
INDUSTRIES
WELL THEN, CHUBA, TSU...
AND..?
T-CHOK.
HIS NAME IS T-CHOK.

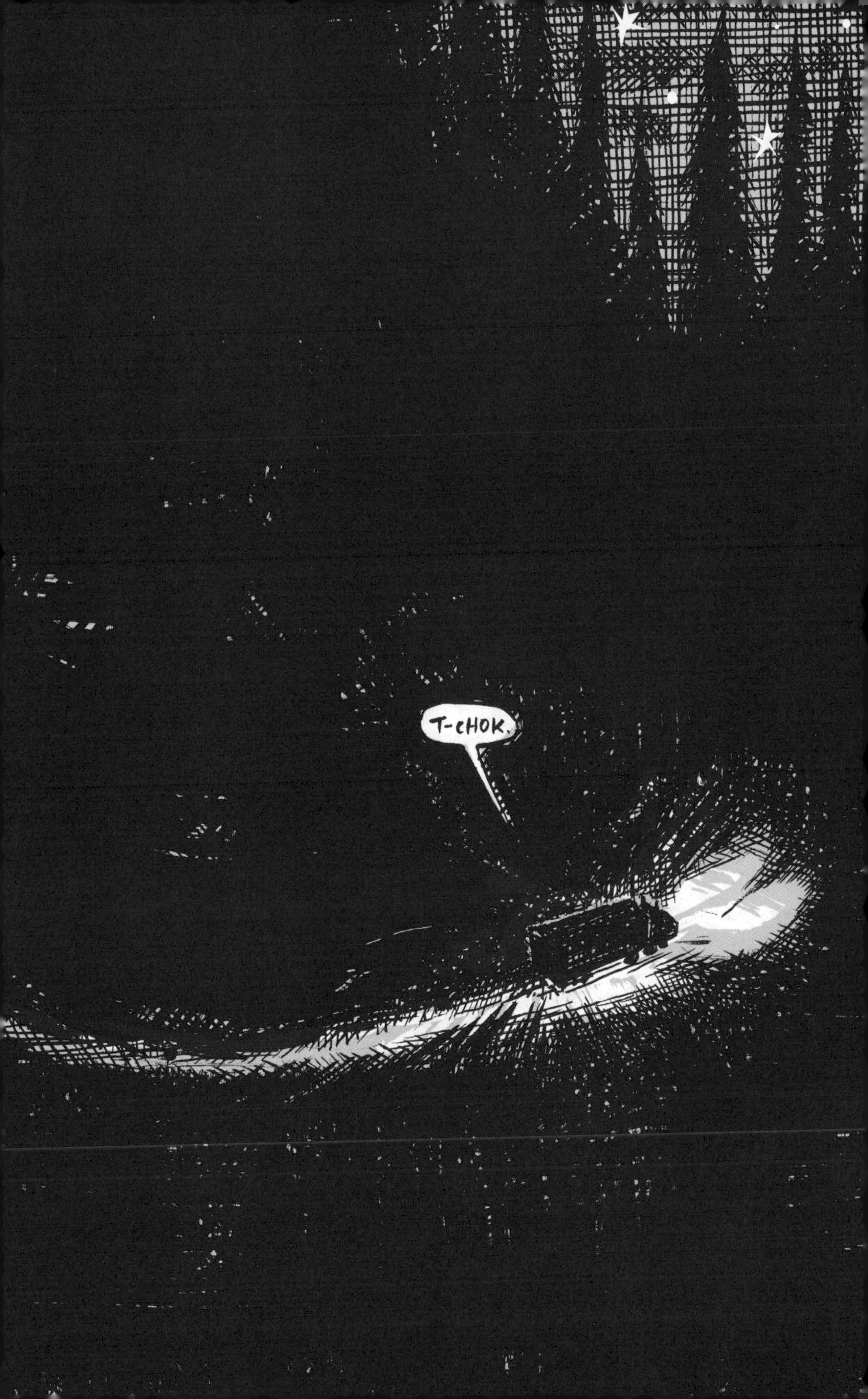
T-CHOK.

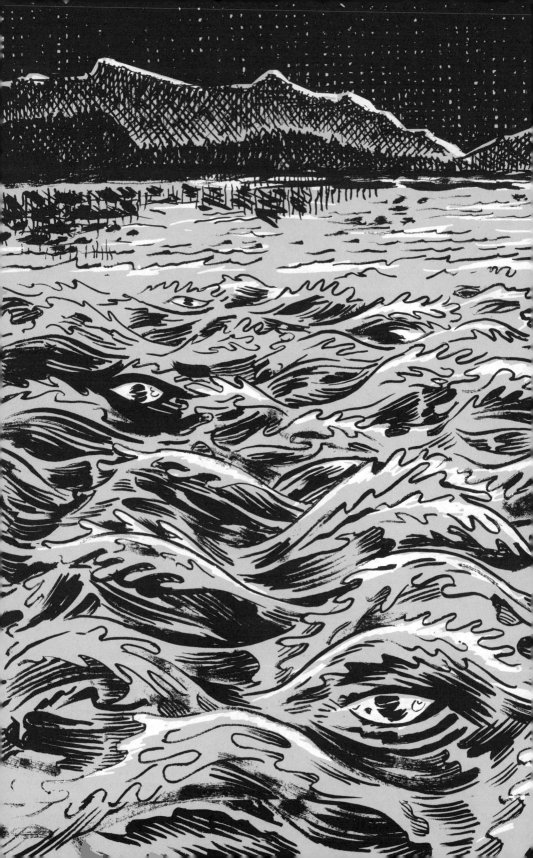

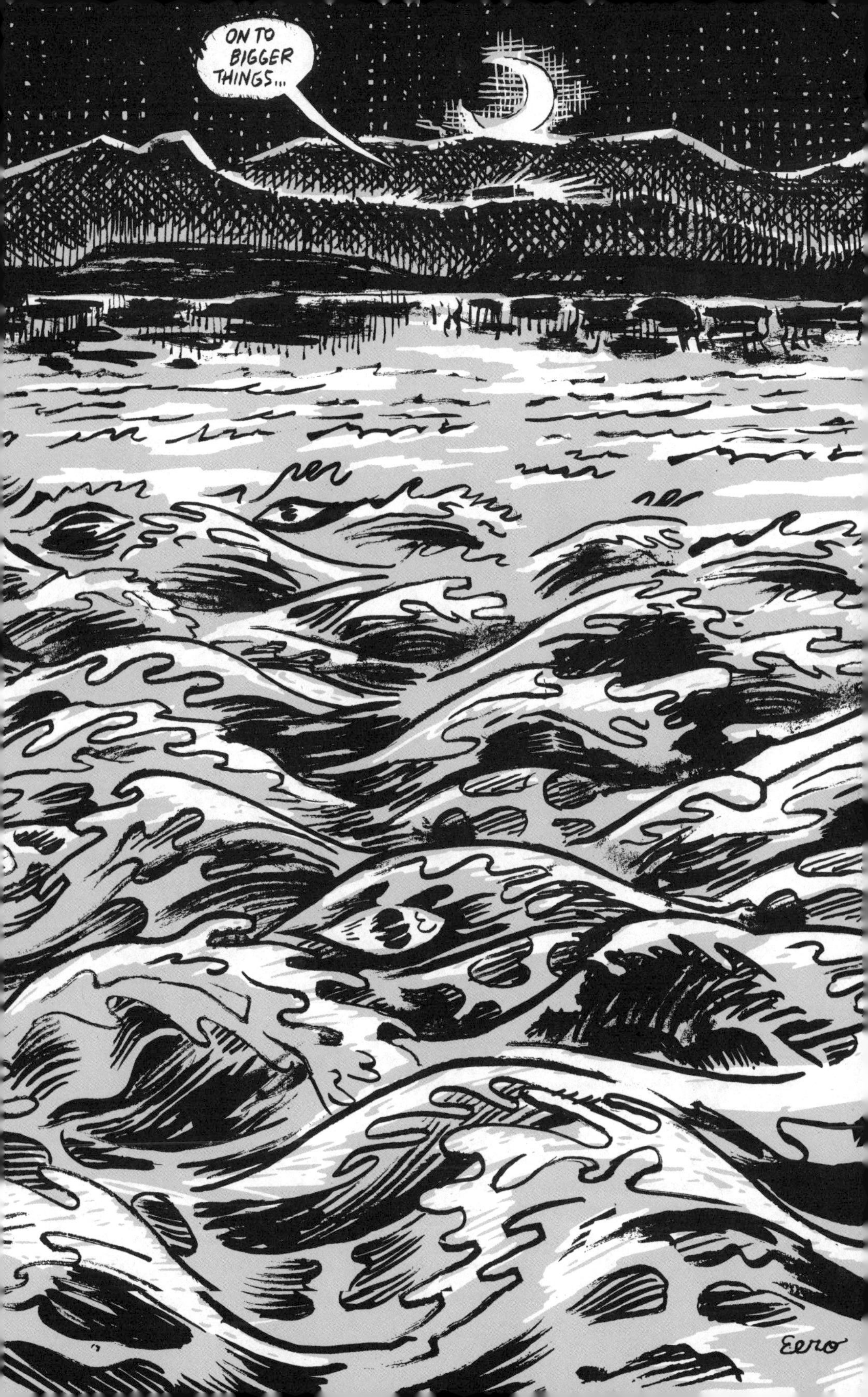
ON TO BIGGER THINGS...
Eero

CREATING A GRAPHIC NOVEL CAN BE A LONG AND SOLITARY JOURNEY IN ITSELF. LUCKILY "TSU & THE OUTLIERS" ACQUIRED MANY FINE COMPANIONS ALONG THE WAY!

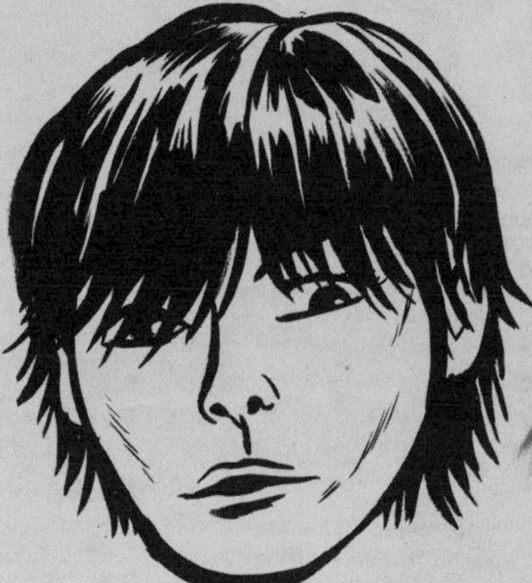

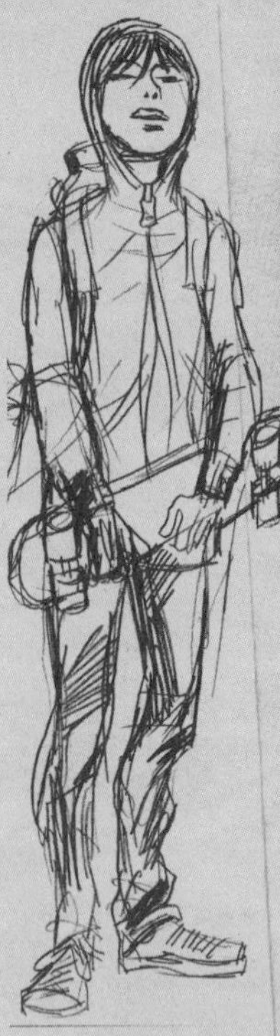

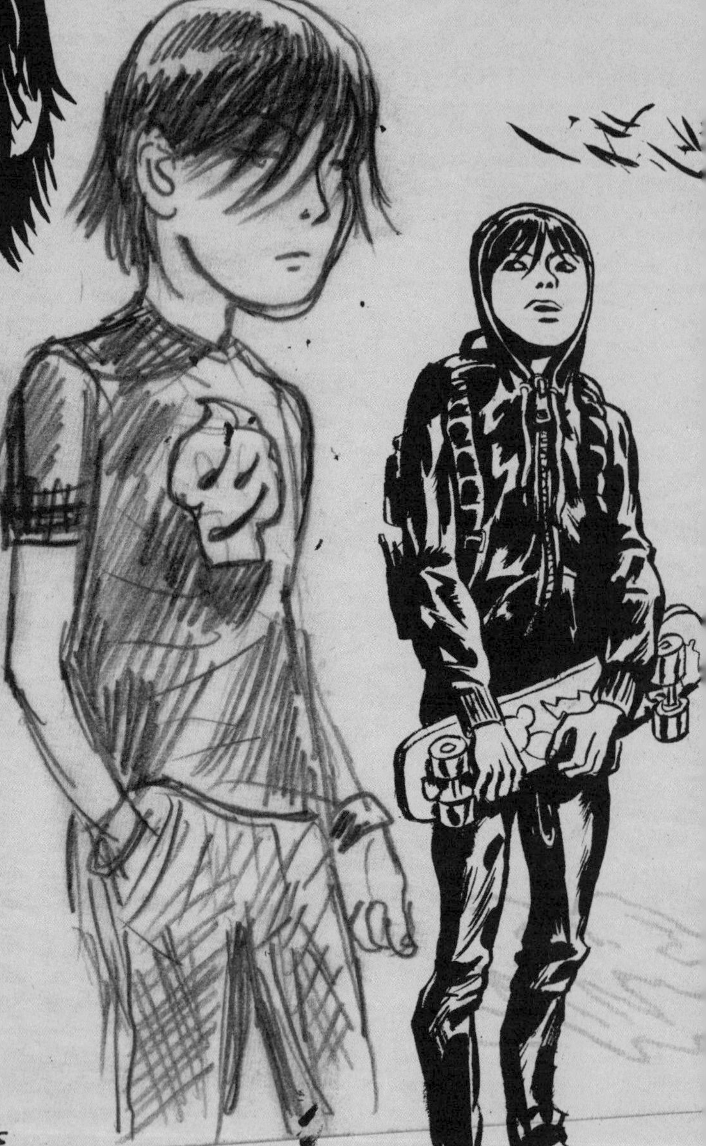

THE FIRST 32 PAGES (MORE OR LESS) OF THIS BOOK WERE PUBLISHED AS A DELUXE MINI-COMIC "THE OUTLIERS" AND WAS SUPPORTED THROUGH A KICKSTARTER CAMPAIGN BY FRIENDS, FAMILY AND A FEW TOTAL STRANGERS – BUT ALSO WITH THE INVALUABLE ASSISTANCE OF DARRELL EAGER (FILMOGRAPHER), ELIZABETH WORKMAN (POET/EDITOR) TIMOTHY PFEIFER (ESQ.), ZAK SALLY (LA MANO), AND MARK ARSENAULT (ALTERNATIVE COMICS).

ALWAYS INTENDED AS PART OF A LARGER STORY, THE MINI-COMIC WAS RECONCEIVED AS A GRAPHIC NOVEL WITH THE HELP OF TOM KACZYNSKI AND HIS UNCIVILIZED BOOKS... BUT NOT WITHOUT A FEW DETOURS...

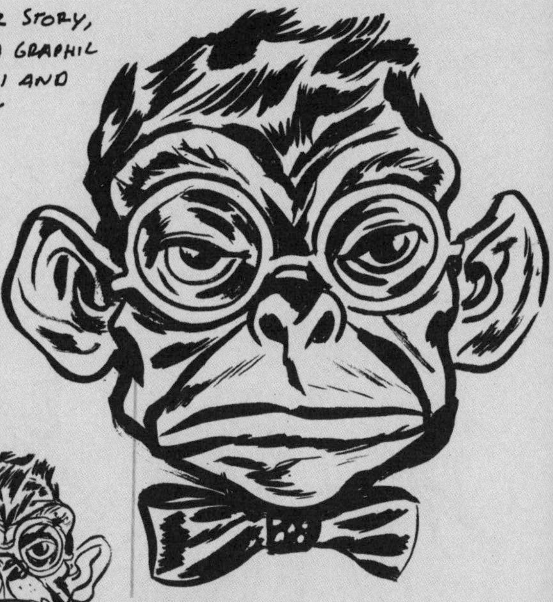

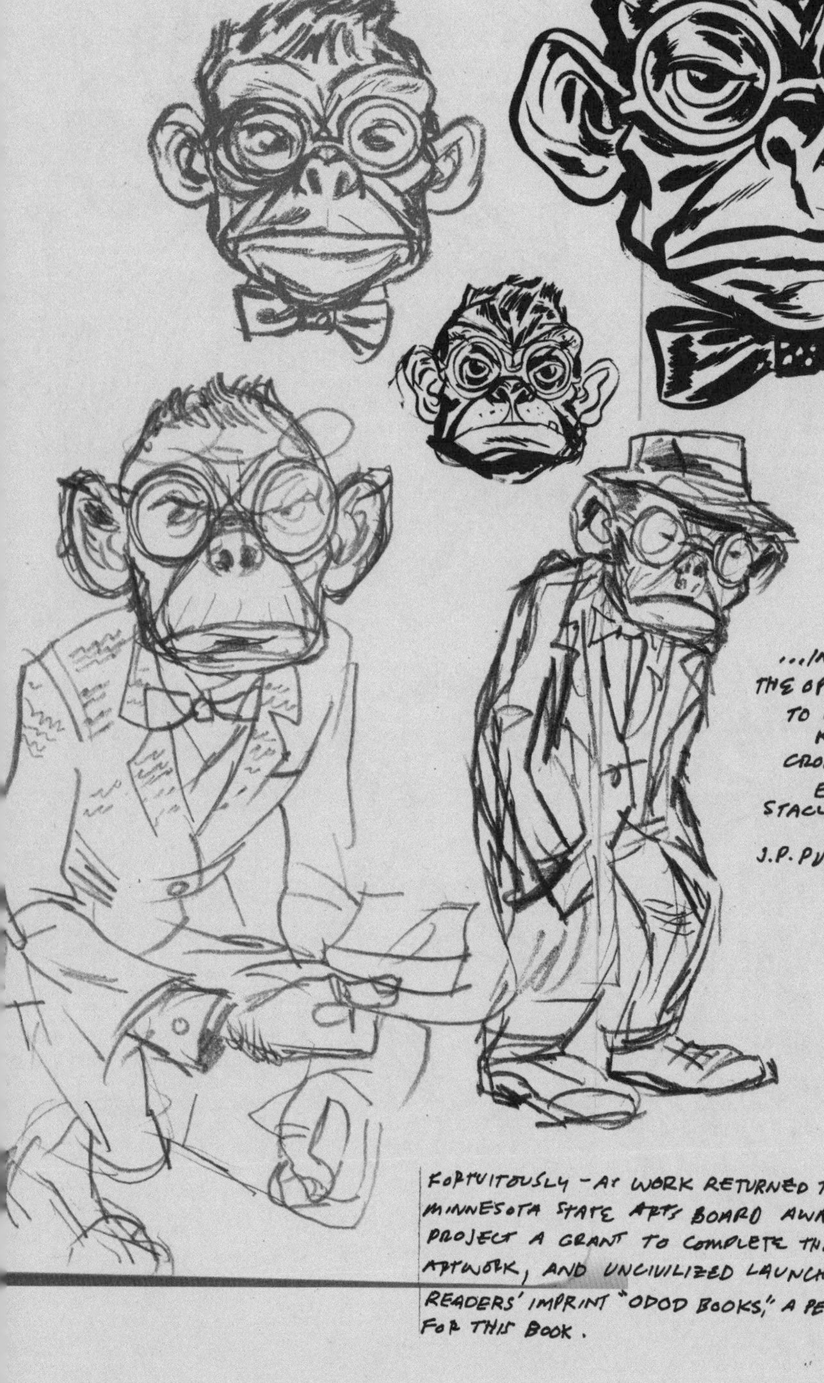

...INCLUDING THE OPPORTUNITY TO WORK WITH KIRSTIN CRONN-MILLS, EDITOR STACY BARNEY, AND J.P. PUTNAM SONS,

FORTUITOUSLY - AS WORK RETURNED TO "TSU," THE MINNESOTA STATE ARTS BOARD AWARDED THE PROJECT A GRANT TO COMPLETE THE EXPANDED ARTWORK, AND UNCIVILIZED LAUNCHED THE YOUNG READERS' IMPRINT "ODOD BOOKS," A PERFECT HOME FOR THIS BOOK.

ARTCRANK, E.BRANDT/MCAD, R.CHRUSTOWSKI, HAMILTON INK SPOT, C. KEEFE, KI-CHAN & ANTONIO, M. LIZAMA, O.O.P.S., C. RODRIGUEZ, S&T SHASLAN, J. STAMPE & A. CADDOCK CHEERED THIS THING ALONG THROUGH HELPFUL ADVICE OR COLLABORATION.

GREAT PATIENCE WAS SHOWN WITH THE PROJECT AND ITS CREATOR BY TAMMY, LITTLE ☾, LITTLE ☆, SALLY AND ERNIE.

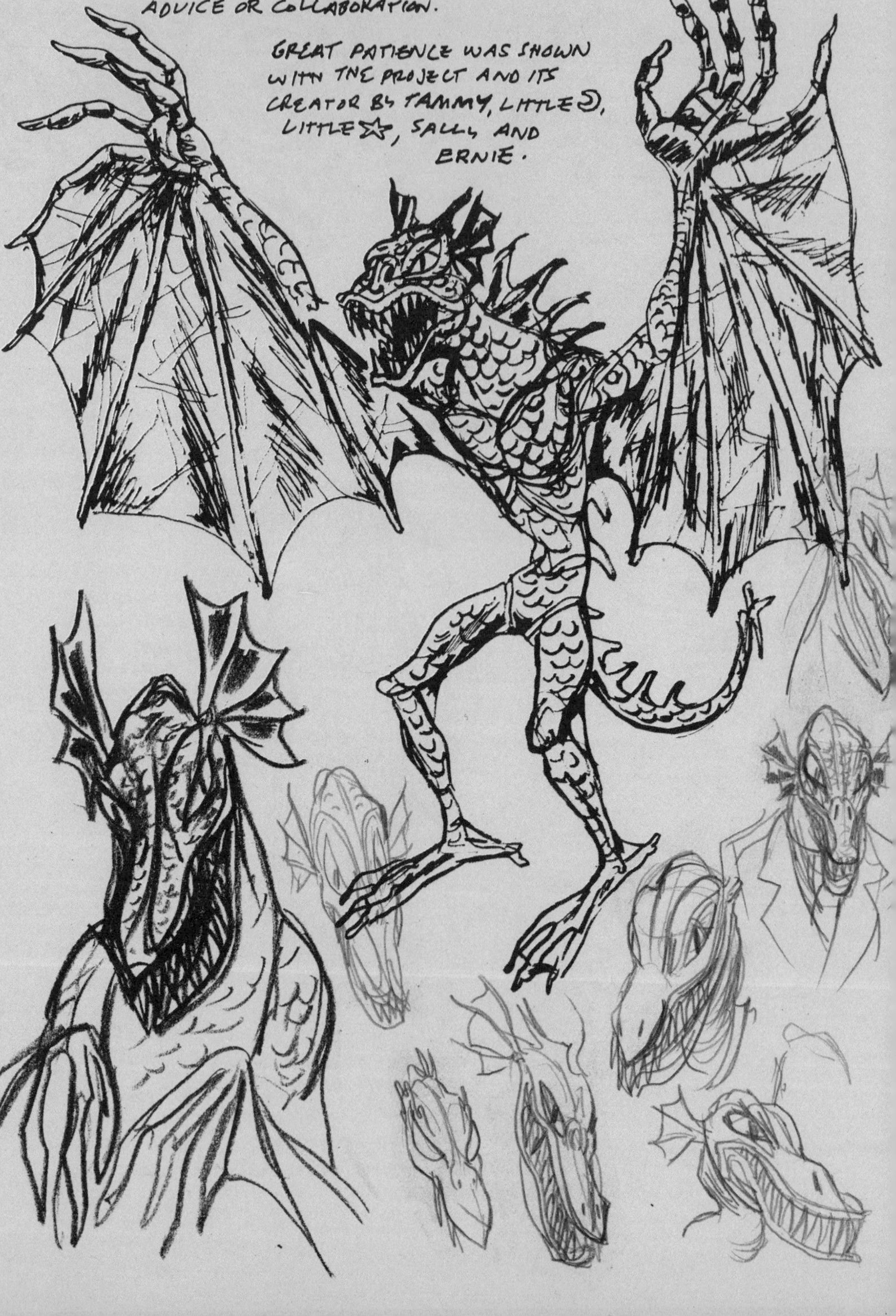

MANY YEARS OF GRATITUDE SHOULD BE EXPRESSED TO THE LIMITLESS CREATIVITY FOUND AT CSA DESIGN (AND THE INFLUENTIAL FRENCH PAPER CO.)

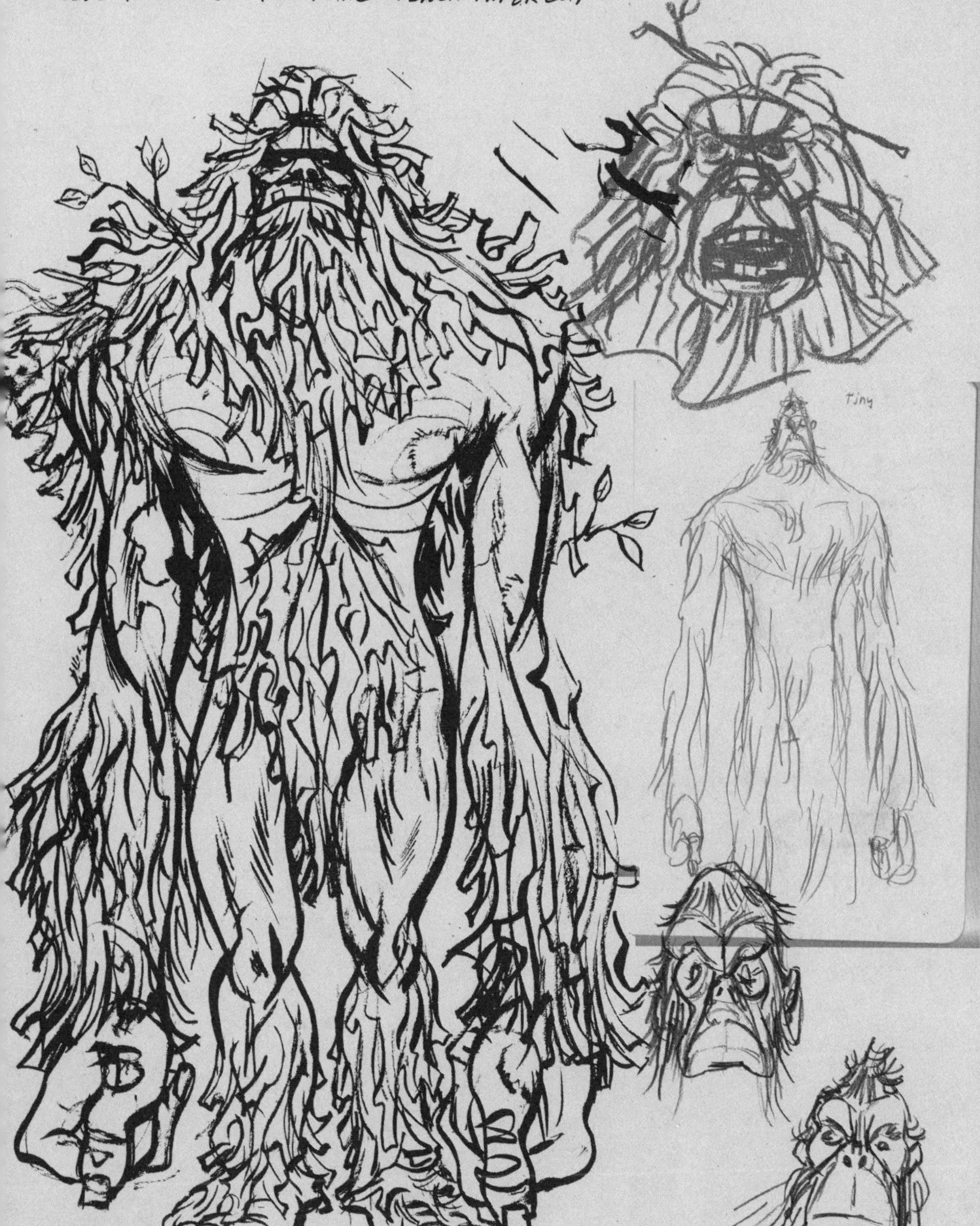
tiny

THERE'S A KERNEL OF THIS STORY INDEBTED TO JOHN HYME, WHO RECOUNTED AN "OTHER-WORLDLY" ENCOUNTER HE EXPERIENCED ON A DARK, SILENT WOODLAND PATH IN SKOWHEGAN, ME.

BUT MOSTLY...

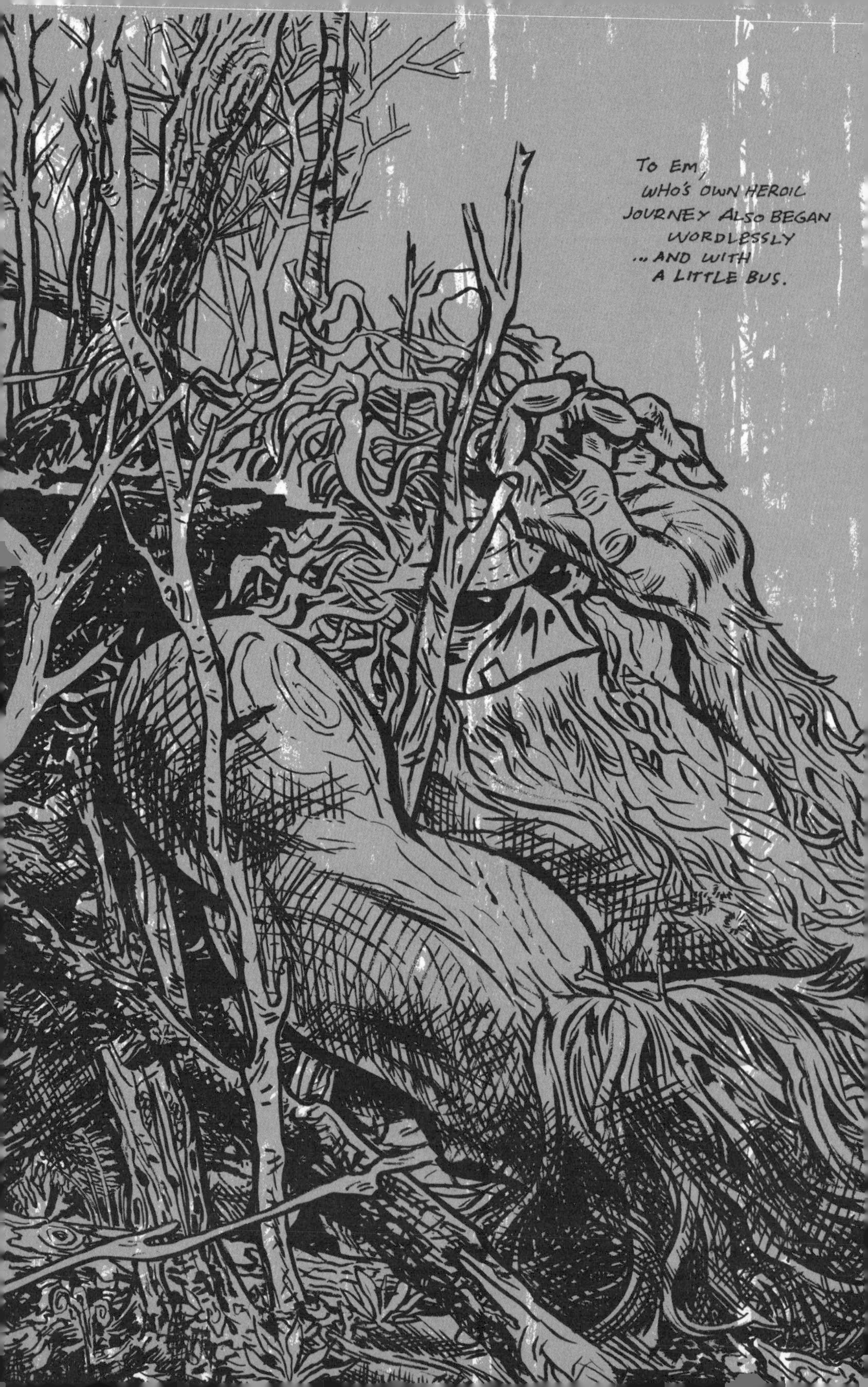
TO EM,
WHO'S OWN HEROIC
JOURNEY ALSO BEGAN
WORDLESSLY
... AND WITH
A LITTLE BUS.